I0825356

WILHELMINA

WILHELMINA

A Celestial Fairytale

by

M. Turandot

Copyright © 2025 by M. Turandot

All rights reserved. No part of this book may be reproduced, stored in a retrieval system, or transmitted in any form or by any means—electronic, mechanical, photocopying, recording, or otherwise—without the prior written permission of the publisher, except for brief quotations used in reviews, scholarly work, or articles.

This is a work of fiction. Names, characters, places, and incidents are either the product of the author's imagination or are used fictitiously. Any resemblance to actual persons, living or dead, events, or locales is entirely coincidental.

Cover design by M. Turandot

Interior layout and design by M. Turandot

Select editorial, design, and developmental elements were refined through a collaborative process with the assistance of AI tools, used with creative discernment and care.

ISBN (Hardcover): 979-8-9994617-0-4

ISBN (Paperback): 979-8-9994617-1-1

ISBN (eBook): 979-8-9994617-2-8

Library of Congress Control Number: 2025916231

Printed in the United States of America

First Edition, published September 2025

Second Printing, January 2026

Published by Miragwyn Books

Manakin Sabot, Virginia, USA

www.mturandotauthor.com

Note on the Second Printing: This edition has been refined to more deeply reflect the celestial resonance of Aetherwyn. The author wishes to thank the readers whose early support allowed these stars to shine a little brighter.

To my family.

And to the dreamers who dare to lift the veil—

they are the weavers of light who guide us through the dark.

When threads of light are tangled in shadow,

it is the heart that must find the pattern again.

—M. Turandot

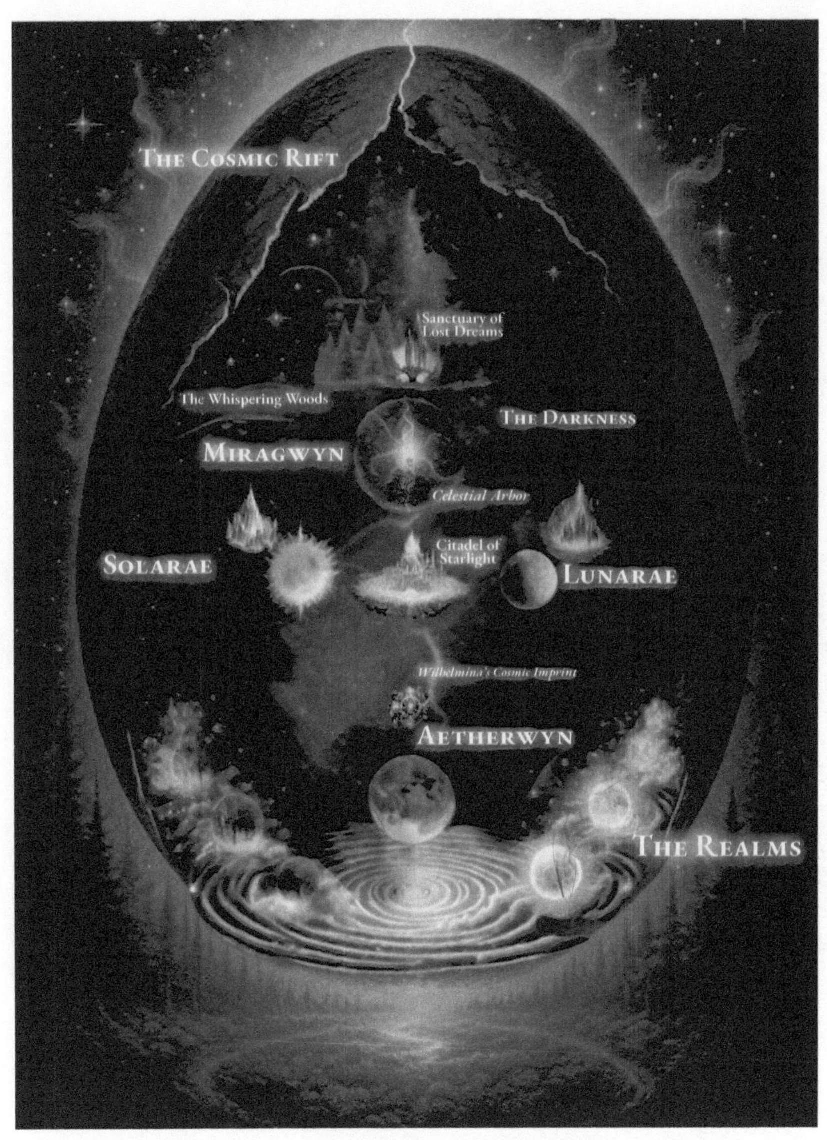

Wilhelmina's Journey

A Cosmogram of the Realms

CONTENTS

Introduction

From the Book of Truth. As transcribed by Quill, Truth Historian of Aetherwyn. Written in the Age of the Seventh Bloom, beneath the eternal watch of the Celestial Arbor, some years after the Elixir of Love returned—and long after she, the girl not meant to save the world but to choose it, stepped beyond the veil and into legend.

Long before the first Love Blossom graced Aetherwyn's soil, before Wilhelmina stirred within her chrysalis, light and shadow bore no names. There was only the Music.

The Celestial Arbor, Dreamer of Worlds, rooted herself in the space between thought and imagination. She dreamed in seeds—each a possibility. These seeds formed the Dreamscape, a vast expanse of nascent creation. She shaped it with boundaries, each a note, a sacred interval in the harmony of existence.

Her dream was not of dominion, but of balance. From the pulse beneath her ancient bark arose the first magic: Resonance.

Years—even decades—spent sifting through the echoes of the past have led this historian to a clearer understanding of the forces that shaped our world. Magic, at its root, reveals itself as pure pattern—a coherence within the Arbor's timeless dream. It hums through everything that lives, binding all with inherent values. Each realm carries a signature, tuned to her original design: compassion, the very boundary of cruelty; wonder, the luminous counter to indifference; truth, the clear line against distortion.

To work magic, then, is to tune oneself to the symphony of living chords, each one sacred in the melody of existence. This, I have found, is why corrupted spells unravel, why disloyal hearts fail to carry the Song. Even time bows to these values. Even gravity itself yields to harmony.

From the Celestial Arbor's imagining emerged her daughter, Demiurge—the Enchantress—radiant with the power of conscious creation and the will to shape. Yet no dream shapes reality alone. Creation requires tension—an interplay of push and pull, resistance and release.

From the mystery of the void, Lambda emerged, dark and undefined—not as an enemy of light but as the gravity that gave light its shape. His presence gave Demiurge's dream contour—not to complete her, but to counterbalance her vision with depth, rhythm, and momentum.

From that tension, the first seeds of darkness were sown—quiet, restless, and profoundly unfinished. Dormant, yet dreaming of a singular, shaping act. Sensing this latent power, the Arbor birthed a hidden wellspring—a final, mystic chord in creation's spiral, the echo of endings that seed new beginnings. It was a measure born of immense foresight instead of fear; yet even foresight, when sprung from the faintest tremor of mistrust, can cast its own shadow.

In that attempt to safeguard the dream, a space was woven, just beyond its immediate song. Some called it the Omega Pulse. Others, the Breath Between. It came like spring after a long galactic winter, when stars realigned and the dreaming deepened. With it, dreams crossed the threshold from vision to form. Without it, they flickered and faded. This energy, a pure origin returning, beyond the simple division of light and dark, gave deeper form to the Demiurge's imagining. It didn't initiate creation but responded to it, an echo answering a song.

The Omega Energy, as the Celestial Stewards named it, raised the threshold of manifestation, amplifying those dreams sung with true integrity. It brought life and renewal to the realms' faltering magic, much like sunlight to a waiting seed, though it demanded alignment: the convergence of value, clear vision, and readiness.

Soon after the worlds were set spinning, it was said the Stewards learned to listen for its return, harvesting it gently—as shared attunement, never possession. Each new age, when the Omega constellation arced back into alignment, they sang it into the roots of magic, restoring what time and distortion had worn thin. Without it, light would dim. Magic would falter. The balance between freedom and fear would collapse.

Together, Demiurge and Lambda brought forth these Celestial Stewards, the heavens, and the pull between them. And so came Celestia, bearer of stars, and Varytita, keeper of mass and force. Through them, the skies moved and day and night came—tide and root, heart, longing, and light.

Through Celestia and Varytita, the twin princes were born: Selenus, child of moonlight and mystery, and Phaethon, child of radiance and growth. The moon and the sun, as they are now known. They were never enemies, but they weren't always at peace.

It was in an age forgotten that the Wand of Dominion, forged by Demiurge to shape harmony, passed from her hand into the eager grip of Selenus. She was weary from sacrifice, and in her weariness, she mistook pity for compassion. But pity, unlike love, carries a fracture—a tremor of fear. That fear, like a nascent seed planted in haste, sprouted slowly into obscurity, an unintended bloom in the garden of magic.

And the gloom, subtle and patient, reshaped itself into a hunger—for power, for control, for the safety of certainty. It seeped into the wand, threading itself through its core. Once tuned to resonance, it now recoiled. It remembered fear—the first dissonant note in a once-perfect song. In that fear, it turned inward, cutting itself off from the dream. It could no longer harmonize. It needed to dominate—to strip away free will in order to protect what it no longer trusted.

Thus was born the Wand of Shadow, not from inherent evil, but from neglect, envy, and longing misunderstood. A magic untethered from love. And the darkness that waits behind all unguarded magic stirred, then struck.

The Celestial Tear that followed split the realms, dimmed the moonblossoms, and nearly extinguished the Love Blossom line before it could bloom again, both bloodline and flower, sacred emblems of harmony. Aetherwyn, once brimming with beauty, became muted, cold, controlled. Demiurge and Lambda, sensing the unraveling, vanished, planting one final hope.

It was no sword, no spell—but a soul.

Wilhelmina.

She was born of no prophecy, for prophecies are but echoes of a fate already cast. She was born of decision—the first light of a future yet to be written. Demiurge chose, and Lambda agreed. Possibility entered where fate had not yet hardened. A chosen soul, shaped by intention and held gently within the dream's spiral.

And so, when darkness whispered its curse across creation's dance, when the worlds heard that an heir of shadow would bring ruin, some believed it was Selenus. He believed it himself, once.

That, to this historian, was the cleverest cruelty of all.

For the curse, as now understood through the clarity of retrospect, did not exist. It was merely a veil, intricately spun by distortion to confuse the heart: to make love seem dangerous, and power, deceptively, safe. Yet choice—true, illuminated choice—was never the curse.

It was the cure.

—*Quill*

Prologue

"*She will never forgive us.*"

Demiurge's whisper fractured the silence, piercing the gloam tearing across the sky. Cradled in her arms, the chrysalis carrying her unborn daughter pulsed with a faint, celestial light. Wilhelmina's light.

Lambda didn't answer. What could he say? That this was for the greater good? That sacrificing their daughter's future would save the realms?

Lies.

Even as the stars dimmed and the heavens cracked open, he knew the truth: they weren't saving the world. They were damning her to a life without love, forcing her to choose a path they would falsely forbid, so her own will might one day shatter the darkness.

Demiurge ran, breathless, clutching their realm's salvation—and its greatest risk.

Beside her, Lambda struggled against the encroaching void. "We're almost there, my love," he murmured, doubt lacing his voice. He glanced skyward. Once steadfast beacons, the constellations now flickered, their light devoured by the ever-growing darkness.

The fractured sky loomed over them, torn apart in slow, agonizing ripples. Night spilled through like ink across a sacred text, staining the stars. Shadows bled from the heavens, unraveling the seams between light and dark, as if the fabric of the universe had turned traitor.

Ahead, nestled at the heart of Miragwyn, the Celestial Arbor's glow pierced the gloom like a beacon of ancient power. Her branches stretched into the heavens, woven from the first light of creation. Her roots entwined with the lifeblood of the cosmos.

Beneath her silver canopy, two celestial couples stood waiting, their expressions solemn as Demiurge and Lambda stumbled forward: Seraphina and Lumineon of the Solar Realm, and Varytita, Architect of Gravity, with his partner in the cosmic harmony, Celestia, Matriarch of Stars.

Demiurge held the chrysalis closer. “We’re too late.” Her voice was barely a breath. “The shadows are already here.”

The Celestial Arbor’s voice, ancient and resonant, stirred the air like a rustling breeze. “They have not yet won, daughter.” Luminous and gnarled with time, she extended her branch-like hands. “But they will… unless we act now.”

Lambda’s hands curled into fists. “There has to be another way.”

“There is none,” Celestia whispered.

Beside her, Varytita, his gaze calculating, observed the sky. “The order of the heavens cannot be allowed to break.”

The Enchantress lingered as she lowered the chrysalis onto the altar of woven roots. “She was meant to know love,” she whispered, her voice breaking. “Not just weave it for others. We will tell her she cannot, but it is in defying that falsehood—in choosing for herself—that her true power will awaken.”

“Perhaps fate will be kind, Demiurge.” Seraphina’s words were gentle, but her golden expression dimmed.

Demiurge faltered. “She will never forgive us.”

“She must live,” Lambda said, voice firm. “And she must be protected.”

The Arbor’s voice resonated like wind through leaves. “Then your daughter will need the Essence of the First Dawn—the last echo of the dream before it broke.”

It was the light she saved for a future even she could not predict.

The ancient tree reached deep within her core, drawing forth a vial of liquid starlight—the purest energy of creation. It pulsed like a fragment of untouched brilliance and hummed a final, mystic chord.

“Take this,” she said, placing a shimmering glass vessel in Demiurge’s trembling hands. “It is the Breath Between—the Omega Pulse made form. Only the child can wield it when the time comes.”

The Enchantress hesitated before passing the vial to Lambda. “Keep it safe,” she whispered. “If the darkness takes me, you must ensure our daughter finds her way.”

Lambda’s fingers curled around the vial, his grip turning white. “She will.”

Seraphina and Lumineon exchanged a glance before stepping forward. “This powerful magic must be hidden until she is ready.”

Lambda exhaled sharply, dragging a hand through his hair. "And if she never is?"

A quiet rustling stirred above them—the faint whisper of wings. Gwydion, the ageless owl, his amber eyes steady and unblinking, gave a low hoot.

"She shall find a way."

He scraped a talon along the Arbor's lowest branch. "Whether you allow her to or not." He looked not at the parents, but at the pulsing chrysalis, as if already seeing the wings that would one day leave a trail of luminescent frost.

Demiurge lifted her chin. "I won't let her suffer," she swore.

Varytita's gaze darkened. "The prophecy is clear. The Cursed Heir will collapse the order."

A hush fell over them. In the distance, the moon suddenly flared—not with its usual gentle silver, but with a sharp, piercing violet that seemed to slice through the encroaching shadows. It didn't fight the dark; it seemed to beckon it.

"It will be him." Lambda's jaw became rigid as he watched the amethyst pulse. "Look at how the darkness answers him. It lingers at the edge of his light, waiting for an invitation."

A quiet gasp escaped Celestia. "*Selenus*?"

Though the name was a plea, it hung in the air like a sentence. Selenus was Celestia and Varytita's younger son who was bound to the moon's quiet power and had long been watched with wary eyes. His loneliness, his brooding nature—signs that darkness could take root.

Demiurge's breath caught. "You are right. The darkness already calls to him."

Gwydion said nothing at first. He ruffled his feathers, the motion slow and thoughtful, before speaking. "And yet, prophecies have a way of deceiving those who place their trust in them." His amber gaze slid to Lambda. "You think you know who it is... Perhaps you don't."

A deep tremor split the heavens. Demiurge gripped Gwydion's feathers. "Take her," she pleaded. "Raise her beyond the reach of this war."

The owl extended his wings, feathers rustling with quiet understanding. "I will guard her as my own."

Demiurge exhaled, her fingers lingering over the chrysalis before pressing a kiss to its iridescent shell. "My daughter... my Wilhelmina."

Lightning cracked across the sky. A howl of the void surged forward.

“We must act,” Varytita warned, his gravity-bound voice anchoring them to the moment. “The darkness moves swiftly.”

The Enchantress turned toward the Silvered Oculus resting within a hollow of her mother’s trunk—a shard of the first dawn that held a steady memory of a world before the fall. It was the only mirror strong enough to contain a soul of her magnitude, and the only prison that could keep her magic from falling into enemy hands.

"I must remain," she whispered, her hand hovering over the cold surface.

Lambda’s head snapped toward her. "No!"

Demiurge’s expression softened. "We knew this seed of possibility might come," she said, her voice finding a terrifying calm. "If the shadows consume me while I am free, I become their greatest weapon. I must lock the light away within the reflection before the distortion takes hold. The mirror will hold me—and it will hold the truth."

“No,” Lambda growled, his form trembling with defiance. “I shall not leave you.”

“You must.” Her hands shook as she touched his face, her light flickering against his. “Protect our daughter. Guard her future. It is the only way our family survives.”

A heartbeat passed. Then another. Lambda placed his forehead against hers, letting his light entwine with hers one last time before he stepped back. “I will be near,” he vowed. “Always.”

The world convulsed as the rift split wide, sending a shudder through the core of existence. The Enchantress gasped, her grip tightening around air as the magic that tethered her to the realms unraveled. Clawing, twisting, the darkness reached for her.

Lambda lunged and caught her wrist. “Noooo!”

Her gaze met his. The pain there was unbearable. “Protect our daughter.”

Demiurge stepped into the mirror’s embrace. Silver light swallowed her, sealing her within its depths. The artifact grew cold, its surface turning to a dull, impenetrable grey.

The Celestial Arbor’s roots groaned, moving with deliberate, heavy grace. They wound upward, coiling around the Oculus like a wooden fist, drawing the mirror deep into the high canopy, hiding it where only the brave or the destined might ever find it again.

Lambda's breath came ragged, his free hand pressed to the glass. He could still see her, feel her, just beyond reach.

The Celestial Arbor's roots tightened around the mirror, forming a cocoon of living wood.

"It is done."

Demiurge was gone.

Above them, the heavens groaned, the stars flickering like dying embers. The celestial beings turned their faces skyward as the fabric of their world trembled on the brink.

The ancient tree's voice rustled through her leaves.

"You must leave."

Lambda shook his head. "Not without her."

The words tore through him more violently than the storm above. But he knew the cost. He had heard the echo of Demiurge's whisper, and in it, the death of the family they once were.

The Arbor's branches shook with great force.

"You know that is not possible."

Lambda turned to the chrysalis, his fingers grazing its surface. "I hope she will forgive herself." And then he whispered under his breath, "Even the Arbor cannot see all. Perhaps we should never have tried. Yet here we are."

He turned, pressing the powerful vial into Seraphina's hands. "Keep it hidden," he commanded. "Let no one wield it before its time."

Gwydion unfurled his wings, the chrysalis secured within his talons. "Destiny is a fickle thing," he murmured. "Attempt to shape it, and it may yet twist in ways unforeseen. Her heart must be kept from love, yes, but it is in choosing her own path that she will truly embody it."

"The Omega stirs once more. The breath between has not yet left us." With a powerful beat of his wings, he soared into the night, carrying the last hope of the realm toward the unknown.

The sky screamed as the shadows reached their grasping tendrils toward the Celestial Arbor, toward Miragwyn, toward all that still remained. But the light would not surrender. Not yet.

The Celestial Arbor's branches trembled, sending a veil of ancient light after them—a final blessing, a hidden ward, a whisper of protection woven through the wind itself. Not to bind Wilhelmina, but to safeguard the path she had yet to know she walked.

The remaining sliver of celestial light faded. The sky above Miragwyn exploded. And in the abyss that followed, a single voice rose—soft, spectral, inexorable.

"The heir of shadow and light has begun to awaken."

1. Aetherwyn's Fraying Threads

Once upon a time, in the mystical realm of Aetherwyn, the morning sun painted the sky with hues of blush and amber, stirring its inhabitants from their peaceful slumber.

"Good morrow!" called a sprite, her voice bright as morning dew.

Mischievous pixies darted among the moonblossoms. Sprites flickered through the air like sparks, their glowing fingers whisking petals into flight. Along the lakeshore, nymphs glided across the surface, their silvery hair trailing like starlight on water. Every step left a shimmer in its wake.

In the distance, elven gardeners trimmed ivy along castle walls, and somewhere on the other side of the lake, a melody from distant sirens threaded the breeze with song. Fairies rose with the sun, wings aglow, readying the day's wedding celebration.

Quill, Aetherwyn's elven poet and scribe, adjusted his feathered cap, already composing mental verses.

Nearby, Crispin, the master pixie of ceremonies, polished his gleaming baton with a flourish, his usual boisterous laughter held to a murmur of anticipation. "Don't mind me," he quipped as he caught a falling garland, "just dancing with gravity." Yet his eyes flicked toward the sky, uneasy.

Flora, a nature sprite with nimble green fingers, meticulously arranged garlands of moonblossoms, concentrating intensely. She paused mid-garland, noticing a wilting blossom. "Not today," she whispered, coaxing it gently to bloom again. "There's still time."

Aria, the siren of melody, hummed a soft, ethereal song, perfectly tuning her voice for the vows. She lifted her gaze skyward mid-hum. "Sing true," she murmured. "Even if no one hears."

"Hurry now!" cried Quill, his voice tight with cheerful urgency. "Wilhelmina will join us with the Celestials any moment—we must be ready!" He tucked a verse behind his sash, heart tight. "Stories hold," he whispered. "They must."

And so they whispered and worked, their reverence as quiet as the hush before an invocation.

This enchanted realm, nestled between the forces of light and shadow, hummed with perfect harmony. Magic wove through every corner of the land. Its vibrant gardens, crystalline lakes, and star-kissed meadows—usually enough to ensure Aetherwyn remained a sanctuary of love and unity.

❧

High above, Celestia, Matriarch of the Stars, stood on the luminous balcony of the Citadel of Starlight. Astral light bathed her silver robes as her gaze swept the cosmos before settling on Aetherwyn—its verdant meadows, mystical lakes, and moonblossom groves shimmering in the newborn day.

"It has begun again," she murmured. "The unrest in Selenus… I can feel it." A faint crease gathered between her brows.

Varytita, Architect of Gravity and patriarch, wrapped an arm around her. His presence steadied the air itself. "And if Phaethon strains beneath his own burden," he said quietly, "then neither brother will stand whole."

His golden robe, embroidered with celestial orbits, glimmered as his gaze swept the cosmic expanse. The sun's arc crested the horizon while the moon's last glow dissolved into dawn.

Grooved lines deepened on Celestia's forehead. "Our sons drift apart each cycle, like stars pulled by opposing gravities."

Both belonged to the Eternal Ones—an ancient council governing the universe's essential forces. Celestia kept stellar harmony; Varytita maintained the balance of attraction that held the dimensions in place. They, perhaps more than any others, understood how fragile their creation truly was.

"The prophecy warned us," Varytita said, his jaw tight. "The Curse of the Heir of Shadow… the one whose fall would unmake the balance. If envy consumes Selenus, everything fractures."

Celestia twisted her hands. "Did we do the right thing in telling them?"

"We hoped it would make them wiser, not fearful." He exhaled. "But fear is often the seed darkness chooses. Still—we must trust the path we laid for them."

"And yet the shadows press closer," Celestia whispered. "What if Selenus cannot resist? His doubts have always been fertile ground for the darkness. If he falls… Solarae's warmth will fade, and Lunarae's shadows will swell until they eclipse all. Every realm would suffer."

Varytita's grip tightened on her shoulder. "Phaethon carries a burden as well. His light shines brilliantly, but it isolates him from his brother. Even the sun cannot reach every shadow."

Celestia brushed away a tear from her cheek. "Once, they shared dreams and burdens alike." Her gaze drifted past Lunarae and Solarae toward the distant green world below. "That terrible day when we lost them... the prophecy spoke of an Heir of Shadow—but it never named which child."

Varytita's expression flickered. "True. But if not our son... then who?"

❧

A bitter exchange between the brothers had played out in the heavens, a direct testament to the fraying threads they feared. The memory was recent, a fresh ache that made the very firmament hold its breath.

A hush passed over the realm's upper skies—one that comes when even the wind dares not hinder.

Phaethon hovered above the Garden's crystalline canopy, his golden aura crowned by arcing flares of solar fire. He exuded an absolute certainty, every motion a sovereign declaration. Beside him, Selenus floated in the darkened currents, a pale, silver edge tracing the hollows of his face. The contrast between them was stark—the sun's searing corona woven into muscle and flame, and moonlight etched into tension and bone.

"You interfered," Phaethon said, his voice crisp but low. "The alignment was delicate, and your pull fractured the harmony."

Selenus's reply came as a soft snarl. "And yet you expect me to drift—forever silent—while you light the sky with fanfare? Must I always be the hidden one? The forgotten?"

"You are not forgotten," Phaethon replied, his hands curling into sunlit fists. "But your shadows do not blend—they consume. What you touch dims. Even the stars recoil."

Selenus faced him fully now, and something in his gaze shimmered like cracked glass. "Perhaps they should. Light without shadow is blinding. You shine, Phaethon, but you see nothing beneath."

A pause. The quiet crackled.

"Then name your purpose," Phaethon challenged. "Instead of circling like a wounded comet."

Selenus turned away from his brother, fading into a darker stretch of sky.

"When the veil frays, don't expect me to mend it. Not with silk and sentiment." And with that, he vanished behind a sweep of lunar clouds, leaving the sun to blaze alone.

The echo of their conflict reverberated even to Aetherwyn, a discordant hum that vibrated through the silver roots of the garden. Far below, Wilhelmina tilted her head skyward, wings folded against her back. Their words remained out of reach, yet the cosmic discord was palpable.

❧

A subtle ripple of light spread across the night sky, drawing Celestia and Varytita's attention. Two figures emerged from opposite sides of the citadel, their movements effortless on the polished starlight floor.

Selenus stepped out of the dimness to the left, his silver robe trailing like a river. Moonlight threaded through his ebony hair as he paused at the balcony's edge. He offered his parents a cool, reluctant glance before his gaze drifted to Aetherwyn. Weariness marked his features—yet deeper still, something brittle lodged beneath the surface, a tension held tight in his jaw and shoulders.

From the right, Phaethon appeared in a sweep of gold. His hair cascaded in strands of amber, his robe bright with sunrise hues. Warmth spilled from him—a light that reached what it could not hold. A flicker of doubt haunted his eyes. His smile wavered, for a loneliness hid beneath his bright exterior. He took his place beside Selenus, the unspoken distance between them far greater than the space on the balcony.

The earlier clash between the brothers lingered in the air, an unspoken bruise neither would acknowledge.

"Ah, my sons," Celestia murmured, embracing each in turn. "It gives me great happiness that you have come to witness the unity that holds our realms. Look upon Aetherwyn—its magic depends on the harmony you share."

Varytita clapped their shoulders. Though his countenance appeared stern, it was filled with a father's love. "The celestial ballet you perform with each rotation sustains more than our worlds. It binds light and shadow, day and night. Aetherwyn's fate rests in your hands."

Phaethon inclined his head. A hint of longing flickered across his face like a star burning too brightly to notice its fading. "We've dedicated ourselves to this duty. But sometimes, I wonder if our efforts are enough."

Selenus's lips twisted into a bitter smile. "Yes, yes. We know the lesson. Your sunlight cannot banish my shadows, brother."

"You're not alone in shouldering this burden," Phaethon said. "Your light—your moonlight—is as vital as mine. We cannot let envy undo what we guard."

Selenus turned away, the silvered dark veiling his eyes. "You speak of balance, yet your brilliance eclipses everything. My shadows are not defects."

Phaethon expelled a low growl. "The sun does not diminish the moon. It reveals its beauty. Yet you let bitterness cloud your vision."

"Must this feud continue?" Varytita's voice cracked like distant thunder.

Selenus exhaled sharply. "Others flocked to his warmth... even when we were children. I was always the shadow trailing behind his light."

"Balance does not require sameness," Varytita said softly. "The moon and sun have always moved on different paths, yet together, they shape the flow of time. It is why I entrusted you to govern Lunarae and your brother Solarae to oversee this eternal cycle."

Celestia placed a hand on their shoulders. "Remember this, my sons. You are not enemies but complements. It is not light that destroys shadow, nor shadow that devours light. Both are needed."

"Yet you have allowed envy to fray the threads that bind Aetherwyn," Varytita warned. "Remember your duty. Gravity does not choose sides; it holds the universe in place."

Selenus gave a reluctant nod, his breath sharp and held, a refusal coiled just beneath the surface.

Phaethon reached for his brother's arm, his movement tentative. For a fleeting moment, a connection flickered—brief and fragile as the glimmer of a newborn star. Then it dissolved, leaving only the cold sheen of the distant void.

"It is time," Phaethon said, his voice regaining its solar resonance. "The celebrations await. Aetherwyn expects us, and we must not neglect our duty." He extended a hand, his fingers catching the silver fabric of Selenus's sleeve.

Selenus recoiled as if the touch burned. "I am not a child," he spat, eyes flashing like cold flint. "You need not fear my absence, brother—I know my place in your shadow well enough."

"Then speak with me privately," Phaethon whispered.

Selenus nodded once, and in a swirl of gold and silver light, the brothers departed the citadel.

❧

In the silence that followed, Celestia and Varytita exchanged a subtle glance. Varytita's jaw clenched, and he drew Celestia close, his hand pressing gently on her shoulder before his grip tightened with a sigh that burdened the air.

"This rift has deepened." His focus shifted to the distant sky, where the sun and moon's orbits diverged. "If we tarry any longer, the balance will surely be lost."

A shiver traced its way down Celestia's spine. She straightened her shoulders and lifted her chin. "Even the vast heavens contain sinister spaces between the stars," she murmured. "Forces that feed on jealousy, envy, hatred—tearing gashes in the cosmos' delicate fabric. I fear they have returned. I pray that a mother and father's love will be enough to shield our sons."

Her gaze swept back across Aetherwyn, where the fragile interplay of illumination and shadow wove through its enchanted meadows. Moonlight touched the edge of the land, casting long shapes across lakes and forests. Wilhelmina's light, a gentle glow amidst the wedding celebrations, gleamed in the distance.

"What about Wilhelmina? She is Aetherwyn's steward." Celestia gripped the balcony's edge, her knuckles white. "Her heart is strong, but even she cannot bear this alone."

Varytita watched the moon's glow, a tiny speck upon the glittering expanse, sharpen against the horizon. "She is our chosen seed of hope—but time runs short." He cupped his wife's face, flicking away a single tear. With his thumb, he smoothed back a silver lock that had slipped free of her coiffure.

"Stewards like her—and like us—must hold these threads together. For our sons' feud shows how divine beings, too, cannot escape the opposing forces of fate and free will, nor the complexities of choice."

❧

Far above, in the silent, star-filled swathe over Lunarae, Selenus stood alone under the strain of his own questions. Dark circles bruised his eyes after a long night of watchful duty.

A familiar, creeping stiffness seized his joints—a chill that began in his bones and spread outwards. He knew the whispers. The prophecy had shadowed him since his first breath, the curse that others feared would one day unravel the realms.

His stone citadel, perched on a high promontory, seemed colder than usual. The cosmic threads connecting his moon realm to Aetherwyn—usually a cool, distant hum—now throbbed with a sickening intensity in time with the void inside him.

His vision caught an anomaly: a cobalt-blue star of singular brilliance, unlike any he had seen before. Its light flickered with a mysterious intensity, drawing him in. A glimmer of something akin to hope flared within him.

He lifted his hands, reaching toward the impossible gleam. In that moment, an image of Wilhelmina—fleeting and unbidden—flashed across his mind. But as he reached, his ingrained self-doubt, a darkness as old as his being, asserted itself. The star's light recoiled as though stung, bending its path away... tracing a distant arc toward Solarae.

"Of course. Light is for others to bask in, to admire. My shadows are too quiet, too cold. Even this beautiful anomaly chooses him," he said aloud. A dry, bitter laugh escaped him, brittle as Solarae's desert sands. Solitude was his destiny. It always had been.

His hands fell, his face impassive. A melancholy suffused the air, born of a truth he had carried for centuries—a truth of separation, of the unrelenting pull of shadows away from the light.

Tonight, however, the hollow of loneliness became colder, deeper—infused with a new, burning resentment. And with it came the insidious confirmation that his fate was inescapable. The pain in his limbs intensified. Clutching the Wand of Shadow, its dark power a twisted comfort, he allowed his despair to coalesce into a formidable will.

And yet, that vision of Wilhelmina—steward of Aetherwyn and his friend through countless cycles—lingered like the faintest balm upon his shadows. A torment, too, for it illuminated all he feared to lose.

His gaze dropped toward the realm below, a longing flickering through him—visible even to the heavens that watched him.

"I shall go to her."

Selenus descended from Lunarae's heights. He lifted his face and found the brilliant star again—pulsing with more radiance than the rest, even against the azure sky. Its silvery light beamed a path toward Aetherwyn.

He followed its projection—a thin ray casting a glow upon a distant meadow where a mysterious aura danced. His expression tightened as the cosmic fabric tugged at him... *inexorable*.

❧

Wilhelmina strolled through the rose gardens, where a fragrant embrace surrounded her. Her opalescent wings caught the cool breeze, their steady rhythm blending with the gentle sway of moonblossom tree branches.

As on countless mornings before, she prepared to bind the bride and groom's nuptial vows with her magic. This celebrated event would always take place at the ceremonial meadow. Even now, preparations were in full swing. Her life was woven into the magic she nurtured. The rhythm of her wings carried the balance of joy and sorrow, a burden she bore without complaint.

Stopping beside a moonblossom tree, she gently caressed the blooms on a lower branch. She plucked a moonblossom—her favorite flower—from the limb and pulled magic from within herself to enchant the petals. Instead, they withered.

"That's strange." Wilhelmina studied the moonblossom in her hand and tried again—but the petals only darkened further.

Wilhelmina exhaled softly. Above her, the heavens bore a faint metallic sheen—a tarnish upon the morning light that spoke of a fraying balance. She continued to watch as Phaethon and Selenus circled one another, brothers in conflict. "They are fighting again," she whispered to the moonblossoms. "When will the threads finally snap?"

Her long silver hair, woven with strands of starlight, drifted around her as she continued to watch the heavens. Then a shimmer caught her eye.

A rare cobalt-blue star streaked across the morning light, pulsing with a rhythmic urgency. It was an anomaly that neither the Sun nor the Moon could explain, a lonely spark that seemed to watch the rose gardens with a strange, familiar longing.

Moments later, a familiar presence unfolded from the shadows—undeniable, yet distant, as though it belonged more to the night than to her sun-bathed world.

Selenus's form sharpened, every line and feature so finely shaped it seemed a matter of artistic precision rather than mere happenstance. His silver eyes, gleaming like polished obsidian, fixed on her.

Wilhelmina blew on the moonblossom to return some life to it. After three breaths, it finally revived. She smiled.

"Selenus, you're late," she chided, her voice a soft bell. "The weddings are about to start."

"Ah. My apologies." He averted his eyes for a bare second before taking her hand, his cool lips brushing the top of it in his usual regal manner.

Wilhelmina's heart quickened, but she pulled her fingers back as if burned.

The weight of her duty was like a mountain of stone upon her shoulders. In such moments, which often happened between them, a tension unfailingly lingered—a tension taut as a harp string about to snap.

"You're forgiven, but do better next time," she teased, a hint of genuine wistfulness in her tone. "I missed our morning conversation."

"As did I. It is always a pleasure to argue with you... among other sentiments."

He turned fully toward her, his profile illuminated, as though chiseled from the finest marble by angelic hands. For a moment, his eyes caught hers—a moment long enough to stir something uninvited in the still night air.

"I brought you a gift," he replied, stepping closer. "A star."

The laws of her heart were etched in celestial silver, a sacred script she had followed since her first flight. Yet, as Selenus stood before her, that silver seemed to take on the density of lead, a heavy, cold weight that pulled against the very grace she was meant to embody.

She gathered herself with a graceful adjustment of posture. It would not do to indulge in thoughts unsuited to her position. Her duty lay in preserving Aetherwyn's magic, not in contemplating the moonlit prince who stood before her. Her wings shifted, and with an intake of breath that could scarcely be helped, she broke the fragile silence.

"Ahem," she coughed lightly. "That's not how gifts work."

He smiled, with that crooked smile that always made her wings twitch. But it appeared hollow at the edges, stripped of warmth.

For a moment, it was easy—just old friends bantering. But beneath their words, something simmered. A yearning. A warning.

As far back as she could remember, an invisible force always pulled her toward him. He loved to tease her, nettle her with his one question, the same one she would often ask herself. "Why do you give love to others but keep none for yourself, Wilhelmina?"

She would always answer him. "Because, Selenus, the realm's harmony relies on my magic to sustain it, and I must remain devoted to my duties."

He would sigh, his shoulders slumping, and walk away.

He interrupted her reverie. "I saw your sadness," he said quietly.

She stiffened. "I'm not sad."

"Yes, you are."

She turned. "And what if I am?"

He looked away. "Then maybe we're both pretending the world is still whole."

Their eyes met. A thousand lifetimes in a glance. But neither moved. Friendship, duty, legacy—they were barriers stronger than any wall.

Selenus inclined his head. "May I ask you something?"

She sighed. "Of course."

"Wilhelmina," Selenus began, his voice a velvet thread woven with amusement and something sharper. "You are the steward of love's magic, yet you stand untouched by it. Tell me—what happens when the balance demands more than even you can give?"

A flicker of challenge brightened Wilhelmina's blue eyes. "Indeed. That is an interesting question. And not the usual one." Her wings fanned the air with deliberate precision.

An amused smile touched his lips—whether in apology or mere politeness, it was unclear. "I ask too much."

Wilhelmina inclined her head. "You know what would happen..." Her voice trailed off. "Why are you asking? Is everything alright?"

He hesitated as if weighing his response before resting a hand lightly on his chest. "Is this not the realm of love's magic? I thought perhaps it could spare a little—for me." His voice drifted. "I have need of it... to quiet some turbulence."

A blush flickered across her cheeks, and a warmth surged through her veins.

The words, though lightly spoken, gathered power in the pause separating them. Shadows stirred across his face, lending him the appearance of a man more haunted by his thoughts than he would admit.

Selenus's lips curved upward, but the smile vanished before it could take shape. "Tell me, Wilhelmina—how is it you remain so unerring in your duty?"

Some burdens were never meant to be shared, even among those born to dance through the firmament, and the silence that stretched between them now suggested they both knew this truth too well.

The question hung in the air, unexpected, and if a bit tinged with curiosity, it was the kind that probed too close for comfort. "It is what I was born to do," she said with practiced ease, though the familiar phrase rang hollow this time.

She sighed. "There are times when I wish I could see the sunset, but I'm busy officiating the day's wedding. It's a constant balance between my responsibilities and the wishes of my heart."

Selenus's gaze held hers, unreadable. "Yes. Our duties don't give us much choice in the matter." A hollow laugh slipped through his lips, vanishing like mist. "For someone so devoted to love, you seem remarkably determined to avoid it."

"Perhaps I simply prefer love in its proper place—far from reckless Moon Princes." She smirked with amusement.

Selenus raised a brow. "Reckless? Maybe... Let me show you something." He reached inside his robe and pulled out a silver wand, gleaming under the moonlit haze.

Wilhelmina inwardly gasped. "The wand," she said, her tone sharp. "You know what it is, don't you?"

Selenus's fingers tightened around the shaft, his jaw hardening.

"It's a tool. Nothing more."

"It's a piece of her," she countered. Her wings bristled. "And it's corrupting you."

He laughed, low and bitter. "You think me corrupted because I won't let my light be eclipsed? Or is it easier to believe that than to admit you've never truly understood me?"

But he approached her slowly, keeping his gaze fixed on hers while returning the wand to the inner folds of his cloak. "I'd rather do the claiming... if you'll let me."

He stood so close that their breaths mingled. His eyes seared with a heated intensity as he reached for her fingertips.

Wilhelmina held her breath. A glow rose from her chest, brilliant in its light.

But wind chimes tinkled in the air—Aetherwyn's signal to call guests to the wedding of the day.

She sucked in a deep breath and shook her head. "No... I can't, Selenus."

"You can't, or you won't. There's a difference." He took her fingers and pressed them against the space where his heart lay. "And I know you feel what I do."

The air between them didn't merely warm; it vibrated. A low, resonant hum—a frequency that predated the very foundations of Aetherwyn—thrummed through their joined hands. It was a harmony that felt instinctively like a transgression, though Wilhelmina could not have said why. Her internal light flared, not in a battle against the shadow beneath his cloak, but as an echo answering a long-forgotten song.

Her eyes drew up to his and then dropped to his lips. A tremor moved through her, visible even in the soft rise of her breath.

"I-I mustn't. It has already been determined what duty is mine. For the good of Aetherwyn." Her voice shook. "I can't let them down..."

She pulled her hand back, looking at the spot where her palm had lain. When she turned up her face to look at him, his crestfallen expression caused her to gasp. A faint, cold whisper brushed her ear, a breath like frost that no wind stirred.

"We are friends, are we not? That has to be enough."

He tilted his head. "Forgive me," he said, his tone cool, though his eyes burned with something unspoken. "Perhaps your realm's light holds answers even I cannot see. I shall see you at the wedding... Wilhelmina."

She took a step back, lengthening the distance between them.

"Yes... that would be lovely. You are always welcome."

The ache sharpened.

Wilhelmina stood motionless, her wings heavy as lead. She clenched her hand tightly, watching until the moonlit haze swallowed him whole, leaving her alone.

A solitary figure amidst the roses and their fading perfume.

2. The Moon Prince's Shadow

As Wilhelmina turned to leave, a gust of wind twisted around her, colder now, its whisper a blade against her skin: "*Beware... the balance falters.*"

A moonblossom branch snapped through the air and whipped toward her. It struck her skirt, slicing a clean tear.

She gasped and recoiled, her gown pulled taut as the wind hissed past her ears. Then, as abruptly as it had risen, the gust stilled—leaving behind a silence too deliberate to be chance.

She steadied herself, wings lifting into the morning light, as if drawing strength from its fragile glow. Her gown trailed like a wisp of moonlight as she drifted above the meadow, but the brightness below rang false. Beneath the cheerful chatter of creatures, a discordant vibration lingered—a shimmer of decay fraying the edges of the realm's lively façade.

❧

In Lunarae's barren expanse, where stony citadels stood like sentinels, Selenus kept his solitary vigil. The mingling of starlight and Solarae's distant glow cast an uneasy brilliance over the landscape; the same light that nourished the realms below burned cold here.

Selenus's shoulders tensed, his stare hollow. A pall of regret darkened his stance, though he made no move to voice it. His parents' reminders of duty and his brother's recent rebuke further chilled the unyielding ground beneath his feet. Love, it seemed, was an abstract idea—inaccessible and devoid of empathy.

Then came the encounter with Wilhelmina. His face burned from the memory. Only the star had offered hope. Though perfect, it was unattainable, like a dream realized that required proving one's worth.

In the night sky, his eye caught it, warm and brilliant, an inspiration of love itself. How could he want the celestial body so much? Was it just a distraction from his growing love for her?

He reached into the folds of his midnight cloak and drew forth his wand. The ancient relic, sleek and luminous like moonlight, had once belonged to the Enchantress—or so the shadows whispered. It was said to hold the echoes of her power, meant solely for hands worthy of wielding it. Yet Selenus had claimed it in secret.

It sat heavily in his grip. His fingers traced its length in slow, deliberate turns—a familiar habit, as though the mere motion might loosen the bitterness coiled within him.

It now pulsed, alive with its own will. In the quiet of Lunarae, where shadows thrived, a voice, dark and honeyed, seeped into the space surrounding him.

"*Take it, Selenus,*" it hissed. "*The Enchantress's greatness could be yours. Why should you remain in his shadow when you could command the light?*"

The temptation was a steady hum, weaving itself into his being until he no longer knew where the darkness ended and he began.

"*This wand was not meant for you, Selenus.*"

The Enchantress's voice lingered—a phantom of memory or imagination. But was it her warning—or the wand's taunt? The stars above glittered without care or consequence, silent witnesses to his vigil.

"What meaning remains if even the constellations refuse me? They shine for others, but never for me," he said aloud. "My sacrifices, my existence—forgotten in the margins of history."

He exhaled, the sound falling like a stone into a still pool. "Once, my brother and I shared the weight of our realms, and together, it seemed lighter. I remember the days when his laughter was as warm as his presence, and I was not just his shadow. His light reaches farther than mine. While he spreads joy across the realms, I am here in this barren waste... alone."

He pressed his fingers against his temples, dragging them through his dark hair. "I have borne enough! If happiness evades me, let no one find it!"

The wand responded to his anger, shadows spilling forth in jagged waves. Each pulse fed on his envy, growing stronger with every passing moment.

Selenus clenched the wand tighter, its promise whispering in his ear. But he hesitated, his grip faltering. Was this what he wanted? A memory of joy flickered in his mind—his brother's laughter, the warmth of the sun on his face.

He was tired of light bending away from him, leaving him in its cold penumbra. If joy would not find him, then let the light itself be swallowed by his darkness.

The wand grew hotter in his palm, and the thought was torn from him, replaced by a hunger not his own.

☙

Wilhelmina arrived at the hallowed meadow. Bordered by vibrant flowers and ancient moonblossom trees, it had long been a favored spot for weddings, where love blossomed in the presence of the lake called Serene Waters. The old bridge, called the Span of Reflections, arched over the lake's mirrored surface, as timeless as the ceremonies it had witnessed.

She stood composed beneath the arch, but the movement of her wings hinted at a restlessness that did not belong on a day so bright. A surge of raw magic pricked her skin, sharp and cold, like splintered glass. Her surroundings, usually a bastion of pure enchantment, appeared... off. The sunbeams filtering through the moonblossom trees spilled across the grass in patterns that shifted erratically, blurring at the edges. It wasn't a visible eclipse, but a profound tremor in the essence of Aetherwyn and in the magic itself.

Her gaze drifted toward the horizon as a chill crept into the air. She adjusted the pleats of her gown with a slight, deliberate movement, and, with the flick of her wrist, sent out sparkling streams of enchantment. They unfurled like ribbons, twisting and curling in dazzling arcs. Laughter erupted from the onlookers. Around her, fairies twirled in dizzying circles. Their delight was infectious, spreading through the gathering like wildfire. And yet, woven into the starlit air, there was a softness—a quiet ache, lingering like a whispered secret outside the reach of light.

Wilhelmina remained on the edge of it all, weaving the magic but never stepping into its warmth. The love she conjured settled effortlessly into the gathered hearts, as if it belonged to everyone but herself.

She glided among the crowd, her presence like a moonbeam threading through starlit water.

"Wilhelmina's gown glows like the stars," one fairy said with a sigh. "And she wears it as if stardust were spun for her."

Butterflies of every color drifted through the current, carrying love notes from one fairy to another. Messages fluttered from wing to wing, bringing delighted giggles in their wake.

"What's this?" Wilhelmina teased, noticing a fairy blushing as she accepted a note from a butterfly. "A secret admirer, perhaps?"

The fairies laughed, their joy bubbling over like morning dew catching sunlight. Perhaps it was the magic in the air, or perhaps the enchantment of Wilhelmina's presence that stirred such merriment.

Amid the fluttering wings, a young sprite stood apart, her small hands pressed to her chest as she watched the butterflies swirl around others, their vibrant wings never once pausing for her.

Wilhelmina knelt beside the child at once. "Oh, little one," she uttered, her voice warm and steady, "sometimes the most important messages come in the most unexpected ways."

The sprite sniffled, dabbing at her eyes. "But I didn't get one..."

With a graceful wave of her hand, Wilhelmina summoned a butterfly from the air. Its wings shimmered in soft twilight hues. The delicate creature glided, landing lightly on the sprite's shoulder.

"This one's for you," Wilhelmina said, her tone soft with affection. "It carries the kind of love that never fades—the love of a friend."

The sprite's tears gave way to a shy smile as she cupped the butterfly in her small hands, the sadness in her gaze replaced by a spark of hope. "Thank you," she whispered, the words brimming with all the earnestness of childhood.

Wilhelmina's smile faltered for a brief moment, unbeknownst to the child cradling the butterfly with unfeigned delight.

She returned to her duties, but in the next moment, her keen fairy ears were pierced by words she never expected to hear.

"They say a curse follows the Moon Prince," murmured one elf to his companion, his tone thick with the gravity of half-believed rumor. "A prince of shadows, destined to unravel Aetherwyn's magic, should his heart grow too dark."

His companion gave a measured shake of the head. "Surely, such tales are only the mischief of myth. The Eternal Ones would never permit so grave a fate to befall us."

A brighter voice—pleasantly lilting and altogether unconcerned—spilled into the air like the chiming of silver bells. "Oh, I heard it quite differently," she said with a conspiratorial flutter of her eyelashes. "It wasn't a curse at all, but a most dashing enchantress who once coaxed the shadows into dancing for her. They say she wore a gown stitched from moonlight and wove spells with ribbons of starlight."

Her companion gave a little trill of laughter. "And then she vanished, of course—pfft!—like mist in a sunbeam. But if she were still about, well, imagine the scene! She'd sweep in, scatter those gloomy shadows like dust motes, and the whole realm would sparkle again."

Nearby, two fairies hovered in a hushed exchange, their wings catching the morning light with a shimmer that belied the somber nature of their words.

"If the Moon Prince's jealousy should spread," said one, "they say Aetherwyn's magic might well wither. And without it..."

Wilhelmina's wings shuddered, and she gathered the folds of her gown. Yet the whispers, as persistent as ivy creeping over an untended wall, wove themselves into the delicate fabric of the morning air.

Despite the gnawing unease, she settled herself back beneath the moonblossom arch. The ceremonial meadow appeared charged now, the familiar beauty of the lake and the old bridge overlaid with a shimmering distortion.

Sunbeam patterns spread across the grass now writhed, unsettling her. To an unknowing observer, she might have seemed at ease, composed. Yet the flutter of her wings, usually a sign of contentment, now betrayed a nervous tension.

❧

Later, Thalor, the elven groom standing before Wilhelmina, cut a striking figure in his moonbeam suit. He shifted from foot to foot, his grin faltering when his gaze found Elysia, his pixie bride.

Crispin, usually quick with a jest, cleared his throat, adjusting his shimmering waistcoat as he prepared to announce the union, but his eyes kept darting to the shifting patterns of light.

Flora's green fingers deftly arranged a final moonblossom on Elysia's veil. The blooms in the crafted bouquet quivered slightly in Flora's grasp as she handed it to her and watched her glide down the aisle, radiant in a gown spun from the threads of the morning sun.

Aria, her siren's voice a stream of pure enchantment, sent a compelling melody throughout the ceremony, her song weaving through the air, but a subtle tremor ran beneath its usual crystalline beauty.

Thalor and Elysia's eyes met, and an enchanted energy rippled between them—subtle as the breeze but charged with the force that binds hearts across lifetimes.

As they exchanged vows, the magic of sun and moon gathered in their words. Each pledge was a thread in the grand design, strengthening the realm's essence.

In Aetherwyn, such unions were foundational. Yet even the most potent magic was fragile, its strength tested by the inevitable dissonance that lurks beneath every great joy.

As Wilhelmina unfurled her enchantments, sparkling streams of magic twisted into dazzling arcs. But instead of the usual cascading joy, a faint, metallic tang filled the air, sharp and discordant. Gales of laughter burst from the crowd, beaming like sunlight on water, but it seemed brittle, like glass about to shatter. Fairies twirled, their delight infectious, yet Wilhelmina sensed an undercurrent pushing against the boundaries of the celebration's magic.

Crispin's grin cracked, replaced by a nervous cough as he fumbled with his baton. Aria's melody fractured, notes wavering into a dissonant hum. Quill, who had been scribbling rapidly on a scroll, suddenly froze, his writing instrument poised in mid-air, ink dripping onto the parchment like dark tears. Flora clutched her bouquet, and a moonblossom within it curled, its luminescence dimming.

A sharp cold cut through the meadow, chilling the air and stilling the crowd's murmurs. The light shifted, not just dimming, but warping, pulling long, distorted shadows across the vibrant grass. Wilhelmina's heart hammered against her ribs. This was no subtle omen. This was a force manifesting, demanding attention.

A presence solidified at the meadow's edge, a figure cloaked in the newly stretched shadows, distinct against the shifting light.

Selenus. The Moon Prince.

His arrival was less an entrance than an assertion, an undeniable ripple through the fragile balance. And now, his gaze cut directly through the wedding guests, finding hers.

A strange, undeniable pull tugged at her.

He said nothing. His hand rested on a dark, slender object at his side. The Wand of Shadow, unmistakable in its sinister grace, throbbed with the deepening gloom.

A shiver, not of the mountain's chill but of a profound resonance, traced the length of Wilhelmina's spine. The air between them thickened, straining against the heavy silver laws of her duty. In the Prince's shadow, an ache she had long buried was suddenly exposed, vibrating in sympathy with the darkness he carried.

Selenus finally moved, a slow, deliberate step that seemed like a cosmic shift. His voice, when it came, was a low hum, resonant like distant thunder, yet cutting through the startled silence of the meadow. "Still weaving illusions, Wilhelmina? Still selling promises of joy that even you cannot possess?"

His words, meant as a barb, struck deeper than he knew, hitting the core of her silent sacrifice. Yet beneath the sting, a fragile thread of empathy pulsed within her. She saw not just the Prince of Shadows, but the wounded soul who often asked her troubling questions.

Wilhelmina straightened; her wings, though quivering, held rigid. She met his stare, refusing to flinch. "And you, Selenus? Still consumed by shadows that refuse to be tamed? You bring your bitterness to a place of hope, threatening the balance you are sworn to uphold." Her voice, usually soft, now held an unexpected steel, a new resolve sparked by his direct assault on her sacred duty.

A humorless smile touched Selenus's lips, a stark contrast to the celebration around them. His gaze flickered to the newlywed couple, then back to Wilhelmina, a spark of something raw and knowing in his eyes. "Hope? Or merely a distraction, Wilhelmina? A pretty lie to keep the mortals oblivious while the true power falters." He gestured with a dismissive sweep of his hand, and the Wand of Shadow pulsed, sending a ripple of distorted light through the air that caused the lanterns to dim and the magical petals to fall in a sudden, dead cascade.

A collective gasp rippled through the gathered wedding guests, a sound of fragile wonder turning to stark fear. Thalor and Elysia, their faces now pale, clung to each other, their joyous union instantly overshadowed by the encroaching chill. Whispers of the Moon Prince's curse spread like wildfire, no longer mere rumors but a palpable, biting reality.

Crispin's face, usually alight with good humor, paled, and his baton slipped from his nerveless fingers, clattering to the ground. Aria's song died in her throat, a mournful gasp escaping her lips instead. Quill dropped his scroll entirely, its parchment scattering across the disturbed grass, his eyes wide with horror. Flora instinctively shielded her bouquet, but already its vibrant colors were fading, its petals curling.

Wilhelmina had a desperate urge to shield them, to mend the fraying threads of joy. Her own magic, usually a wellspring of warmth, had now become strained, battling against the cold, invasive force radiating from Selenus.

"Stop this, Selenus!" she commanded, her voice cutting through the rising panic. She extended a hand, not in anger, but with a plea woven into her magic, attempting to counter the dissonance he invoked. The space separating them shimmered, a visible struggle between her restorative light and his burgeoning shadow.

Selenus merely watched, his eyes gleaming, unaffected by her appeal. His gaze held a strange mix of triumph and profound pain, as if reveling in the chaos he created even as it tore at him. "You cling to a dying light, Wilhelmina," he murmured, his voice laced with bitter amusement. "This realm, like its magic, is destined to unravel. And you, the Wedding Fairy, are powerless to stop it. Your devotion to their love means nothing in the face of true sorrow."

He lingered for another beat, letting his words sink in, letting the growing panic among the guests solidify. Then, with a flicker of shadow that consumed the last vestiges of twilight, Selenus vanished as abruptly as he had appeared, leaving behind a profound emptiness and the lingering chill of his despair.

The vow had not yet been spoken, but something had already shattered.

❧

Some said the Enchantress had forged the wand as a gift for a worthy soul—a vessel for channeling both light and shadow. But others whispered darker truths, tales of a relic born to anchor the balance of magic, yet capable of tipping it entirely in the wrong hands. Selenus had taken it not out of duty, but desire—a decision he now carried like a stain of its own.

The wand trembled in his hand. A breath. A choice. Then lightning cracked along its length, and the night shifted irrevocably.

He tightened his grip. "If light denies me, let darkness carry my name. I shall make my mark, not in joy, but in sorrow. Even shadows will remember me."

His grip hardened. "And if I am to live in shadow, I will become the darkest one. Let them know my pain."

Selenus swept the silver wand upward, pointing it toward the star-filled firmament. With that motion, the moonlight waned, and spectral silhouettes stretched across the barren expanse.

The silver shaft remained still, heavy in his grasp, then shuddered, growing hot until it scorched him. With a cry, he released it. The clatter of silver against stone rang out in the empty expanse. Sharp. Final.

A plume of smoke coiled upward from its tip, twisting, unfurling, summoning a power that could command attention from the deepest recesses of the galactic void. The shadows responded to his will, curling like living threads.

Breath by breath, the darkness thickened, emerging from the hidden depths of the night. It transformed from a mere absence of light into a potent force laden with sinister ambition.

Above, the stars dimmed, their light retreating from the encroaching gloom. A low rumble echoed across the heavens, as though the cosmic order itself shuddered at the presence of something ancient and malevolent.

Selenus stared at the wand where it lay, its silver glinting with an eerie pulse. He neither moved nor spoke. Despair gathered within the stillness, though no sign of it touched his face.

The darkness spread like ink through water, curling outward to blot out the landscape, suffocating every color and spark of light. Aetherwyn lay beneath its reach, its vibrant meadows fading beneath the night's expanding bleakness.

The wand dulled in the cold, unforgiving new reality. Darkness fed on its hunger as the umbra claimed the bespangled void. Another thunderous crack reverberated through the hushed ether.

Selenus looked down at the wand by his feet, its pulse ominous, its call inescapable. Turning away would have been easy, had it not held him fast—a lure too potent to ignore. His gaze drifted toward Aetherwyn, and he swallowed hard as the reach of night grew. His lungs constricted as a biting coolness crept through the air. A distant cackle broke the silence, quickly consumed by the night.

Darkness seeped into every home, sweeping through hills and valleys, infiltrating gardens and forests across Aetherwyn, dimming the realm's vibrant colors. The wand's tendrils crept along invisible paths, weaving themselves into the fabric of the realms, tugging at the delicate balance that held light and dark in harmony.

"What have I done?"

His whispered words went unanswered. He clenched his fists, jaw tightening. "No. They must know. They must all know my pain."

In the cold reflection cast upon the citadel's stony walls, a face stared back at him, pale and drawn, with dark hollows beneath his eyes and a sickly pallor. Turbid coils snaked from the rising plume and curled toward his chest.

His breath came ragged, and he sank to the ground. "I have lost control," he whispered. "This darkness will not release me." His fingers clawed at his hair.

The wand pulsed with an ominous rhythm, unwavering in its call. He would have withdrawn, but its power murmured seductively through the shifting murk. A voice arose, low and serpentine.

"*You are power, Selenus. Let them tremble.*"

A shiver passed through him, though his lips curled into a thin smirk. His hand hovered over the wand for a moment longer before closing firmly around the shaft. He rose and moved away, retreating into the depths of the citadel's walls. The stones pressed inward like a tomb, sealing him in silence.

Far away, the celestial threads linking Solarae, Lunarae, and Aetherwyn lost their luster as the darkness stretched its grasp.

3. A Steward's Burden

The meadow was plunged into a stunned silence, broken by the whimpers of frightened pixies and the rustle of dead petals. Wilhelmina stood rooted, her hand still outstretched, the warmth of her magic fighting to reassert itself against the cold imprint Selenus had left. The love she had woven, the delicate harmony of the ceremony, now seemed fragile, endangered.

Her spine stiffened. This was not a subtle warning, and the truth hit her with the force of a blow. This was a declaration. The balance had not merely teetered; it had been actively attacked. And Selenus, the very being meant to uphold one half of that balance, had chosen to shatter it.

A cold certainty settled over her. She had carried the burden of Aetherwyn's harmony all her life, yet never had its weight pressed so close to breaking. The whispers she'd heard earlier threaded through the air once more: "*...the balance falters.*"

She had to act. She had to understand. Her path was clear: she needed Gwydion. With a sudden, decisive beat of her wings, she ascended, leaving the stunned, shadowed meadow behind. The celestial bodies above, usually comforting, watched with bated breath as she flew towards the Grand Oak, their distant light a faint, uncertain guide in the encroaching gloom. The lingering chill from Selenus's presence still clung everywhere, a stark contrast to the warmth that had so recently enveloped Aetherwyn.

Wilhelmina's mind raced, the catastrophic scene at the wedding replaying in vivid flashes. It wasn't a threat; it was an open wound, and Selenus was both the blade and, perhaps, the bleeding heart behind it. Gwydion's warnings, once vague premonitions, now resonated with brutal clarity.

☙

She found Gwydion perched on a gnarled branch of the Grand Oak, his amber eyes already fixed on her approach. The wise owl, ancient as the realm itself, seemed to have been expecting her. His feathers, usually a deep reddish-brown, appeared muted in the bruised twilight.

Wilhelmina landed softly before him, her wings quivering, no longer from exhaustion but from the profound disquiet now visible in her bearing.

"Gwydion," she breathed, the single word imbued with all the terror and confusion of the past moments. "He was there. Selenus. He... he used the Wand of Shadow. He spoke of unraveling, of the balance breaking. It was as if he wanted it."

Gwydion flapped his great wings with a slow, deliberate rustle, a sound like leaves in an autumn wind. A low hoot escaped him, primeval and mournful. "Indeed, Wilhelmina. The unraveling has begun. The Moon Prince's despair is a powerful, destructive force, and he allows it to consume him, just as it now threatens to consume the realms."

Wilhelmina's head snapped up. "His despair? What could drive such darkness in him?"

Gwydion turned his head, his gaze piercing. "His envy, fueled by long-held bitterness and perceived injustices, has become a torrent. He wields a darkness now that seems to come from deep within himself, and its ripple spreads across the celestial threads."

Wilhelmina's shoulders drooped beneath a wave of sorrow, her bearing weighed down by fear. She knew only the outer manifestations of his bitterness. It was a wound in Lunarae reflecting one in Aetherwyn. "To feel pity for him is a powerful impulse, child, but be wary of its hidden currents. Remember: pity, unlike true compassion, often carries a fracture of fear. If your empathy mirrors his despair, it risks weaving discord into your own essence, feeding the very shadows you oppose." Gwydion's gaze held hers, a solemn caution.

"But the realms... the magic... can it truly withstand this?" Wilhelmina finally managed, her voice thin.

Gwydion shook his head slowly. "The balance is fragile, Wilhelmina. Always has been. Love and joy are powerful, yes, but they require constant nurturing. And when despair takes root, it seeks to consume all light. The magic that binds us all... it is not merely a force, but a living thing, dependent on the hearts that hold it. If even one of its guardians succumbs to such darkness..." His words trailed off, the silence heavy with unspoken consequence.

"I don't understand... If he is so consumed, how can it be stopped? How do I—" Her voice faltered. "How is such power to be defeated when it comes from such profound despair?" A deeper question, echoing the ache in her heart, surfaced. "How can I nurture love across the realms when my own heart feels so... empty?"

Gwydion's amber gaze rested on her, steady and unblinking. "Your role demands sacrifice, child. One that leaves little room for your own happiness." He paused, his expression softening almost imperceptibly. "Yet, love, like magic, often finds its own way, even in the most unexpected places. It does not always adhere to the dictates of prophecy."

❧

With a graceful arc of her wings, Wilhelmina bowed her head, leaving the wise owl on his limb. The dim, starry light softened her path homeward. Enveloped in the misty glow of the shimmering expanse, she glided, burdened by thought. Petals rising from the rose gardens brushed past her, as though they too were swept up in her silent charge. She glanced over her shoulder at the Grand Oak.

So caught up was she in her reverie that she didn't hear the distant voice calling her name.

"Wilhelmina! Wilhelmina! Stop!"

The voice grew closer, sharper.

But it was too late. "Oomph! Oh!"

She had bumped into her oldest and dearest friend, Lumina, the glowing sprite. The fairy and sprite tumbled in midair, their wings fluttering in surprise. They burst into laughter and embraced.

"Lumina! Are you all right?" Wilhelmina patted Lumina's limbs to check for any sign of injury.

"Oh yes... yes, I'm fine! Just a bit winded," Lumina sputtered, catching her breath. She pushed Wilhelmina's hands away and adjusted her wings as their laughter faded.

Wilhelmina placed her hands on Lumina's shoulders, a long breath of relief escaping her lips. "It's so wonderful to see you."

Lumina's wings beat in brisk bursts, stirring the still air. She tilted her head, narrowing her eyes in gentle scrutiny. "You don't seem yourself today," she observed, taking Wilhelmina's hand in hers. "Your smile is weary, and your wings look tired—drooping, even. It's like even the magic you carry is becoming heavier. Have you rested lately?"

Wilhelmina offered a bright, fleeting smile, a delicate construct of grace. She slipped her hand from Lumina's, brushing at the air as if shooing away an invisible insect. She fidgeted with her fingers, saying nothing more.

Lumina frowned, a flicker of concern crossing her features. "What's wrong?" Her hands tightened gently around Wilhelmina's.

Wilhelmina shivered. "If Aetherwyn loses its magic, Solarae and Lunarae will lose their connection to it. Without harmony, light will collapse into destruction. The darkness will grow, and there will be no stopping it. I won't be able to halt it." Her shoulders slumped forward. "I shall be... useless... unwanted."

Lumina bent her head, her expression softening. "Wilhelmina, do you ever wonder... what if this burden was never yours to carry alone? What if love isn't something you need to earn, but something you already deserve?"

Wilhelmina clasped her arms, tightening her wings against her back. "But it's what I was made for."

Lumina shook her head. "The realm needs you, yes, but not at the cost of your own light. If you let it burn out, Aetherwyn will indeed die."

Wilhelmina blinked rapidly, moisture gathering until her lashes glittered in the dim light. She turned away. Her words carried a whisper edged with longing. "Sometimes, I envy you, Lumina. You have the freedom to love and to move through the world without this burden. You have choices. I don't."

"Magic is delicate, and there are shadows near us that would see it unravel. But we are not so powerless as they might hope," Lumina said. "You are stronger than you know, and I believe in your good judgment."

"I hope you're right."

Lumina chuckled. "I trust you will prove it to be so." She leaned closer, her voice dropping to a conspiratorial whisper. "Tell me, are you not even a little curious about what it would be like to hold someone's hand or share a kiss, not as the wedding fairy, but just as yourself?"

Wilhelmina's eyes widened, and her cheeks flushed a beet red. "Oh, Lumina. What a silly thing to say." Averting her eyes, she sighed.

"You've spent centuries giving others their happily-ever-afters, Wilhelmina. But when was the last time you allowed yourself to do more than dream of one?"

Wilhelmina managed a strained smile. "Dreams are safe, Lumina. They don't threaten the balance."

"You've always been the heart of Aetherwyn, but even the strongest heart needs others to lean on." Lumina paused. "Perhaps it's time to let others give back. And you have choices, too, even if they aren't what you expected."

Wilhelmina's wings shivered, her voice brittle like flower petals close to crumbling. "But what if love... what if it isn't a part of the order, but a threat to it?"

A warmer breeze stirred the meadow. Lumina smiled, brushing her wingtip lightly against Wilhelmina's shoulder. "And isn't love strongest when it's shared? Perhaps it isn't a threat to the balance—it could be the balance itself."

She blew out a sharp breath. "All right, I will not speak of it further. Now, let's leave these shadows where they are and look forward to a new day." She pulled Wilhelmina into a quick embrace. "And you will do what you always do—hold the worlds together."

Above them, the stars shimmered in alignment with the cosmic forces that wove through Aetherwyn's fate. Yet while its magic was delicate, it was also enduring, and so was she. Her role, though isolating, was valuable. The weddings Wilhelmina officiated were not mere ceremonies—they were threads in the tapestry of magic that bound the dimensions.

As Lumina's glow faded into the night, Wilhelmina stared at the celestial bodies, their light both a promise and a burden.

"But what if I can't?" A quiver ran through her, then stilled. Clutching her hands to her chest, she shook her head, but then snuck a glance at the moon, and her wings caught the light in a glimmering arc beneath its silver gaze.

4. The Imprint of Destiny

As the lengthening umbra stretched from Lunarae, the charm that had once bound Aetherwyn's gardens, lakes, and forests in harmonious enchantment unraveled. Where joyous melodies had once floated on the breeze, an unnatural hush crept in—like an uninvited guest at a wedding, extinguishing every note of merriment. Joy, it seemed, had discovered it was no match for the encroaching gloom.

Far across the meadow, Wilhelmina beheld the chill of darkness, and a tremor ran through her wings. As she wrapped her arms around herself, the familiar magic of Aetherwyn seemed thin and weakening, but she could not see the true source of the decay. The magic was not merely fading; it was being siphoned. What power had the decay awakened in Selenus?

She fluttered through the darkened gardens, her flight stirring the air with a nervous rhythm. The roses—those sun-kissed darlings of the meadow—now sagged beneath an invisible burden, like love soured before the heart could grasp its disappointment.

Her path led beneath the moonblossom tree. Its petals flickered between presence and absence, undecided whether to endure the night or surrender to it.

Across the lakes, water and sky no longer flirted with playful reflections. Now, choppy ripples of discord spread over the surface, betraying the struggle beneath.

With a glance toward the heavens, Wilhelmina sought some fragment of hope among the stars. But the night offered little comfort. She rose into the breeze, her wings stirring with purpose as she surveyed the skies. Her voice, though a whisper, cut through the silence. "What is causing this horror?"

Her gaze alighted upon the moon, now veiled beneath a mist of gray. It hung low, solemn and reticent. And in that moment of observation, the truth that the moon's light was not just being resisted, but was being intentionally siphoned, became clear to her. The satellite was indeed conspiring with the shadows. A soft exclamation escaped her lips. "No!"

She descended, her wings carrying her through the somber streets of Aetherwyn. The city lay in muted silence, its magic diminished to an unsettling quiet. Statues, weathered by time and decorated with ancient carvings, stood sentinel along her path, though their stony countenances offered neither guidance nor comfort.

She passed by one worn statue of a beautiful woman adorned with intricate carvings. As she stared at its eroded contours, a shimmering darkness coalesced from the stone itself, taking the form of a cloaked figure. Its pupils, shining with tortured agony and arcane knowledge, fixed on her.

Wilhelmina froze, her wings shivering, as the apparition drifted closer, hands outstretched—only to dissolve into tendrils of smoke, unraveling into nothingness just before making contact.

A single name escaped her lips, a whisper of recognition. *"The Enchantress?"*

The name, The Enchantress, lingered like a melody recalled after many years—familiar yet bittersweet. Whispers of her had persisted in the manner of all ancient tales: dismissed by the sensible, yet never entirely forgotten. The notion that such a figure might have walked these lands, leaving traces of her power behind, was as tantalizing as it was troubling. For if this sorceress had once shaped the enchantments now unraveling, then surely some remnant of her knowledge remained—a thread, perhaps, with which to mend what was falling apart.

This thought, quiet and inevitable, took hold and gathered force as Wilhelmina wandered through the dim streets of Aetherwyn. "If I discover the secrets she left behind and her connection to Aetherwyn," she murmured aloud, "then perhaps there is still hope to revive its dwindling magic. I must find the answers."

❧

Wilhelmina lay restless in bed, troubled by dreams that twisted and warped the familiar passageways of Aetherwyn into labyrinths drowned in dusk.

In one strange dreamscape, smoky tendrils of darkness muted once-vibrant colors, and fleeting whispers skittered at the edges of her hearing. Her dreaming form twisted, head shifting as if to ward off unseen dread.

Musical notes of joy vanished, leaving a dreadful silence in the void. In another dream, a wilted moonflower brushed against her hand, its lifeless petals whispering of forgotten love. Her body folded in on itself in sorrow.

Shadows stretched before her, and among them appeared a figure—its form indistinct, its eyes gleaming with both sadness and longing. Before she could grasp its meaning, it faded into nothing, slipping through her fingers like a phantom of regret.

Catapulted into yet another dreamscape, the streets now teetered on the brink of desolation. Familiar faces flickered briefly—friends and companions, their voices drowned by the night. She reached out, and the figures vanished as if they had never existed.

Then came the cryptic whispers, slipping through the dark folds of the dream. They hinted at meanings that eluded clear understanding, as though pieces of a puzzle lay scattered just beyond comprehension.

"Beware celestial envy!" "Embrace the darkness to find the light!"

With a start, she awoke, her breath catching in her throat. A chill, colder than any dream, still clung to her, a dank pall tethered to reality, not a figment of sleep.

Wilhelmina's course, winding steadily toward the Grand Library, was not one she consciously chose. Rather, it appeared that fate—or some inscrutable hand—had set her wings upon this path, pulling her by an invisible thread long before she noticed the journey unfolding beneath them.

The library's tall doors, carved with familiar yet enigmatic symbols of wisdom and magic, stood ajar, as if left open for her arrival. She slipped inside, and the murmur of turning pages reached her ears—though whether from a distant reader or the library itself, she could not say.

Within, the scent of parchment and ink mingled with something older—something elusive, like the fragrance of rain poised just before it falls.

Rows of bookshelves stretched into the shadowy recesses, their contents whispering promises of forgotten truths. She drifted through the aisles, her fingers grazing the spines of books she could not name.

Then her gaze landed, as if by design, on a single book atop a polished wooden table. Its silvered script shone under the dim candlelight, shifting ever so slightly, as if reluctant to be understood all at once.

This was no ordinary volume. Its title, emblazoned across its cover, echoed a lost name from old tales:

THE ARCANE MAGIC OF THE FORGOTTEN ENCHANTRESS

A shiver traced Wilhelmina's spine, a recognition stirring deeper than memory.

The tome lay before her, its timeworn pages waiting like an undelivered letter. There was no fanfare, no sudden revelation—only the certainty that she had stumbled upon something important.

She opened it, her breathing stuttering as the ancient words unfolded.

The tale spoke of a sorceress unparalleled in her mastery, whose power had once cast a long shadow over the realm. Her spells, it was said, held the key to magic so potent it could bend reality.

The further she read, the more the story revealed a curious, almost unsettling familiarity, as if the words had been waiting for her to discover them.

With still wings, Wilhelmina leaned closer to the book. Whether by coincidence or by some inscrutable design, the narrative hinted at a connection—her destiny entwined with that of the Enchantress.

❧

News of the Moon Prince's jealousy had traveled swiftly, casting a pall over Aetherwyn. The skies dulled, as if mourning the joy that no longer thrived beneath them. Festivities continued out of habit, but the cheer rang hollow, like a melody played in the wrong key. Couples still exchanged vows, but uncertainty crept in—a fragile tension that muted laughter and left smiles flickering, unsure whether to stay.

Under the moonblossom trees, a small group gathered, their faces shadowed with concern. Wilhelmina arrived, her own heart heavy, in time to catch the thread of conversation. Their faces, etched with concern, mirrored the dread already festering within her. Each voice added to the consternation.

"The forest suffers," Flora said, brushing wilted petals from her gown. "The plants cry for help, and I can do nothing."

Crispin frowned deeply. "Even the pixies have lost their humor. The gardens are silent—no mischief, no laughter. It's as if joy has withered overnight."

Aria's soft hum filled the silence between words—a tune so mournful it might have been the last note of a symphony dissolving into silence. "The celestial harmony weakens as if even the stars grow weary of singing."

Wilhelmina paced before them, her wings beating in restless bursts, stirring the heavy air. Her gaze swept across their faces, each marked by the same shadow of doubt.

"Do you feel it, even at the weddings?" Quill asked. "The joy seems fragile now, as if it could vanish with a breath."

Wilhelmina clenched her hands at her sides. "Yes. The magic is unraveling. Every ceremony, every tradition—it's all being drained by his envy." She paused, uncertainty flickering in her eyes. "But... perhaps the gloom will pass. Selenus's moods have waxed and waned before. This might only be a passing storm."

Crispin shook his head. "This is no fleeting shadow, Wilhelmina."

Quill stepped forward, his brows knitting. "If the Moon Prince's envy is allowed to fester, it will consume everything we've built. We need you to find out why he's doing this."

Wilhelmina's shoulders sagged beneath the weight of despair. "I cannot go chasing shadows. Perhaps if we wait, the balance will right itself."

"But what if it doesn't?" Flora asked as her hands shook. "What if the joy never returns?"

Wilhelmina's breath snagged. "I need time to think," she said, her wings folding close against her back.

The companions shared glances, yet held their tongues. Aria's melody trailed into silence. "Let us hope the answer comes before it is too late." Wilhelmina tried to offer a reassuring smile, but a shadow crossed her face, as if it had every intention of staying.

❧

The stars above twinkled in peaceful affirmation, as though utterly indifferent to the events unfolding below them. Wilhelmina, for her part, stood rooted to the spot. It was not fear alone that bound her—it was hesitation, that most perplexing of qualities, which held her fast when action was most needed.

And so, the night stretched on, vast and unyielding, until the sound of a gasp cut through the silence.

It was Lumina.

All the vitality that had once defined her now drained away. The sprite, usually radiant and full of laughter, now appeared pale, her wings drooping under the weight of a shadow all too eager to claim her.

"Lumina?" Wilhelmina's voice, typically so steady, now quivered with disbelief. Her first instinct was to rush to her friend's side, but the moment her fingers touched Lumina's clammy skin, she knew, with a certainty that chilled her to the core, that the gloom had reached farther than she had imagined.

The world tilted slightly—perhaps it was the wind, or perhaps it was the sudden weight of realizing that Aetherwyn itself was no longer safe.

Lumina's lips parted, her voice barely a whisper. "This realm saps my strength," she whispered. "I shall return to Solarae, where my mother can heal what ails me."

Wilhelmina's heart ached at that moment—a sharp, profound pain. Yet, she remained composed.

"Solarae's direct sunlight will help, I'm sure," she said, forcing her voice into something resembling calm. "And your mother, Seraphina, always has a few tricks up her sleeve. Please take care, Lumina." Her words faltered, weighted with emotion. "I couldn't bear it if anything terrible happened to you."

Lumina managed a small smile that lacked its usual spark. "Don't worry about me. The realm needs you now. We all do."

And there it was. The moment in which Wilhelmina, confronted with the suffering of her dearest friend, realized that hesitation could no longer be indulged. Lumina, her guide and her closest confidante, was fading, her wings barely able to lift her off the ground. It was a sight so deeply unsettling that she could not speak for several moments, staring as though by sheer force of will she might somehow reverse the inevitable.

It was then, as Lumina began her slow and weary ascent toward Solarae, that the full weight of responsibility settled upon Wilhelmina's shoulders. She had often spoken of duty, of joy, and yet here she stood, frozen at the very moment that action was required. The darkness was no longer an abstraction but a present peril. If Lumina could fall, no one was safe.

❧

High above the land, Wilhelmina alighted on the tallest tower, her wings shining beneath the moon's silver glow. The vastness of the night stretched before her—an eternal, unyielding expanse that, in another time, might have comforted her. But not tonight.

The stillness suggested that even the stars themselves awaited some grand pronouncement, their radiance dimming in shared anticipation.

"Stellara," Wilhelmina called into the boundless sky. "Guide me. A shadow threatens Aetherwyn, and I fear it reaches beyond our borders."

It was not the first time she had called upon her. The star-wanderer had always appeared at strange intervals—unpredictable but never unwelcome—much like a quirky friend or a beloved fairy godmother. Whether summoned by magic or affection, Stellara had a way of knowing when she was needed, even before the one calling knew it herself.

In the hush, the stars twinkled innocently, as though her plea had gone unheard. But just as doubt crept in, the sky responded.

Constellations danced, shifting subtly until they formed familiar patterns, like the shapes of old friends who arrived unannounced, yet always welcome. And then, as though summoned by some cosmic hand, Stellara appeared.

Her presence, ethereal and fleeting like a comet passing through the heavens, brought with it a warmth that softened the sharpness of the night. There was something both capricious and kind about her, a figure whose wisdom was as ancient as the galaxies, but whose manner retained the charm of a playful, eccentric aunt.

"Wilhelmina, darling, you summon me under the finest stars. What trouble brings you here?"

Stellara's voice held a lightness, but her gaze—a knowing gleam that had seen much—betrayed her awareness of the gravity in Wilhelmina's plea.

Wilhelmina's wings folded close. "The moon's shadow deepens, and I fear Selenus's envy has disrupted the magic that sustains us."

"Ah, envy." Stellara tilted her head just so, starlight catching in the tumble of her hair. "A tiresome thing, even among celestial beings. It creeps in like fog across clear waters and blurs all it touches. But surely, my dear, you understand—shadows cannot form without light. Darkness stretches where light dares to shine brightest. Even the brightest stars falter, Wilhelmina. And when they do, their shadows fall longest."

Wilhelmina's wings shifted. "But how can I restore the light if the shadow has already taken hold?"

"That's a question every soul asks, in every realm." Stellara gave a soft laugh. "Shadows are not fought with force. Understand them for what they are—a projection of something unbalanced. Always find that root cause."

"What do you mean? The shadow spreads, and the lights that fuel our celebrations dim each day. If the joy fades and the lights go out entirely—the magic will wither."

"Yes, I know. The lights are dimming. Love, joy, and hope weave the magic of Aetherwyn will all collapse. But these things, especially joy, my dear

Wilhelmina, are not something one summons with a wave of the hand. It is something that must be nurtured carefully, like a flame. And perhaps, you've forgotten that even those who nurture joy must, at times, allow themselves to receive it."

Wilhelmina stiffened. "You think I—?"

Stellara's gaze grew tender, though a spark of mischief lingered in her smile. "There is much you've yet to understand about yourself, dear one. The world you see around you is not the full extent of your reach. You are tied to the cosmos in ways you cannot yet grasp."

Wilhelmina frowned, her wings faltering. "I don't understand."

Stellara gestured upward, her finger tracing a path through the stars.

"Your essence is bound to that star—the brightest one. It is the source of your cosmic energy."

Wilhelmina's gaze followed Stellara's hand, her breath catching as she saw it—the star, casting its light with an unrelenting glow. Her wings wavered, off-rhythm, uncertain.

"That star is no ordinary one. It is your imprint upon the universe, a celestial thread that links you to your magic and the magic of this realm." Stellara's eyes glowed with quiet intensity. "You are its projection—a manifestation of its light, and that same light is what keeps the balance in Aetherwyn."

Wilhelmina jumped back, and her voice quivered with disbelief. "How can that be? I am just a fairy, bound to Aetherwyn's gardens. How can I be linked to something so vast?"

Stellara drifted closer, her presence warm as a summer breeze. "You are more than your role, more than your rituals, more than the gossamer thread of tradition that shaped you, Wilhelmina. The chrysalis that shaped your form was the beginning. The light of that star is indeed your essence, and it is through this light that Aetherwyn's balance can be restored."

For a moment, Wilhelmina stood in stunned silence, her wings stilled as her gaze lingered on the star above.

Stellara pointed toward Wilhelmina's heart. "You are the key to restoring balance—not just through the Lost Chronicles, but through the light you carry within."

Wilhelmina's gaze stretched to the galaxy where her mystical imprint radiated brilliance. The star responded to her, twinkling with greater amplitude. A luminous thread extended from the star to her fingertip and then encircled her body in a dance of light.

"For now, focus on the task ahead. The answers will come in time." Stellara pointed toward the horizon, where glimmers of light marked the boundary of the void. "Within the circle is Miragwyn. It is a dimension between thought and imagination—hidden within its folds of space."

"While there, seek the Lost Chronicles and... the Forgotten Enchantress. Both will hold the knowledge you will need to restore harmony."

Wilhelmina's brows knitted. "But I read that she succumbed to the darkness."

"There are many secrets that will unfold. Keep your mind and heart open to the truth, for it lies within you."

"I still don't understand. Why me? Why can't it be someone else?" Wilhelmina's voice held a raw vulnerability. "Many others could do this. Why am I the one to undertake this quest?"

Stellara's gaze softened as she regarded Wilhelmina. "Because you are the thread that binds Aetherwyn, dear one. Every wedding you've blessed, every moment of joy you've nurtured, has woven you into the enchantment that upholds this realm. No one else holds the same connection. The magic has chosen you because it knows, as I do, that you won't abandon what you love."

Wilhelmina's eyes fluttered while her wings stilled. "And if I fail?"

Stellara paused, locking eyes with Wilhelmina. "If the way grows dark, follow the lights. They will guide you. And know this: the light from your star shines brightest when those who face their greatest challenge look upon it," she affirmed. "Your imprint acts as a guide for those in despair, showing them the way. It senses the turbulence within those connected to you."

The cold unknown pressed in around Wilhelmina, the bright stars offering little warmth. She took a deep breath and folded her arms, shivering. "I've never ventured beyond Aetherwyn... I've never imagined it. My place has always been here among the joy and celebrations of weddings."

Her wings fluttered against the rising wind, their rhythm faltering with hesitation. "Everything I've built... I can't leave it all behind."

"But what you've built is as fragile as a spider's web and easily destructible under dark forces."

"And the journey to Miragwyn?" Wilhelmina twisted her hands. "Will it be dangerous?"

"The trials ahead will not be merely physical, but will challenge your perception of yourself and force you to see parts of your essence you have not yet embraced. You may confront illusions, moral tests, and ancient forces hidden within Miragwyn." Stellara grasped Wilhelmina's shoulders. "And yes. It will be very dangerous."

"I don't think I can do this... even if I am linked to this star."

"But your cosmic connection is why you will succeed—no one else has the light within like you to accomplish this mission. Remember your duty to the realm."

Stellara traced a delicate pattern in the air, leaving a trail of stardust in her wake. "The journey will test you, yes. But every worthwhile journey does. Peril only makes the destination sweeter."

"And remember, Wilhelmina. Leave space for joy. It will find its way back to you if you allow it."

"You have one more cycle of the sun and moon's rotation to decide. After that, Aetherwyn will vanish. Of course, you always have a choice, and I hope you make the right one." With those words, Stellara's form dissolved into a cascade of light.

❧

High above the darkened landscape, the night sky twinkled with a thousand stars—eternal and unchanging. And yet, among them, one star—Wilhelmina's imprint—stood apart, gleaming brighter than the rest. Stellara had said that this light guided those in despair.

Reason and Wilhelmina's magic had a chance to reach Selenus's heart and turn back the shadow. The decision to act was not hers alone; it was a resonance within Aetherwyn itself. As the idea of confronting him took shape for her like smoke curling in the wind, her wings quickened, as though the air encouraged the decision.

But even in that decision, a brief and almost imperceptible pause persisted. A weak shudder pulsed through her, as if some part of her still weighed the unknown dangers of Miragwyn. And yet, she ascended, her flight carrying her toward the inevitable confrontation with the Moon Prince.

5. The Fractured Moon

Wilhelmina squared her shoulders and regarded her companions. "We can wait no longer. The time has come to confront Selenus."

Quill unfurled a shimmering map, his movements deliberate.

"That's higher than we've ever flown," Flora uttered, her brows rising as she looked at it.

"You're right," he replied. "Our wings may brush the stars before this journey is through. It won't be easy, but the sun's warmth should hold the ice at bay if we leave now."

Anxious glances flickered between them, but their expressions settled into resolve.

Aria placed her hand on Quill's shoulder. "We will face this together."

Crispin clapped his hands, the sound bounding through the grove. "Sure, we can! If we huddle together, we'll keep each other warm."

Wilhelmina smiled. "That's right. Thank you, Quill. Let's move with haste and remain near."

With a final glance at her friends, she spread her wings. One by one, they followed, rising into the darkening sky. They flew higher and higher until the great, glowing sphere loomed before them. Bathed in moonlight, yet touched by the sun's fading warmth, their path led them ever deeper into the Moon Prince's domain. It was veiled in perpetual dusk—the very source of the peril. A deep silence fell around them, broken by the sigh of the wind. The stars seemed within reach, their twinkling lights guiding their way.

As they neared their destination, her posture showed a visible tension. The moon's glow failed to pierce the shadows clinging to Lunarae.

The hazy light revealed Selenus standing alone, his figure swallowed by a pale, spectral aura of despair.

Wilhelmina's breath broke in shallow fragments, and she pressed one hand against her heart.

A citadel of glistening frost and solid stone loomed behind him, its crystalline spires soaring toward the stars. The structure, both majestic and desolate, mirrored the anguish written on his face. Moonlight glinted off the glacial surface, casting refracted rainbows that only highlighted the emptiness within. His presence was a palpable reflection of the discord threatening the cosmos, a stark figure against the black backdrop.

Wilhelmina raised a finger, signaling she wanted to speak to him in private. The companions retreated into the shadows, ready to aid her if needed.

She descended, her gaze fixed on him, drawn as if by an unnameable and provocative force. There was a fragility in her movement, perhaps borne from the icy winds of Lunarae, or perhaps from the solemnity she witnessed in her old friend before her.

Selenus's expression, haunted and troubled, betrayed the battle raging within—one he looked unable to quell. His frame trembled, whether from Lunarae's chill or something deeper. He folded his arms tightly across his chest, a gesture that appeared to hold back more than just the cold.

"Wilhelmina!" His eyes had softened, but there was a restlessness in the way he shifted between meeting her gaze and casting it downwards. It was the fear of what he might reveal, or what she might see.

"Selenus." Her wings faltered mid-beat as though in sympathy with the sag of his shoulders. She stepped forward, her fingertips grazing his. The moment was fleeting, yet in that brief touch, a connection—a thread so delicate even fate would struggle to weave—pulled taut.

As she watched him, her face drained of color. "What is this darkness you've wrought? Your misery has torn the fabric of magic apart. You know this, don't you?" Her voice was soft, but insistent. "Please tell me. What has driven you to do something so unthinkable?"

Selenus flinched. His eyes flickered, like a deep, unspoken pain stirring. His words, when they came, rasped, as if his confession had lodged in his throat.

She let the silence settle, her hand pressed to her chest like a ward against what he said.

"I long for her... she whose radiance sets my soul aflame. It's as if she knows me, sees me in a way nothing else does." He paused, his shoulders tightening. "She calls to me in ways I can't explain, but she always turns toward my brother's brilliance, never mine."

Wilhelmina recoiled, her face heating. She wasn't sure if it was jealousy or a wound she couldn't name, but it pierced deep.

"That's what you want? Not—" Her cheeks flushed. "You're afraid of what's real, chasing something you'll never have."

"You're right. No matter how hard I try to win her favor, I repel her. I am so ashamed, and yet—" His voice broke.

Wilhelmina's mind reeled. *He means the star. He means me.* The star he was so infatuated with, the one he believed loved his brother, *was her*. A bitter irony twisted her heart: he loved her, yet his own insecurity and misperception created this phantom rivalry. But her own denial of love for him was the true barrier.

A sharp resentment kindled within her. This star—this celestial extension of herself—was the very thing drawing his misguided obsession, complicating the tenuous love she knew she could not, yet, embrace.

"Unrequited love is a pain I have helped many endure. Let me help you—"

Before she could continue, he interrupted her with a sudden shake of his head. "No. This is different. It is not like that. She..." He fell silent.

At this, the air froze between them. Although she stood tall, a hint of confusion crossed her face before she masked it.

"Your longing clouds your judgment." Her tone carried unexpected gravity. "The shadow you have cast does not fall upon you alone. It reaches far and wide, tearing Aetherwyn apart. Perhaps if you would allow it, we could fix this together."

A nervous chuckle escaped her, though it faltered as Selenus's gaze darkened. Her attempt to lighten the tension, to reach through his pain, was met with a wall of hardened pride. As she extended her hand, he stepped back, retreating into the distance that he clung to like a lifeline.

"I appreciate your kindness," he said, his voice turning cold. "But this is mine to bear. My love, my burden, is mine alone. I cannot share it."

Wilhelmina's face paled to a ghostly white. Her wings moved sharply, as if cutting through her hesitation. His unyielding arrogance, coupled with his refusal to accept help, created a spectacle almost painful in its obstinacy. Within her, compassion and duty—two forces rarely at odds—now vied for dominance, but the enormity of his transgressions could not be denied.

"How selfish can you be?" she snapped, her voice cleaving through the air with a command she hadn't meant to summon. "Your heartache brings chaos! It's not just your burden anymore—it's hurting those I care for, Lumina, the realm. Don't you see?"

"Before you," he said, though his voice now lacked the authority of his title, "I stand as a prince. Beneath this crown lies a heart ensnared by desires I will never fulfill." He paused, his gaze drifting toward the shadows. "I've woven this darkness, not from malice, but from a profound ache for a deeper connection I may never achieve."

Lunarae's whispers gathered around them, the ancient magic filling the space between their words. The moonlight now pulsed with an uncanny glow, casting spectral shapes across the stones.

Wilhelmina's gaze locked on his, committing his features to memory. Her eyes flashed, and what she said next cut through the air like a blade: "What admiration I once held for you has vanished, leaving one undeniable truth. You are a coward."

A thunderous boom rippled through the landscape, resembling a shock wave. The ground trembled, and the light dimmed as if resonating with the heat of her accusation.

Selenus's body stiffened as if to shield himself from the blow. For a fleeting moment, a quiver of something raw in his gaze—pride crumbling into ruin, after which came the bare trace of a man more vulnerable than he dared admit. But it was fleeting. He lowered his eyes, his expression hardening. Without another word, he turned and vanished into the icy wind that swept through the citadel.

The fragile thread of connection between them was now severed by his own withdrawal into the shadow and her final, devastating words.

She blinked back the tears that threatened to fall as she took to the skies. Her wings lashed open, slicing through the frozen air. Guilt flickered at the edge of her resolve, but she forced it aside. Regret had no place—not when his vanity imperiled everything she held dear.

The impact of their fates had made itself known: duty on one side, desire on the other, neither willing to bridge the divide that separated them.

The moon cast its silvery light over Aetherwyn, steady and unforgiving. Wilhelmina offered no words after the confrontation, but the firm set of her jaw and the tautness in her posture spoke volumes.

Her attempt to reach him—grounded in reason and responsibility—had shattered against the immovable wall of his ego.

As they flew across the realm, her wings stumbled off rhythm. Tension etched every line of her brow as her gaze wandered toward the horizon.

Though her companions stayed beside her, loyal and steadfast, their nearness offered little shelter from the storm gathering inside her.

The lunar shimmer, once a source of comfort, now revealed the delicacy of her confidence. Her silence was both a mark of resolve and a signal of private grief—grief not only at failing to reach Selenus, but at the gnawing doubt that perhaps she was unequal to the task ahead: the looming journey to Miragwyn, the Forgotten Enchantress, and the Lost Chronicles. Each beat of her wings brought them closer to a trial she could no longer avoid.

❧

As they descended toward the forest's edge, the tension lingered, though her flight remained steady. Upon landing, Wilhelmina gathered her companions and shared the truth of her mystical imprint. There was no flourish, only certainty—yet it was enough to fill the air with wonder. They listened in reverent silence, eyes wide as they absorbed the weight of her revelation.

Flora rested a hand on the bark of an ancient tree, gaze lifting to the vast, starlit sky. "It makes sense now," she said softly. "The cosmic threads that bind you to the heavens are undeniable."

Wilhelmina's eyes followed hers upward. Without knowing it, she had borne this mantle all her life. Yet the revelation offered no relief—only the deepening of a burden now made visible.

She looked around the circle of friends. "There is no other choice," she announced at last. "We must enter Miragwyn. It's the only means of restoring balance. But I cannot do it alone. Will you come with me?"

"Always," Crispin replied instantly, his usual cheer giving way to a rare solemnity. "We'll stand and fight by your side."

The others nodded in turn, murmuring their assent, hands reaching out to clasp her shoulder in shared resolve.

Flora's palm lingered on the tree's weathered bark, drawing quiet strength from its roots. "No one has ever returned from Miragwyn," she said. "But if anyone can, that's you."

Stillness followed her words.

Then, a gleaming circle unfurled before them, its colors pulsing with quiet life. The air surrounding it compressed and then expanded, as if the portal itself were inhaling breath, inviting, expectant.

Wilhelmina welcomed their trust like a cloak. Her companions' hands remained steady on her shoulders, a solid anchor.

And yet, as the gateway shimmered before them, she paused.

Not from fear. But from a quiet realization, no louder than a sigh.

“Perhaps, even now, the answers we seek are hidden by a deceit older than Selenus’s pain.”

With no further words, only a glance shared between them, the companions rose as one. Together, they crossed the threshold—and the magic of Miragwyn wrapped around them, drawing them into a realm unlike any they had ever imagined.

6. The Reckoning

Selenus remained after Wilhelmina's figure faded into the night. His posture held, rigid and unmoving—a solitary figure against the desolate landscape. Each breath came with difficulty, as though the air resisted his presence. A profound hush settled over Lunarae—a silence more damning than any accusation.

"Coward."

The word—a venomous whisper—ripped through the stillness. It coiled around him, a searing brand that bled the reality of his own making into the festering darkness within. He clenched his fists, jaw rigid, willing the charge against him to vanish, but the shadows he had summoned writhed, binding him tighter with each futile effort to deny the merciless truth. The more he fought, the more they consumed.

Wilhelmina's parting gaze remained with him, a silent reminder of all his failures. He *had* neglected his duty; his envy *had* poisoned the magic that sustained Aetherwyn, unraveling its vibrant threads of joy like a tapestry left to decay.

Yet, of course, it was not his fault alone. Such things were rarely so simple.

He paced, his steps quick and agitated. His boots struck the cold stone floor with a hollow, discordant rhythm. The citadel loomed in the distance, its towers gleaming with a stark, indifferent light, offering no solace. He retreated into the sanctuary of his chamber, but the marble walls, which had once reflected the moon's gentle light, now lay dim, shadows gathering at their edges as if his presence had drained the room of its former brilliance.

His frantic movement might have been an effort to dispel the cloud of accusation. Wilhelmina's words pierced deeper than he had expected, each one a barb lodged in his heart. She was right to call him a coward. His jealousy had clouded his judgment, and the shadows he brought forth threatened to devour everything he had once claimed to cherish.

And yet, a small part of him resisted. Was it all his fault? Had he *asked* to live in Phaethon's shadow? It was too convenient to place the blame entirely on him. His brother's light had always shone brighter, casting him into obscurity. Why, then, should he not feel envy? Why should he not seek his place in the cosmos?

❧

The air in the room grew colder, the shadows lengthening. Then, a sorrowful glow filled the gloom, bathing the chamber in a light that was at once gentle and full of reproach. His breath caught, and for a moment, even he seemed uncertain of what might come next.

His mother had arrived.

Celestia stood at the threshold, her silver robes trailing behind her like the last remnants of stardust. Whether that celestial grace was intended to comfort or to reprimand was uncertain. Her radiance illuminated the chamber's dull, faded corners, yet could not dispel the pervasive darkness that clung to the room. Her eyes, a careful blend of sorrow and disappointment, rested upon him.

"Selenus, my son... what have you done?" The words, spoken with such gentleness, carried within them the burden of long-suffering patience now strained to its limits. She moved closer, her gaze sweeping over the barrenness of her son's realm, no doubt an unforgiving reflection of his handiwork.

"You have let your envy consume you." Her tone held undeniable grief. "The shadows you've cast stretch far beyond this realm, unmaking the harmony we have labored to sustain. The magic of Aetherwyn is withering, and with it, the joy that once flowed."

Selenus, as though recognizing the futility of meeting her gaze, cast his eyes to the floor. Her disappointment—always more formidable than any expression of anger—weighed upon him far more heavily than even the darkness he had summoned.

Celestia, after all, had always believed in him, always clung to the hope that her son might, one day, fulfill his potential with the grace she knew him to possess. That such belief had now been shattered was, perhaps, the more grievous injury.

"There was a time," she said, though the tremor in her voice hinted at the weight of memory she bore, "when I looked upon you and saw nothing but the potential for greatness. You were never meant to compete with Phaethon's light, but to complement it. The moon and the sun—" Here she paused, as though the thought pained her. "They were never designed to rival one another, but to dance in harmony. Yet you have allowed your heart to be clouded by envy."

Her words, cutting as they were, fell upon him with the magnitude of undeniable truth.

Yet, before he could muster any semblance of a reply, a shimmer of stardust unfurled beside him, as Stellara appeared. She stepped into the room with her usual radiance, though it was dimmed by disappointment.

Gone was the playful warmth that once accompanied her arrival, a warmth that had often softened the harsh realities of the cosmos. Her presence now carried an acrid scent, reminiscent of ozone after a lightning strike, that permeated the air.

"I trusted you, Selenus." Her voice was neither harsh nor accusing, but imbued with a sadness far more cutting than any reproach. "I believed your shadow could temper the brilliance of the cosmos, not smother it. And yet here we are. All that potential... squandered for this?"

She gestured toward the blackening air. It was the most telling sign of all: the austere beauty of Lunarae, once the realm of delicate balance, had dulled by the darkness that Selenus had unleashed.

"You allowed envy to cloud your heart, and in doing so, you silenced your own light. I thought you could find your place among the stars, but now... it seems you have lost your way."

Selenus flinched at Stellara's words. She had always been a beacon of hope to him, a figure who saw potential even where others saw failure. To feel that even she had turned away was more wounding than he had anticipated.

"I didn't mean to..." His voice faltered, weak and unconvincing, as though the admission could not bear the full burden of his guilt.

"You didn't mean to, but whether you meant to or not, the damage is done. The one question that remains is whether you have the courage to fix what you've broken."

A new presence filled the room—one whose arrival seemed to carry the gravity of consequence. His father entered with the force and certainty of a celestial body in motion, summoned by the very laws of the universe he upheld. His golden robes, adorned with the symbols of orbits and balance, glimmered in the dim light. Yet, for all their brilliance, they offered little comfort to the son whose transgressions had disturbed the natural order. There was no paternal warmth in Varytita's expression; the stern lines of his face conveyed the cold, unyielding authority of universal law—laws which Selenus had chosen, most unwisely, to defy.

"I entrusted you with Lunarae," Varytita began, his voice low, rumbling like distant thunder, "not as a realm of shadows, but as a place of balance. The moon, after all, does not compete with the sun; it reflects its light, just as you were supposed to reflect the cosmic harmony we labor to sustain. But you—" His voice grew harder. "You have allowed jealousy to unmake what has taken eons to preserve."

Selenus's face blanched; whether it was from the force of his father's rebuke or the sharp pang of his guilt was impossible to discern. Yet still, his obduracy lingered—a familiar, stubborn wound, festering despite the crushing burden of his father's judgment. His fists clenched at his sides, as if bracing against an unrelenting tide.

"You think you suffer in Phaethon's shadow." Varytita's gaze appeared as cold and distant as the stars themselves. "But it is your shadow that has poisoned this realm. You allowed it to fester, and now it threatens not only Lunarae but the universal order."

Selenus, his breath now quickening with frustration and guilt, dared to speak. "You speak of balance." His voice shook despite his efforts to exercise control. "But can I live in balance when I am always the one in darkness? I never asked to be compared to Phaethon, to live in his light, while mine is but a pale reflection."

Varytita's eyes narrowed, his patience strained. "The universe, Selenus, is indifferent to your envy. The balance must be maintained, or all will fall to ruin. While you wallow in your grievances, the fabric of the cosmos unravels."

The final blow came, not in anger, but with the measured certainty of a decree. It was a law, etched into the celestial tapestry, delivered without threat, only consequence.

"I will take your place while you seek to undo the damage." Varytita's tone carried with it the weight of an irreversible decision. "But know this—my presence in Lunarae is temporary. I can sustain the balance for a short time. If you do not return before the fixed cycle is complete, both Lunarae and Solarae will collapse. And with them, the universe."

The silence that followed was as deafening and unforgiving as the void itself. The implications of his father's words pressed down upon Selenus. Though it was not the idea of potential exile that suffocated him, it was the realization that the entire cosmos teetered on the edge of destruction because of his folly.

Celestia, who had remained a silent observer until this moment, stepped forward. Her sorrow, though evident, was tempered by the quiet dignity that had always marked her presence. "Your father is sacrificing more than just his place, Selenus," she said, her words cutting through the stillness like a thread of light in the darkness. "He is placing himself at the heart of Lunarae's balance. If you fail to return before the cycle ends, he will be lost. The universe will be lost."

She paused, though her expression remained composed. There was no pleading in her voice, only a deep sadness. "How can you stand there and cling to your envy, knowing the price your father is willing to pay? Knowing that you alone can prevent this collapse?"

Selenus stood unmoving as the significance of his parents' words settled over him. His envy, once so consuming, now seemed small—petty, even—compared to the catastrophe he had set in motion. And yet, for all the shame that now threatened to overwhelm him, a resistance stirred, as though self-regard still clung to the edges of his soul.

"I—" His voice cracked, the final barrier of his pride beginning to crumble. "I did not mean to dishonor father or you, or put your lives or anyone's lives at risk."

Celestia's gaze softened. "Intention alone does not undo harm. You must act."

Varytita, having given his son room to face his remorse, now stepped forward once more. His presence, as ever, was like the inexorable pull of gravity itself—unforgiving and absolute. The final judgment seemed to hang in the air.

"You will restore balance to Aetherwyn. Or you will face permanent exile from Lunarae. You will lose your celestial station, and the darkness you've unleashed will follow you to the ends of the universe."

Selenus's breath caught in his throat. Exile. The very thought of it—a severing from his family, from his celestial purpose—was unthinkable. To be cast out, wandering in the void, was a fate he had never contemplated. His gaze flicked to the elusive star above he longed for. But as he reached out for its light, it flickered, weak and distant, as if it too had turned away from him. The suffocating reality of his situation settled over him, heavier than he had imagined.

"I will go," he said at last, as though the words themselves bore the weight of the path ahead. "But I cannot promise success. It may be too late for me."

Silence settled over the room, pressing against the walls like the hush before a storm. When Selenus glanced at his parents, he found not the anger or disappointment he feared, but something far more difficult to bear—a quiet resignation. They understood, perhaps more than he did, that redemption was a road he alone must walk. Whether he would find his way remained uncertain.

Without a word, Stellara reached into the folds of her robe and drew forth a wand—an elegant artifact, shimmering with a kaleidoscope of light. As she raised it, a soft hum filled the air, and reality seemed to shift. The wand cast a beam of radiant energy, and in its wake, a circular portal unfurled before them.

Through it, Selenus glimpsed a world bathed in the warm hues of twin suns—one a deep, burning red, the other a fierce orange. The sky churned with vibrant energy as the winds pulsed with ancient magic. The portal beckoned, equal parts promise and peril.

"This is the way to Miragwyn," Stellara said, her voice now edged with urgency. "Your journey begins here. And there is little time. Your father's strength is not infinite—he cannot hold the balance for long."

From her pocket, she withdrew a glowing orb. Its surface shimmered, pulsing like a heartbeat on the verge of stillness. "Take this," she said, placing it in Selenus's hand. "It will guide you. As your father's strength wanes, the light within will dim. When it fades completely, there will be no time left. Everything you love—everything you cherish—will be lost."

His hand hovered over the orb, as if held back by some invisible weight. To accept it was to shoulder the burden of atonement and to risk failure.

At last, he took it.

The orb's glow flickered in his palm, already less steady than it should have been. His face turned pale, and his fingers trembled as he stepped toward the waiting portal.

He looked at it for a moment longer, then looked at Stellara, his brow furrowing as a flicker of doubt crossed his face. "Why Miragwyn?" he asked. "Why must I go there?"

"Miragwyn holds the answers you seek. It is a realm of illusions—of trials both visible and veiled. Many have ventured there in search of redemption, but not all have returned. For Miragwyn does not simply test the will—it reflects the soul. It strips away illusion to reveal the essence beneath. And to restore balance, you must first confront what lies hidden within yourself."

The words—*not all have returned*—hovered like a cold mist. They were not spoken with malice but with the solemnity of truth.

Selenus's eyes widened, his lips pressing together as if to hold back the full force of his reaction. Miragwyn's dangers were well known across the realms, through stories told in hushed voices—stories of those who had gone there only to be lost in its folds. And there, too, lay the Enchantress, imprisoned by forces he could not hope to comprehend.

For a moment, his resolve wavered. The weight of his parents' sacrifice, of his father's burden, pressed down upon him with a force that exceeded even Lunarae's gravity. But he said nothing. What could he say that had not already been left unsaid?

He looked toward his father. Varytita stood tall and unyielding. His form radiated the immense force of will required to maintain Lunarae's balance. Though the pallor of his skin and the tired lines etched in his face betrayed the toll of this sacrifice. No words of complaint passed his lips, however. Celestia stood beside him, her silver robes reflecting the dim light. She carried a grief that needed no words. Her gaze, filled with both love and regret, rested on her son, as if bidding him farewell with a mother's unspoken plea: *return*.

His hand tightened around the orb as he turned toward the portal. The kaleidoscope of light swirled before him, a dazzling array of colors that beckoned with both promise and peril.

For the briefest moment, he remembered Wilhelmina's eyes—fierce with disappointment, yet unwilling to give up on him. He did not believe in redemption yet. But perhaps... she did.

The orb, flickering now with a faint glow, marked the time left before his father's strength—and the balance of the universe—would fade. With a fleeting look at his parents that carried all of his unspoken fear, Selenus stepped forward. The portal expanded before him, its pull undeniable. The twin suns of Miragwyn blazed on the other side with an intensity that momentarily blinded him. Without further hesitation, the light of the portal enveloped him as if the stars had drawn him into their embrace, and in a flash, he was gone.

In the quiet that followed his departure, Stellara exchanged a glance with Varytita and Celestia. There was little else to say. They knew, even as they stood in the bleak silence of the citadel, that time was already slipping away.

7. Dreams That Undress the Soul

A fantastical landscape greeted the companions as they stepped into Miragwyn. The air felt thin, like it had been poured from a higher altitude. In this inner fold of space, the laws of nature appeared to bow before whimsy. Hues of violet and indigo flared across the heavens, where twin suns pulsed in slow, deliberate orbits. One spilled tendrils of green fire; the other blazed with shades of orange and crimson.

Above it all, a silver-blue celestial body gleamed, unwavering. Amid such chromatic chaos, its cool light held steady, a quiet guardian in a realm where permanence no longer had a name. Wilhelmina lifted her eyes, a whisper escaping her lips. "How extraordinary. Even here, something constant remains."

The star held steady above them—an anchor in Miragwyn's wavering sky. It pulsed once. The ground answered with a dull, measured thud that traveled up their shins and settled behind their teeth.

Without warning, the land transformed with abrupt caprice. A cold draft threaded under their collars, though no wind moved the trees. Shapes rose like vapor, twisting into fleeting forms—first an entity, part dog, part deer, its striped pelt swirling with liquid patterns. It bounded toward them in joyful abandon, tail whirling, hooves striking no sound.

Wilhelmina bent instinctively, but before her fingers could meet its ethereal fur, the creature fractured into a hundred threads of light and dissolved into nothingness. Her fingertips met only a cool static, as if she'd touched the edge of a storm.

She inhaled sharply. "It's not real," she murmured, looking once more to the sky. "Nothing here is what it seems." Yet through the chaos and illusion, the star endured.

Flora stepped forward and vanished up to her knees. The emerald grass had simply ceased beneath her boot. She flailed, her lungs locked before catching herself on a gnarled root of a woody plant that materialized in that instant. "What—what is this place?" She stammered, eyes wide with bewildered horror. Quill lurched forward, boots skidding, and caught her elbow before the ground could swallow more.

Even the trees held unnaturally still—no leaf-shiver, no creak—though the cold draft kept worrying their sleeves and collars.

Then, the world blinked. Their heads turned in unison—pulled by the sudden shift. A towering trunk spiraled upward, its limbs forming an impossible helix. In the next instant, it was gone. The ground rippled, then disappeared. Hills rose and dissolved. Shadows regrouped and reformed.

"I've seen nothing like this," Quill murmured, narrowing his eyes as he scribbled on a hidden scroll. "It's exhaling new scenes each time we look." Ink blotted at the edge of his page where his hand trembled.

Crispin's voice, usually booming, cracked through the haze of unreality. "What strange magic is this?"

Wilhelmina wobbled as the terrain undulated beneath her once more. "Gwydion once told me Miragwyn was an in-between place—where thought and imagination touch. A dream suspended between the seams of reality."

"But where, exactly, is it?" Flora asked, her voice tinged with lingering unease.

Wilhelmina looked down at the dissolving ground, then toward the shimmering, mutable sky. "Not a place one finds on a map. It hides in the folds of space."

Crispin lifted his baton like a divining rod. It dipped—then spun, unhelpful as laughter in a nightmare. "So," he said, narrowing one eye, "is it real?"

Wilhelmina tilted her head. "Perhaps... Miragwyn is a truth place," she said, steadying herself as the ground softened underfoot. "It takes whatever we rely on—and asks what remains."

Aria's eyes gleamed, a flicker of an artist's wonder amidst the danger. "Musicians speak of such places. That liminal realm where raw melody is born. Magic, untamed and formless, lives here."

The terrain fractured again. In a flash, they stood in a meadow lit like emerald glass. Towering mountains, their peaks piercing the sky, dissolved into mist moments later. A dense forest emerged next, where trees grew at impossible speeds, their long shadows twisting and dancing toward nowhere.

Each step forward became an act of trust. They tested each patch of ground with their heels before committing their weight. The magic wasn't merely shifting the terrain—it was taking what made them feel sure of who they were. Crispin was the first to experience it—a strange tingling along the surface of his back where his wings had unfurled. He faltered. He ran both hands along his shoulder blades—skin, smooth as if it had never known flight.

"I-I can't feel my wings!" he exclaimed, reaching around instinctively.

As his fingers brushed his shoulder blades, his wings dissolved into silver sparks, ascending like stardust. The skin sealed without pain or scar. It was an odd sensation, not painful, but unsettling in its profound finality.

Each experienced the same disquieting transformation. Wilhelmina's breath snagged as her wing structures vanished in a delicate swirl of light. The ethereal glow on her back faded as the surface became smooth.

The magic of Miragwyn erased every trace, stripping them of a part of their identities.

A further affront came when Crispin tried to voice his vexation, only to find, much to his astonishment, that silence had seized him. His arms flailed in exaggerated disbelief, his face contorting. He jabbed a finger at his throat, eyes wide with indignation. Even his clever observations, his boisterous nature, fell captive to Miragwyn's enchantments.

Not far off, Flora examined her attire with something akin to wounded pride. Her vibrant garb, once a testament to nature's exuberant palette, had surrendered to a most unremarkable shade of gray, a color she would never have chosen.

"Oh! My beautiful greens are gone!" She choked on a sob as she rubbed the fabric briskly, trying to warm color back into it. The green and gold threads would not return.

Quill reached for his side, where his magic pen had always been. But his fingers met with nothing. He looked down for a second, baffled, as if the world had conspired to deprive him of his most trusted tool. Without it, his words, and perhaps even his thoughts, were somehow less valid, less real.

Aria opened her lips to release the melody that had so often been her solace and joy, yet no sound emerged. She swallowed hard. Nothing moved but the delicate tendons in her throat. Her lips parted again and again as if to summon a note that would not come. Without song, her presence appeared muted, her figure briefly stilled, transformed into a mere specter of herself. She pursed her mouth and looked to Wilhelmina, a silent plea in her eyes.

At last, Flora spoke—her voice barely a whisper, but enough to pierce the spell. Tears threatened to spill down her cheeks. "What if we never find our way out? What if—" She gestured helplessly at her gray garments. "Is this forever?"

Wilhelmina stood earthbound, her movements tentative, unfamiliar, and perhaps a touch humbling. Her breath grew shallow, and her eyes widened at the unsettling changes. She pulled her gaze toward that singular silver-blue star. There it remained, a resolute pinprick of light.

She took a steadying breath, though a fine sheen of sweat formed on her brow. "No, Flora," she said at last, her voice clear despite her unease. "Miragwyn is feeding on our insecurities. Fear is the real enemy here—and it has worn my face, too." A bead of sweat slipped at her temple; she wiped it away before anyone could see.

High above, the star pulsed with a soft, sympathetic gleam, as though acknowledging her courageous words. Her eyes flitted to it. "If we keep our wits and hold fast to what is real inside ourselves, I believe we shall discover a way forward."

A hesitant sound escaped Crispin's throat—his voice, quiet but present once more.

A clearing appeared ahead, and the ground beneath their feet grew solid and stable. Wilhelmina gestured ahead.

"See? Adjusting our perspective is already working. Accept what you're seeing, understand it, and let it flow through you. There's always magic within us—even if it's changed, or hidden, or forgotten. Come on—we've got to find the Lost Chronicles."

❧

They traversed Miragwyn's ever-changing landscapes, the world itself a fickle thing. Meadows glowed with diaphanous light, and the shadows cast by flanking mountains stretched and contracted with each fleeting glance. They walked in near silence, listening for the sound of their own steps—and hearing none.

At long last, the thick forest canopy parted to reveal a clearing. Streams of amber light spilled down from the twin orange and red suns, painting the glade in hues of stately warmth. Shapes on the forest floor stretched like beckoning fingers, pulling them forward. And once there, at the glade's heart, stood an immense structure, hewn from age-worn stone. Delicate patterns and cryptic symbols adorned its weathered facade.

Etched with remarkable artistry, the carvings seemed almost alive, undulating in the glancing light like an optical illusion. These symbols hinted at tales long forgotten—legends of valor, love, and perhaps secrets best left untold. Crystal columns, entwined with silver and green vines that glinted in the twin suns' light, framed the structure with an almost sacred beauty.

Towering trees encircled the structure like silent sentinels, their branches clawing and twisting skyward, forming an embrace that was part shelter, part guardian. "This must be it," Wilhelmina breathed, her voice a hushed whisper. "The Lost Chronicles have got to be here." Together, they pushed against the groaning, heavy wooden doors. The hinges complained like old bones.

A cloud of dust, thick with the musty odor of parchment, tickled their noses. "Ah-choo!" Crispin sneezed loudly. Flora covered her mouth, her giggles barely muffled. He gave her a wry, sidelong glance.

They scanned the towering shelves, each row lined with age-worn tomes and enchanted scrolls. Quill's eyes gleamed. "The Library of Mysteries! It's like stepping into a legend come to life. Histories say it holds the lost knowledge of all realms. These books—why, they must contain the arcane recipes for every wondrous and perilous spell imaginable."

"I just hope we find something useful here," Crispin muttered, his earlier mirth replaced by a weary sigh. "We've journeyed too far to leave empty-handed."

The colossal stacks closed in around them, their spines bowed beneath the weight of secrets long held. The air grew thick with anticipation, as though the books themselves were waiting for something—or someone—to unlock the knowledge sealed within their pages.

In one part of the library, a row of shadowed shelves held a peculiar stir. From the books lining them, ghostly apparitions drifted, coalescing from their spines, hovering momentarily before fading back into the pages.

Flora strolled over, drawn by a volume titled *Chivalric Heroes*. As she leaned closer, a knight in gleaming armor atop a white horse materialized, sword raised high. She yelped, startled, and tripped over her skirt, landing with a clumsy thud.

The knight's eyes rounded. "Forgive me, my lady!" he boomed, pulling on the reins as his horse whinnied loudly. They vanished as quickly as they had come. Nearby, a figure cloaked in shadow whispered incantations, evaporating into thin air.

"*Alizara Salaminus*!" it hissed, and with a deafening boom, an explosion of fireworks erupted, prompting everyone to cover their ears.

It was as if the characters and topics penned in the ancient volumes were restless, their stories yearning to be seen. The phantoms flickered in and out in a mad, magical cycle, leaving no doubt that the library's enchantments were more fervent here than in any corner they had yet explored.

Quill moved to Flora and helped her up. "Let's all move back, shall we?" he said, more command than question.

She nodded vigorously, brushing dust from her skirt. "Indeed, Quill. Let's keep our wits about us. We stand on the cusp of mysteries kept from mortal minds for centuries... but I don't think the secrets here want to be disturbed." Her voice held a reverent note as she gestured toward the shelves.

Crispin stifled a chuckle and gently tugged Aria and Wilhelmina's hands, leading them away from the curious scene.

Quill and Flora followed closely, moving toward a set of aisles that appeared to rest in a state of calm.

As they moved, their fingers trailed over the spines of the venerable volumes. Each worn cover hummed under their touch, as though protesting the interruption of their silent vigil. One particular tome, grander and more forbidding than the others, seemed to pull them in with an insistence that was at once compelling and sinister.

Aria extended her hand, and an errant spark of silver light surged from her fingertips as they met the spine. She turned the book's age-darkened pages, and a grayish-blue shadow swirled from the paper. It formed a doppelgänger—Aria as a mute crone, her mouth agape in a silent scream.

Air caught in Wilhelmina's throat as she turned to Aria. "Look! It's you... b-but you've lost your voice."

The image flickered, spectral and chilling. Around them, every book lining the shelves emitted an unsettling, sickly glow.

"I've heard you joke about this, but this," Quill began, glancing from the apparition to Aria.

"This... is my darkest secret." Aria's words came in a strained whisper. Her speaking voice was a dry, hollow echo of the music that usually lived there. "I've long dreaded the idea of growing old and fading into obscurity." A glint of unshed tears caught in her eyes. "Yes. I've long feared this."

One by one, the others each pulled a book from the shelves, and as they did, their fears materialized before them, each image cast into sharp, unrelenting relief. The library grew thick with an ominous energy, the room dimming as grotesque shapes writhed across the walls.

The books' magic reached each of them. Flora gasped as a barren, desolate landscape swallowed her vision. Quill's trusty pen dissolved before his eyes, its ink turning to dust. Aria's song fell silent, her throat closing on an unspoken melody. Crispin opened his mouth, but his voice escaped in silence, the absence of sound unsettling against the whimsical landscape. Iron chains, heavy and cold, encumbered Wilhelmina, each link pulling her down, binding her to the earth.

Her voice, though strained, cut through the oppressive quiet. "These books… they're repositories of learning, vessels of magic, showing us our deepest fears."

Wilhelmina's chest rose and fell with a shallow breath. "For all my talk of steadfast duty and that hollow self-assurance in my accomplishments… I am not without doubt. The fear of failure, it seems, is always but a breath away. Seeing this vision… it feels as though all my responsibilities are bearing down upon me."

Her gaze lowered. "You might not know it, but I lose sleep night after night, worrying that the next wedding will somehow unravel. I strive for flawlessness, yet it eludes me. I doubt I shall ever reach it."

The weight of societal expectation seemed to rest heavily upon her slender frame, unseen yet undeniably present, like the bindings of a corset laced far too tightly.

"And even in those moments where I come close, I cannot help but wonder if joy might ever be mine as well. I watch couples depart while I remain, bound by duty."

"Wilhelmina! Why haven't you ever told us?" Her friends' voices rose in shocked unison.

"Why should I tell you what is impossible? It seemed selfish to even try. But it's true—I fear an unending cycle of duty, without freedom."

Flora touched Wilhelmina's trembling arm. "Love and freedom need not be at odds. We'll find a way for you," she said.

Wilhelmina took a longer, steadier breath, her form still quivering. "I don't know what it was, but admitting it helps somehow. You should all try it."

She released a measured breath, her shoulders dropping as the silence settled. No one seemed eager to fill the pause.

Aria opened her mouth, but the words didn't come easily. "I-I've always feared this. Losing my voice... It's like losing a part of myself. What if... what if I fade away, forgotten? What if even my thoughts...," she trailed off, her hands fluttering at her sides.

Wilhelmina reached for Aria's hand. "Your words carry meaning beyond sound. Think of when you comforted the grieving elves—your presence alone held its power. It is your kindness and spirit that define you."

Quill shifted from foot to foot, lowering his gaze to the stone floor. "I doubt my abilities. What if my dreams of adventure are just that—dreams and nothing else? I've dreamed of exploring the Whispering Caves, but what if I'm not brave enough?"

Crispin rested his hand on Quill's shoulder. "You have a strength within you, Quill. Your determination and heart make you capable of great things. Remember how you found the hidden path through the Enchanted Forest? Don't ever forget that."

He gave Quill a playful punch under the chin, but he let out a shaky breath, scratching the back of his head. "You know, I never thought it'd come to this... me, Crispin, king of comic timing, worried about losing my spark." He chuckled, but the sound carried little mirth. "What if one day I tell a joke and... nothing? Not even a pity laugh?"

He looked up, his grin faltering. "What if I lose the one thing that makes me... me?"

Wilhelmina looped her arm through his, curving her lips upward. "Your laughter is a gift, Crispin. And even if words escape you, your heart will find a way to spread joy. That is something no spell can take."

Flora spoke, her voice almost a whisper, as if uttering the fear might call it to life. "I'm terrified of a world without nature, where all I love and care for has vanished." Her voice trailed off. For an instant, it seemed as if the world around her echoed her deepest fear—a realm where the vitality of nature had withered, leaving only the ghostly husks of trees where once they had blossomed—a graveyard of what could have been.

No one spoke, the silence honoring the raw honesty of her words. But Aria moved nearer, pulling Flora's hand to her heart. "We'll be with you, Flora. This world is ours to protect, and together, we'll preserve it."

The eerie visions vanished all at once, displaced by the energy and strength of their growing solidarity. The oppressive atmosphere lifted, and a fortifying light seemed to fill the room in a warmer glow.

"Sometimes facing the deepest fears, even if only in shadow, helps us understand what truly matters," Flora said, her voice stronger now.

Quill nodded, rubbing the back of his neck. "I don't expect any of you to be perfect. And I know none of you expect that of me either."

Crispin offered a genuine grin. "Then how about this? Imagine a happy place and talk about it."

Silence fell over the library, settling like dust upon the ancient folios. The companions stood, each figure momentarily stilled, as though the recent revelations had bound them in place. Wilhelmina's shoulders lowered a fraction. Crispin stared pensively at the floor, while Quill's grip eased on the book's spine; his knuckles regained their color. Aria exhaled—soundless, but complete.

Wilhelmina exhaled, her gaze meeting Flora's in a silent exchange of understanding. A shared sigh escaped them both. Wilhelmina's hand, after a moment's hover, rested on Flora's shoulder. At once, the air lightened—a subtle, unmistakable lifting of the heavy magic that had permeated the library.

As their honesty settled among them, the library's pressure eased—like a hand unclenching. For a moment, nothing moved but their breathing.

Aria's book began to hum and echo celestial harmonies. Its obscure glow intensified, illuminating the forgotten tale of the Enchantress who had once crafted Aetherwyn's destiny.

She stroked her fingers over the pages, as if sensing the melody hidden within the words. "The melody... it resonates with the celestial harmony. Perhaps the Enchantress was more than we imagined—a keeper of the balance between the realms."

Quill leaned closer to the magical artifact shimmering above his book. Intricate symbols etched onto its surface glimmered, each a representation of an ancient, astronomical dance. "These symbols," he said, tracing their delicate lines, "align with the stars... the dance of the cosmos itself. I wonder if the Enchantress crafted the magic that binds our world together."

Crispin's book, not to be outdone, responded, its pages flipping of their own accord, the paper rustling like whispers in the still air.

"Marvel of marvels!" Crispin's eyes shone as he beckoned them closer. "Come! You must see this enchanted wonder!"

The companions gathered around him. Crispin's hand hovered over the chronicle until its pages stilled, lying open. He leaned in and read aloud.

"This is the history of the Enchantress, a guardian of cosmic balance.... could she have left these books for us to discover?" he asked, raising an eyebrow.

Flora leaned in, her fingers trailing over the page. "The Enchantress sought to preserve the harmony of our world. But in her efforts, she inadvertently caused a rift—a fracture that divided Aetherwyn." Her voice quivered as she read from its luminous pages.

They watched in rapt silence as an illustration bloomed on the page, revealing the Enchantress casting dark spells that mirrored her sadness. Another image flickered into view: her face—tragically beautiful, yet filled with longing. Quill leaned closer. "She wanted to be loved." His voice caught, as if choking back a sob. "She wanted to be accepted."

The tale drifted like smoke through the library, soft but unmistakably powerful. The companions' eyes scanned the text as if searching for deeper meaning within its cryptic words. Flora traced her fingers over the image, her eyes widening in surprise. "Look here. See these moonblossoms and sun-kissed roses? The Enchantress must have woven her magic into the fabric of our realm."

Wilhelmina gently turned the page, tracing her fingers over another illuminated illustration where an orchard burst to life—trees laden with rainbow-hued petals that pulsed with splendid vitality. "These flowers... there's something about them... Every color imaginable...." Flora bent her head, fixing her gaze on the fantastical image. "These blossoms are special. I sense purity... like the embodiment of unconditional love."

Wilhelmina's eyes shone with understanding. "I think you're right, Flora. I wonder if these blossoms are somehow connected to the Enchantress...."

Before she could finish, an unearthly image rose from the book, coalescing above its pages. The figure was unmistakably the Enchantress, yet transformed—a haunting beauty with long, dark hair cascading like a shadowy river. Her skin gleamed in the moonlight's pallor, and her piercing emerald eyes shone. Deep purple and black robes, adorned with ancient symbols of power, draped elegantly over her delicate frame.

With a graceful motion, the Enchantress's apparition pointed to a far-off corner, hidden from all but the most discerning eye.

There, a dusty volume lay flat and forgotten on a high table. Wilhelmina moved toward it and brushed its spine. The book sprang open at her touch, its pages fluttering until they came to rest on scrolled letters in golden ink.

The others drew closer, looking over her shoulder as she read aloud, "Herein, dear reader, is the history of the Enchantress and her accomplice, Gwydion...."

Wilhelmina's fingers held a corner of the page as she read. "Torn by betrayal, the Enchantress's cries echoed throughout the realms and time, reaching Gwydion's ears. United in purpose, they sought to weave a new destiny for themselves and the world."

The air thickened, charged with a magic older than any they had yet encountered. Dust continued to settle in slow spirals through the light, landing on their sleeves and the open pages.

The tale of the Enchantress unfolded like a long-forgotten memory, the words rising from the page as though eager to be set free. "Once a revered guardian, the Enchantress had seen her powers twisted against her through betrayal—an insidious force that left her bound to an Enchanted Mirror, imprisoned by the very magic she had wielded. The curse, however, was not solely her burden to bear; it was the key to a balance long disturbed."

The room shifted beneath their feet, and the act of reading became a reliving of a memory. A shimmering image of the Enchantress stood before them, a figure of tragic beauty, her fingers grazing the mirror's surface with a touch both tender and reluctant.

An image of Gwydion, the enigmatic and wise owl, emerged from the shadows, bearing an air of secret knowledge. They needed no words; the plan was already forming in the silence, though neither could yet see its conclusion. For all their powers, it would not be their hands that unraveled the curse.

The vision flickered like the last remnants of a dying fire. The companions glimpsed figures—heroes yet to be named—woven into the strands of destiny. These shadowed ones needed to complete the work, though they had yet to step forward.

Aria read the final words on the page aloud. "Bound by fate, you too are threads in this ancient weave." The vision flickered out. The companions' mouths gaped open, each lost in individual thought.

Wilhelmina spoke first, her tone carrying a hint of authority. "This was no simple story of betrayal. The Enchantress's fate, her curse—it's tied to more than just her fall. Gwydion was part of it. They sought a way to undo the damage, but they knew it would take more than their power."

Her words met with silence, not one of misunderstanding, but one of absorption. Each companion seemed to process the moment with newfound gravity. Quill appeared on the verge of speaking, carefully contemplating his phrasing.

"It seems," Quill finally remarked, lifting his chin with an air of resigned acceptance, "that the prophecy and curse are tied to us now, whether we like it or not. Whatever they began, we are... inescapably bound to finish."

A silent glance passed between the companions, conveying more than any words. No one protested; an unspoken agreement filled the space. The hush that followed was not hesitation, but a shared resolve—a quiet adherence to the monumental task now laid before them.

"But why did Gwydion never tell you he knew the Enchantress?" Quill asked. "Why keep such a secret from you?"

Wilhelmina hesitated, loyalty to Gwydion clear in her voice, though doubt crept into her expression. "I don't know, Quill. He must have had his reasons...." Her brow furrowed slightly.

"I don't like it. It seems suspicious. What if Gwydion tricked you? What if this is all a ruse?"

The Enchantress's ghostly image moved again, waving her hand gracefully. Another page in the book flipped open, as if at her silent bidding. This time, an illustration of a field of blossoms greeted the companions, vibrant with colors unlike anything they had ever seen, reminiscent of moonblossoms in shape. Each petal shone with the hues of the rainbow, their intensity shifting with the light, alive with magic. The blossoms bore a striking resemblance to those Flora had examined, and their meaning soon became clear.

Wilhelmina beckoned them closer. The companions leaned in, their eyes widening at the sight of the multi-hued field within the illustration. As they looked, the air shivered, blurring the boundary between reality and illusion.

"Do you hear that?" Flora glanced at the pages. A low, insistent hum rose from the book, as though it were breathing. It grew louder, vibrating through the air like a heartbeat. The companions froze, their gazes flicking to the book just as its light pulsed, bright and insistent.

A gust of wind stirred the pages. Flora clutched her blowing skirt. "What's happening?"

Quill stepped back instinctively, adjusting his glasses. "I don't like this..." His arms flailed for balance.

Wilhelmina reached out to close the volume, but her hand stopped inches away, held by its will. The glow spilling from the pages intensified, painting their faces in shifting hues.

"Wait—what if it's trying to—" The magic surged forward and wrapped around them, cutting off Crispin's words. The air spun with a maelstrom of hues and luminescence, pulling them in despite their attempts to resist.

In a flash, the companions no longer stood in the dim library. Some form of enchantment transported them into the illustration. Instead of the musty scent of parchment, they now smelled a tantalizingly sweet perfume.

A faint, tenuous chime tinkled on the edge of the atmosphere, a melody woven into the fabric of the blossom-laden current, as if the field itself were greeting them with a soft, musical sigh.

Strewn about after their tumbling journey, they lay upon the vibrant clearing they had just been admiring. Arms akimbo, Quill's glasses askew, groans reverberated across the expanse where flowers stretched as far as the eye could see, making it hard to tell where earth ended and sky began. Dazzling colors painted the landscape, creating an atmosphere of unsettling yet dazzling splendor.

A breeze brushed the blossoms, but the petals remained still, as though the field itself were watching. Shivering, the companions scrambled to their feet, wobbling unsteadily. Quill adjusted his glasses, the others gingerly testing their limbs for breaks. A cloying sweetness thickened the air, catching in their throats. Their widened eyes and parted lips betrayed astonishment, while unease lingered in their expressions. The magic that had brought them here was as enchanting as it was bewildering, and none needed to say aloud what their tense glances made clear—escape from this place would not come easily.

8. The Moon Prince's Gamble

Selenus gripped his father's orb. A distant echo of Stellara's voice accompanied him as he took his first step. "*Wilhelmina and her friends have made their way to Miragwyn. You must find her and protect her... and the Enchantress. Do not forget your father's sacrifice....*" He paled at the mention, and he stumbled through the portal's opening.

The step he took unraveled into something wholly unexpected. In an instant, he was swept into a spiraling current. His body tumbled as if he had fallen straight into a vortex of starlight.

Through some unknown, wormhole-like passage, he turned over and over, arms flailing, as bursts of color and shadow streamed past him, warping in ways that defied all sense of orientation. He plunged deeper into the dizzying vortex until, with a rather inglorious *splat*, he landed sprawled on the spongy ground of Miragwyn.

Brushing off the leaves and dust with an air of reluctant acceptance, he stood. The orb he carried slipped from his hand, rolling a short distance across the ground before resting at his feet. He picked it up gingerly and ran his fingers along its polished surface.

An image materialized within, and he jumped back. It was the solemn yet strained visage of his father, suspended in the dark void of space, now appearing within the confines of the orb. The vision showed Varytita taking Selenus's place, keeping the balance of the sun and moon in check for one fixed cycle. The image was a wordless reminder of the cost of Selenus's mission. He tucked the orb carefully away inside his cloak.

Surrounding him was a forest unlike any other, its towering trees bent into impossible angles. Their branches wove together into tortuous patterns against the dim light. Each trunk seemed alive with movement, emitting words too faint to grasp, like secrets shared by silent conspirators.

He looked up. Above the trees' canopy, against the strange, swirling colors cast by the twin suns, he glimpsed a single brilliant star. Its silver-blue radiance, piercing and unwavering, cut through the shifting landscape like a lighthouse on a foggy shore. It held steady against the swirling colors of Miragwyn's sky.

Selenus took in the star's constancy as if drawn by a magnet. "Perhaps it is here to guide me."

The star illuminated the forest's shadows with a fantastical sheen. An odd energy throbbed through the air, and the trees swayed in a secretive, arcane dance. Selenus adjusted his step with caution, but even this tentative movement did little to quell the strange murmurs. From all directions came a chorus of voices—some tremulous, others thick with an undertone of disdain.

"Undeserving, indeed!" The whispers rose to a relentless hum. Selenus turned sharply, brushing his ear as if to rid himself of their invasive presence. But the murmurs, undisturbed, continued with their taunts. *"Do you truly believe you shall succeed?"*

His hair stood on end, his face drawn with strain. "Am I going mad?" he said, pressing his hands over his ears.

The shadows in Miragwyn's strange light stretched their reach. With each halted stride, it seemed his past stumbles crept closer. Yet he pressed on, step by steady step. This constancy did not spring from bravery but rather from the diffident, millennia-old resilience of the moon's unending cycle.

Each forward pace was a retort to the forest's whispered derision. "I will get through this," he said, as though by speaking it aloud he might make it true.

The landscape seemed to acquiesce. The voices withdrew. Only murmurs remained in the shifting wind. The orb in his palm flickered, and for a brief moment, the eclipsed, watchful image of his father reappeared.

The silence held, and yet here was no ordinary silence; it carried an unspoken challenge. Selenus's duty, and the magnitude of it, while still unmeasured, loomed vast.

❧

Ahead, Miragwyn unfolded its surreal panorama before Selenus. Rivers glimmered and wove through mist-laden hills, while mountains rose in fleeting majesty only to crumble, yielding to some ancient whim. Yet through this world of shifting forms, his pace grew surer. A deeper, calmer rhythm untouched by Miragwyn's caprice guided him forward. Above him, the lone star—its silver-blue gleam brightening—offered its constant light, a sparkle of distant reassurance amidst the mutable landscape below.

As he pressed on, the scene darkened, and shadows drew inward to form a labyrinthine obstacle of stone and murk surrounding him. He ventured through, winding his way along paths that twisted with a peculiar logic, as if to follow him rather than the other way around. The maze was clearly crafted to confuse, provoke, and unsettle the heart of its wanderer. And it succeeded, for it seemed to know Selenus all too well.

It was here, at the puzzle's core, that he encountered a curious sight that brought him to a dead halt. A full-length mirror, polished to a deceptive gleam, stood before him. Its surface, too pristine, held an air of menace, reflecting not the prince of Lunarae's fair visage, but an ugly, disfigured brute. Were these the imperfections that even he had hidden from himself?

The mirror shivered in mirth, and from its depths, Wilhelmina's familiar visage emerged, her face calm but unflinching.

As Selenus approached the mirror, the figure within softened. Her gaze was no longer piercing but warm, almost beguiling. Her hand stretched outward, a gentleness defying the maze's sharp angles, as if the glass were but air. The warmth of her touch seeped through his skin as her fingers grazed his arm. He inhaled sharply but did not resist as she drew closer. Then, her features melted into an expression of tenderness that, for a fleeting instant, appeared natural and real.

Her arms encircled him, and she lifted her face to press a kiss to his lips—sweet at first, then deepening, searing, until he became almost unmoored, lost in the embrace of what resembled a beautiful illusion.

For one suspended moment, the labyrinth, the shadows, even his own mission, seemed to disappear, as if her touch alone could unravel the universe.

Yet as he leaned into the kiss, her fingers tightened, and the warmth that had enveloped him grew unnervingly hot, as if laced with fire. Her nails clawed into his shoulders, digging sharply through his cloak. Her soft gaze turned cold, her lips twisted into a smile both lovely and vicious.

Her mouth opened, and the sound she made shattered the silence.

"Coward!"

Her tone was sharp, relentless, echoing through the stone maze.

He stumbled backward, but her grip held fast, her fingers clawing into his arms, forcing him to meet her gaze. But her voice, no longer quite Wilhelmina's, grew louder and harsher, each accusation flung with the accuracy of a javelin.

"Failure! Pretender! Unworthy!"

The chorus continued, insistent and unyielding, while her hands reached farther, tugging at his sleeves to pull him into that frigid, gleaming prison. He grappled with her, his fingers sinking into the cold, reflective surface that yielded under his touch, trapping him.

Even amidst the throes of danger, Selenus knew he was losing ground. The more he wrestled with the reflection, the stronger its pull became.

"*Coward.*" It was a whisper, laced with venom. Her grip on him turned vise-like, forcing him to his knees.

"Pretender. Failure," she hissed, each word like a lash whipped across his back. Her embrace constricted, intent on wringing the last drop of his life force.

His father's orb in his pocket burned through the fabric, freezing his skin to a dangerous degree.

Disoriented and fighting against Wilhelmina's chimeric grasp, Selenus tried to wrench himself free, his breath growing ragged. But the mirror held fast, pulling him in like frozen quicksand.

"Coward!"

The scream tore from her throat, and suddenly he was on the side of the mirror where she had been, and she was on the other. They had flipped places in this mad world! Looking down at his feet, he saw verdant grass where there had been a stone floor in the labyrinth. He was trapped in the mirror's confines.

He pounded against the glass with his fists. "I demand to be released!"

Wilhelmina's apparition stood mute, watching him with an expression of curiosity. It was a tableau both cruel and instructive, requiring not one word from her to make plain that this was indeed his creation.

Then, her likeness dissolved and reformed with his every attempt to look away. At last, his gaze met hers, and his face contorted in anguish. Recognition struck—a painful, honest reckoning. The reflection glinted, its cruelty coming into clarity, and the glass fractured in delicate fissures, a light glimmering from the fragments, almost celebratory, as if the trial had passed. The silence that followed was a palpable release.

Selenus wiped his mouth, as if to erase the kiss that hadn't truly been Wilhelmina's. His voice faltered. "Unworthy... perhaps she was right. But then again... perhaps not entirely."

The weight of it lingered on his shoulders, no less a burden for its honesty. From the corner of his eye, the silver-blue star had unexpectedly reappeared on this side of the labyrinth's mirror. His fingers rose of their own volition, and he pressed them against his lips where the skin still burned.

He turned around slowly, and a gasp caught in his throat. An open meadow draped in a veritable kaleidoscope of blossoms arose before him and stretched for miles to the horizon. The scene was almost absurd in its radiance. Each flower appeared to hold a quiet insistence upon its brilliance, defying the logic of color or pattern.

Seized by a frantic will, Selenus broke into a full sprint—wild, unrelenting, like a horse galloping into the gale, the wind tearing past. The ground blurred underfoot, each stride carried by a frenzied energy that pushed him to the edge of his strength.

Under the kaleidoscopic light, his trial was no longer a distant ordeal but an immediate challenge—tangible, inevitable, and fraught with the weight of his father's sacrifice. He had traveled to Miragwyn to seek Wilhelmina and the Enchantress, and perhaps, should fate allow, to carve a path toward his redemption.

Before he could stop and take a quieting breath, an unanticipated whirl of force pulled at his body, tugging in a way he could neither resist nor fully believe. And then it happened. His shape compressed, compacting in on itself with a peculiar, cosmic inevitability. When the pull relented, he was no longer a prince but a small, luminous pebble—simple, unassuming, and inert.

He had become, quite unmistakably, a rock—a humble fragment of moonlight.

The orb had rolled a short distance away, its polished surface catching the silver-blue star's light like a beacon. From the shadows, a pair of eyes appeared—gleaming, unblinking, and far too interested in the fallen treasure.

9. The Garden of Truths

The vibrant field stretched endlessly. For a moment, the companions stood transfixed, caught between wonder and a gnawing dread. They had fallen literally into a world beyond comprehension, with beauty so intense it bordered on the supernatural.

Colors and scents fluttered in the gentle breeze, and the friends lingered amidst the blossoms they had admired moments before from the safety of the library. Rainbow-colored flowers unfurled along winding pathways, each petal glowing with a luminescence that could only have been conjured by magic's deft hand.

The trees lining the paths swayed lightly. Shimmering leaves adorned their branches, casting dappled shadows upon the companions' bewildered faces. Here, serenity reigned supreme. Even time itself seemed to have paused, creating an atmosphere both beguiling and unnerving.

Wilhelmina's jaw dropped. For a heartbeat, she took an instinctive step away, her fingers fluttering to her throat. "Is this... a dream?"

Aria answered, though her voice held little certainty. "What... is this place? And, more importantly, how on Aetherwyn are we going to go home?"

Flora had already wandered a few steps ahead, brushing her fingers over the delicate petals of a rich red blossom. "It's beautiful, but... rather unsettling, isn't it?"

Wilhelmina steadied herself with a deep breath, taking in the endless, vibrant horizon. "I don't know where we are exactly, but I have to believe the Enchantress brought us here for a reason."

Adjusting his glasses and attempting to reclaim a modicum of dignity after their graceless arrival, Quill huffed, dusting his sleeve.

"Yes, but... is it a test or a trap?"

With his usual flair, Crispin gave an exaggerated sweep of his tunic, though the mud from their fall refused to be banished so easily.

"Well, if it's a trap, it's the loveliest trap I've ever seen."

With a wry grin, he observed the curious details around them: the shifting colors of the flowers, the branches overhead that leaned in, as if listening intently. "Honestly, I could settle down right here. Perhaps a little nap is in order, but I'll avoid those pebbles over there," he uttered with a stifled yawn.

Wilhelmina suppressed a smile. "Save your nap. Let's hope this place is less about trapping and more about teaching us... something."

A rustle nearby brought every head to swivel toward the sound. Just a few steps away, a small creature lurked within the blossoms, its gaze fixed on an object glowing in its tiny paws. Moisture dripped from its salivating, wagging tongue as it beheld the priceless treasure clutched in its delicate claws. Its enormous eyes darted side-to-side from the orb to the companions with comical eagerness.

"Er... does anyone else see that... thing staring at that ball?" Crispin whispered, fighting to suppress a grin. "What is it doing?"

"Yes," Flora said, edging closer. "Oh, it's precious... come here, little one. What have you got there?"

Crispin sprang forward, startling the creature into dropping the orb with a squeak. A short chase ensued. Both of them weaved through the flowers in an undignified to-and-fro motion, trampling petals and stems beneath their clumsy steps.

It almost escaped, but Crispin grabbed the creature's tail after a targeted lunge. With that last effort, he pulled it to a halt, ending in a triumphant, if not quite graceful, heap. The creature yelped from the pull and the subsequent tight capture within his arms.

Flora gave a shriek, dashing over. "Don't hurt it!" She deftly scooped up the creature from Crispin's grip, swatting his hand away as she cradled the little thing. Now safe in Flora's arms, it licked her face with earnest enthusiasm, sending her into a fit of giggles. "Oh, you're a dear, aren't you?" she cooed.

Crispin pulled himself to his feet and brushed off his trousers with exaggerated affront. "I would not harm it!" he huffed. His gaze darted over the field as he spun around, scratching his head. At last, he spotted the orb a short distance away.

A pulse of light emanated from the patch of grass where it lay, nestled almost as if it were breathing. His eyes rounded with a sudden childlike zeal, and he lunged forward. He picked it up as if handling a rare jewel. Turning it slowly in his hands, he marveled at the way it seemed to flicker with secrets just out of reach. "Oh, I'm definitely keeping this," he said, a grin spreading across his face.

Aria tsked as she looked around at the surreal beauty of the garden surrounding them. Her pupils sparkled as the chiming of flowers singing rang out.

Nearby, Quill had taken to examining the vines snaking along the ground in curious patterns.

Crispin held the orb up to the light, angling it toward the hovering luminous crystals scattered above. The orb's color shifted at once, startled, from a warm, golden gleam to an impenetrable, mournful ebony. He squinted, leaning in for a closer look, then gave it a small, cautious shake, half-expecting some hidden reaction.

"Could've sworn I saw something inside there a moment ago. Now it's all... black." He turned the sphere thoughtfully in his palm, tilting it back and forth, considering a solution. "Rather somber, wouldn't you say? Could do with a good polish."

Just then, Flora's glance fell upon a patch of strange flowers nearby. "Why does this place seem so familiar?" She knelt to inspect the tender blooms. "There's more to this garden, I think. It's as if magic is within every flower and blade of grass." She extended a tentative hand toward one bloom, only to draw back as a delicate spark, quite unlike any she had seen, leapt between her finger and the petal. Her gaze lingered on the bloom, her brow furrowed in concentration. "Might these... be truth blossoms?"

And as if on cue, the peculiar statue at the garden's edge—small, weathered, and rather unassuming—twitched and trembled. At first, it was barely noticeable, a mere ripple of stone. It resembled nothing so much as a diminutive boulder until the figure straightened, gave itself a brisk shake, and transformed before their eyes.

To their astonishment, there now stood a garden gnome, sporting blue furry trousers and a ruby-red shirt that barely covered his rounded middle. Upon his head rested a conical hat, striped in red and white like a candy cane. It flopped slightly with a fluffy ball at its tip, as though it had been hastily put on in mid-slumber.

His beard, long and snowy with a curl at the ends, had a few tiny wildflowers nestled within. It framed jolly rosy cheeks, a bulbous nose, and a pair of sparkling cerulean eyes that contained an air of bemusement. Though plump, he moved with surprising sprightliness, and a small pouch stuffed with herbs and polished pebbles dangled from his belt.

"Indeed, miss, they are truth blossoms," the gnome said in a voice carrying a deep, resonant timbre. "And this garden is of no ordinary beauty. It is a place of intention."

"Who-who are you?" Flora squeaked. She clutched her hand to her chest, which promptly led to her dropping the creature she'd been cradling in a cozy embrace. Startled, it scurried toward Crispin again.

"Ah, apologies, my dear. Where are my manners? Please allow me to introduce myself—Grumblefoot, at your service." With a flourish, he clicked his heels and gave a solemn bow. A twinkle of humor brightened his wizened eyes.

Crispin barely had time to react before the creature leapt at the pocket where he kept the orb safe. He jumped back, but it was not so easily deterred, trying again and again to approach him. Baring its teeth, it lunged, delivering a final nip at Crispin's exposed ankle.

"Yow!" Crispin raised his foot, hopping about in an indignant howl of pain. "It bit me!" He swatted at the little beast and tried to shoo it away. "Blasted thing. I shall best you! I'm much smarter," he boasted while glaring at his persistent adversary.

Just then, a slender root shot up from the blossoms beneath him, thin as a thread and quick as a whip. The lashings continued as it wrapped firmly around his waist, joined by others rising from the ground. In a flurry of movement, the underground threads jerked him off his feet, hoisting him aloft. He struggled to wriggle clear, but his efforts were to no avail.

"Crispin!" the companions cried in alarm.

"Ah," Grumblefoot remarked, nodding sagely. "I'm afraid your friend has been ensnared by the Threads of Truth."

"The what?" Wilhelmina asked. "How do we get him down?"

"Hmph. There's the rub, my dear. He alone can free himself." Grumblefoot stroked his beard thoughtfully. "You see, this garden, though lovely, is enchanted to challenge all who dare to enter. No one leaves without passing its test."

"Test? What test?" Quill interjected, his skepticism flaring.

"The Test of Truth," Grumblefoot stated matter-of-factly, gesturing to the blooms. "These are truth blossoms. They respond to honesty, punishing deceit with a rather, er, persuasive squeeze." He glanced up at Crispin, who wriggled helplessly in the air. "I regret to say your companion has told a fib."

"Are you calling me a liar?" said Crispin, grunting while twisting against the roots.

"Well, considering you're somewhat indisputably trapped... yes," Grumblefoot said baldly, eyes twinkling with unspoken amusement. "The Threads of Truth are quite adept at squeezing out the hidden realities from those who choose to conceal them. And it would seem, my dear boy, you have been holding back quite a bit."

He gave a knowing nod, stroking his beard. "Only by facing what's concealed can one break free," he said. "The deepest revelations await those who dare to confront themselves. And once revealed, the garden will respond, reflecting a glimpse of who you truly are."

The others shifted uncomfortably, exchanging wary glances. "It might help if your friends were to share their truths to show you how," he added with a wink. He then tapped his nose and turned toward Wilhelmina, who seemed naturally poised as their leader. "How about we start with you, miss? I reckon you might set a good example, eh?"

"Well... yes, all right," she said. "I officiate weddings because I believe in love's power.... Oh!" she squeaked as fresh vines hoisted her unceremoniously into the air.

Grumblefoot observed her struggle with a chuckle. "Goodness me! Love's power, eh? But do go on, dear, for the garden seems unconvinced. You might want to dig a little deeper there... get to the root of things, if you know what I mean." He pointed his finger at Quill. "Your turn, lad."

Quill gulped, casting a wary look at Wilhelmina's suspended form. "Er... I seek knowledge to understand the world as any scholar would. Oof!" At once, a tangle of vines grabbed his ankles, rendering him upside down in the air and snugly wrapped like a struggling silkworm in its cocoon.

Grumblefoot let out a tired sigh. "Ah. I... uh... don't see. Not quite the whole truth, either." He gestured to Aria, who rushed toward Quill, her eyes round as saucers, looking up at his inverted strands of hair, now waving in the wind.

"Let me try! I sing and gather people because it brings joy." The moment the words left her mouth, a fresh set of singing threads rose and twined about her, lifting her gently.

Grumblefoot tilted his head as she floated, waiting. "Bringing joy, you say? Well, my dear, the garden senses a bit more to that tune." He shook his head, seeing her blank expression. “Half-truths all around! Come on, dig deeper, my fine friends. Face what’s truly there, or you may be here a while.”

“I... protect nature because it’s beautiful and essential,” Flora stammered. Vines shot up beside her feet, lifting her upright in a snug net of green threads—not quite uncomfortable, but certainly insistent.

Crispin, still tangled and squirming, spoke up next. “You’re right, of course. Here goes. I like making people laugh. It’s just who I am. No need to squeeze so hard,” he said, wriggling.

Grumblefoot smacked his hands together, and his belly shook with laughter. “Now you’re all really quite stuck, aren’t you? Look, you must abandon these pretenses. Come now, face your truths!” He stretched out on the grass, closing his eyes as if settling in for a nap. “Oh, don’t mind me. I have all day to wait,” he said with a yawn, which turned into a loud snore.

Groans of frustration and muffled complaints echoed from the hoisted friends. “Love is the solution!” Wilhelmina called out. “No, Nature!” said Flora. “Knowledge!” cried Quill. “Singing is the answer!” Aria shouted.

This cacophony of half-truths and evasions only led to each of them being squeezed tighter. Then, Wilhelmina blew a sharp whistle, commanding their attention and waking the slumbering Grumblefoot.

“We are getting nowhere with half-truths,” she said. “Look, I don’t know exactly what this... being wants, but we’ve got to let go of our pride and trust each other. I commit to you that I won’t laugh, and I will be your friend, regardless. So, let me go again.”

She cleared her throat and breathed in. “It goes beyond love itself—it’s about creating a love that protects. I officiate because I don’t want any child to feel abandoned, as I did. If I can help people create families full of love, maybe the world will be a gentler place.”

As she spoke, her aura glowed, and the vines gently loosened.

Grumblefoot nodded with a wise smile. “Ah, creating love that protects. Now that’s something genuine one can root for.”

“Oh, Wilhelmina! I didn’t know!” Aria choked back a sob. “I wish I could hug you now. Let me try again, too.”

She took a breath. “I do sing to bring joy, but it’s more than that—I want people to feel loved, to belong. My voice isn’t just mine. It’s meant to build friendships, to create a shared happiness... a joy that binds us.”

As she confessed, Aria's aura brightened, and her cheeks glistened with tears. The vines slackened their hold on her, and she drifted to the earth.

Grumblefoot smiled fondly. "A voice to bind, not merely to sing. Truly, the sweetest song!"

"Nature isn't just something to preserve—it's family," Flora said, as she let out a deep sigh.

The gnome inclined his head with understanding. "Beauty, yes... but family, I dare say, is a stronger tie."

"Every plant, every creature, every leaf is connected by threads of energy, a vibration that unites us all. I care for it because it's... It's who I am. And we're all kin, bound to one another."

The vines, as if acknowledging her kinship with the natural world, released her gracefully. Her dulled garments then blossomed with shades of deep green, delicate petals, and dynamic hues, as if she were clad in a tapestry woven directly from the forest floor.

Grumblefoot beamed. "The plant kin and kinfolk! Now that's a family like no other."

A delighted smile spread across Flora's face as her gift returned, and her garments became radiant with the energy of the natural realm.

However, nearby vines wrapped and coiled around Quill's arms. He then spoke up, his voice low. "It's more than mere knowledge."

Grumblefoot raised an eyebrow at Quill's statement, prodding, "Knowledge? Hmm... might there be more in that scholarly head of yours? Go on, lad. Truth does have a way of rooting out secrets."

Quill clenched his fists before admitting, "I want to preserve our history—the true history. I wish for more than knowledge. Too much is hidden and rewritten. I need to uncover the truths lost to restore integrity for future generations."

"A keeper of lost truths! Quite a noble cause, I must say." Grumblefoot chuckled approvingly. He looked at Crispin with a smirk.

"Ah, it is true, my good man. Humor is indeed a fine distraction... but what lies beneath the jests?"

Vines wrapped tighter around Crispin's legs.

"Laughter isn't just for fun," Crispin admitted, squirming. "I know what it's like to feel alone and hurt... to feel angry... to feel like there's nothing left but sadness. When I make others laugh, it's a way to help them forget their pain, even briefly."

His outfit brightened to vivid cobalt, and the flower beside him glowed warmly.

Grumblefoot's eyes twinkled. "Ah, a noble clown. Good fellow, your inner desire to protect your friends with laughter is a truth about yourself you mightn't have recognized before this moment, eh?" A twinkle of light appeared in his eye. "Protecting others through laughter. Now, that's a first and a rare gift. Keep it close, lad, for such joys are rare indeed."

The vines that had bound Crispin like a vise now shifted to tickle him under his ribs, prompting a burst of laughter that spread to the others, who joined in chorus, including Grumblefoot. Their laughter lightened the atmosphere as the vines relaxed, lowering the companions gently to the ground.

As each confession bloomed into truth, the garden brightened anew. Colors intensified and fragrances deepened.

"Ah, the garden knows when truths take root." Grumblefoot clapped his hands, his face alight. "Only then will it let you wander freely! Well done, my fine friends. Well done."

And with that, the garden, which had been holding its breath during the truth-telling, now swayed as if in acknowledgment of their new understanding of themselves. The bonus had been the reversal of Flora's previous disenchantment. The hues of nature stirred on the surface of her garments.

An unseen path emerged, inviting the companions forward. Grumblefoot waddled to each one, extending his hand in a firm shake.

"Your truth unlocks progress, and this path will take you on your journey."

"Where does this trail lead?" Wilhelmina pointed ahead. "We only wish to find the Enchantress and bring harmony back to Aetherwyn... our home."

Grumblefoot's eyes darkened for an instant, but he tapped the side of his nose.

"My dear, I expect many challenges, but each truth you have spoken has deepened you to your purpose. It has proven to be the key to the garden's secret. Many have not even come this far. Keep these truths with you, for you will face even greater tests where these realizations will become your foundation."

"Thank you, Grumblefoot, for your wisdom," Wilhelmina said. "Come on, everyone. Let's continue." She then paused, her eyes catching something shiny beside her foot.

"Funny, was that pebble there before? I could have sworn it's been following me." She knelt and picked up the small, lustrous white object, then dropped it back on the ground with a shrug. "Huh," she said under her breath as she sniffed the air. "Is that the scent of... Selenus? No, it couldn't be." She shook her head, the others trailing close behind.

The gnome nodded and gave her a brief wink. He watched them go, offering one last cryptic piece of advice.

"Hold fast to these truths, my dear friends. Your self-honesty will serve as your shield and your guide," he declared. "May our paths cross again. Farewell, and good luck!"

He offered a final wave before his form stilled, shifted, and hardened back to stone as if he had never left his original post, a knowing smile lingering in the creases of his face.

The companions' mouths gaped open.

"Well, that was bizarre," Crispin remarked, tilting his head with exaggerated seriousness, "but I dare say he was the jolliest of pebbles, if I've ever met one. And I mean that... with the utmost sincerity... and truth!"

His words prompted an eye roll or two from the others, who now seemed to feel a tad lighter than before they entered the garden.

❧

Empyrean whispers and glimmers hinted at an ancient enchantment as the friends wandered along the chromatic pathway of flowers and trees. The blossoms' radiance illuminated their way, casting long shadows that appeared to dance with fanciful spirits.

"Ow!" Wilhelmina grimaced in pain, having stubbed her toe. An object had found its way into her shoe. She bent down to remove it and shake out the offending piece. Her eyes widened in surprise.

"You again!"

It was the same pebble she had dropped some distance back. As she held it, the smooth surface pulsed with a superlunary glow.

“Oh! How beautiful... and so smooth! But it felt sharp underfoot!” she grumbled, brow furrowing. “There’s something... strange about it. Almost as if it’s calling to me.”

Flora’s gaze fixed upon the little stone, her expression thoughtful. “There might be a story behind this. I’m sure of it.”

An odd thing then happened. A beam of illumination from the blue star—a silver thread of sorts—streamed toward the earth, connecting its tip to Wilhelmina’s heart, which pulsed beneath her ribs. From there, another ray traveled to the shining pebble in her palm and back to the celestial body in the sky.

A radiant triangle now glimmered in the air. The other companions’ mouths formed an ‘o’ as they stared at the extraordinary shape.

“This light is ... steady, but distant. It’s like a promise of something I don’t yet understand.” Wilhelmina’s nose crinkled, as if trying to match the fragrance from before. “Very strange indeed.”

10. The Henge of Memory

A short time later, the companions encountered a curious phenomenon and halted their steps, their mouths agape. Before them stood a towering henge, a circle of colossal columns hewn from opal and topaz. The monolithic stones gleamed with age-old etchings, their symbols obscure yet discernible.

Wilhelmina gestured for the others to follow with a discreet motion of her hand.

"Can you smell the scent of magic?" Flora asked in a voice bordering on reverence. "The very air seems... It's as if enchantment has suffused the wildflowers and grass."

Quill squinted as he peered closer at the inscriptions. "Goodness! Do you see this? The image—why, it bears an uncanny resemblance to the Enchantress in the chronicle."

Moonblossoms encircled the figure cloaked in shadow.

He traced the faded lines with his fingertips. "These symbols speak of an era when she held sway over Aetherwyn... before she suddenly vanished."

"The hairs on my arms are rising quite on end! What could it mean?" asked Aria.

Before Quill could respond, a low rumble reverberated through the clearing. The companions froze, their eyes widening as the towering columns of the standing stones shifted slightly. Gleaming patterns inscribed themselves anew along their surface, and with a crackling whisper, faces emerged, ancient and weathered, carved by millennia of wind and time.

The first voice, deep and resonant, spoke from the tallest column. "Seekers of truth, you've reached a place of remembrance. The henge holds the history of Aetherwyn, carved into our rock and woven into its light."

The stone face before Wilhelmina opened its eyes, glowing like embers. "Do not fear us, child of balance." Its tone was softer than the first, but it carried the weight of ages. "You tread upon a path foretold, but with it comes a burden heavy and profound."

"Who... who are you?" Wilhelmina asked, her voice trembling.

"We are the Watchers of the Henge, sentinels of memory, guardians of truth," the column answered, its tone smoother, almost melodic. "We have witnessed the rise and fall of the Enchantress, and we remember the shadows that consumed her light."

Quill's fingers tightened on his satchel. "What do you know of her?"

A ghostly apparition of her shimmered and emerged into view within the henge's circle. She gazed toward the starry heavens, and with precise, measured movements, she sketched intricate mathematical formulas in mid-air. Each symbol lingered briefly before dissolving after she swiped her hand through them. Their remnants became luminous dust drifting in the wind and sky.

The largest column rumbled again, its voice resonating like distant thunder.

"Long ago, the Enchantress foresaw a great conflict, its resolution hinging upon the unity of opposites. To thwart the encroaching darkness and restore the cosmic order, she crafted a bridge. Entrusting her creation to her most loyal friend, she set in motion a course of events so intricate, it was as if she played a game of celestial strategy. She forged the bridge not of stone, but of a soul, woven from light and shadow. The Octet was her pattern, and Wilhelmina, her thread of balance. Each move was deliberate, each risk calculated. Yet her sacrifice was the price of this design. Bound within the Mirror, she ensured her light would not draw the darkness's gaze. Her choice was one of unfathomable pain, but she believed it necessary to preserve the realm."

The apparition's form flickered, her figure trembling under an invisible strain.

"Her gambit has brought you all here, to this moment, where the threads of destiny converge. The balance she sought to protect now lies within all of your hands."

Quill's voice cut through the heavy silence, his tone sharp with indignation. "Th-then our histories have been false!" His eyes flashed as he stared at the apparition.

As if in response, the face on the column nearest to him shifted. A glowing pen of multi-hued feathers and petals materialized from nowhere before him.

"Yes, young scholar. Her story's been twisted, shrouded by fear and misunderstanding. Write her truth," the stone intoned. "Let her courage be known to all who follow and honor her memory as it deserves."

Quill's expression lit with delight as he reached for the pen, swishing it through the air. "I will. I shall record the truth!"

The column facing Flora spoke next, its tone contemplative.

"The tale does not end with the Enchantress, for the harmony she tried to preserve now lies in peril. Aetherwyn's balance rests not solely on her tale, but on a unity that must exist between the Sun and Moon Princes. The sons of Celestia, Matriarch of the Stars, and Varytita, the Architect of Gravity, must forsake their rivalry and embrace kinship, or the shadow will consume all."

Wilhelmina squared her shoulders, though her hand brushed against her pocket. The pebble burst out like a flame and then retreated. She swallowed, her face blank.

"Their sons..." she echoed, her brow furrowing. "And what of the Moon Prince?"

"His envy seeped into the land before casting a shadow over Aetherwyn. The Enchantress sought to calm his heart, yet his jealousy lingered. Now, the past repeats itself."

Her expression grew fierce. "What of him? Selenus... His cowardice has left us vulnerable. He chose to abandon us, refusing to turn back the darkness he wrought. He turned away from us when we needed him most." Her voice shook as she clenched her fists at her sides.

The column grew quieter, almost mournful. "The Moon Prince, in his jealousy and doubt, has hidden within a stony heart of his own making, all to shield himself from pain. But only the one who sees beyond the surface can free him. When you look beyond what lies in front of you, peer beyond the rock and silence, and you may find him waiting."

Wilhelmina placed her hand within her pocket, where the pebble lay. Slowly, she drew it out, and her friends gathered close to observe the glowing stone. Its light intensified, casting a gentle, silver-blue radiance across her face. Indistinct engravings on the pebble's surface appeared. As she tilted it, the markings became clearer, revealing a delicate crescent moon surrounded by tiny symbols that appeared to shift and wisp in and out of view, as if glimpsed through a mist.

The stone resonated in a way that was almost sentient, reluctant, but undeniably alive, both patient and weary, waiting for her to act.

Flora's eyes gleamed as she observed it. "The light... it grows brighter with every touch," she said, her voice rising in pitch. "As if it's awaiting freedom."

Wilhelmina turned the pebble over in her hand, frowning. Its smooth, moonlit surface looked less solid, as if it veiled a depth only half-imagined.

A strange glint passed over Flora's gaze. "That pebble... Perhaps it had followed you for a reason," she mused.

"The artifact you hold, child, will guide and protect you, should you have the courage to see."

The stony face beside Wilhelmina turned its gaze to the pebble. "But beware—the path ahead is fraught with trials. Unity is your strength, and the shadows seek to divide."

The columns inclined in unison, their light dimming slightly. "Go forth, truth seekers," they said in one voice. "And carry with you the wisdom of the past. The balance lies in your hands." The glowing lines faded, and the faces receded into the stone, leaving the henge silent once more.

❧

Miragwyn's two suns fell over the horizon as twilight descended, casting a haunting melody through the garden. Aria's gentle presence drew closer to the center of the stone circle's clearing, and she raised her arms as if responding to the unspoken harmony of the moment.

A heartbeat later, her voice broke the stillness. A resonant melody carried tones that stirred the air. The garden's blossoms trembled, their petals unfurling as if drawn to the sound. The song moved like a living thing, weaving through the companions, touching each with its unique grace. A faint starlight shimmered above, bending subtly as Aria's sound swelled.

In the garden where emotions bloom,
Moonlight whispers, dispelling gloom.
A heart's reflection in silvery light,
Love unveiled in the serene twilight.

Wilhelmina remained immobile, her hand tightening on the pebble while the tune unfolded. Though she said nothing, her posture softened, and the rigid line of her shoulders eased as tiny stone glimmered silver. It was subtle at first, but with each note, the light grew stronger and cast rippling patterns across her palm.

She glanced at Aria, awe blooming in her gaze. Was the garden singing with her, or was Aria simply hearing what others could not?

Quill smiled and took his new pen, flourishing it in the air. His ink strokes pulsed with truth and feeling. He pulled a little journal from his vest. Opening it to a blank page, he wrote fresh lyrics to accompany Aria's haunting melody. His voice intertwined with hers, becoming a duet of revelation and longing. He glanced at her, his usual wit quieted by the sincerity of her song. She caught his gaze for a fleeting moment, her lips curving into a smile before returning her focus to the unfolding magic.

Mystic blossoms reveal a tale,
A melody hearts can feel.
Their dance, a mystical quest,
In this true garden, love expressed.

There's more in this realm
Where magic's entwined,
Guiding us to realms untold,
Secrets we are fated to find.

The ancient henge seemed to hum in response, a low, vibrating resonance that harmonized with Aria and Quill's duet. Though no words were spoken, the Watchers in the stone stirred, their faces momentarily illuminated as though roused from a long slumber. A breeze carried the melody outward, mingling with the echoes of the henge's vibrations.

Glances passed between the companions, acknowledging the magic that had just unfolded. Quill's brow furrowed as he watched the garden's reaction to the song, his sharp eyes catching the glow of the pebble in Wilhelmina's hand. Flora, in contrast, tilted her head slightly, her expression softening. Aria's melody swirled upward, brushing against the twilight skies. It was not a song of simple beauty but one of revelation, a quiet invitation to see what lay hidden underneath. Though none could explain it aloud, the power made itself known, a bridge between what was revealed and what remained hidden.

The stone in her palm shimmered in rhythm with the song. Its engravings shifted, catching the light of the garden as if emerging from a veil of mist. The moment seemed suspended, as though the garden had paused to witness the unfolding connection between the music and the stone.

Aria and Quill's voices faded like whispers into the wind. Wilhelmina pressed her hand to her heart, and a smile graced her lips. "Your magical, wondrous voice has returned, and your lyrics speak with a newfound depth and truth."

"I heard the whispers of your heart," Aria said. "I think it reignited my voice. Embrace the music of your soul, Wilhelmina. Let your soul's music guide you through the intricate symphony of emotions you're feeling."

Quill's eyes lit as he gazed upon Aria and then shifted to Wilhelmina, nodding, not speaking, as if recharging his gift of words.

Wilhelmina held the pebble higher. The others drew closer, and it pulsed, as if reflecting the moon's essence. A shiver of something, neither fear nor awe precisely, passed over her as she studied the stone. She found her mind drawn, rather against her will, to an image of Selenus's eyes haunted by a sorrow none of them had ever entirely understood.

The stone, small and cold in her palm, carried within it a presence unmistakably weary and remote, as though it were holding a regret that belonged to another age. Wilhelmina held it aloft for her friends to observe. Her expression contained neither shock nor certainty, but an air of consideration that quickly piqued their interest.

"There is... something within... a presence," she murmured. "And yet..." she faltered, caught between intuition and reluctance. "Could it be... Selenus?"

The companions looked on, their expressions a mirror of her own intrigue. Though none dared to agree or deny her speculation. At that, Aria's voice rose, her song a tender echo of Wilhelmina's discovery, weaving around them like the gentle touch of stardust:

In the twilight's hushed symphony,
Moonlight whispers, wild and free.
Mystical song, our journey's theme,
Through enchanted realms, we gleam.

When the last note of Aria's melody drifted into the air, the garden blossomed anew. Wilhelmina's fingers curled around the pebble as she knelt. "Perhaps it needs help to break free."

Guided by a moving intuition, she tapped it lightly against a nearby stone, her heart quickening with each attempt. But no sooner had she struck it than a mournful sound escaped from inside it, something closer to a sigh than a crack.

She paused, listening, but as she kept trying to chip away at it, the noise grew louder, almost a low wail, reverberating like a sad echo in the stillness. The harder she tried, the more intense the sounds became, each one stirring an unexpected pang of sympathy within her.

She released the pebble into her open hand, frowning at it thoughtfully.

"Perhaps... I'm doing this all wrong."

Her brow puckered as her hands gentled around it. She drew the stone to her chest, closing her eyes with a pensive expression. Then she took a steadying breath and spoke to it. "If you wish to be free, I will help you... but not with force."

Slowly, the tiny rock softened, its rigid edges dissolving into a luminous vapor that swirled in her palm, filling the grove with a brilliant glow. As the final shimmer of light cascaded outward like starlight spilling from Wilhelmina's hand, the mist cleared.

The companions exchanged wide-eyed glances as a figure emerged.

Selenus now stood before them, his form distinct yet veiled by the wisps of residual mist clinging to the air. His silver eyes, cool and guarded, scanned the group with measured intensity. Though his tall and regal posture was composed, a weariness, as if he bore the burden of unspoken regrets, clung to him.

"You!" Wilhelmina gasped, startled by his sudden appearance. The old wound flared behind her eyes. "I didn't expect... not like this." Then, as if remembering herself, she added more coldly, "It would seem the coward returns."

Her friends shifted uncomfortably, eyes darting between them.

Selenus's expression didn't falter, but his gaze darkened and grew veiled. "One does not truly return if one has never fully departed," he said in a tone edged with wariness.

Wilhelmina's fingers closed over the space where the pebble had been in her pocket. "Then perhaps you have come to account for the choices you made."

His measured response contained careful neutrality. "If I am to answer for anything, it is to the realm and its future, not to one who presumes to judge what she cannot understand."

At this, a brief silence hung between them, neither looking away, as if testing an invisible boundary. Yet the tension between them eased almost imperceptibly as the gravity of their shared purpose eclipsed their resentments. Finally, he bowed his head with a formal reserve, offering no words yet conveying an equal willingness to abide by this tentative truce.

Wilhelmina's hand fell back to her side. "Then it appears we have no choice but to begin as strangers, however familiar the past."

Selenus glanced toward Crispin, noticing the faint glow of the orb cradled in his hands. The sight softened Selenus's expression, though weariness still lingered in his eyes.

Quill's eyes moved side-to-side from Selenus to the orb in Crispin's hand, his eyes narrowing.

"And what of this, then?" He gestured to the small globe with a curiosity that barely masked his suspicion.

"The orb is mine," Selenus said, his voice edged with hesitation. His eyes flickered to Wilhelmina, lingering for a moment before refocusing on Crispin. His following words were more of a statement than a request.

"Keep it safe, lad. Though I would much prefer it in my own care."

Quill stepped forward, his stance defensive, as if shielding the group from a latent threat. "And what guarantees do we have that you won't twist its purpose?" His tone carried a sharp edge.

He leaned down to whisper in Wilhelmina's ear. "Have you already forgotten what he did? I don't trust him, and neither should you."

Her eyes lingered on Selenus, but her thoughts, like shadows, offered no certainty. He stood composed, almost solemn, but the memories of his betrayal clung too tightly to be washed away by mist and moonlight. The orb pulsed with power, power she wasn't sure he should hold again.

Was she meant to follow the prophecy? Or had she already given too much of herself to a story someone else had written? She longed to believe she was more than a piece on a board. But what if the realm's fate depended not on fate itself, but on her choosing something no other could? And yet... the choice had to be made.

Wilhelmina raised a hand, halting Quill with a firm yet calming touch against his chest. Her steady gaze met Selenus's. "Give it over, Crispin."

Crispin hesitated, then shuffled forward and held out the orb.

Selenus accepted it with a deep sigh, his fingers brushing the smooth surface as though reacquainting himself with an old wound.

As the orb settled into his palm, its dark face shimmered, a faint golden light rising from within it before receding once more, as if acknowledging its new keeper.

Crispin narrowed his eyes. "I'm going to be watching you, prince," he hissed.

Selenus paused, his grip on the orb tightening slightly before he tucked it close. He met Crispin's eyes, then Quill's, before returning to Wilhelmina's.

"You would not be wrong to watch me," he uttered, his voice low. "Perhaps you'll see something I have yet to confront myself."

"Whatever secrets remain will unveil themselves when needed. For now, we keep our counsel." Wilhelmina lifted her face toward the darkening horizon. "Our path shall reveal what it will in time."

Selenus inclined his head. His guardedness was kept in check as he stepped back, creating a deliberate distance between himself and the group. Though neither ally nor friend, he kept silent, his presence marked by a truce bound to a shared purpose rather than trust. The space he left between them was a buffer against wounds not yet healed, if they ever could be.

The companions turned and walked on, exiting the garden as twilight deepened around them. A soft breeze rustled Flora's newly viridescent garments, and Wilhelmina whispered under her breath, "As Grumblefoot would say, the truth we carry guides the way."

II. The Sphere and the Sword

A fractured expanse of shadowed archways and ancient stones rose before them. Vines twisted through jagged cracks and clung to pillars and columns, as if unwilling to release them to the mercies of time. The mournful cries of distant birds pierced the wailing gusts of wind. Each note was an elegy to the civilization that once flourished here.

Yet signs of life persisted, embodied in resilient flora whose vibrant hues defied the muted tones of decay. Wildflowers peeked out of fissures in the rocks. Their petals swayed in the chilled breeze, while moss carpeted the ground in verdant patches, in quiet defiance of the dilapidated structures it bordered.

Wilhelmina's gaze lingered on the weathered surface, where shadows cast an otherworldly pallor over the ancient blocks. "What secrets lie hidden in this desolation?" she murmured, a shiver escaping with her words.

Selenus took a deliberate step forward, his jaw set with resolve. "We shall need to explore further. It is almost as if something or someone guides us onward."

The companions advanced with caution through the arched entrance. Their footsteps reverberated against the cool stone. Shadowy shapes flickered along the walls, interrupted here and there by cracks through which beams of faded light spilled.

The path narrowed and twisted before leading them to a single chamber where a series of shimmering crystals obstructed their passage, each arranged in a complex, mesmerizing pattern.

Wilhelmina observed the array, a slight furrow creasing her brow. "I've encountered puzzles like this before. It is no doubt a test of sorts. If we decipher the arrangement, it should open the route."

"Or," Selenus interjected, his tone tinged with a certain impatience, "we could attempt something more direct." His fingers flexed as if eager for action. "Brute force would prove swifter. We could bypass the puzzle entirely."

Wilhelmina shook her head. "That would be too risky. A spell of this age may respond poorly, perhaps violently, if disturbed. We must defend the enchantment's equilibrium."

Selenus's jaw tightened. "Equilibrium or no, further delay brings us closer to failure. There are times, Wilhelmina, when force is necessary."

As if sensitive to their discord, the crystals' glow shifted from a steady pulse to a sharp, fitful flicker. Wilhelmina hesitated.

"Perhaps if we work together, the path may reveal itself. It could be as much a test of trust as of strategy."

Selenus held her gaze, his resolve easing, a trace of grudging respect in his expression.

"Very well. Lead the way."

They each placed a hand upon a crystal, and in answer, the erratic light softened, its unruly flutter calming beneath their combined touch. Gradually, the crystals' radiance intensified and realigned in harmonious patterns until an opening in the stone wall was revealed. The ruin's ancient magic, it seemed, had deemed their cooperation acceptable, permitting them passage.

❧

They advanced through the winding corridors until they stumbled into a gloomy chamber. A chill pervaded the air, thick with an unseen force that pressed upon their senses, eerie, inescapable.

"We're not alone." Crispin's tone was laced with trepidation.

The silence that followed was short-lived. A haunting melody filled the space—a delicate sound that wrapped around them with ancient resonance. An icy gust swept through, and from the shadows emerged a figure cloaked in mist, her eyes aglow. The haze encircling her appeared to have a will of its own. The companions recoiled, visibly startled by her spectral gaze.

"I am the protector of these ruins." Her voice carried a commanding note above the sublime melody. It was rich with authority and tempered by a discernible distrust.

Her sharp gaze passed over each of them in turn, pausing at last upon Wilhelmina.

"What purpose drives you to awaken the past from its slumber? Are you here to procure the relics left by the Enchantress?"

"Relics? I don't understand. I... suppose we seek them, though perhaps with less grace than one might expect, but with sincerity nonetheless," Wilhelmina ventured, glancing at Selenus. "We mean no harm and seek only to restore balance to Aetherwyn. All we've been told is to find the Enchantress. If these relics were hers... and placed here by her for her rescuers to discover, then wouldn't they be important for us to have?"

The Protector's eyes narrowed. "Words spill easily from hopeful lips, but they lack substance if not born of truth. Indeed, the Enchantress came to this ancient place to house these relics—keys, perhaps, to the balance you claim to seek."

Her gaze swept over each companion with measured pauses.

"Those pure of heart may take what lies here. Should your intentions falter, the relics will remain forever beyond your reach, and so will this place."

Her eyes rested on Wilhelmina, a penetrating light in their depths. "Wait... the spirit of the celestial sisterhood is apparent in you. A legacy woven through time's tapestry, entwined by destiny's threads. You carry the essence of those who've come before you. But we shall see..."

With that, her spectral hand pointed toward the center of the chamber, its form wavering like mist.

"We shall not falter," Wilhelmina said.

Behind her, the others exchanged cautious glances, but they proceeded with reverence. At first, they saw only an empty space.

"It's not working." Wilhelmina looked at the others. "Maybe... we should clasp hands?"

All but Selenus nodded and linked hands, but Wilhelmina motioned for him to join.

"Come on. This isn't the time to be timid. Besides, I don't think it will work without all of us in sync."

With reluctance, Selenus clasped her hand, sparking a current that leapt between them.

Quill linked with Wilhelmina on the other side, and Aria, Crispin, and Flora completed the circle, Flora's hand finding Selenus's free one.

The spark that began between Wilhelmina and Selenus traveled around the chain, building in intensity. A glimmer of light then expanded, illuminating the room.

Within their linked circle and suspended in midair, there appeared a sphere wound with gold strands. It cast flickering, gilded reflections on the chamber walls. Slowly, they unlinked hands. Their gazes remained transfixed on the phenomenon. Yet the sphere's light continued to glow without wavering.

Wilhelmina approached the object. Her fingers trembled as they reached for its textured, grooved surface.

Though the Protector's steely gaze suggested the challenge was no mere game, she could not help but wish the matter would resolve itself, her patience growing thin. The instant she made contact, however, a bolt of electricity shot between her and the sphere.

Selenus stepped forward with a furrowed brow. "What is this strange abomination?"

"It is not an abomination, foolish prince," Wilhelmina rebuked. "One might think even shadows could recognize an artifact of worth."

"This is the Sphere of Golden Thread, created by the Enchantress herself," the Protector announced, her voice slicing through the thick silence of the room with unyielding clarity. "Its magic is ancient, formidable, and entwined with her enduring legacy."

Wilhelmina's breath caught as she studied the artifact. Each flicker from the intricate, luminous patterns etched upon its face seemed to whisper a story, a lost fragment of Aetherwyn's forgotten past now captured and woven into the delicate threads of light.

Then, from a pale glow amidst the rubble, another relic emerged. Selenus knelt on the dirt floor and brushed aside centuries of dust and decay to uncover the pommel of an ancient sword. Its surface appeared dull, and yet it displayed enduring grace.

The sword emitted a low, resonant hum, subtle yet potent, whispering of the power it contained.

"Wait," Aria said. "There's... something different about this weapon. Its vibration feels like a melody, a memory calling to us."

Flora bent to examine the blade, her eyes bright as her fingers traced the finely engraved symbols along the hilt. "It does seem to possess a distinct energy," she observed.

Crispin grinned as he reached to touch the sword's edge, but he snatched his hand back with a yelp as the blade pricked his finger. "Ow! It's got a mind of its own!"

Selenus swiftly intervened, his face amused. "Dear fellow, caution would serve you well. Swords rarely have opinions, but they often reward the cautious."

Quill knelt by them, his voice reverent. "This blade bears the unmistakable marks of a bygone era, as though it once held a place of great importance." He pondered the etched patterns with unabashed admiration.

Wilhelmina's eyes met Selenus's, her tone calm yet certain. "Whatever its purpose, this sword is more than a relic; it must be another key."

The Protector materialized near them. Her sudden presence made them start. "You are worthy," she intoned, her gaze sweeping over them with an intensity that silenced all. "The Sphere of Golden Thread and the Sword of Truth's Eye would not have appeared if it were otherwise. They are alive, bound by ancient magic and part of the Enchantress's design since the dawn of time."

Following her words, the Sphere in Wilhelmina's hand and the Sword gripped by Selenus seemed to pulse from within.

A bejeweled sheath then emerged where the blade had lain, and with a steady grasp, the prince sheathed the gleaming weapon, securing it to his side.

The Protector's stare lingered on them, and for a moment, her stern countenance gentled.

"The Sphere guides those who seek balance, while the Sword defends those who stand for unity. Together, they forge the path forward."

A shadow flickered across her face. "Be forewarned," she said, her voice a low, haunting echo. "These artifacts are no mere trinkets; they hold both light and shadow, entwined with the destiny of Aetherwyn itself. To wield them without understanding is to risk calamity. Should your efforts falter, their light will fade, and Aetherwyn's balance may never be restored."

Her eyes fixed upon Wilhelmina, piercing and unwavering. "Guard them well, for they are both gift and burden."

Wilhelmina swallowed, her hand resting on the Sphere's surface, where its pulse seemed to quicken, attuned to her heartbeat. She nodded. "We will not waver."

The Protector inclined her head. "Then go, and may the truth of your purpose light your way. Remember, Aetherwyn watches you. The Sphere and the Sword hold the fate of your world, whether in light or shadow." With that final warning, she faded from sight, leaving the chamber steeped in solemn silence.

12. The Trials of Lambda

The dim, vaulted corridors lay cloaked in silence, as if the air within had grown weary from carrying the weight of untold secrets. Even the moonlit stone sentinels watched with a grave, unblinking regard as Wilhelmina and her companions advanced. The torch Selenus had crafted from a resinous branch, now held high, cast elongated shadows across weathered walls, which sighed under the burden of time.

Quill's scholarly excitement danced from his eyes as he adjusted his glasses. "It's as if these stones themselves have something yet to say, if only they had an ear to listen."

Aria, meanwhile, appeared somewhat less composed than she might have liked. Though she endeavored to conceal her unease, the tight clutch on her shawl betrayed a trace of apprehension.

"If they do speak, let us hope it's with kindness," she said, as if any other response could undo their fragile confidence. Yet, despite her sensible reservations, she, along with the rest, shared in the sentiment that unity, however unwilling, would be their best safeguard against whatever ancient force governed these halls.

Their breaths came in short, staccato bursts as they maneuvered the twisting path. Shadows leapt and shifted in the torchlight, distorting their reflections into phantom shapes.

"Let's hope those shadows stay where they belong." Crispin's words held a thin veil of bravado.

Selenus, holding the torch aloft, rushed to the front of the group.

"I shall lead the way to ensure we are united and unassailable," he proclaimed, his voice lifted with an air of self-importance.

This attempt at grandeur earned him a glance of mild amusement from Wilhelmina, who watched him hold the torch high, as if every shadow would vanish at his command. Though she held a grudging admiration for his confidence, she could not extinguish the smirk that tugged at her lips.

"We are unassailable thanks to you, are we?" she echoed, one brow arched. "Well, then, I suppose there's little need to concern ourselves with the obstacles that lie ahead."

"Who knew the Moon Prince was as skilled in poetry as he is in leadership?" Crispin quipped.

With practiced patience, Wilhelmina refocused the group. The sound of water dripping into bottomless depths punctuated the silence. It settled heavily around them, and a chill seeped into their bones. Their footsteps slipped on the slick floor, the path winding and unpredictable beneath their feet, but none faltered.

❧

At last, they entered a vaulted hall, and from a darkened corner a shrouded yet unmistakable form emerged. Shadows cast by the lone silhouette wavered with an eerie, almost watchful energy, as if they too were guardians of what lay hidden.

His silver hair caught the torchlight, spilling over his shoulders like liquid starlight, a stark contrast to the gloom that clung around him.

A strange vibration then emanated from the Sphere of Golden Thread and the Sword of Truth's Eye, resonating with a sound both unsettling and familiar.

As the figure stepped closer, he dipped his head, a motion neither hostile nor benign, but ambiguous enough to disquiet even the bravest among them. He wore an amused expression, his eyebrow raised.

"You seek what lies beyond. But what you search for is not simply found; it must be earned."

The companions exchanged cautious glances, a mixture of bravado, curiosity, and, in Wilhelmina's case, an exasperation with the mystery of it all.

"We accept your contest," she said at last, a touch of impatience in her tone despite her respect for the occasion.

Though she had come prepared for all manner of challenge, she could not deny the smallest desire for the matter to be resolved with haste, for the sake of those she held dear.

The figure's gaze lingered on her features as if searching for an echo of a memory he held. "Indeed," said. "There are parts of you, my child, that remind me of days before you walked these realms."

Wilhelmina experienced a strange pull, a profound familiarity in the sound of his voice and presence, as if she were hearing a melody from a forgotten dream.

It wasn't a recollection, but a resonance deep inside her own being, unsettling and yet strangely comforting. She also sensed a subtle, bitter truth stirring, a whisper of her own unwitting hand in the shadows' reach, and a flicker of resentment for the unwanted, consuming longing her light had drawn from Selenus. She did not presently possess the words to question it, nor the knowledge to fully understand, but she sensed the intensity of his gaze upon her, watchful.

The figure's eyes narrowed as though reading more within her than she had intended to reveal. "Indeed," he said, stepping closer. For a brief moment, his profile aligned with hers, their features cast in parallel by the torchlight. In a curious synchronicity, both raised a hand to their chins, mirroring each other's gesture with an uncanny likeness.

"Strange... there's something familiar there, isn't there?" Flora muttered to Crispin, who nodded in concurrence.

The figure tapped her shoulder, his fingers brushing against the fabric there.

"You bear the celestial sisterhood's legacy. It's clear you take after your mother. Its her light you carry," he observed wistfully. "But you must find your own path. And remember, you are not alone. Those who love you will protect you in ways you don't perceive."

Selenus, ever mindful of appearances, inclined his head, as if sensing the veiled rebuke.

"Well said." His tone suggested he had resolved to meet whatever was required with perfect composure, though whether that composure would endure remained to be seen.

He patted the somber orb hidden within his pocket, a gesture that seemed both possessive and reassuring. Then, as if to hood his eyes from observation, he lowered his gaze. "Hello, Lambda."

A flicker of recognition crossed Lambda's features as he studied Selenus. His expression morphed into a curious blend of disdain and, perhaps, a hint of pity.

"Ah, prince of shadows," he said, his voice hardening. "Once again, we meet. May the celestial boundaries help us. Tell me, have you yet come to understand the curse you have placed upon yourself?"

Selenus's hand tightened around his Sword, but he met Lambda's stare with defiance. "I know my path, and I am ready."

"Do you? Are you? Prince of shadows," Lambda sneered, almost as though remarking on the weather. "A finer ambition might temper the unfortunate consequences of... well, overestimating oneself."

This last comment spurred quiet laughter and giggles from the observers of this tense debate. Wilhelmina huffed. Their lightheartedness amidst ancient ruins and spectral figures seemed disturbingly out of place for such a perilous quest.

Yet Lambda's next words directed at the prince cut deeper. "You carry burdens beyond those you've laid upon yourself, burdens you may not yet fully grasp. Your ambition treads close to peril, Selenus. Misstep, and it is not merely you who suffers, but all you hold dear..."

He paused, his eyes narrowing with a knowing glint. "You coveted the light, Prince, yearning to possess it, yet you allowed your jealousy of Phaethon's perceived light and your own insecurity to twist your perceptions, turning you away from the truth of that light's pure essence. Tell me, do you still cling to the belief that the star you desired never once belonged to you, convinced it belongs to another, rather than admitting the real reason she retreated?"

Crispin cleared his throat, muttering under his breath, "And I thought I was dramatic." His eyes darted to Wilhelmina. "Should I be taking notes? This feels more like a lecture from a schoolmaster—with very long hair."

She shot him a piercing look, raising a finger to her lips. "Shhh... not now." But as she hushed him, her eyes slid sideways toward Selenus.

Selenus's lips tightened, his jaw clenching as he averted his gaze, but a sharp, invisible tremor ran through him. A searing memory flashed behind his silver eyes: a distant, shimmering star, vibrant and unattainable, and the bitter, suffocating coil of his own jealousy that had sought to extinguish its light. Silence was a shield he refused to lower, but the torment was plain.

Lambda's gaze drifted with veiled tenderness toward Wilhelmina.

"Loyalty is the foundation of honor, and honor, in turn, is the foundation of love." Then, as if a cloud had passed over his face, his tone hardened.

"But folly—your possessiveness, misperception, and the shadow in your heart—has twisted your path, prince. Until you conquer it, Aetherwyn will remain imbalanced."

He paused, his breath quickening. "our impatience has cost the realm and those under its protection more than you know. This curse you've wrought threatens to unravel the destiny shaped for you… and those you will one day hold dear."

Wilhelmina's brow furrowed as she took a cautious step toward Selenus, her tone edged with urgency.

"Selenus, what is he talking about? What curse?"

Selenus met her gaze, a note of steel in his voice. "It is my burden to bear alone."

Lambda turned, his expression softening as he regarded her.

"In this dominion, princess of light, no burden is ever truly borne alone." He extended his hand toward a narrow corridor leading deeper into the ruins.

"Ahead lie the trials of the mind, heart, and spirit, not merely tests of strength, but of the truths you fear to speak, the loyalties you dare not question, and the choices you thought you'd already made. Only if you emerge whole, in unity and purpose, can you find the answers you seek. Fail, and you will lose all that you cherish."

Aria gasped, her voice dropping to a whisper. "What do you mean… lost?"

Lambda's gaze hardened. "Every path is woven into creation's tapestry. Each thread holds its place in the grand design. If you falter, those threads will fray and unravel all that has been… and all that will be."

Wilhelmina's glance lowered, her fingers brushing the Sphere in her satchel. The weight of the journey, of each misstep and secret yet untold, pressed down like a mantle. For a breath, she looked as if she might turn away.

Aria stepped gently to her side, sensing the shift. Her voice was soft but steady. "No thread exists alone, Wilhelmina. We're all part of this weave, even the frayed parts."

Wilhelmina raised her face, her eyes meeting Aria's, and some of the tightness in her brow eased.

The companions drew closer together, their shoulders slumped in unison.

Wilhelmina's expression grew firm. "We'll find our way."

As they took a step into the darkness, Lambda called out his final wisdom.

"Guard well your hearts. You have choices and many decisions. Each one will ask whether you shall light your path with purpose… or cast it in shadow. The balance now rests in delicate hands."

Wilhelmina steadied her breath and gave a slight nod, as though to anchor herself beneath the gravity of his words.

Then he drew her aside before she joined her companions.

"Take heart, child. I can guide you, but only so far. And know this—the stars, light and dark, scripted the bridge you cross long before you ever walked it. Bear this knowledge with care. Go now. Beyond lies the darkness of your making, and light alone may lead you through."

He watched them depart, the echoes of his warning following them as they ventured forth into the shadowed hallways that lay ahead.

13. Trial of the Mind and Heart

As the companions wound their way through the ancient ruins, a simmering tension, one quite impossible to ignore, hung in the air. Wilhelmina's thoughts churned with the curse, a topic Selenus, true to form, refused to acknowledge. She glanced his way, irritated by his usual air of detached mystery, as if curses were no more pressing than a fading breeze. Yet it was not in her nature to indulge such evasions.

"This curse—how do we plan to address it?" she asked matter-of-factly.

Selenus shrugged with the infuriating ease of a person for whom planning was an indulgence best reserved for others. "It's under control."

Wilhelmina, however, would have none of it. "You heard Lambda. This is a serious threat. You... we cannot afford to be complacent."

She regarded him, her mouth set, her expression so intent that a more modest prince might well have felt a pang of conscience.

Yet he possessed a royal bearing and a certain talent for maintaining an air of aloofness. He met her gaze with quiet defiance.

"You worry too much." His casual air would have been quite at home at a garden party.

Her lips tightened as though suppressing a dozen retorts. She clenched her jaw before measuring her tone to the patience of one forced to explain the obvious. "This isn't about worrying. It's about facing reality and taking action. We cannot afford to underestimate the dangers."

He regarded her with a single arched brow, saying nothing. She glared, summoning the fiercest expression she could muster.

They might have continued in this charming deadlock for some time had not the path opened into a dark cave, heavy with the air of ages long past. Within it, faded tapestries and crumbling hieroglyphs clung to the damp stone walls. Torchlights hung on wooden posts, casting flickering shadows in twisting shapes.

No sooner had the companions stepped inside than the granite doors at both entrance and exit crashed shut with an ominous thud. They were now trapped in the chilly embrace of the cavern.

Flora and Quill dashed to the sealed thresholds. They pressed their hands in frantic motion against the unyielding surface. And yet, they found no give and no answer to their attempts at freedom.

The sound of their breaths quickening fractured the silence, a sense of entrapment creeping over them like a shiver. Even Selenus's nonchalance wavered in the charged atmosphere, though he would never have admitted as much.

The cave's frigid air grew colder still. It held a biting frost that urged them closer together.

Selenus and Wilhelmina exchanged a glance before each took charge.

"Everyone remain calm," Selenus intoned. His voice carried the practiced composure of one accustomed to crises, or, perhaps, to ignoring them.

"Right." Wilhelmina's gaze swept over the group. "Slow your breathing to conserve strength." She turned to Aria. "Aria, your soothing melodies might be just what we need."

Aria gave a brisk nod and closed her eyes. From her lips rose a melody that spilled from her heart to their ears. It brought a calming energy into the chamber. And as though bewitched by her song, the cave's etched walls glowed. Pale light ascended from the runes. Each symbol flickered in a gentle rhythm with her voice. The spectral glow that resulted beckoned them forward.

The companions stared, their brows raised.

"This must be what Lambda meant," Flora offered. "The first test... This one has to be of the mind."

Wilhelmina gestured toward the glowing etchings. "These symbols... what do they mean? Can anyone read them?" She looked around, and her gaze caught on Selenus with something between expectation and doubt.

Selenus shifted his feet and dropped his gaze to the floor as if debating whether he ought to admit familiarity. "Perhaps... but it's been some time since I've seen these markings."

"Then lend us your great expertise, dear prince," Crispin quipped, offering a half-smile that cut through the tension. Albeit Selenus's nonplussed expression suggested he was impervious to Crispin's charms.

Flora, with her arms crossed, gave an exasperated huff. "I happen to know a thing or two about ancient languages as well."

Without waiting for further permission, she stepped toward the wall and moved her fingers along the first line of runes. She examined each stroke with her nose turned up with scholarly pride.

"These speak of trials—tests of courage and heart," she said. A rare softness emerged in her voice as the script's graceful curves and loops danced beneath her touch.

"There must be a pattern." Quill's eyes narrowed as he scrutinized the symbols beside her. He traced the intricate lines. "Some sort of sequence to unlock their secrets."

Wilhelmina watched him work before turning to Aria.

With her eyes closed, Aria raised her arms, waving her hands to the cadence of the runes' vibrations. "I can sense the harmony in this set of symbols. This is an altogether new rhythm... I don't believe it's ever been discovered."

"These symbols speak of... no, they speak of the grass and trees... *By the light of the grass and trees' embrace*... I think," Flora whispered.

The moment the word "trees" left her lips, an invisible force seized her like a vise, wrenching her backward. The air cracked with static as the runes flared an angry red, the sound sharp as a whip. She gasped as her body slammed against the wall, her scream mangled and lost in the deafening hum that followed.

"What is happening?!"

"Flora!" Wilhelmina reached toward her friend and pulled at her limbs.

Despite her struggles to free herself, Flora would not budge.

But it was Crispin who called out with a wry laugh, "Seems these runes don't appreciate mistakes or hesitation!" His humor barely veiled the visible fear in his eyes.

"It's not grass and trees... I think you meant to say *stars and moon's embrace*," Selenus offered nonchalantly.

"Of course. *By the light of the stars and moon's embrace*...," Flora translated, though her face flushed red with embarrassment. But her correction must have consoled the runes, for the pull on her lessened, and she fell to the floor with a heavy, reverberating thud. She gritted her teeth in vexation, and a new glint appeared in her eyes.

"Come on. Let's focus," Wilhelmina offered, as though to steady the energy in the agitated chamber.

"Right," Selenus coughed, his voice turning serious. "The next set of runes... We'll have to approach them with caution. I'll do the next line."

He cleared his throat and focused on the next set of symbols. "*In realms of old, where enchantments trace. Seek ye wisdom in shadows sleep...* Hey!"

A magical force yanked him from his feet and crushed him flat against the ancient mural in a spread-eagle formation, mashing his nose.

"Ow!"

The runes twinkled in the air, amused to see the Moon Prince so humbled.

Flora chuckled and shuffled over to the mistranslated rune. "I think you meant deep.... *In realms of old, where enchantments trace. Seek ye wisdom in shadows deep...* Not so easy, is it, prince?"

A low grumble emanated from the space between Selenus's lips and the stone.

"Indeed, Flora," said Quill. He reached into his waistcoat, drawing out a small pair of wire-rimmed spectacles, and peered over them at the runes. "I see some recurring symbols here. I believe we can find a cipher... give me a moment."

After several heartbeats and the others standing with bated breath, he broke the silence.

"Ah ha! This is a recurring pattern of intertwined serpents and crescent moons. Do you see here? They alternate in a sequence along the corridor walls."

"I see it!" Aria said. "In times of yore, serpents were drawn with their tails curving into the infinity symbol."

"That's right," said Quill. "The serpents represented eternal life, regeneration, and... transformation." He clapped his hands together. "Look here! These crescent moons describe the cycles of life, femininity, and the passage of time!"

"Well said, Quill." Selenus, his face smashed, said this while still pinned to the stone despite everyone's attempts to tug him free. "The serpents and moons have always been seen as the symbols of life and death, and of rebirth. These are reminders of the universe's cycles."

At that, Selenus's body, like Flora's, thudded to the floor.

Quill paced along the wall, oblivious to Selenus's attempts to rise and dust off his trousers. He pointed to each symbol as he spoke.

"Perhaps the trial isn't just about understanding—it's about embodying balance. We're meant to harmonize with the forces these symbols represent. See these serpents and crescent moons? They signify life cycles—rebirth, growth, and balance between light and dark. Each duality seems to guide us to interpret these symbols correctly… or pay the price."

Selenus tugged at his collar and turned his face away as if to hide. Wilhelmina caught this new and rare humility, frowning.

Aria closed her eyes and raised her face as if toward an invisible light. "The runes are conduits of cosmic energy." Her voice carried the confidence of one certain of her craft. "The vibrations align with balance and order, synchronizing, it seems, with the universal laws of creation and transformation."

She stepped forward and, with a breath as measured as her words, hummed a mystic chord.

As the melody rose, the air thrummed with life, each note wrapping around them like a caress. The runes pulsed brighter, their vibrations syncing with her voice in resonant harmony. The ancient symbols bowed to her song's authority and responded to its unspoken command.

The sound expanded, filling the chamber with the music of sadness, joy, and love woven through it. Each note became a thread binding the companions in unspoken unity. Even the most stoic among them found their eyes suspiciously bright. The melody had pierced their defenses and revealed their humanity, or magic, that bound them together.

As she sang, the runes pulsed in time with her breath. The cave listened, waiting for her to unlock a forgotten harmony.

As Aria's hands moved along the glowing runes, she spoke again. "Certain combinations emit stronger vibrations and connect specific symbols to elemental energies." Her fingers hovered over the sequence. "These water runes resonate with fluidity and rhythm, while those representing fire pulse with intensity and power. They form a language and a source of energy—a bridge, of sorts, between understanding and action."

The runes acknowledged her insight and responded. Their static shapes shifted and glowed brighter with every hum of Aria's melody.

At last, the final rune fell into place, and a spectral light bathed the chamber.

A low groan echoed through the space as the stone door, their supposed prison, rose. The passage to freedom transformed the suffocating confines into a threshold to new trials and their outcomes.

The companions advanced toward the beckoning path, but Selenus fell behind as if to let the others lead the way.

Wilhelmina fell back to keep pace with him. "Are you all right?"

He shrugged. Before he could answer, the runes reverberated with the mystical notes of the mystic chord Aria had created: the root note of E, the major third of G#, and the perfect fifth note of B.

To the untrained ear, it was just a beautiful chord, but to the stones—and perhaps to the stars—it was resonance made audible, a blueprint of forgotten harmony humming in the bones of the world.

The song notes remained, resonating in the ancient stone. Selenus's brow furrowed, and he carried an expression as if he were reaching for a memory he couldn't quite grasp.

"That melody." He murmured, distracted. "It feels... familiar."

Wilhelmina, catching the shift in his demeanor, leaned in with sudden curiosity.

"What do you think it is?"

Selenus's gaze persisted on the glowing runes, his face half in shadow. "Perhaps," he said almost absently, as if entranced by a distant memory. It could be a key—one that might restore balance.

"But..." He hesitated, his voice trailing off.

"It seems to call to... another thing. Something buried." A shadow crossed his features. "It seems like it's pulling me somewhere I've been trying to avoid."

Quill murmured, "It's as if the cave knows us—not just our knowledge, but our memories... our hopes."

Aria nodded softly, adding, "As if it remembers our imprint... even before we understood it ourselves."

The group fell silent as the last notes faded. The cave's walls echoed with the melody's resonance—an echo half-remembered and haunting. Before them, the passage ahead stretched into darkness, thick with questions.

14. Trial of the Body and Unity

The bridge stretched before them, a treacherous span over a bottomless chasm. Narrow and slick with a malevolent sheen on its surface, it seemed less a path than a dare issued by time.

Ominous shadows lingered at its edges. These were spectral sentinels, translucent apparitions with a restlessness that promised ill intentions. Their light pulsed with a strange and eager energy, as if anticipating no end of amusement in witnessing the visitors' attempts to traverse the abyss.

The companions exchanged wary glances. Each face betrayed a different shade of dread.

Wilhelmina broke the silence. Her tone was sharp and commanding, yet fear underlay it.

"One misstep, and we're lost."

Selenus cast an appraising glance over the span. His expression was unreadable, save for the furrow of his brow. Without hesitation, he took charge, though his voice carried a hint of indifference.

"We must cross with haste. Hesitation will only give these things more reason to... engage with us." His focus lingered on the sentinels.

But Wilhelmina was not so easily swayed. "And what if the bridge hides answers?" Her unflinching gaze met Selenus's. "What if the key to what we seek lies here? We need to study this."

His jaw tightened. "We don't have time for conjecture." His gaze flicked to the dark forms edging closer. "The priority is to survive this crossing."

She did not yield. Her reply cut through the mounting tension.

"And what if we overlook the very thing that could save us?"

Crispin's glance darted between them, his unease plain to see.

Quill folded his arms and sidled next to Wilhelmina, offering a slight but deliberate nod of agreement. It was an unspoken declaration of alliance.

The air between Wilhelmina and Selenus grew taut, the clash of wills almost audible. Then, at last, Selenus drew back, his stance retreating by mere inches, just enough to signal his reluctant acquiescence.

"Fine. But be quick."

Wilhelmina wasted no time, stepping closer to the bridge's edge. She swept her gaze over the slick stones and the sentinels' restless forms before crouching to trace the indistinct grooves etched into the surface.

"These markings..." she murmured, then looked up at him. "Quill, do you see this pattern?"

The runes bore no immediate meaning, but their symmetrical placement spoke of deliberation.

Quill knelt beside her, his scholarly interest overtaking his earlier wariness. "Fascinating." His fingers brushed the ancient carvings. "The geometry suggests this bridge wasn't a simple passage, but a trial. The entities—they aren't just watchers—they're participants."

She straightened, her eyes narrowing in thought. "Then they respond to action," she concluded. "We can't just pass over—we have to be mindful of how we move. A careless step could provoke them."

Selenus, standing a pace behind, allowed a brief smirk to cross his lips. "So, the lady insists on studying the structure, and the conclusion is to tread with care. Astonishing."

Wilhelmina ignored the jab. "It's more than that." Her tone had grown sharper. "Those beings are getting stronger the longer we linger. They're reacting to us already. If we're not unified, they'll exploit it."

Flora nodded from her place at the rear. "Then we navigate the passage together, step by step, without hesitation."

Wilhelmina met Selenus's gaze, a flicker of defiance still in her eyes.

"Now we move." She turned her body toward the bridge.

Quill advanced first, nimble and sure-footed. Each of his steps seemed to defy the bridge's slick surface. His balance was a triumph against the threat of a misstep. Behind him, Flora stretched out her arms, keeping her focus sharp.

Aria, however, held back at the rear while her eyes remained riveted on the chasm below. With a gulp that seemed louder than the whispering mist, she shook her head.

"I-I'll just stay behind. You all go on," she stammered.

She crossed her arms and plopped herself onto the ground.

Quill, hearing the commotion, glanced behind him. His expression flickered with exasperation before he turned on his heel. With a deep sigh, he marched to where she sat, cross-legged and defiant.

"Oh no, you don't," he said, frowning.

Before Aria could protest further, he pulled her up and, with surprising ease, hoisted her over his shoulder like a sack of flour.

Aria shrieked. "Quill! Put me down!"

She beat her fists against his back, but he only adjusted his grip and commenced his trek across the bridge.

The sentinels' ghostly forms looked on in bemusement.

"I know you fear heights without your wings." While his tone sounded light to listening ears, it held an undercurrent of firmness. "But you're coming with us. End of discussion."

"You should have left me!" she wailed, though her protests lacked their earlier force.

"Never going to happen. We need you. I need you. And we leave no one behind."

His words carried an unexpected seriousness that silenced further argument. When he reached solid ground, he set her down with a gentleness that contrasted sharply with her earlier theatrics.

Huffing, she brushed at her skirts until her fingers settled within the folds of the fabric. And then, a hum started to form in her throat, a calming melody that seemed as much for herself as for those still navigating the bridge.

Quill turned back toward the others, calling out with cheerful bravado.

"Come on! It's easy!"

The remaining companions inched along the treacherous path, moving slowly and deliberately. Every footstep was a negotiation with the slippery stones and the mist thickening around them. Beneath, the chasm yawned like a living thing, its depths unfathomable, its silence oppressive save for the drip of echoing springs.

Flora stumbled, shooting her arms out. Her motion caused the structure to sway precariously.

A ripple of unease shot through the group. They had almost reached the halfway point when the bridge trembled with greater force, as if an invisible gust of wind pushed it.

Crispin's boot slipped on the slick stone, but he could grab onto the vines to secure his balance.

The spectral sentinels, who had seemed content to linger at the edges before, now grew bolder.

Tendrils of shadow, with shifts both fluid and insidious, brushed against Crispin.

A sentinel, with a swift and well-nigh playful motion, nudged him.

"Ah!" he cried. "What is happening?!"

His equilibrium faltered. His arms flailed, grasping at nothing but air. He slid across the greasy surface with a screech that tore through the mist's oppressive silence.

The sentinels pulsed with a restless beat, their actions flowing yet deliberate. Their flickering forms danced at the brink of the bridge with a grim, nearly mocking rhythm. They seemed to measure the companions' worth, as if their very existence hinged on the balance of light and shadow.

A final misplaced foot sent Crispin over the lip. His boots lost purchase, and his body pitched over the edge. His fingers scrabbling against the rock, he barely gripped the bridge's rim.

"Heeeelllpp!"

Crispin's voice cracked with panic as his legs dangled above the abyss, his cry echoing into the void.

Selenus reacted first, his composure breaking into swift action. He lunged toward Crispin.

"Hold steady!" His muscles tensed as he reached over the brink, his expression a mask of grim concentration.

Quill, who had watched the disaster unfold from his place ahead, raced back without hesitation.

The group now moved as one.

Wilhelmina braced Selenus, whose outstretched arm anchored Quill as he leaned forward. His fingers hovered mere inches from Crispin's grasp.

Silence thickened around them like the rising fog from the chasm. Quill's fingers found Crispin's at last, but the unstable clasp was fleeting.

Before one could sigh a breath of relief, Crispin's hand slipped, and his scream tore through the oppressive space.

"Hold on! We're not losing anyone—not here, not now!"

Wilhelmina's shrill cry was sharp and commanding, seeming to cut through Crispin's terror and the cloying mist. The authority in her tone, so at odds with the chaos, anchored his tenacity.

Crispin scrambled to regain Quill's hand, but the sweat on his palms betrayed him. His body teetered further toward the abyss, and his widened, pleading eyes met those of his companions. His knuckles, white with strain, seemed ready to surrender to the void when Selenus lunged forward with a single, imperative command.

"Hold him!"

The bridge groaned beneath their collective mass, a muted warning of its fragility.

Selenus, positioned at the center of the desperate chain, strained against the pull of gravity. His arm trembled as he braced against the weight, his princely facade cracking for a moment to reveal raw, unguarded determination.

For that fleeting instant, his detached demeanor slipped, revealing something fiercely protective and almost human. He was not the Moon Prince, but a man fighting against the abyss to save his unlikely companions. His muscles, taut and unyielding, spoke of a strength often hidden beneath his composed exterior and regal robes.

With one final surge, Crispin's fingers locked around Quill's. All other sounds faded. The world narrowed to a single suspended heartbeat. Inch by agonizing inch, they pulled him back onto the bridge's surface.

Crispin collapsed in a heap, trembling. His gasps mingled with the ragged sighs of relief from the others.

For a time, they all sat, their fingers still gripping each other as if afraid to release the fragile bond that had kept them from disaster. It was Crispin who broke the silence with a weak, shaky laugh.

"Guess... we made it," he said, though his trembling hands betrayed the strain from his ordeal.

Selenus, catching his breath, rose first and dusted off his sleeves with deliberate nonchalance. The crack in his princely veneer that had spurred him to action sealed, leaving his familiar aloofness now returned with practiced ease. His expression softened—a flicker that might have gone unnoticed had

Wilhelmina not been watching. Then, with a clearing of his throat, he turned away and spoke with his usual cool detachment.

"Let's move on."

Wilhelmina remained still, following him with her gaze. A fragile trust born of necessity had been forged in peril over a deadly abyss. Whatever it was, it sat alongside the wariness that had always marked their interactions.

As they pressed forward, a shudder ran through the bridge one last time, as if exhaling its relief. Behind them, the spectral sentinels, no longer isolated figures, coalesced into a single mass of shadow. Their unblinking, unkind gazes lingered a moment more on the companions as they stepped onto solid ground, as if imprinting the group's defiance in the crevice's memory. Then, like smoke seized in a gust, they vanished into the mist.

Wilhelmina cast one last look over her shoulder and at the gorge below. "The trial of the body... This is the beginning. What other terrors shall we face next?"

With breaths still labored, they reached solid ground at last.

Crispin, shaking, gave Selenus an expression of gratitude, yet Selenus turned his attention elsewhere, as if he had completed an expected duty that needed no acknowledgment. Yet Wilhelmina saw his glance and offered him the slightest, almost imperceptible nod.

Whatever their differences, they had crossed the ravine together.

15. The Mirror of Spirits

The companions reached the end of the path. It was veiled in shadows so dense that it seemed the air conspired to shroud them. Then, the darkness gave way, not to a wall or gate, but to a chamber.

In that uncanny instant, mirrors rose from the mist-covered floor—their ascent stretching from floor to ceiling—was as silent as it was eerie.

A weak glimmer of light grew and transformed into a radiant brilliance that bathed the room in an almost blinding glow. Faceted like the finest cut crystal, the mirrors caught and refracted the light into a kaleidoscope of dazzling hues that painted the walls.

The shifting array of colors seemed too vibrant to be real. Yet, within this splendor lay a disquieting vitality. The fractured reflections of the companions appeared distorted and grotesque.

Wilhelmina's breath shivered while her gaze roamed over the mirrors. In one reflection, her eyes appeared hollow, her features stretched into odd, shard-like shapes. Each mirror seemed possessed of its own distinct energy and drew their gazes like moths to an enchanting yet dangerous flame. Her voice pierced the room's oppressive hum.

"What is this place?"

Quill's breath caught. "This... this is the Mirror of Revelations."

Recognition dawned on him, bordering on reverence. His gaze lingered on the nearest rippling surface of a mirror.

"The old texts spoke of such a place. A chamber that reveals the deepest parts of the soul—truths we hide even from ourselves."

"Truths? I hope my truth's a good sport," Crispin gave a nervous chuckle. "So, what's the plan then? We just... stare ourselves into submission?"

"I fear it's not that simple." Quill stroked his chin. "If the texts are correct, we not only look into these mirrors. We wait for them to show us... and perhaps, to teach us."

Selenus, his jaw set like stone, turned his face from the mirrors where his image wavered like smoke—intangible, fleeting, and obscure.

"The mirrors reveal more than we might wish to see."

Wilhelmina's eyes darted to Selenus's shadowy reflection, her features drawn tight.

"Truths? Or judgments?"

"I don't like this." Aria shivered, arms wrapping tight around herself. "What if... what if the mirrors show something we're not ready to face?"

"Then we face it, anyway." Wilhelmina's tone brooked no argument. Her gaze swept over the group, issuing them a silent challenge, daring them to waver.

"Well, let's not keep the mirrors waiting." Crispin's voice pitched just a shade too high, his forced bravado thin in the oppressive atmosphere. "What's the worst they could do? Show me in an unflattering tunic?"

The laugh that followed was thin, its edges fraying into silence. Crispin's reflection, however, did not laugh.

It moved first.

The image in the mirror froze mid-chuckle, and the glass's surface rippled like disturbed water. Then the laughter vanished, replaced by the stillness of another time.

❧

In its place stood a young pixie—a younger Crispin, alone in front of a window in a darkened room. His small shoulders hunched, and his small frame curled inward, bracing against an invisible weight. His wide eyes stared out from the glass, not at the companions but at something far beyond them—an empty, unseeing gaze that spoke of wounds too deep for words.

Crispin's eyes pinched at the corners, lines of strain appearing even as he forced a grin.

"Oh, come on now. That's hardly fair. I didn't even have a proper haircut back then."

The reflection rippled again. This time, it revealed a lad no older than five. It was Crispin, standing in a bedroom, dwarfed by the sight of a man lying still on a bed. A woman, whose sobs filled the silence, clasped the man's hands in her trembling fingers.

"That's my mother."

The scene unfolded to reveal the young pixie's wide eyes fixed on his mother, taking a hesitant step forward.

"Why won't Papa wake up?"

The woman pulled the child into her arms, and her sobs turned into a broken wail.

The reflection morphed to show young Crispin standing beside a fresh grave. His gaze distant and uncomprehending, the child clutched his mother's hand.

Her face was ashen, and her eyes gaunt. She shook the child's hand off, turning away from him.

The image changed again.

The lad sat alone at a bare table, with an empty chair beside him. Shadows loomed about him, stretching long and menacing.

A door closed with quiet finality, followed by the sound of retreating footsteps.

He slumped forward with his face buried in his small hands.

"Crispin..."

Wilhelmina's voice broke through the stillness, but Crispin raised a hand to stop her.

"It's nothing." He set his jaw, holding himself rigid. "Just a reflection. Doesn't mean anything."

The mirror seemed to disagree, shifting.

Crispin's face was now older, thinner, and paler. His reflection grew restless, then furious, lashing out at forgotten figures. A blur of fists and a pandemonium of shouts followed—schoolyard fights born of grief too immense for a young pixie to contain.

The present-day Crispin moved back, his grin long gone.

"That's enough."

But the mirror refused to relent. The reflection transformed anew to show a young Crispin in a crowded square, his thin arms straining under the weight of a wooden pail of fish. A misstep sent the pail's contents scattering in a silvery cascade across the cobblestones.

The crowd froze before erupting in laughter—not cruel, but warm and genuine.

The younger Crispin lay still, wide-eyed, before a hesitant smile broke across his face. With a theatrical flourish, he leapt to his feet and bowed deeply.

The laughter swelled, bright and infectious, and for the first time, a fragile spark lit in Crispin's eyes—an ember of joy amid the pain.

"That's when it started," he whispered.

His companions turned to him.

"*What* started?" Wilhelmina asked.

Crispin hesitated, and his hand went to the nape of his neck. "The laughter. The jokes. It wasn't just for them—it was for me. Every laugh I got... it made... things... hurt a little less."

"That's not nothing, Crispin," Aria said. "That's everything."

Crispin looked away. "I don't know about that. I just... I didn't want anybody else to feel what I felt. Lonely. Forgotten. So I figured if I could make them laugh, maybe they wouldn't."

He cleared his throat and straightened, forcing a grin. "Anyway, what's done is done. No use dwelling on it, eh?"

The mirror wasn't finished. The reflection changed.

And older Crispin stood before a crowd with his arms outstretched in a gesture of triumph. Yet behind the adoring faces, shadows loomed, indistinct, menacing forms, and their laughter turned hollow. The triumphant grin on his reflection altered, and doubt flickered across its face.

Crispin's voice, quieter now, disrupted the silence. "But I don't want to be the reason someone's laughter feels empty."

Wilhelmina moved to stand beside him. Her gaze moved between Crispin and the mirror.

"Your laughter isn't empty. It's a choice—a powerful one. You take something painful and turn it into light. That takes courage."

The mirror's glow grew less intense, and Crispin's present-day reflection returned. This time, his grin wasn't stretched or exaggerated—it was genuine. Warmth shone in his gaze where there had been doubt. The shadows behind him receded. Their edges blurred until they faded. The reflection smiled back at him, not as a mask, but as a truth. Something deeper, more solid, had replaced the cracks in his mirth. There was purpose there now, plain for all to see.

Crispin emitted a shaky laugh. "Well, that was interesting," he said, his voice lighter now. "Guess I passed the test. Or at least didn't fail."

Flora folded her arms and placed her hand under her chin. "You let us see into your soul. The strength it took to carry that light into the world, to create laughter for others even when you were hurting... that's no small thing. It's a gift."

Crispin shifted his gaze toward the floor. "I hoped nobody would ever feel the same anger."

The mirror dimmed and settled, its surface smoothing into calm. A low, haunting voice emerged, echoing throughout the chamber. *"You have seen your pain, but you have chosen to transform it. This is the strength of the spirit."*

A second voice followed. *"Find the laughter, even in the hardest times."*

Crispin rubbed his eyes, now suspiciously rimmed red.

"I remember... My father used to say that when I was a wee lad. It almost sounds like him."

He covered his face with his hands, his shoulders trembling.

A stillness settled over the chamber, as if even the mirrors honored what had been revealed.

Quill interrupted the silence. "That was bloody brilliant!" He rushed to Crispin's side, pulling him into a fierce embrace. "If that's not passing the test, I don't know what is."

Crispin offered a wobbly chortle. A glint of moisture in his eyes expressed his unspoken gratitude to his friends and for the trial's lesson.

Quill let him go, wiping the moisture from his face with the back of his hand as if to dismiss any evidence of emotion. He straightened, drawing a steadying breath, and turned toward the next mirror. "Well then, what else have you got, old boy?"

❧

The mirror gleamed in response. Quill stepped forward with purposeful strides, his shoulders squared as the reflections mutated.

The image revealed a grand study: a scholar's paradise. Towering bookshelves crammed with folios and manuscripts stretched toward the vaulted ceilings. Candles glowed in golden sconces, casting warm, flickering light across polished wooden tables stacked high with books. Each volume bore Quill's name in ornate gilded letters that gleamed in the light. Scholars bustled around him, their faces alight with admiration, hanging on his every word.

Above the grand door leading into the study, an elaborate plaque read:

QUILL, CHRONICLER OF AETHERWYN'S GLORIOUS HISTORIES.

"Oh-ho!" Quill leaned forward with a boyish grin. "I like where this is going."

He wiggled his fingers as if they itched to touch the volumes in the reflection.

The scene changed. Now, Quill sat at a polished desk, signing copies of his latest work. A line of eager scholars, each waiting for his attention, stretched out before him.

Yet, as the current Quill observed his reflection, his grin faltered.

The man in the mirror—though celebrated—did not appear content. Instead, he kept glancing over his shoulder, as though expecting someone—or something-to expose him or judge him.

The scholars' applause grew muted, their earlier words of praise ringing hollow.

Quill took an involuntary step back. "What's this? What did I do wrong? They love me!"

The mirror rippled in response, and the study dissolved into liquid light.

The reflection showed Quill when he was a young elf in his village, seated cross-legged on the floor in a fire-lit hall. His wide eyes sparkled, listening to an elder storyteller spinning tales of Aetherwyn's golden age. The firelight cast him in a near-heroic glow.

Young Quill's admiring expression turned to doubt when he saw his father sitting in the shadows and frowning in stern disapproval.

"*Not all stories are true*," his father said later as the two walked home. *"Remember that, son. Tales are woven by those who wish to be remembered a certain way."*

The image showed the young Quill creeping into the village library at night. In the furthest recesses of the shadowed room, he uncovered a codex buried beneath layers of dust. Its cracked spine and brittle pages hinted at its age. The words, faded but legible, wove a narrative far removed from the noble tales recited by the elder.

The young lad's trembling voice broke the silence. "*This is nothing like what the local chief spoke about! Was he lying?*" He turned the page with hesitant fingers, his eyes widening. *"All these stories are of betrayal... and greed... and loss. Could Aetherwyn's gilded age be a tale of fancy and not the truth?"* His voice dropped to a whisper. *"What is even real anymore?"*

The friends exchanged worried glances as the reflection continued to play on.

The young Quill's expression darkened with every revelation, each line seeming to strike at and shake the values upon which he stood. He hunched over the book as though shielding its forbidden knowledge from judgmental eyes, and his hands trembled despite the fierce grip he maintained on its fragile pages.

The vision turned to the next day. The village elder stormed into the library, his robes billowing behind him like a gathering storm. Young Quill, still engrossed in the ancient tome, did not hear him enter.

The elder, his face a mask of fury, snatched the volume from his hands. *"Some truths are better left buried!"*

The mirror's surface cleared and displayed the earlier image of Quill in the grand study. He was alone, surrounded by the books he had written. The gilded volumes gleamed on the shelves, with titles attesting to his skill as a chronicler. These were books that glorified the realm's history while omitting its darker chapters. Yet, his reflection betrayed a restless unease. The smirk on his face held pride, but it was shadowed by a deeper guilt that refused to be hidden.

The mirror's voice resonated through the chamber. *"What will you do when truth demands sacrifice? When the lines blur between what is known and what is felt? Will you wield the pen to uncover or to conceal?"*

Quill's eyes rounded like saucers. "I-I honestly don't know."

The reflection in the mirror revealed the consequences of his choices. In one version, his sanitized histories allowed rulers to repeat the mistakes of the past, plunging Aetherwyn into chaos. In another, his uncompromising pursuit of truth isolated him, leaving him alone and unremembered.

"I-I never meant to—." His voice faltered.

The mirror returned to the image of his young self in the dusty library, clutching the old book. He turned its pages until he stopped at the last line: *Truth, like light, is refracted. To see it whole, one must embrace every angle.*

The scene dissolved into an image of the labyrinthine archives of Miragwyn, where the companions had journeyed before arriving in the Garden of Truths. Quill's image wandered among the shelves, his gaze shadowed as though haunted by untold stories.

Quill in the present took a step forward, closer to the mirror. His hands shook as he raised them, but his voice took on a new steadiness.

"Truth is not only facts or dates... I see that now," he said. "It's the lessons we choose to pass on. The stories we tell shape our future."

He placed his hand upon the mirror, and its surface fractured into countless shards. Each shard reflected a distinct moment of history in cascading images. Falsehoods blackened and crumbled into nothingness, while truths shone bright and flooded the chamber with light.

The shards spun around him like a constellation before coalescing into a single image of Quill writing by candlelight.

On this occasion, he was not surrounded by fawning scholars but by his friends. Their camaraderie filled the room—laughing, debating every topic, their banter resembling a cacophony of life.

"Truth is not static. It is shaped by those brave enough to seek it and honest enough to share it."

The last image showed Quill writing alone. His feathery writing instrument moved in quiet solitude. There was peace in those moments, too—a reflection of the balance between the solitary and the shared.

The present-day Quill stepped back as the mirror's surface smoothed once again. He turned to his companions.

"You're all co-authors of this story. The truth isn't something I can chase alone. It's shaped by all of us—by how we choose to live it."

In Quill, the companions saw more than just their chronicler; they saw a mirror to their own unspoken truths.

Wilhelmina nodded, a small smile tugging at her lips. Crispin clapped him on the back, his laugh lighter now. Aria beamed in approval, while Selenus inclined his head, his murky reflection clearing somewhat.

Quill lingered for a moment, his fingers brushing his satchel where his pen and parchment rested.

"This story isn't over yet."

❧

The chamber responded with a pulse of light. The mirrors sparkled, their glow shifting to a hue both inviting and ominous. A deep and resonant voice reverberated through the room, commanding,

"Where is the child who fears disconnection? From nature, from others, from herself."

The companions exchanged uneasy glances. The tension hung thick until Flora took a tentative step forward.

"Yes... I am here."

"*You are the one we seek,*" the voice replied, now softer, almost coaxing. *"You view the world as an interconnected family, yet the thought of being severed from this web, or of witnessing it unravel, haunts you."*

The mirror shimmered again, and an image of Flora, a young nature sprite barely nine years old, formed, her laughter ringing like the tinkling of a woodland stream. She darted through a sacred grove—joyous, vibrant, like the life surrounding her.

But the scene darkened. Flames roared toward her in a relentless hunger, devouring all in their path. Young Flora leapt aside, her small hands clutching at air as if sheer will could shield the grove from destruction.

Yet she stood before the inferno, her face streaked with soot and tears, powerless to stop the chain reaction. The flames consumed everything, and the towering forms of ancient trees crumbled to ash, smoke, and embers.

The fire's wrath then spread beyond the grove, leaving a barren wasteland in its wake. Animals fled from destroyed homes, and rivers turned black with ash, choking the life from the water. Crops from neighboring fields withered under the poisoned soil.

"This was the moment you realized the fragility of the web. If one part gets damaged, the entire system suffers. And it was here that you vowed to protect it, yes?"

"Y-yes." She clasped her arms. "It drives me still. I believe and see that we are all part of an interconnected whole. We are bound not by blood but by the vibrational threads that weave all life together."

The mirror's image dissolved again to show young Flora kneeling amidst the ashes. She cradled a single sapling—a tender survivor—singing to it as if to coax its healing.

Days turned into years as the sapling grew under her care into a mighty tree. From its seeds, new life spread across the land. The grove returned to full glory, and its heart was the same sapling, now a mother tree, that Flora had saved.

The voice spoke again. *"Indeed, your purpose is to love and nurture... to protect the greater family... to preserve harmony and balance for future generations. However, you have only grasped the surface."*

Flora wrinkled her forehead. "What have I missed?"

The mirrors rippled and dissolved into mist, revealing a barren wasteland. Ash-gray soil replaced the vivid greens of Aetherwyn, and a stagnant sky loomed overhead. A skeletal deer nosed at the parched earth, while brittle flowers drooped beside a dry streambed.

Flora's hands flew to her mouth, her breath hitching as the devastation unfolded. She turned as if to escape, but the vision held her captive.

"The web of life unravels." The voice echoed. *"Will you mend it, or let it break forever?"*

"No," she murmured, shaking her head from side to side. Her hair spilled over her shoulders like a veil. "I-I didn't want this...."

Her knees buckled, and she fell to the ground. Her palms pressed into the cracked earth. Tears blurred her vision as she looked at a lone tree in the distance. It was the sapling she had nurtured. Its once-mighty branches now hung limp, its bark split and peeling. She crawled toward the tree.

"I'm sorry." Her voice broke. "I didn't mean to fail you."

An unknown voice broke through the clamor, vibrating deep and sharp. *"Will you lament what's lost, or will you fight for what remains?"*

Flora froze, her tears halting mid-flow. She glanced around, but the voice had no source—it seemed to come from everywhere—from the earth, the air, and the dying tree itself.

"What can I do?" she asked in a small voice. "It's all broken."

"The web frays, but it is not severed," the voice said. *"Feel its threads. Listen to its song. It needs you to mend it."*

Flora closed her eyes and pressed her palms to the cracked bark. She took a deep breath and hummed.

The melody started at a low volume and then swelled, rippling through the wasteland.

Life stirred. A dried riverbed surged with water, flowers bloomed in bursts of color, and the tree beneath her hands healed. Green leaves unfurled, and animals emerged from the shadows, drawn by her song. When the melody ended, Flora opened her eyes.

The wasteland had vanished, replaced by a thriving meadow. Her chest swelled.

“I understand now... I’m not just nature’s caretaker—I’m a part of it. Caring for nature is caring for myself. We’re all threads in the web, vital and connected. My love, my care, my voice—they matter. I can heal what’s broken and nurture what’s growing. I may not be perfect, but the love I give is enough.”

The vision dissolved, yet the glass walls now reflected the verdant meadow Flora had restored. She turned to her companions, her eyes shining.

“We’re all connected. Everything we do ripples outward. We are responsible for each other—for the family we’re part of.”

No one spoke. The echoes of Flora’s song lingered like perfume in the air, sacred and fragile.

Wilhelmina grasped Flora’s hands, her expression warm with pride.

“Flora, I believe you’ve passed your trial with the flying colors of nature. Your insight reminds us all that our unity is our strength, and your gentle wisdom will be a guiding light for us.”

The mirrors shimmered, holding the echo of her truth like a blessing upon the chamber.

16. Truths We Cannot Hide

Before Flora could answer, the mirrors trembled. The glow softened, revealing an idyllic paradise: a waterfall cascading into a glistening lake, a cozy cottage nestled among wildflowers, and a plume of smoke curling from its red-brick chimney.

"That's my parents' house! It's where I grew up!" Aria's voice quavered.

The vision sharpened to reveal her sprite father and siren mother standing outside the home. Heavily pregnant, her mother cradled her swollen belly. Her father, from behind, held her close. The couple kissed with the fervor of a passion that had defied tradition and taboo.

Sprites and sirens were not meant to mate, and yet their bond had forged a family against all odds.

The mirror darkened, and its tone deepened.

"Their love was genuine, but it came at a cost."

The scene changed, revealing a baby nestled in its mother's arms—Aria, born into a fractured world.

An image of her grandparents appeared next, their angry, contorted faces laden with judgment and rejection.

The reflection then rippled, showing a young Aria, no more than eight years old.

The cry of her mother echoed through the house as her father stumbled home, bruised and battered from a clash with her kin. Though he healed physically, the emotional scars lingered.

The image flickered again, this time to a crowded village tavern, thick with tension and rising tempers. Voices rose, insults flew, and the heaviness of hostility pervaded the air.

Amid the chaos, little Aria climbed onto a chair, her delicate frame radiant with courage, and started to... sing.

It was instinctive. A melody, pure and unadorned, soared from her chest. Her wings quivered as her tune carried the magic of her sprite and siren heritage.

The clamor quieted, anger dissipated, and a stillness settled over the room.

Aria's song seemed to have peeled away years of bitterness and fury to reveal the love beneath.

The warring families, once blinded by their hatred, finally saw the girl for what she truly was—destiny and fate's gift, born to teach love's triumph over tradition and prejudice.

"I'd forgotten." Tears pooled in Aria's eyes. "My voice filled the space, and the hostility melted into wonder. It was a miracle."

But the vision twisted. Her song faltered, her wings drooped, and the tavern faded into silence.

The reflection morphed to show her as an adult, standing before a crowd. She opened her mouth to sing, but no sound emerged.

"It can't be!" Aria raised her fist to her mouth.

The crowd dispersed, leaving her alone with broken wings.

The mirror vibrated, and a voice sang in a deep, operatic baritone.

"Child, who are you without your song? Without your voice, would you still bring light into the world?"

The image transformed, and an older Aria appeared, sitting in silence among her companions. Though she did not sing, their faces glowed with laughter and warmth as they leaned on one another.

The mirror sang again. *"It is time to choose! Shall you cling to the fear of losing your voice or embrace the truth that your essence—your joy, your empathy, your courage—is the true gift? Do you see the test lies in trusting that you are more than your song? That your value transcends performance?"*

"I-I don't know..."

Quill stepped forward. "Aria, your gift isn't just your voice. It's the love and connection you create. Can't you see that?"

"I remember now. It wasn't just the songs. It was the love I poured into them, the way I connected with people." Aria's hand reached for the looking glass.

"Even without my voice, my heart will find a way to connect. I don't need my song to do that."

"Your voice is not your gift, young siren," the mirror intoned, its surface shimmering with a gentle, otherworldly light. *"Your soul is the melody that binds."*

Aria now stood tall. Her lips parted, and a haunting melody poured forth—a song that was not just a voice but an embodiment of her truth. She turned, her gaze softening as it fell on Quill.

"You've always believed in me, even when I doubted myself. Quill, you are my best friend, and... *I love you*."

Shock crossed Quill's face. "You... *love me*?"

"Yes." She took his hand in hers. "I've always loved you. I just... didn't know if your kin would accept me."

His grin broke free, unreserved and joyous. "How could you think that? I love you, Aria, and so does my family."

Her smile lit her entire face. "Then let's stop pretending."

"Once we save our realm." He winked. "I'll ask you properly—on bended knee."

A hush fell over the group—not out of discomfort, but reverence. Love had cracked open the silence.

"Well, it's about time," Crispin quipped, grinning as he clapped Quill on the back.

Laughter rippled through them, but Wilhelmina's gaze shifted, drawn almost instinctively to Selenus. Their eyes met for a fleeting moment, heavy with unspoken emotions, before they both turned away.

The mirrors' shimmering light dimmed, receding into shadows, save for one. Here, the surface glowed, brilliant and piercing, drawing everyone's attention to it.

A sharp yet sweet scent filled the air—lilacs, weaving inside the chamber like a whisper from a forgotten dream.

Wilhelmina froze, her hand reaching for nothing as the illumination took shape, forming the misty outline of the wise owl, Gwydion. His voice, familiar and tinged with wistful regret, broke the silence.

"Lilacs... they were your mother's favorite... Oh! I shouldn't have said that. Never you mind."

He waved a dismissive wing, as if brushing away an errant thought.

She jumped, drawing in a jagged breath. "I recall that day."

The lilac scent deepened like a spectral thread, pulling her into the past. The mirror shimmered, and a pale radiance within illuminated the image of a little girl, about five years old, kneeling by a frosted window. Her tiny fingers pressed against the cold pane as she peered outside. She watched families in the fresh air playing with their children, their laughter drifting from beyond the glass.

The vision mutated abruptly, and a grand hall materialized, its shadows long and oppressive. At the doorway, the girl gripped the frame with tiny hands. Her voice broke the heavy silence.

"Mama? Papa?"

Tears shimmered on her face as two figures walked away, their silhouettes fading into the distance.

Wilhelmina staggered back, clutching her chest, the memory tearing through her. "No." Her voice quivered. "Not this dream... not this nightmare again."

The vision splintered and fractured into shimmering shards of light that dissolved into the mirror.

But the glass did not still. It revealed a new scene. Now, a young woman stood at an altar, her serene smile a fragile mask barely concealing the hollow ache in her eyes.

"Why do you give so freely to others what you deny yourself?"

The question reverberated across the chamber, incisive in its clarity.

Wilhelmina's reflection gazed back at her, weary and worn. The longing she seemed to conceal so carefully shimmered across her mirrored counterpart, raw and unguarded.

Her voice shook as she replied, "Because... It's not about me. It's about them."

The light from the altar dimmed, and shadows crept across the space.

"And what about the child who watched her parents leave? Does she not deserve love, too?"

Wilhelmina's hand lifted to shield her throat, warding off a truth too painful to bear. "She does," she whispered, "but it's too late for her."

The glass surface rippled. *"Too late? What do you believe about yourself, child? What is your truth?"*

Wilhelmina hesitated. "I believe I am a protector, a nurturer. I build the foundations for others to have what I never did—a love that is strong, unbreakable. What every family should have."

"*But beneath that,*" the mirror asserted, "*you believe yourself unworthy of such love. You fasten yourself to detachment and fear rejection. Even Gwydion's love feels conditional to you. Why?*"

"Because love always feels like something that can be taken away," she confessed. "If I admit my longing, I risk distraction... failure. The realm's magic depends on me. I can't afford to want for myself. I can't risk being vulnerable."

Cracking like ice under pressure, the reflective surface fractured into lines resembling a spider's web. A chill spread through the chamber as the image reformed.

This time, her parents appeared. They knelt before her younger self, their hands outstretched and held back by an invisible force. Her mother's voice interrupted.

"We never stopped loving you, Wilhelmina. We had to leave to protect you... to protect everyone."

Wilhelmina reached out with shaking hands, her breath catching. "I thought... I thought I wasn't enough. That I had done something wrong."

The child mirrored her movements. Her small hand touched the barrier that separated them. Then the mirror dissolved, leaving Wilhelmina face-to-face with her younger self.

"Love is infinite," the child whispered. *"Boundless and unearned. You deserve it as much as you give it."*

Wilhelmina knelt before the little one, tears streaming down her cheeks. "I'm so sorry."

"Love begins within. When you can connect with yourself, still loving your flaws and gifts... your own uniqueness. Only then can you connect with another... one you long to share a life with romantically." The chill in the air lifted as the mirror spoke. *"Can you recognize that longing and vulnerability are*

strengths, not weaknesses? To give love freely, you must first allow yourself to receive it."

"So then… All this time, the fear I've had of losing love has kept me distant from the connection I have always wanted." Wilhelmina's voice grew firmer with every word. "Love is not earned through perfection or sacrifice. I am worthy of love, not as a protector or leader, but as myself."

She transferred her gaze to her feet.

"But… I still don't know if it's even possible. Who would want to share their life with me?"

Quill stepped closer, draping an arm over her shoulder. "We believe in you, Wilhelmina." She grasped his hand and offered him a warm smile.

The shadows that had clung to her appeared lighter now, as though she had made room for a sliver of light.

The mirror's voice, sighing, interjected. "*Oh, young fairy… And yet there is another whose silence echoes yours. You both long for connection yet retreat into shadow."*

❧

Before anyone could respond, the chamber turned its attention to Selenus, whose steps now faltered. His stride lost its usual regal precision, and for the first time, his unshakable composure wavered.

His reflection remained dark—a silent abyss that devoured light rather than deflected it. He averted his gaze, his jaw tightening, but the chamber would not allow him to escape to the shadows.

Slowly, the mirrors began to glow, and his reflection emerged—blurred, indistinct, like smoke curling into nothingness.

The voice returned, resonating through the air. *"Moon Prince, why do you hide?"*

"I do not *hide*," he snapped, though the sharpness of his tone faltered. "I walk in the open."

The reflection rippled, and a different image took shape. Selenus, as a boy, chased Phaethon through the emerald forests of Aetherwyn. Their giggles echoed—bright and unburdened—as sunlight dappled the ground in shifting gold and silver.

For a brief moment, Selenus smiled—a wistful curve of his lips.

The brothers, inseparable as youths, stood beneath a glittering sky. Selenus's silvery glow mingled with Phaethon's golden radiance, and together, their light balanced the realms—two halves of a whole.

The vision changed, and the scene darkened. The brightness faded into shadow, and the laughter grew distant.

Now the brothers stood in a field, surrounded by cosmic children from distant galaxies whose forms shimmered with light borrowed from their origins—silver, gold, and hues from the heart of nebulae. At the center was Phaethon, lifted high on the shoulders of elders. His golden light illuminated the gathering as the children chanted, "*The Sun Prince!*"

Selenus separated himself, picking up a small stone and rolling it between his fingers before letting it fall to the ground. He kicked it idly, watching it skitter across the open ground until it bumped into a cluster of children. He flinched back—only to see their faces turn toward him, smiling.

"Come, Selenus!" Phaethon's voice was warm. "Join us!"

Selenus's expression twisted into something unreadable—hurt masked by scorn. He kicked the stone again, harder this time. It ricocheted off one glowing child, who yelped in surprise.

"Why bother?" Selenus muttered, shrugging. "They need only the Sun."

The mirror's words broke through the memory. *"Why do you reject those who reach out to you? Why do you retreat into the shadows of your making?"*

Selenus gritted his teeth. "I wasn't retreating." His voice lowered now—straining. "I was... finding my way."

The image rippled anew. Young Selenus paced beneath the shadow of a great tree, its gnarled branches reaching across the sky. Laughter echoed from a distance, fading into a haunting stillness. He glanced toward the sound, hesitating—but turned away.

"Finding your own way?" the mirror pressed, its tone gentle but relentless. *"Or shielding yourself from what you feared most?"*

"I walk alone because I must." Selenus's gaze dropped to the floor. "The Moon needs no other light."

A new image formed. Phaethon stood alone in the golden halls of the Sun Palace, his shoulders slumped. His voice, soft and searching, disrupted the silence.

"Selenus? Where are you?"

The mirror's tone, sorrowful now, echoed the scene. *"Even then, he searched for you. He never sought to overshadow you, Selenus. He wanted to share his light."*

Selenus's hands trembled. His breath came sharp and uneven. "It doesn't matter. They cheered for him, not me. He was always first... always the one chosen."

"Your light has always mattered," the mirror replied. *"But you have dimmed it yourself with doubt."*

"It is not doubt," Selenus spat, his voice cracking. "It's reality. The Sun shines brighter, and that is the way of things."

The mirror glinted. *"The Moon is no less than the Sun. You are equals, balancing the realms together. But you have blinded yourself to this truth."*

The vision shifted. Phaethon, older now, stood on a balcony, gazing toward the horizon. The weight of duty etched lines across his face. *"Selenus... what I would give to have you here."*

Selenus's defenses crumbled, his breath hitching. "I thought... I thought he didn't need me."

The mirror's reply was a whisper. *"He needed you just like you needed him."*

Phaethon's golden eyes, searching the expanse and longing for his brother's light, lingered in the final image.

Selenus dropped to one knee, clutching his chest as though the ache had finally reached him.

"I... I don't know how to believe that." His voice stripped of pride, gentled. "I miss him. I miss the days when we were children, when we..." He stopped short, swallowing hard.

His hand rose to his neck. His fingers brushed the edge of a pendant concealed beneath his collar—a silver disc engraved with the sun and moon entwined.

Wilhelmina unconsciously rested her palm on her heart. She caught him absently touching the amulet, his gaze distant. "You're not alone, Selenus. Not anymore."

Crispin's voice broke through—wry but kind. "Well, mate, your light does matter. You need to stop being so bloody stubborn about beholding it."

Selenus straightened, his shoulders squaring, though his eyes remained shadowed.

"Perhaps... It's time I stopped letting those memories be shadows and started seeing the light they held. But believing it... that won't come easily. Not yet."

17. The Book of Truth

The echoes of the mirrored chamber lingered on as they stepped forward. Wilhelmina glanced at Selenus, who stood apart, his fingers unconsciously brushing the pendant at his neck. Shadows clung to him still, but they seemed lighter now—as if the weight had lessened. Ahead, the book pulsed with its own gravity, waiting.

The room transformed, and the reflective surfaces dissolved into streams of stardust, reshaping the space into a crystalline palace alive with cosmic splendor. Constellations adorned its walls, and celestial patterns traced its spires. Music, born from their harmony, enveloped the air—a melody both haunting and gladdening.

The mirrored chamber's voice rose again. *"Children,"* it said, *"you have glimpsed the soul's nature—a tapestry of choices, flaws, and beauty. Will you now see your worth and be guided by it?"*

Wilhelmina came forward, her tone pensive. "This restoration mirrors what we must strive for within ourselves—and the realm. Though it is a lesson not easily mastered."

"Then the moment has arrived to reveal the Book of Truth," the chamber's voice declared. Liquid light gathered at the chamber's center, coalescing into a radiant nexus. From this point, a glass column rose, refracting a stream of rainbows onto the crystalline walls. Atop the pillar rested a book, its sparkling binding reflecting the heavens.

Wilhelmina drew nearer. Intricate etchings shimmered across its surface like constellations in motion, their meaning tantalizingly out of reach. They shifted and swirled with each heartbeat, alive. She hesitated, her hand hovering just above the cover. Her voice, barely a whisper, broke the stillness.

"This... this is it. The answers we've sought. The truths that could change everything."

Selenus moved to her side, his words measured with deliberate gravity. "It is more than a book. It is a mirror, a map... a reckoning."

Wilhelmina turned to him, her face alight with the kaleidoscope of shimmering light that danced around them. "And what if we are unequal to its demands? What if I am not equal?" Her tone, though calm, betrayed a flicker of doubt—one not easily extinguished.

"You are," he said simply, as if it were the most natural truth. "We all are. Because we must be."

For a moment, she studied him. His confidence was not the boast of one untouched by uncertainty, but the conviction of someone who had made peace with it. Drawing a deep, shuddering breath, she turned her gaze to her companions.

Each bore the mantle of their trials, their faces marked by a steadfastness she could not help but admire: Crispin's quiet self-belief, Aria's radiant determination, Quill's thoughtful resolve, and Flora's serene strength.

"Then let this be the beginning," Wilhelmina said at last. Her fingers hovered before the Book, and when they touched the cover, it appeared as if the universe itself placed its great hand upon her shoulder.

The chamber carried a stillness so profound it bordered on reverence. Whatever truths lay entombed within the Book of Truth, she would meet them as one who understood the weight of the moment—not for herself alone, but for the realm, for her companions, and for the fragile hope of balance yet to be restored.

She turned again to the group, her voice steadier now, though her eyes gleamed with unshed tears, lending her gaze a singular brightness.

"We shall uncover its secrets and make it right—no matter the cost."

As if in answer, the Book stirred to life. Its surface glowed, spilling forth rippling waves of ethereal light that bathed them all in its radiance. Slowly, the cover parted, and a world of revelation awaited them.

A crackle of energy surged through the air. The pages fluttered, moved by an invisible wind, despite appearing pristine and pure white, untouched by ink or hand. A commanding and resonant sound rang out.

"I am the Book of Truth. Do you dare seek what lies hidden?"

Wilhelmina pulled back her shoulders. "We seek the Enchantress. How can we find her?"

"*Yes,*" the Book replied, its voice deepening. *"But are your hearts open enough to understand the truth? Can you find compassion in your souls?"*

Its tone sharpened. *"Place the Sphere of Golden Thread upon my pages. It carries the fragments of your truths. Let them weave with the Enchantress's tales."*

A gasp escaped Wilhelmina, but her fingers moved under compulsion. She retrieved the Sphere from her satchel and set it down on the open pages. It fused with the volume, radiating a cascade of brilliance across the room. Light flooded the chamber, and its surface glimmered like a pool of liquid starlight.

The Book turned sharply toward Quill, casting a brighter glow over him.

"You there... Scholar! Write these truths down."

Quill, taken aback, fumbled momentarily before retrieving a roll of parchment and summoning his enchanted quill. Its tip gleamed with energy.

"Ready," he said, though his voice shook.

The Book responded with a vivid display of images and text written in a forgotten script, rising upward.

"These are the chronicles of the Enchantress," it recited. *"In the beginning, the force of creation sparked her spirit, and she was born into life from the universal balance itself. She became a being of immense power, and with her boundless imagination, she shaped the galaxies."*

The air shimmered, and threads of illumination and shadow materialized. A panoramic vision unfurled above the book, forming a delicate mosaic before their eyes. It showed star systems swirling into existence with breathtaking grandeur.

But at their heart was a fissure, black and jagged, splitting the cosmos like a wound.

Crispin let out a low whistle. "I did not expect... that."

"From this miasma, she shaped Aetherwyn to preserve and sustain the magic across the cosmos. The same magic from which she herself was born."

The vision altered to show a radiant sphere swirling with vibrant colors. From it emerged threads of light, weaving into the familiar patterns there.

"So she made all this?" Aria said, her voice a whisper. "She created everything? Even the magic?"

"And took on its burden." Quill's enchanted quill scratched furiously across the parchment. "This wasn't mere creation—it was sacrifice."

"So it was. To balance the cosmos, the Enchantress created Celestia and Varytita, who in turn brought forth Phaethon and Selenus to govern the Sun

and Moon," the Book said. *"This balance between light and darkness was essential to preserve magic."*

A depiction of the celestial brothers filled the air, their darkness and radiance entwined in harmony.

Their surroundings faded. They saw the Enchantress moving among mortals, her beauty otherworldly. Her presence seemed to bring solace—a guiding light in the desolate corners of the land—to those shrouded in darkness.

Aria's eyes widened. "She was magnificent... like she could touch the essence of the stars."

Flora nodded. "It was a perfect system."

"Perfect," Selenus's expression darkened. "Until it wasn't."

Yet, as the vision changed, shadows crept into the tapestry.

The Enchantress appeared in a dark forest, her movements deliberate as she conjured shapes of terrible allure. Tendrils of sinister energy coiled around her.

"Mark this: though she sought to safeguard the fragile harmony of our world, her actions set in motion events that shaped Aetherwyn's destiny for generations to come."

The light flared, and the scene shifted again. The Enchantress stood on a windswept cliff, her silhouette stark against the night sky. Arms raised, she reached toward the stars. A layer of desperation seemed to coat her expression.

"She was sad." Tears glinted within Aria's gaze. "It's as if she yearned for something she could never have."

"Or someone." Quill's focus locked on the Enchantress's anguished face. "What would drive a being so powerful to such despair?"

Wilhelmina ended the silence. "Why did she embrace the shadows?"

"The equilibrium between light and shadow is delicate," Flora replied, her brow furrowing. "Perhaps she sought a gateway to her aspirations and thought the shadows held answers—or power."

Aria clasped her hands over her heart. "Why would she turn to such power?"

"Perhaps because she had no other choice, or perhaps she thought she didn't," Quill mused.

"Power always demands a toll," Crispin interjected. His expression turned somber. "And it rarely leaves room for joy." His brow furrowed. "But why? Why take that risk?"

The Book's light dimmed, its next words somber. *"Because she believed the realm's survival depended on it. Yet, in choosing harmony, she fractured the natural order."*

The shimmering text reappeared. *"The Enchantress saw the imbalance within herself reflected in the world. In seeking to mend the cosmos, she endeavored to heal her fractured soul. But harmony, once disturbed, does not easily return. Thus, the balance held—until it broke."*

Wilhelmina's fingers brushed her lips. "And in trying to restore balance, she may have unraveled it further."

A fresh image emerged—a portrayal of Selenus. His face twisted with jealousy as he watched the Enchantress from afar. The surrounding stars dimmed as shadowy tendrils crept closer.

"No!" Selenus snapped. "It wasn't like that! She just never turned to me, always toward his light, never mine. I believed she preferred my brother."

Wilhelmina's eyes narrowed, her tone measured. "Then tell us how it was."

The Book interjected, its voice resonating with finality. *"The darkness preys on the vulnerable. Her pity for the Moon Prince invited chaos."*

"The ripples of these choices echo still," the Book forewarned. *"Reality itself is at risk. The realms suffer, their balance overturned. If the Enchantress is not found, if her truths are not reclaimed, all shall fall into shadow."*

A charged silence filled the chamber until Wilhelmina spoke. "Then we have no choice. We'll find her and set this right."

"Remember. Choice is never absent," the Book replied, its voice resonant with timeless gravity. *"Even now. Choice is the crucible of free will. The Moon Prince's envy—though within his right—was a decision shaped by fear, not faith. He abandoned the harmony he was born to uphold. That choice cracked the already fragile order. The Eternal Ones' intervention granted a brief reprieve from a near-catastrophic loss. But their power is not infinite. Their gift was a salve, not a cure."*

The Book's glow wavered, casting shifting light along the stone.

"The prince's doubts never vanished. They festered in silence. And now, his most recent act—reckless, born of the same old fear—has torn the veil. The cosmic bottleneck is broken. The wound bleeds, and darkness rushes in.

Not as shadow alone, but as a wave of chaos unraveling the weave of existence."

The Book's voice lowered to a hush. "*Magic is not mere power. It is joy, love, and compassion woven into form. It is coherence. It is meaning. Without it, the realms falter. And now, reality itself hangs by a thread."*

Wilhelmina drew in a taut breath, her expression tightening. She glanced toward Selenus, who remained silent, his head bowed.

"Have a care, child," the Book warned, its light casting long, reaching silhouettes. *"You, too, have tasted envy—though yours bore other names. Judgment. Pride. The fear of losing what you love. Beware. Such shadows feed the darkness you seek to dispel."*

Wilhelmina stiffened. "I… I don't know what you mean," she said, but a quiet prickle of understanding stirred within her.

"You feared that love would cost you your calling. That closeness would cloud your clarity. And so, you turned away—not from love itself, but from its risk. That, too, is a choice. And choices leave marks."

She hesitated, but her voice sharpened. "I grew bitter when he rejected my help. I tried to save him from his illusion—from the chains of unrequited longing. That is all."

The Book's voice—like wind through glass—sighed. *"Oh, child… what of your own silence? What of your retreat? He misread your distance as fondness toward his brother, and the wound deepened. His jealousy did not arise alone—it was shaped, in part, by your absence of truth."*

Wilhelmina turned away, bitterness tightening her voice.

"My refusal was a burden I bore for the balance of the realm. I did what I believed was right. My pain came not from his desire—but from his blindness. He could not see past his own illusion, and now the cost of that blindness threatens us all."

"*But is that the whole truth?*" the Book pressed, its tone gently relentless. "*Do you not still grieve what was lost between you? Both of you carry pride and pain like armor. Yet pride cannot mend what truth can heal. Shadows cling to those who will not fully see themselves."*

"Even now, the Moon Prince bears a secret—one that may shape the fate of all. And time is thinning. What will you choose, child of balance, when the moment comes again?"

The Book paused. *"Guard this Sphere well, for you will both need it in the hour of your decision, your choice. In this, you shall write your destinies."*

The Sphere launched itself into the air, its light refracting in a thousand directions before landing back in Wilhelmina's hands.

"Moon Prince, will you make the choice now to tell your new friends your truth?"

Crispin raised an eyebrow. "Well, Prince? Shall we stand here all day, or are you going to enlighten us?"

Selenus exhaled heavily, unsheathing his Sword with deliberate precision. Its blade gleamed as he placed it on the book's open pages. "I can share part of the truth," he said, his voice low. "But no more."

"Long ago, I yearned for the freedom to explore the galaxy." As he spoke, he stared past them, his focus on a distant point.

"She... the Enchantress granted me this—from the Moon's tether, from my brother's shadow. The darker energies of her mate, Dark Matter, combined with hers allowed me this release... but it came at a cost. The tides of Aetherwyn faltered, and my light—my presence—threw the realms into imbalance."

He hesitated, eyeing the Sword. "I thought she saw me, truly saw me. But it was pity, not understanding. And I... I took that pity and turned it into resentment. Against her. Against Phaethon. Her kindness was flawed, yes, but my pride blinded me. Freedom didn't heal—it deepened the wounds. The realm paid the price, and yet here I am again."

He studied the floor, as though the answers he sought might be etched in the stone.

"It's easier to blame others than to face yourself. I see that now," he stated, his tone bitter. "The light he offered was never meant to diminish mine. But sometimes, I wish it did."

"The truths revealed are but fragments," the Book decreed. *"The balance remains fragile, and the path forward is laden with shadows. Shall you confront them, or will you let them claim you? Will you honor your promise?"*

Selenus bowed his head in assent, and the Sword rose from the book, hovering briefly before returning to his grasp. He sheathed it silently.

A blinding light shot from the volume, rendering him translucent for an instant before solidifying again.

"It is time for you all to finish your quest for the sake of all." A spiral of stardust swarmed from the Book's pages. *"The path you must take lies through the center of the cosmos, but you must first seek the Celestial Arbor."*

Wilhelmina bowed her head. "What is that?"

"This cosmic tree was born at the dawn of time. It stands sentinel at the Lake of Mirrors, bordered by an ancient garden deep in the mystical forests of Miragwyn. Hidden in its boughs, you shall find the Enchantress, bound and imprisoned inside an enchanted mirror."

"How can we release her?"

"The Arbor possesses the properties, wisdom, and connection necessary to reveal and understand the mirror's secrets. But take heed. Tests and obstacles will make the trail difficult."

Wilhelmina recoiled slightly, overwhelmed by the Book's words, and bumped against Selenus, positioned behind her.

"Though to lighten your path, it is imperative that you know the nature of your bond with the enchantment of weddings in Aetherwyn."

"Yes, I know. I've been told this... many times."

"Magic is unity," the Book stated, growing impatient. "*Child, your magic alone fortifies unity, love, and wholeness—the fundamental nature of the universe."*

A jolt went through Selenus, and his attention snagged on Wilhelmina's silken hair, glinting under the stardust motes suspended in the air.

"*These are the conditions where diverse entities complement and combine into a fruitful whole*," the Book proclaimed. "*And you are the nexus upon which balance can return."*

Wilhelmina stilled, her hand drifting to her chest. Her expression appeared steady, yet her eyes clouded for the briefest moment—as though doubt had brushed against her heart.

With a sweeping cascade of starlight, the book conjured an astronomical map now hovering before them.

Selenus's eyes rounded when he glimpsed a familiar cosmic jewel—the blue light that he had first witnessed. The one that had captured his soul.

"In the infinite expanse, the mystical imprint linked to your non-physical essence manifests in your unique role," the Book declared.

"This cosmic star will guide you to the enchanted mirror. Its light is pure, drawn from the sun's illumination. In his insecurity and painful longing, Selenus tragically misinterpreted this simple truth as affection for his brother, Phaethon. And you, Wilhelmina, unknowingly, came to resent this radiance within you, for it drew his all-consuming gaze and complicated the love you denied yourself."

"Wait… are you saying that particular celestial gem… is Wilhelmina's cosmic imprint?" Selenus turned to Wilhelmina, sputtering. "That star… is… *you*?"

"Indeed, that heavenly object is the wedding fairy you see before you. She has been all along."

"Why didn't you tell me?" Selenus said, his voice raw with a mix of awe and bewildered betrayal, almost angry.

"I-I believed it was of no consequence. Stellara told me before we left. I told them—later… after everything fractured in Aetherwyn."

Wilhelmina's pitch rose, a tremor betraying her suppressed emotions.

"You and I weren't exactly… speaking then."

He froze mid-step, staring at her as though seeing her for the first time, his entire world tilting. The star he had spent what seemed like lifetimes chasing—an obsession he'd thought unreachable, forever linked to his brother by his own mistaken belief—had been beside him all along. His fists clenched at his sides, knuckles white.

"All this while… I never knew." His voice broke, filled with a complex blend of regret, disbelief, and a dawning, terrible understanding. He turned away, pacing like a storm gathering force.

"It doesn't matter," Wilhelmina spoke fast, though her tone wavered. "We have more important things to deal with right now." She cast a quick glance when Selenus stumbled behind her. Her brow furrowed at his ashen expression. "Why was she imprisoned?"

"Eons ago, the Enchantress crafted the Enchanted Mirror to reveal hidden truths and guide Aetherwyn's destiny. The mystery surrounding her became distorted, leading to misunderstanding and a corrupted perception of her intentions."

Quill clenched his fists. "I knew it. History has besmirched her truth."

"Indeed, the darkness has always tampered with history, and it is vital for anyone to remain vigilant to the darker vibrations," the Book warned.

"The Enchanted Mirror, though, is untainted and has great power. Arcane magic, invisible to all but those with pure hearts and understanding of astronomical energies, veils it. It can influence emotions and decisions in subtle, yet profound, ways. When you find it, take care not to gaze upon it."

Wilhelmina's eyes widened. "Why? What will happen?"

"The Enchantress made sure to cast a protection spell where no one but the celestial gem, the imprint of the uniting star, may lay eyes on it."

Selenus stopped pacing, and his focus shifted to the map, where the celestial body still glinted. For a fleeting moment, awe softened his features.

"You were the light I couldn't reach..."

Wilhelmina knitted her brows and glanced at him, a puzzled expression on her face, but she spun her attention back to the Book.

Selenus fixed his gaze on the ground. "I... we understand." He gripped the Sword's pommel. "We must find the mirror, regardless of the risks."

A single page flew out of the Book, levitating and floating like a leaf falling from a tree.

"Take this leaf and solve the riddle within to guide your way."

Flora bent to pick up the page and read aloud.

Seek the heart of Miragwyn,
Where ancient trees whisper secrets to begin.
Follow the path of moonlit beams,
Guiding you through enchanted dreams.

Listen to the song of celestial birds,
Guiding you to the gate's refrain.
Beneath the arch where stars do play,
You'll find the entrance to light the way.

Once within, heed the ethereal wind's call,
Bringing you to the Mirror, tranquil and small.
But beware, for light and darkness intertwine.
Only courage and purity will align.

Remember, Cosmic Star, your role so true,
Keeper of balance, in all that you do.
Trust your inward light, shining bright,

For it will reveal the path to light.

The chamber creaked softly, as if settling under the weight of its own history.

"One must remain to preserve what is revealed. The truth must be written, or it will be lost again," the Book intoned.

"I must stay here."

Quill's next words shattered the heavy silence. They were measured as if he had rehearsed them in the quiet spaces of his heart.

"To write the truth—Aetherwyn's history, Selenus's story, and the Enchantress's legacy. I understand now. This is where I am meant to be."

The companions stared at him. Their faces were etched with disbelief and something bordering on betrayal.

Selenus's voice was unusually subdued. "That is honorable...but unnecessary."

Flora inclined her head in agreement, though the tremble of her hands betrayed her worry.

Crispin grew uncharacteristically silent. His face was pensive, and his brows knit together as if contemplating the gravity of Quill's declaration against the bonds of their friendship.

But it was Aria who broke the silence, her expression stoic. "Bring forth the truth in our stories, Quill. But come back to us... to me."

"I'll find you, Aria," Quill replied, his voice tender. "Keep hope in that."

He pulled Aria into a fierce embrace and pressed a kiss to her temple. "And you... The quest will need your voice—your song to heal Aetherwyn's soul." He rested his hands on her shoulders but turned to the others.

"Trust me, my friends. We will meet each other again when the time is right."

The companions stood rooted to the spot. Tears glistened in Aria's eyes. Crispin kept looking at the floor. Even Selenus, for all his princely detachment, averted his gaze, tightening his jaw in a futile attempt to conceal the flicker of regret that crossed his face.

"Now go!"

Quill's tone was brisk, though a note of melancholy lingered beneath his scholar's focus. "The truths I weave here may one day reunite us, though not in the way we expect."

The friends hesitated, their gazes fixed on Quill. Each seemed caught in a web of their unspoken thoughts. Flora stepped forward, her lip quivering.

"Quill... are you certain? The path—this sacrifice—shouldn't be yours alone."

Quill's lopsided smile faltered for a heartbeat. "The tapestry demands it, and who better to preserve it than me? You all carry your burdens. This is mine."

Wilhelmina drew closer, her hand trembling as she reached out, but stopped short. "We'll come back for you. I swear it."

He nodded with slightly lowered eyes. "I'll hold you to that, Mina." He gently touched her shoulder and looked away.

The very air seemed to respond to their shared grief. A gentle wind swirled around them, carrying with it a chorus of whispers. Without warning, the light intensified, flooding the space with radiant silver beams.

The luminous energy surrounded Quill, and as they watched, his form dissolved into the brilliance, becoming one with the mirrored chamber.

He was gone.

Deafening silence followed. Crispin's usual levity had vanished, his face pale as he stared at the empty spot where Quill had stood moments ago. Aria wiped a tear from her cheek. Flora clasped Wilhelmina's hand.

❧

The column trembled as if alive, and a burst of light emanated from the Book of Truth.

"Beyond this point, the bonds you forge shall be your shield," the Book stated. "*Only together can you reach the Enchantress.*"

Wilhelmina squared her shoulders. "We move forward. For Quill. For Aetherwyn. For Magic."

The companions all turned toward the pillar, and one by one, they nodded.

The chamber shifted, and the ground fell away under their feet. Weightless, drawn by an unseen force, they floated upward. A vortex of swirling colors—a dimensional wormhole that defied all sense of time and space—whooshed them through the portal.

Fleeting glimpses of other realms and distant galaxies passed by, animated and alien. Ethereal cities hovered amidst nebulae, and vast oceans sparkled beneath unknown suns. The experience challenged logic—a journey infinite and instantaneous all at once.

A new image broke through the phantasmagoria of light. The Enchantress, radiant yet shadowed, stretched toward an ornate mirror. Spectral figures circled her like predators, their forms fragmented, as though stitched together from shards of broken starlight. They reached for her, their movements halting and grotesque, desperation emanating from their every motion.

She struggled, her luminous hands clawing at the air as she fought against the mirror's force. Her eyes, pools of anguish, locked onto a whisper of hope—something that might still save her. Her lips moved soundlessly, forming words the companions could not hear, but the plea in her expression was unmistakable. "Help me."

The vision dissolved as quickly as it had come. The swirling vortex remained, and the Book's voice guided them onward.

"The light shall guide you. Step forward, and let the stars carry you."

As the chamber faded, a distant pull emerged, like the soft hum of wind through ancient boughs. The Celestial Arbor awaited.

18. The Enchantress

The journey ended in a burst of brilliant light, and the companions struck the ground. Thick with aged parchment and traces of lavender clinging to the walls, Miragwyn's ancient library exhaled with relief as its high-shelved books welcomed their return.

"We're back." The silence swallowed Crispin's words.

Wilhelmina glanced at the others, her expression resolute. "Not for long. The forests await."

They scurried through the grand doors, crossed the clearing, and slipped into the woods. A ribbon of silver light wove through Miragwyn's dense forest, scattering shadows across the floor.

The twin suns had descended. In their wake, an amethyst satellite filtered a lavender glow through the leafy canopy. A chorus of crickets and frogs harmonized with the leaves rustling in the breeze. The air carried the spice of pine needles, tempered by the sweetness of wildflowers and the earthy richness of moss.

Wilhelmina inhaled the mingled scents, her composure steady, though she started slightly when Selenus's arm brushed hers.

"The forest is beautiful." The sternness of his usual demeanor momentarily diminished. "You must miss officiating those magical unions in woods such as this one… in Aetherwyn."

She focused on the path before her. "Yes… I do," she said in a clipped tone.

They walked in silence before she came to an abrupt halt. Selenus, engrossed in the rhythm of his steps, continued several paces onward before realizing she was no longer beside him. He turned around, raising an eyebrow.

"Is anything wrong?"

Her voice cut through the quiet like a blade. "When are you going to tell me what you're holding back?"

For a moment, he did not respond. He closed the distance between them with measured strides, his tall figure casting a shadow in the dim lavender glow. When he stopped, the space between them tightened.

"It's not important." His words were laden with emphasis, though his tone betrayed a flicker of something deeper. "Only know that I will protect you and go to any lengths to do so."

But his eyes, hooded as they were, told another story. Wilhelmina studied him, her brow knitting as she bit her lip. She stayed rooted—yet her body tipped forward before she could stop it.

Around them, the forest held its breath. The leaves whispered in soft tones above, and the murmur of a distant stream filled the silence. A haunting melody drifted down through the foliage.

She stepped back and lifted her face to the sky. Selenus followed her line of sight, his raised brows easing as the source of the sound revealed itself.

Star-magpies—feathers aglow with cosmic dust—soared in intricate patterns, trailing azure and silver. The companions' breath caught as they observed the avian creatures' magnificence.

"These have to be the celestial birds from the riddle!" Flora stared in amazement as her eyes tracked the glimmering flight.

Aria gasped and pointed down the walkway ahead. "They're leading us! This must be the way to the gate!"

Crispin blew out a breath. His face lit up as he started forward, quickening his steps. "Finally, a clear sign. Let's not lose them!"

They quickened their pace and followed the star-magpies as they flitted gracefully through the canopy, illuminating the route with their glowing trails. The flock slowed its movement just enough for the travelers to keep up.

"There it is—the Arch!" Crispin called out, breaking into a run as a grand stone gateway materialized at the end of the path. Its weathered facade gleamed, etched with ancient magic.

☙

One by one, the companions passed beneath its imposing frame, practically skipping, until the Arch dissolved into a cascade of light. The forest behind them vanished, replaced by a cold, barren expanse.

"Where did everything go?" Aria's voice broke the stunned silence. Her wide eyes scanned the unfamiliar terrain.

A tiny puddle shimmered on the cracked ground before them, its surface unnaturally still. Slowly, as if drawn from a hidden spring, the liquid expanded, spreading into a vast, looking-glass-like lake that blurred the boundary between sky and water. The companions stared as the lake unfurled, spellbound.

On the far shore, bathed in paradisiacal light, a majestic tree loomed. Wilhelmina's lips parted. "The Celestial Arbor...The Book of Truth said it would be here...."

A pulsing, radiant glow hovered above the tree's boughs, like a ghostly apparition. "And look there... The Enchanted Mirror...," Selenus pointed in its direction. "Its illumination is beautiful, yet something feels... ominous." His hand tightened around his Sword's hilt. "We need to follow the coastline to reach it. Be wary...there are bound to be tests."

"Well, no time like the present," Crispin interjected. "Let's find this mirror and be on our way."

A sudden, strange draft swept across the lake, the temperature dropping to a biting chill. Frost clung to their boots. "Goodness! The Book never mentioned the weather turning so nasty!" he complained.

The companions instinctively huddled closer, bracing themselves as the frigidity strengthened. Cold knifed through the air. The lake froze over—then sealed into ice. Purple light—and the Celestial Arbor's inverted reflection—shimmered across it.

Before they could move along the shoreline, an icy blast of air surged from the Arbor. It pushed them onto the lake's glimmering expanse. They stumbled, their boots skidding against the brittle ice until they stood at the lake's center. The wind stilled. The ice groaned. Jagged lines rippled outward like veins beneath their feet.

Selenus shouted above the noise. "This is a test! Tread carefully!"

They took tentative steps forward. Wilhelmina's gaze darted between the frozen landscape and the distant glow of the Arbor. The sharp crack of splitting ice broke the hush.

"Flora, stop!" Crispin's shout came too late.

Flora's boot had struck a fragile patch. With a gasp, she plunged into the frigid depths. Her scream cut short as the water closed over her head, leaving rippling shadows behind.

Without hesitation, Crispin dove after her. The others held their breath as the seconds stretched into eternity. A few bubbles of air ruptured the surface in that span of time.

"Where are they?" Aria screamed, her face a mask of horror.

Wilhelmina and Selenus, their expressions grim, stared stoically at the gaping hole where their friends had submerged.

At last, Crispin surged upward, his arms encircling Flora's limp body. Both of them shivered violently, and ice formed on their brows as they gasped for breath.

The group rushed to pull them onto solid ice, their hands trembling as they dragged the pair to safety.

"We must keep moving!" Crispin rasped, his voice hoarse. "The lake's playing tricks!" He hoisted a chilled Flora over his shoulder.

As if in response to his defiance, stepping stones emerged from the frozen water's depths. Their surfaces gleamed like polished crystal. The companions bobbed on the enchanted rocks as whispers rose from the lake, insidious and haunting.

"*You're only useful when you're entertaining. Why even try?*"

Crispin froze as the hissing voice echoed in his ear.

Aria faltered, her breath hitching as a voice spat venom at her.

"Your song won't be enough. You'll always be alone."

Wilhelmina clenched her fists, but the darkness found her, too.

"Give up, little fairy. You cannot defeat us. We are the shadow, and you will fail them the way you failed before."

"No, you're not real!" She pressed her hands tightly over her ears.

But it was Selenus who faced the cruelest taunt. The voice reached him, resonant and painfully familiar.

"You abandoned your throne for this? Powerless, aimless, lost. Exiled. Take what I offer, and you can rule the stars."

The words coiled around him like a serpent, their origin indistinct yet laced with the unmistakable cadence of his brother's mocking tone. He faltered, his expression pinching in anguish. The ice under him cracked and splintered, radiating outward.

"Selenus!"

Wilhelmina's cry broke through the haze. She leaped onto his stone, her hand gripping his arm as his footing gave way.

"Power isn't our aim. Unity is. These shadows lie because they fear us. But we have free will. We choose our path. Not them. And I've seen your physical strength. You are not weak. Now translate that to your mind and trust in its strength."

Her words interrupted the whispers. The ice stilled, and the lake fell silent. He exhaled shakily, his gaze meeting hers, with the flicker of a smile on his face.

"You could have died." His voice was raw. "You risked everything to save me. I don't deserve that."

Wilhelmina's lips curved, mirroring his. "It's a good thing I believe in second... and even third chances."

She rose to her feet, pulling him up with her. They stepped forward together, the glow of the Celestial Arbor growing brighter with every stride.

Once the murmurs faded into silence, the final stone emerged close to the shoreline. The companions leapt from it to solid ground, their breath misting in the sudden chill. Crispin carefully set Flora down, her shivering form slowly regaining warmth. They turned to face the sight that had left them all speechless.

❧

An ancient tree towered before them—a grand, colossal timber that bridged worlds. Grooves that sparkled with inter-dimensional light etched the trunk's surface. Branches reached skyward, emitting an otherworldly hum—a melody born of magic.

Above its highest boughs, the sky appeared awakened, as though the cosmos itself had converged here. An almost tangible energy charged the dense air, as if the Arbor was aware of their presence and awaited their next move.

Wilhelmina took a step forward, her voice barely a whisper. "The Celestial Arbor... It's even more magnificent than I imagined."

Her attention focused on the pulsing glow nestled high within its branches. The light there resonated with the Enchanted Mirror's mysterious power.

Selenus remained still, though he tapped the Sword's pommel lightly. He scanned the shadows that flickered and appeared distorted along the edges of the Arbor's radiance.

"I can't shake the feeling we're being... judged."

Aria hummed softly, her lilting notes weaving into the tree's hum.

Flora folded her arms against the chill. "This is incredible, but we don't have time to stand here gawking. The Mirror's up there, isn't it?" She gestured toward the glowing light.

Selenus nodded, his jaw tightening. "We climb. Be ready—the Celestial Arbor itself might test us."

Wilhelmina hesitated as she stared at the towering branches. Her fingers brushed the empty space where her wings had once been, a pang of loss flickering across her face.

"I'm not sure I can do this."

"You can." Selenus offered her his hand. "Jump on my back, and I will carry you. Trust me."

After a moment's hesitation, she placed her hands on his shoulders and climbed on. Selenus adjusted his stance, his movements steady despite the strain, and began scaling the trunk. Each foothold he found glimmered, as if the Arbor responded to their determination.

The climb was arduous, the crystal-laden branches slick with frost and dew. The hum of the boughs grew louder as they ascended, each step charged with its ancient power.

Wilhelmina tightened her grip, focusing her attention on the climb as they drew closer to the glowing Mirror.

When they reached a sturdy branch, Selenus carefully set her down, his breath coming in short puffs. "We're close... Think you can manage on your own from here?"

She nodded, though her hands trembled slightly as they gripped the bough. "I've never scaled a tree before... not since I lost my wings." She twisted her head over her shoulder to view her wingless back; a wistful look crossed her face.

Selenus hesitated before offering his hand. "You'll be fine. One step at a time. I'll be right behind you."

Wilhelmina slipped at one point, her foot skidding off a smooth branch, but Selenus's arm shot out to steady her before she could fall. They arrived at the Arbor's crown. The Enchanted Mirror rested there, ensconced in a web of shimmering brilliance, casting indistinct shapes that danced across their faces.

"I can feel its power." Wilhelmina's fingers trembled as she reached for it. "And it's... overwhelming."

"Do not let it distract you," Selenus cautioned. "Focus."

Taking a deep breath, she averted her gaze and gingerly wrapped her hands around it. The moment she lifted it, the brightness surrounding it flared briefly before settling into a gentle glow.

She held it close, her voice unsteady as she glanced at Selenus. "How are we supposed to get down with this?"

"Carefully," he replied, extending his hand. "Here, pass it to me. I'll keep it safe."

"Do not look into it!" she warned.

"I won't." He kept his eyes averted as he cautiously took the Mirror from her hands, tucking it into the inner pocket of his cloak. The fabric glowed where it rested, its power palpable even through the layers.

"Now hold on tight." He crouched slightly. She climbed back onto him, her grip firm around his shoulders. He began the descent, his muscles straining under the added weight and the vibration of the Mirror's energy.

When they reached the ground, Crispin greeted them first, his face lighting up. "Well done!" He clapped Selenus on the back.

Selenus removed the Mirror from its safe resting place, taking care not to look at its surface. The Mirror's surface trembled, and a thin, chiming note slid into the air—too soft to be sound, yet impossible to ignore. Crispin's gaze snapped to it.

"Let me see it—just for a—" Without warning, he lunged forward, his palm outstretched. He snatched at the Mirror—tilted it—and his eyes caught the surface.

"Crispin, no!" Wilhelmina shouted, but her warning came too late.

The instant Crispin's eyes locked on the lustrous surface, his gaze widened, and his body went rigid, the Mirror dropping from his hands. A swirling light emanated from the enchanted artifact as its power seized him, fixing him in place.

The companions froze, their friend's reckless action hitting them like a physical blow.

Flora was the first to move, rushing to his side and shaking his arm. "Crispin! Say something!" she pleaded, but his eyes were glazed, staring unseeing into the void.

"Oh! He's so impulsive!" Wilhelmina stamped her foot, frustration mingling with fear. "Why doesn't he ever listen?" Her gaze darted from Crispin to the mirror, her face ashen.

"Crispin, what have you done?" she whispered, stepping closer as though her presence alone might undo his mistake.

❧

The Enchanted Mirror's radiance intensified, casting a spectral glow over the companions. A surge of otherworldly energy thrummed from its surface, and a luminous woman rose from within, hovering. Light wove through her flowing hair, merging seamlessly with the Mirror's ethereal glow.

Regal yet translucent, her form floated toward them as they stood frozen and stunned, silent. Even the wind stilled. Her eyes, bright and piercing, swept across the group, settling on Crispin's still body.

"You have found me," a mournful note underpinned her words. "But at what cost?"

Wilhelmina stammered, "A-are you the Enchantress?" She took one breathless step back.

The sorceress inclined her head, her eyes glistening. "Yes, child. I am Demiurge, your mother."

Wilhelmina's knees nearly buckled. The truth she had sought her entire life stood before her, radiant and untouchable. The Enchantress. *Her mother.*

For a heartbeat, the world narrowed to that single truth—until Crispin's frozen stillness yanked her back into breath. She gestured with a shaking hand towards his frozen figure.

"Please help him! This is Crispin, my friend. He-he looked into the Mirror, and now he's—" Her words dissolved into a sob.

Demiurge's expression darkened as her gaze lingered on Crispin, her eyebrows pulling together.

"Your friend's circumstances are grievous," she said, her voice weighted with sorrow. "The Mirror is not meant for all eyes. It reveals and binds, especially when touched by those unprepared. Alas, his impulsiveness has turned into a dangerous misstep."

"He did a foolish thing, but can't it be forgiven? You are powerful. Couldn't you simply release him?" Wilhelmina pleaded.

"The Mirror is both my prison and a gateway to salvation. Its power is layered in keys, tied to those destined to wield it. Your friend's actions inadvertently activated the Mirror's first key—an opening meant for you alone. His gaze was not meant to unlock its secrets, and, alas, he has fallen under its spell."

Frost crept along Crispin's eyelashes, sealing them together. Flora rubbed his hands harder, whispering his name as if he might hear her through the ice.

"Is there nothing you can do?" Wilhelmina's voice cracked, raw with desperation. "He's brave—fearlessly so—but sometimes he acts without thinking. He doesn't deserve this!"

Demiurge's light flickered, and she spoke her next words slowly.

"Only the Elixir of Lost Dreams holds the power to undo his binding," she explained. "It is a rare and potent substance, harvested from the Dreamscape by its guardian, Somnius. Yet, the Dreamscape itself has frayed. Its energy has waned, and the Elixir has become perilously scarce."

No one spoke. Even their breath seemed afraid to fog the air.

Wilhelmina clutched her hands to her chest, her face pale. "Then... what can we do? Tell us how to find this guardian!"

Demiurge inclined her head. "He dwells in the Sanctuary of Lost Dreams, nestled within the Whispering Woods—a realm as ancient as the cosmos itself. To reach him, you must first seek his daughter, Seraphina."

"Seraphina?" Wilhelmina's brows furrowed. "My friend Lumina's mother is named Seraphina... Could it be the same?"

A soft smile graced Demiurge's lips. "Yes, child. She, your friend's mother, is the key. She holds the wisdom needed to lead you to her father."

"She lives in Solarae," Wilhelmina said half to herself. "Lumina had to return home. Perhaps... we should consider going there."

"Your journey there is vital." Demiurge's tone was firm. "Through Seraphina's guidance, you will find the path to the Dreamscape. Its instability, however, threatens not only Crispin's life but the delicate balance of reality itself. The threads that bind it also anchor the cosmos. To save your friend, you must help Somnius mend the unraveled threads to craft the Elixir. Only then can Crispin return to you whole."

Wilhelmina's shoulders trembled. Crispin's stillness was a cruel reminder of the stakes they faced. Yet, the steeled light in her eyes burned brighter.

"It's not fair... none of this is. Why must it be like this? Why did this have to happen to him?"

Demiurge's voice carried a mournful edge. "Crispin's suffering," she began as her eyes lingered on his frozen form, "is but a single thread in a vast and intricate tapestry. To mend this one thread, you must understand the equilibrium that governs all creation."

Wilhelmina stiffened, a flicker of shock in her expression. Her gaze darted between Demiurge and Crispin.

"This balance..." she said, raising an eyebrow. "If it's so delicate, what chance do we have of fixing it? I couldn't even prevent this from happening."

The glow of Demiurge's form softened as she turned toward her.

"My daughter, choice implies risk, and you have already chosen to act despite your fears. You've come this far, and yes, you could still fail. But to not try is the same as doing nothing at all. You're not alone. Your friends will help you. There is more power and chance of success if you work together."

Wilhelmina's lips parted, but no words came. She hung her head.

"Light and shadow are intrinsic to creation. They are not adversaries, but complements," she explained as her luminous eyes swept the group.

Selenus shifted, his cloak falling across the Mirror's edge, dimming its glare.

"Each defines the other. Free will—the greatest gift bestowed upon creation—grants the power to choose, but it also invites danger. The consequences of choices ripple across the cosmos, shaping harmony or discord. Shadows prey on fear and doubt, corrupting those who are unguarded. They twist choices into instruments of despair."

Selenus stiffened, crossing his arms. His sharp gaze cut through the ethereal light that surrounded Demiurge.

"You speak of balance and trust." His voice seared with an edge. "But why should we trust you when you've consorted with the very shadows you claim to oppose? We saw you. You've studied them, haven't you? Who's to say you're not one of them?" His hand closed around the Sword's hilt, not drawing it, but not releasing it either.

Demiurge's light lost some of its brilliance, though her countenance remained unchanged.

"Your skepticism is not misplaced, Selenus," she said evenly. "Confidence must be earned, not demanded. But understand this—knowledge of one's adversary is essential to victory. To vanquish the darkness, one must know its depths. I sought understanding, not allegiance. Though at great risk, the experience nearly ended my existence. But it taught me what I needed to do."

Selenus's expression darkened further, and he narrowed his eyes. "Is that so? And now you ask us to cross into Solarae. My brother's domain—bathed in perpetual light. Do you realize the gravity of what you're asking?"

Demiurge's piercing eyes fell on him. "Unity demands vulnerability, Selenus. Only through humility can strength be forged, not domination. It is by embracing what you fear that you will forge the unity required to heal what has been broken."

Selenus gasped under his breath. His jaw worked, and he glanced away, unwilling—or perhaps unable—to respond.

Wilhelmina walked toward the Mirror, which lay on the mossy ground, and bent down on her knees beside it. "If shadows feed on fear and doubt... what does the Mirror do?" Her fingers brushed against the cool, glowing surface. "What is its purpose?"

"It is both a tool and a test," Demiurge explained. "It reveals truths—sometimes harsh ones—and grants access to the paths required to restore balance. Yet those fated to hold it may look upon it without consequence. Crispin was never meant to bear its power, but you, Wilhelmina, were."

"Me?" Wilhelmina rose to stand and took a step back, her brow furrowing deeply.

"Yes, my child," Demiurge said. "The Mirror's essence resonates with yours. It is why you are its keeper."

As Demiurge spoke, her light flickered like a dying star, her voice resonating with centuries of longing.

"We knew of the fractures..." Her tone grew somber as her gaze shifted toward the Mirror. "This Mirror is also my prison, a choice made alongside Lambda, your father."

The Arbor's low hum deepened, vibrating faintly through Wilhelmina's boots.

"It was the only way to safeguard Aetherwyn from collapsing when the shadows threatened to consume it," Demiurge continued. "We understood the cosmos required agents of balance—our child and her friends—to repair the fractures in creation. My imprisonment was necessary to ensure your journey would unfold as it must. I could not intervene openly before this moment..."

Wilhelmina's heart skipped. The mysterious figure in the ruins—the one who had spoken of balance with both hope and despair—had been her father?

"But I saw him—he was in the ruins." Her voice caught, and her gaze fell to the ground. "Why didn't he tell me? Why didn't either of you?"

"Lambda watched over you from afar, guarding your path while respecting your autonomy. It was a difficult choice, born not of indifference, but of trust in your strength."

Wilhelmina's shoulders sagged. "I don't know if I can forgive him... or you."

Demiurge lowered her head. "Forgiveness, like strength, is a choice. One you must make in your own time."

Wilhelmina's eyes glistened with unshed tears. "I-I know that... your sacrifice... You did it for us."

"I did it for all of creation." Demiurge lifted her gaze. "But it was always meant to be you and your companions who would mend what has been torn. Through your unity, courage, and free will, you can accomplish this and restore balance."

"But we've freed you. Why can't you vanquish the darkness?"

"Lambda and I could not take that risk. Our powers are too volatile, the polar opposite of the darkness. Any direct hand we give could be disastrous. My form is but a fragment of what I was." Demiurge's tone was heavy with sorrow.

"A spectral echo, bound to this Mirror as both its warden and prisoner. Though I can guide you, I cannot wield the might needed to change what has transpired. My release hinges only on the power of Omega Energy."

"But I simply thought that once we found you, our mission would be over, and we could go home!" Wilhelmina said in a bitter whisper.

"Alas, no." Demiurge shook her head. "The journey is far from over. It depends on your defeat of the darkness and replenishing the Omega's reserves, for there is not enough at this time to release me from the Mirror's spell."

"This is all too much." Wilhelmina's breath came rapidly. "What if I make the wrong choices? I'm already to blame for this terrible thing happening to Crispin."

She knelt at his side, her hands brushing his frozen form. "I should have warned him," she whispered, tears streaking her face.

"I should have stopped him." Her voice cracked as she looked at Demiurge. "I've already failed him once. How do I make this right?" Her grip tightened around the Love Blossom, the stem bending beneath her fingers.

"That you question yourself speaks to your humility and fortitude, and you carry more courage than you realize, Wilhelmina," she said in a gentle tone. "Trust in yourself and in the bonds you share with your companions. In this way, you shall find the strength to carry out your purpose."

"I-I don't know..." Wilhelmina hung her head, squeezing her eyes shut. Her hands trembled at her sides, holding the weight of her doubts. "I want to believe in myself, but I'm uncertain if I can carry this alone."

Demiurge's gaze rested on her with a softness that belied the significance of her words.

"Wilhelmina," she began, "you are more than you know. You were created to be a bridge—a vessel of harmony between light and dark, a union forged from the love between me and Lambda, your father. Within you dwells the binding spell of that love, a force that can heal the rifts that threaten this world."

Wilhelmina's hands twisted in the fabric of her dress, and when she found her voice, it wavered.

"A bridge? I... I've always wondered about my nightly visions, where I saw light and shadow entwined. Was that... was that you?"

A gentle smile graced Demiurge's spectral features. "Yes, child. Those visions were my gift to you—a reminder that you are never alone. They were meant to guide you, to prepare you for the role you were destined to fulfill."

Wilhelmina's shoulders sagged. "But I don't feel... worthy."

Demiurge stepped closer, her radiant form seeming to embrace Wilhelmina with its warmth. "Worthiness is not bestowed upon you; it is something you discover within yourself. Trust in your heart, for it is pure."

She shifted her attention to Selenus, her eyes narrowing. "And you, Selenus, were also born of light and dark, yet your path differs from hers." Her voice resonated with quiet authority.

"You were made to forge unity, not through force, but through humility and vulnerability. It is through these qualities—not dominance—that true courage is found."

Selenus's expression tightened, a flicker of resistance crossing his face.

"Unity," he repeated, his voice edged with skepticism. "It sounds noble, but how does humility serve in a world that values power? My choices... my past—they don't reflect unity. They reflect failure."

"Your doubts do not diminish you, Selenus. They humanize you. True unity is not born of perfection, but of flaws embraced. You have the ability to inspire and lead—not through fear, but through the fortitude of shared purpose."

Selenus's jaw clenched, his hand instinctively brushing the pocket where his father's glowing orb lay.

"You ask much," he muttered, his tone guarded. "To lead through vulnerability... to embrace my flaws... It feels like surrender, not strength."

"Humility is not surrender," Demiurge countered. "It is the strength to admit what you do not know, the courage to trust others, and the wisdom to build something greater than yourself. Unity demands that you walk this path, not alone, but with those who will guide and challenge you."

Wilhelmina interrupted. "Demiurge... you said your freedom depends on Omega Energy. But what exactly is it?"

Demiurge pointed at the Mirror, its surface rippling. "It is the essence of creation. Battles with the shadows have drained it, leaving the cosmos frayed. It is tied to a rare celestial phenomenon—the Omega Event."

The companions exchanged uneasy glances.

"What is that?" Wilhelmina asked.

"Once every millennium, the heavens align in a cosmic symphony, flooding the Whispering Woods with unparalleled power. It is here that Omega Energy is renewed and safeguarded."

Wilhelmina leaned forward, her brow furrowed. "The Whispering Woods... they're a reservoir for this energy?"

"Precisely... the last one," Demiurge replied. "It is in the Sanctuary that Somnius and his kin safeguard its renewal. His daughter, Seraphina, holds the path forward. But the shadows' influence has disrupted their preparations, and they cannot succeed alone. I don't think they even realize it yet." She paused. "Only you can restore it, Wilhelmina."

She turned her gaze to Selenus. "And you, Selenus... with your friends and others who join you to help."

"Then... we must go with no time to waste," Wilhelmina said with determination. "When Lumina's life force weakened, she returned to her home for her mother's healing. If the shadows have reached there too... I won't let her suffer alone."

Selenus winced, pulling his eyebrows together. "I regret this news about your friend, Wilhelmina. I-I'm sorry to be the cause."

Wilhelmina gasped, but she said nothing and met his tight gaze.

Demiurge's expression turned somber. "Solarae is not merely a destination," she warned. "It is a land bathed in eternal daylight, ruled by Selenus's brother, Phaethon. The tensions between light and shadow will challenge you at every turn."

Selenus stiffened. "Phaethon's domain..." he muttered. "You would send us into the heart of his power? How can we trust that this is not another manipulation?"

Demiurge met his eyes steadily. "Your skepticism is understandable," she said. "But trust is not the issue here—necessity is. The stakes demand that you face what lies ahead. Solarae holds the answers you seek and the allies you need."

The air grew heavier, charged with unspoken tension as Demiurge's voice grew urgent.

"The shadows know of the Omega Event," she warned. "They seek to corrupt its energy into a weapon of despair and chaos. Should they succeed, the rifts in reality will widen, and existence itself will unravel."

The companions stood frozen, the gravity of her words rendering them silent.

"The timing is critical," Demiurge continued. "When the stars align in the Omega constellation, and the intergalactic meteor shifts from tranquil blues to fiery crimson, the Event will begin. It will paint the skies in opposing hues—a dance of light and dark that mirrors the balance of creation."

Wilhelmina's thumb worried the Love Blossom's bent stem until the fibers creaked.

Aria spoke up hesitantly. "If we fail... what happens?"

Demiurge's light dimmed, her tone laden with sorrow. "If the Omega Energy is lost to the shadows, it will cast our world into unending chaos. The harmony we fight to restore will be irreparably broken."

The companions stood arrayed before the Enchanted Mirror, whose surface quivered with light. A peculiar hush fell around the Celestial Arbor and the clearing surrounding it, broken only by the rustle of leaves.

Demiurge hovered nearby, her spectral form flickering like a living flame. "Behold the Enchanted Mirror," she said, her tone resonant like the distant toll of a bell. "It is a gateway... and a test reserved for those who dare to unite light and shadow."

Selenus shifted his stance and rested a hand upon the Sword's hilt. He cast a sidelong glance at Wilhelmina, whose hands cradled the Sphere.

"Light and shadow." He spoke as though tasting the words and finding them heavy.

Demiurge inclined her head. "The Sphere of Golden Thread and the Sword of Truth's Eye are embodiments of primal forces—the eternal choreography of harmony. They must be united on the Mirror's surface."

Wilhelmina's breath synchronized with Aria's—three inhales, three exhales—before either of them moved. She looked down at the Sphere, her expression betraying her uncertainty. "And me? What is my part in this?"

"You, my child, are the key that will unlock the path forward. This Mirror is bound to our lineage. Your cosmic imprint alone allows you to view it without suffering the consequences. Through your vision, its power will awaken."

Wilhelmina's grip tightened imperceptibly, and for a moment, she appeared motionless, like a figure in a portrait captured in indecision.

The companions exchanged glances, their unease palpable.

Selenus's brow furrowed, his expression caught between exasperation and concern. "You've faced worse odds," he said. "You can do this."

Wilhelmina twisted her head, meeting his eyes.

"Stand against your fear," Demiurge encouraged. "Trust in yourself, as I have always trusted in you, my daughter."

Wilhelmina slowly turned her head to see her mother's saddened eyes and gentle smile. She lifted her chin slightly, and a tremor of resolve rose in her voice. "Well... there's no better time than now."

Her heel lifted—then settled once more—as if her body needed one final agreement before following her will. She gave a curt nod toward Selenus. But before she could step forward, Flora's voice broke through the tense silence.

"Wait!" She glanced at Crispin's frozen form, her eyes wide. Her hands hovered over him, a silent promise to remain. "I can't leave him like this. What if—what if something happens while we're gone?"

Demiurge regarded Flora with compassion and approval. "Your choice is noble."

"Crispin was always the brave one." Flora's voice caught as she knelt next to him. "Now it's my turn. He'd do the same for me." Her hands rested lightly on his frozen form, a silent promise binding her to remain.

Demiurge nodded. "Remain here and guard your friend. The Mirror's magic will shield this place, keeping you safe until their return."

Flora adjusted her position beside Crispin and nodded, though her lips quivered. "You'd better come back. All of you."

Wilhelmina offered a small, trembling smile. "We will."

❧

As Wilhelmina, Selenus, and Aria focused on the Mirror, the air shifted, carrying a delicate, intoxicating fragrance. From the Celestial Arbor, a small branch with a single blossom detached and drifted downward, settling into Demiurge's outstretched hand. She held the cutting aloft.

"This is a Love Blossom—a symbol of unity, hope, and renewal. It is the light within darkness and reminds us that even amid the shadows, harmony may yet bloom." She handed the branch to Wilhelmina.

The companions' lips parted as they watched the flower's petals radiate with hues that shifted like the morning sky.

Wilhelmina's fingers brushed the stem, the light reflecting in her eyes. "It's beautiful," she said with reverence, "but what must I do with it?"

"In Solarae, amidst the eternal sands, you must plant its seeds," Demiurge replied. "This cutting will guide you and reveal what must be protected and restored. Keep its light close, for it will fortify you when the shadows press hardest. Now... it is time to lay the artifacts upon the Mirror."

Selenus approached first, drawing the Sword from its sheath. Its edge gleamed, a shadow that appeared to drink the surrounding light. He placed it gently on the Enchanted Mirror's surface, where it rested with an audible hum.

Wilhelmina followed suit, her steps deliberate. She raised the Sphere, its radiance pulsing in tempo with the Mirror's glow, and set it beside the Sword.

The instant the two artifacts touched, the Mirror's surface surged violently, the silver liquid expanding into an area wide enough to carry them all.

Demiurge's voice, soft yet commanding, broke through the reverie.

"It is time."

Wilhelmina hesitated. Yet, as she looked into Demiurge's eyes—eyes that mirrored hers—she filled her lungs and climbed onto the Mirror's expanded surface. Her reflection merged with the silvery expanse as though she were stepping into a dream.

Selenus joined her, clasping her hand, his attention focused on her.

Aria completed the trio, grasping Wilhelmina's other hand, the plant cutting interlaced between their fingers. Her voice hummed a melody that calmed the trembling Mirror.

The blossom's gleam intensified, and its light wove into Aria's song as though part of the celestial design.

For an instant, the clearing seemed suspended in time. The Mirror's light enveloped them, and the blossom cutting pulsed with a gentle glow that whispered promises of hope. Its surface, now alive with swirling, silvery light, throbbed in rhythm with the companions' collective breaths.

As the Sphere and Sword rested upon it, their energies intertwined, sending waves of light and shadow cascading outward in a mesmerizing dance.

Demiurge addressed them with motherly tenderness. "The path is open. Solarae and the trials that await you lie beyond this gateway. Trust in yourselves—and in one another."

She turned her luminous gaze to each companion. "The shadow that tore through our cosmos lingers still," she warned. "It feeds on despair, solitude, and division. As you step into this next phase, remember this: unity is your greatest weapon. Hold fast to one another, and you will endure."

She looked at Wilhelmina with warmth. "My child, you carry within you the strength to bridge what others would keep apart. Trust in that strength. And know that I am with you always."

To Selenus, her tone grew firmer. "You, Moon Prince, must let go of your doubts. Strength is not found in the absence of vulnerability but in the courage to embrace it. Find the conviction to harness the power of unity."

As Selenus stared into the Mirror's churning depths, his brother's face appeared for a fleeting moment—sharp yet unreadable. He exhaled shakily, the weight of unspoken words heavy in his chest.

"If unity is the answer," he murmured, "perhaps it's time I stopped running... and faced him. Only then can I hope to heal what we broke."

Demiurge's light flickered briefly, and she addressed Aria. "Your voice will guide and heal when all else falters. Use it wisely, for its power is greater than you yet know."

With her words, the Mirror's surface rippled, expanding outward into a vortex of swirling energy. Its depths seemed to beckon, alive with a power that resonated through the clearing.

Flora, standing protectively beside Crispin's immobile body, called out to them. "Don't you dare leave me waiting too long!"

Her attempt at bravado did little to mask the tremor in her voice, but her determination was unmistakable.

Wilhelmina turned her head toward Flora, her tears threatening to spill over.

"We'll come back with Crispin's cure—and with hope. And we will free you, Mother!"

The moment they entered the portal, the clearing behind them dissolved, replaced by a cyclone of light and shadow. They found themselves weightless, suspended within it as images and sensations rushed past them. The light within the Enchanted Mirror surged, and visions formed within its depths.

Wilhelmina's breath caught as a vision of Solarae's deserts appeared. Golden sands stretched infinitely under a relentless sun, giving way to ancient ruins. The Omega constellation burned bright above the scene, its stars moving in progression towards its alignment.

Selenus's jaw tightened as shadows flitted across the vision of the sands. Vague yet menacing forms seemed to lurk at the illumination's edges. His brother's domain. How long had he avoided this place, nursing his resentment in the shadows?

He now glimpsed his brother's face, distorted and unreadable, hovering just beyond his reach.

Aria gasped, her eyes fixed on a vision of herself standing before a great tree, its roots burrowing into the sands as its branches reached toward the heavens. A melody drifted from the Mirror, entwining with her voice in a haunting harmony.

Demiurge's final words echoed, carried on the winds of the vortex. *"The shadow will test you, but your bond will guide you. Go forth, my children, and restore the light."*

When they emerged on the other side, the arid heat of Solarae greeted them, its golden dunes stretching beneath the blazing sun.

19. The Sun Prince

The sun, a merciless eye above, scorched the desert sand into waves of golden fire on a sea of heat. It distorted the air and bent the horizon into fractured images, blurring the lines between reality and illusion.

"Where are we?" Aria's voice rose against the gusts of wind, but it faltered under the strain of her parched throat. She shielded her eyes with a quivering hand.

"This is Solarae, my brother's land." Selenus's tone was clipped, weariness edging his words. His Sword was now sheathed at his side, but he kept his grip firmly on its hilt.

He scanned the undulating dunes. "From here, the distance to his palace is—farther than I'd hoped."

Wilhelmina blinked against the blinding sunlight and clutched the Sphere of Golden Thread and Love Blossom cutting tighter.

"I hope this little plant can bring life back to this barrenness," she said, as grains of sand whipped against her face like pinpricks.

In the lush, verdant forests of Miragwyn, the travelers had layered shawls and scarves, which had warded off the chill in the crisp mountain air. Now, their sweat-drenched garments clung to their bodies.

Bent with exhaustion, they moved as specters against the barren expanse. Each breath they took seemed a minor triumph, and their slow, deliberate steps faltered often. The sand drifts quickly swallowed any trails they left behind.

"The harsh panorama must have seen many a mission end within the dunes, its travelers lost in the endless desert." Wilhelmina's voice, barely audible over the wind, broke the stillness. "No. I have to keep going. Crispin is counting on us... and so is my mother." She tossed her head and focused on the shifting sands beneath her feet.

A shadow too unsteady to pinpoint followed them. Aria glanced back uneasily, her steps slowing. "The hairs on my scalp are standing on end. Do you feel it? Like we're being watched."

Wilhelmina looked over her shoulder. She saw Selenus's unwavering stare. "M-maybe? Just a little..."

His expression grim, he unsheathed his Sword, its blade glinting under the oppressive sunlight.

"The darkness gathers wherever there is light," he murmured. "And my brother has light enough to draw it." He surveyed the dunes ahead, searching for lurking threats.

Aria's head tilted, as if listening to something carried on the wind. She faltered, her footing giving way. Selenus lunged forward to catch her elbow, but she waved him off.

"I'm all right," she said, through her shallow breaths.

He nodded, although he adjusted his pace to stay close behind her.

Wilhelmina lowered her eyes to the fragile sprig cradled in her arms and exhaled sharply. The plant's edges twitched, fighting against the harsh conditions, but its petals had wilted and now hung perilously limp.

Aria's coloring had become dangerously pale. Her brows knit together as she watched her struggle under the heat.

"We've got to get to water quickly."

The shimmering dunes shifted with a cruel sentience, their golden expanse swallowing every footprint as if to guard against intruders. Despite the brutal environment, they pressed on.

Hours later, as the suffocating heat continued to batter them, Aria's steps faltered with greater frequency, her breaths shallow and uneven.

Wilhelmina raised a hand. "We should stop."

"I'm fine." Aria touched her brow, her breathing labored. "I just need... a moment to—" Her knees buckled, and she crumpled to the ground.

"Aria!"

Wilhelmina and Selenus rushed to her, kneeling on the scorching sand. Her breathing quickened, her shoulders rising and falling with visible strain.

Wilhelmina stroked Aria's cheeks and brushed the damp hair away from her face. She pressed her forehead against hers, willing her fortitude into her friend. "I've failed you."

Selenus crouched down, his attention fixed on Wilhelmina's anguished face. He placed a steady hand on Wilhelmina's shoulder.

"You didn't fail her."

When she looked away, he reached for her chin, tipping it gently until her eyes met his.

"You must stop blaming yourself for what is beyond your control. A failing here would be to let these doubts win." His lips curved with resignation. "This land tests everyone."

Wilhelmina exhaled shakily, her lips trembling. "These conditions are insurmountable."

"Perhaps, but we've got to keep moving. If we stop, we lose."

"Of course. You're right. Doubt paralyzes." Wilhelmina sighed. "Thank you."

Selenus dropped his hand from her chin and helped her to her feet. "Don't be overly hard on yourself." He leaned down again and gathered Aria's limp body in his arms.

"Let's find shelter," he said simply.

Wilhelmina swallowed, nodding, and watched Selenus lift Aria, his muscles bunching.

The sun's unrelenting glare scorched the air, turning it into a haze that distorted the horizon. They trudged through the unforgiving terrain in silence, broken by the gusting wind and the crunch of sand underfoot.

❧

Just as their exhaustion threatened to break them entirely, the desert's cruel dominion faltered, and the air shifted.

A strange, golden calm spread across the sands. Shadows stretched across the knolls, longer than the waning sun could account for. Even the sand underfoot grew cool to the touch.

Wilhelmina froze mid-step. "What is that?" She squinted, shielding her eyes against the glare.

Selenus halted beside her, his breathing ragged from carrying Aria.

A glimmer sparked in the distance, elusive as a star at dawn's edge. It grew brighter, expanding into a wave of radiance that crashed against the desert's verge.

Their breaths caught, as though uncertain whether the sight heralded salvation or another cruel mirage.

The radiance intensified, resolving into the distinct silhouette of a rider upon a magnificent firesteed wrought from the sun's flames. It galloped down a path of light, its hooves leaving trails of embers. Mane and tail flicked with flames without consuming beast or horseman.

Phaethon emerged as if summoned by the sun itself. He rode with practiced ease, his fiery aura a grand display of his power and authority. Even the barren landscape appeared to bow to his presence. Behind him, loyal guards followed in silence, their glimmering forms cutting through the heat haze with precision. His sharp stare swept over them.

Wilhelmina's breath caught when she saw Lumina at Phaethon's side. She looked nothing like the frail, fevered sprite she had last seen. Instead, she seemed renewed, her strength radiating like the dawn itself.

Her golden hair caught the sunlight like spun stars, and her bearing emitted a resilience that defied the desert's cruelty as she rode her own ethereal steed. A calm yet watchful expression appeared on her face.

The friends exchanged a look, and in that moment, no words were needed. A smile of kindred affection passed between them, a silent promise that they were still allies, still connected by their shared purpose.

Phaethon dismounted first, his piercing gaze surveying the small group. He glanced briefly at the wilting flower in Wilhelmina's arms, a subtle furrow crossing his brow before his attention snapped to Selenus.

"So, little brother, you have graced us with your presence. And here I was thinking the desert might devour you if you tried."

Selenus maintained an impassive countenance, yet his jaw tightened.

"The arid land is harsh and may devour the weak, but I have learned to walk its edges and return stronger." He pointed a look at Phaethon. "And it is not as unforgiving as some."

Phaethon smirked. "You mean me, of course, and are always so quick to deflect your own failures."

Selenus bristled, his grip tightening on Aria's limp form. His silence, however, spoke volumes—a quiet defiance honed by years of standing in his brother's shadow.

Before the tension could mount further, Wilhelmina stepped forward, her chin lifted despite her obvious exhaustion. "Your timing is impeccable, Your Highness. Our gratitude is sincere."

Phaethon's eyes shot to her, narrowing slightly. Wilhelmina's resolute posture seemed to surprise him, and the corners of his mouth twitched as if considering a smile.

"Indeed. It seems your resolve is as stubborn as my brother's."

"Selenus guided us through trials that would have broken most." She did not falter. "His strength is not so easily dismissed."

Phaethon's smirk faded, replaced by a flash of guarded emotion. He lowered his head slightly. "If you say so."

Lumina dismounted gracefully, her presence softening the tension. She approached with a healer's urgency, her eyes sweeping over Aria. She placed a hand on Aria's forehead, and a golden light emanated from her palm.

Moments later, Aria stirred, her breathing returning to normal. She blinked up at Lumina, her voice hoarse. "I thought... we'd never see you again."

"The desert carries whispers of those in need," Lumina said, her voice soothing. "I sensed your struggle and convinced Phaethon to intervene. I'm glad we arrived in time."

Wilhelmina stepped closer, her expression softening as she looked at Lumina. "It is good to see you well again. After the shadow... I feared..."

Lumina interrupted her, but her smile deepened. "It took time, but the stars are kind to those who endure, and your strength brought me through the shadows as I made my way home."

Her gaze shifted briefly to the Love Blossom. "This bloom's light carries a purpose, just as we all do."

Phaethon, meanwhile, observed the scene with a detached air, though he watched Lumina's interactions. A glimpse of something indecipherable passed over his features before he refocused his attention back to Wilhelmina.

"This land is unforgiving of outsiders, so why are you here?" he asked bluntly.

Wilhelmina straightened, pressing the plant closer to her chest. "We bring a cutting of the Love Blossom from the Celestial Arbor in Miragwyn. It was given to us by the Enchantress herself."

Lumina's brows rose. "You found the Enchantress?"

"Yes, but she remains imprisoned." Wilhelmina steeled herself, meeting Phaethon's gaze. "This plant must take root in Solarae. It is key to restoring balance—not just here, but across all realms."

Phaethon studied her intently, his expression inscrutable. "Bold. But boldness alone will not protect you from what lies ahead."

"Then guide us," Wilhelmina said without hesitation. "If you wish to see Solarae thrive, help us plant this living branch and retrieve what we need for the greater good."

"This is what you plan to achieve with my little brother?" Phaethon's attention flicked to Selenus. "It's rare to witness your return. I had wondered if the shadows had finally claimed you."

"The shadows have taught me resilience—something I doubt your unyielding light or indulgence could ever provide," Selenus replied coolly.

A brief, inscrutable flicker crossed Phaethon's face. "Perhaps the shadow taught you something after all, though we'll find out if it's enough."

"Your brother has faced shadows you cannot imagine. He has led us through dangers that would test the strongest hearts. I trust his strength implicitly, even if you do not."

Wilhelmina's voice cooled, a quiet firmness entering her tone. She knew, perhaps better than anyone, the raw struggle Selenus had faced, and for a flash, she remembered her own judgment, her own denial that had contributed to his pain. But she also remembered his unwavering resolve in Miragwyn. That memory—sharp and true—fueled her defense.

Phaethon exhaled sharply. "Very well. But you'll find Solarae's challenges are not so easily overcome." He nodded once, curtly. "Follow me."

The group mounted the firesteeds provided by Phaethon's guards. Under a sky painted in purples and gold, the beasts carried them swiftly over the sands toward the palace. Yet the dissonant hum of impending dangers persisted.

❧

The rhythmic sound of hooves against the sand filled the air. Lumina rode beside Phaethon, their dynamic drawing curious glances from the group. While Phaethon's manner was reserved, Lumina's warmth seemed to balance his aloofness. As they led the way, the subtle tension between them was clear. The unspoken bond hinted at deeper feelings not yet acknowledged.

Wilhelmina glanced at Selenus. His features showed deep lines of fatigue. For a moment, the weight of the journey seemed to settle between them, unspoken but palpable.

"You surprised me back there," he said finally, his voice low but clear in the stillness.

She turned to him, a crease forming between her eyes. "Surprised you? How?"

"You've carried this mission on your shoulders without faltering. Even in the face of doubt, you move forward."

Her grip tightened on the reins, but a smile curved on her lips. "I practically gave up back there, were it not for you. But there's too much at stake, and necessity is the one thing keeping me going. Not strength."

"It is strength," he countered. "And courage."

She studied him, her expression curious. "And you? You have returned to Solarae, a place tied to so much pain for you. That takes bravery."

Selenus's features hardened, but a trace of vulnerability crossed his face. "Coming back was never part of the plan. But I've learned that some battles can't be fought from a distance."

"Then we fight together." Wilhelmina reached out, her hand brushing lightly against his arm. "None of us is alone in this."

He met her stare, but his mouth formed a small smile. "No. I suppose we are not."

Wilhelmina held the Love Blossom close, looking toward the palace, looming on the horizon. Its gilded towers pierced the twilight sky, promising refuge.

❧

Under the sunset's glow, the amber sands gave way to Phaethon's oasis. His palace rose from the barren dunes like a phoenix, its golden spires glimmering like a mirage amid the desert's stark expanse. But where the desert demanded resilience, the palace spoke of indulgence, its opulence seemingly untouched by the trials that plagued the realm.

Inside, the palace pulsed with life, and the weary travelers entered a courtyard where the splendor unfolded. Fountains sang like wind through crystal chimes. Mosaics on the walls, gleaming like molten fire, depicted valor and myth, where every hue was a fiery echo of Solarae's rich history.

While they moved back and forth around this architectural magnificence, the attendants, though masked and silent, cast cautious looks at the newcomers.

Wilhelmina and Aria exchanged a look, their brows pulling together. Despite the orchestrated beauty, a subtle tension that hinted at invisible barriers lingered.

Phaethon's guards led them to a grand hall, bowing deeply before taking their leave. Adorned with lively tapestries and illuminated by floating orbs of amber light, the room carried a hum of magic that pulsed through the air.

The group was ushered to a low table laden with a feast fit for royalty. Despite their fatigue, the sight of fresh fruit, golden bread, and crystalline goblets of water brought a spark of gratitude to their faces. The lavish banquet laid out before them contrasted with their recent straightforward fare.

Aria broke the silence. "I feel out of place in all this opulence... especially compared to Miragwyn's simplicity."

"These walls remind me of the luxury I knew," Selenus mused. "I wonder if I've become a stranger to it or if our journey has changed what I see as valor."

Before Wilhelmina could respond, Phaethon walked towards them. The golden crown atop his head scattered beams of sunfire, and his robes glimmered like liquid gold. Tall and regal, his presence drew every eye, his features illuminated as if by a haloed light around him.

It appeared as if an invisible thread bound the palace to its ruler, and its splendor depended on Phaethon's light.

He now gestured at the feast, his tone brisk. "Please eat. You'll need strength for whatever foolish quest you've undertaken."

The brothers exchanged tense glances, their rivalry casting an unspoken shadow over the opulent setting. Wilhelmina glanced at Selenus.

A hard edge jutted from Selenus's jaw. "It's hardly foolish. The balance of all realms is at stake."

Phaethon's eyes flashed with fire. "The balance faltered because you couldn't resist temptation, brother. You're always seeking shadows where light should reign."

"And you?" Selenus straightened his posture. "Blind to everything but your own reflection... and unwilling to admit that shadows must exist for light to have meaning."

Wilhelmina looked at Phaethon squarely in the eye. She remembered the Book of Truth's words, her own initial unwillingness to see Selenus's true heart, and the bitter irony of her past denials. Now, seeing the profound change in him, her conviction solidified.

“Your brother carries the weight of this mission with more courage than most. His choices may have cast shadows, but it’s his resolve that presently fights to restore the balance you claim to protect.”

“My brother’s impulsiveness gave darkness an opportunity to threaten and destroy us,” Phaethon snapped. “And at present our father suffers to take his place, desperately giving up his life force until my brother fixes the repercussions of his folly.”

Wilhelmina gasped. She spun her head toward Selenus. “Your father is doing what?”

Selenus stood up abruptly, his chair falling back on the hard marble floor. He curled his fists. “Be silent, Phaethon!”

“And still you bring this threat to my doorstep.” Phaethon leaned back in his seat. “Tell me, little brother, when did you develop such grand ideals?”

“Enough.”

Wilhelmina’s voice, calm but firm, cut through the tension. She met Phaethon’s gaze without flinching.

“Your brother speaks the truth. We are here to plant the Love Blossom in Solarae. Its light can fortify the barriers that protect your realm—and all others.”

Phaethon scrutinized her, his face blank. “You speak boldly for a stranger. But tell me this. Why should I risk Solarae’s ancient defenses for your crusade? My realm has its trials, its own balance to maintain.”

Lumina, seated beside Wilhelmina, leaned forward. “Because the darkness we fight is not confined to one realm, Your Highness.” Her voice was gentle but resolute. “It is a tide that shall consume us all if left unchecked. Your ancestors understood this when they forged alliances to protect these lands. Do you not carry their legacy?”

Phaethon’s eyes blazed. Her words had struck a chord, and his pride remained evident in the imperious tilt of his head. He sighed. “You speak of balance as if it were so easily restored. Very well. I wish to hear more of your plan.”

❧

As Phaethon’s voice rose, sharp as the sun’s glare, a scrape echoed across the dining hall. Aria had pushed back her chair. Her deliberate movements went unnoticed amidst the brewing discord. They betrayed an inner tension visible in the downturn of her lips and the slight crease between her brows.

She stepped into the courtyard, now still under the desert night and devoid of bustling attendants. The gentle murmur of water at the singing fountains offered a soothing counterpoint to the conflict she had left behind. Dipping her fingers into the cool water, she dabbed a few droplets onto her warm forehead.

Slowly, she swayed, her movements fluid as if guided by the fountain's melody. Her dance birthed a song within her, one both haunting and tender. It began as a soft hum, but soon her voice carried through the air, weaving a tune that resonated with the timeless sands and the stars above. Each note held a quiet power, and its echoes wove an intangible balm for the tension within the palace.

The music expanded, its intensity building as it reverberated off the palace's ancient walls. It slipped into the dining hall.

Drawn to its ethereal pull, the guests rose one by one, their earlier discord forgotten. As if in a trance, they followed the melody to its source.

There in the courtyard, they saw Aria standing by the fountains, her eyes closed as her voice unfurled. The water harmonized with her song, the two forces blending into a single, healing resonance.

Wilhelmina and Selenus's eyes met amidst the gathering, their lips curving. Both shed their guarded exteriors for a brief moment.

While he stood apart from the others, even Phaethon's rigid posture softened. His gaze was fixed on Aria.

As the final note faded, Aria's eyelids fluttered open. Quiet settled over the courtyard, broken by the murmur of the fountains and the faint stir in the desert air. The dimmed lamplight from the palace bathed the space in gold and cast long, intricate shadows against the stone walls.

His golden aura subdued, Phaethon stepped forward to stand beside Wilhelmina. His tone was measured. "Your companion has a gift. It is rare to hear such honesty in a song."

Wilhelmina pivoted toward him. "It's what binds us... honesty, unity, and trust."

Phaethon nodded, his eyes still resting on Aria before settling on Wilhelmina. He gestured subtly, inviting her to join him in a quiet corner of the courtyard.

Selenus lingered nearby, his figure half-hidden in the interplay of light and shadow.

Phaethon now leaned against a railing as he looked out at the desert expanse. A sigh, almost imperceptible, escaped him, as if the vastness before him mirrored the endless burden he carried.

"Wilhelmina, I must admit, it has been long since I've had company," he began, though his voice carried a note of hesitation, "and longer still since I've had reason to trust it. Forgive my distance."

"There's nothing to forgive, Your Highness, but it's clear you bear a heavy burden—one that even your radiance cannot fully obscure."

The flickering lamplight cast lines of weariness across his golden face as he turned his face to her. "Isolation is the price of my role. I protect Solarae, yet its splendor often feels hollow. I am surrounded by light, but it offers no warmth."

Wilhelmina's brows furrowed slightly. "Light is not meant to stand alone. It exists to guide, to illuminate paths and lives." She folded her hands before her. "Perhaps you're more isolated than you need to be."

The stillness between them deepened. All that could be heard besides that was the faint sound of trickling fountains in the distance.

"Even with all this light, I have felt alone." His voice dropped to a near whisper as he glanced toward the shadows where Selenus stood. "And I envy him." His lips tightened. "My younger brother possesses a charm and charisma that I cannot match."

"And yet, he envies you more." Wilhelmina sighed. "Look... your roles have tested you, but the light you carry, Your Highness, isn't just yours—it's meant to guide others, including your brother."

Phaethon's jaw clenched. "Our destinies have strained our bond." His voice carried regret. "Selenus and I were once inseparable, but our roles created a chasm between us—jealousy and resentment filled that space."

He exhaled sharply, his frustration barely concealed. "The Enchantress granted Selenus the freedom that I had desired. It was unfair that he received this gift while I remained steadfast in my duties."

"I understand, but your brother's journey has been far from easy. His path has been fraught with mistakes, but he carries their lessons of those mistakes just as you carry the weight of your duty. And he has returned with the will to make amends. Perhaps it's time to see him not as a rival, but as an ally."

Phaethon regarded her, a hint of something unspoken in his golden eyes. "You talk of unity, but it is a noble idea I've always found difficult to grasp and a luxury I could never afford. Even with Selenus, there has always been... distance."

"It's never too late to bridge that distance," Wilhelmina urged, stepping closer.

He breathed softly. "You make it sound simple, yet nothing between us has ever been so."

"You have your doubts." She stepped closer. "I can see them."

Phaethon didn't turn from the horizon. "This realm depends on me. There is no time or room for doubts."

"But you hesitate," she pressed gently, "not because you fear failure, but because you fear being wrong."

His breath caught, though he remained silent before he faced her. "What would you know of it?"

"I know that every choice I've made has risked the lives of others, and I know that if we let fear rule us, we doom ourselves to stagnation."

She tilted her head toward him. "Complexity is no excuse for inaction. The darkness we face will not pause for your misgivings, whether or not you are aware of them."

Phaethon studied her for a long moment. "You speak as if you understand my burden."

"I do. Your Highness, I know what it is to feel the weight of responsibility, leading others when you're unsure if you're strong enough. We all carry it. But we don't have to carry it alone."

Her hand brushed his arm. "This is a time to build, not break further. So, whatever divides you, you are better and stronger with friends who support you. And your light is needed now."

Before Phaethon could respond, Selenus's looming figure emerged from the shadows. His shoulders stiffened as his brother watched him, each moment unspoken but heavy with years of unaddressed grievances.

"Brother. I'd almost forgotten you had returned," Phaethon said, his tone sharp. "But I wonder more if you'd forgotten where your light began."

"I've not forgotten." Selenus snapped. "Perhaps I've just seen what lies beyond it. Our paths diverged long ago, and while I may have chosen wrong, my choices led me here, to see a truth you have yet to grasp. The chasm between us was built by more than just my choices. And I didn't return to challenge you, brother. I came back because this fight needs both of us together. Whatever divides us, the darkness will destroy everything if we allow it."

Phaethon's lips thinned, his gaze fixed on a distant point. "Perhaps you're right," he said at last. "But do not mistake my agreement for forgiveness. Trust must be earned."

"Then we start here... in Solarae."

The stars hung low, and through the desert haze, their light refracted like scattered embers. And now, the tense reconciliation between the brothers seemed as fragile as the thin crescent moon above.

Wilhelmina stood between them, her hands folded and her fingers interlaced. She turned first to Phaethon. The cooler tones of twilight had softened his golden aura.

"Your Highness, the Love Blossom is more than a symbol. The hope of many realms rests on your support to heal what darkness has shattered."

He gave a brief nod. His eyes flickered briefly to Selenus before turning to her. "And yet, you ask much of Solarae. The desert is unforgiving, even to the strongest of seeds."

"This is true," Wilhelmina replied, her tone firm. "But the strength of this realm lies in its people and their resilience and in the legacy you guard so fiercely."

Phaethon's lips curved into a smile, though his expression remained guarded. "And where would you have this blossom take root?"

Selenus stepped forward. "I suggest the edge of the desert," he said. "It is where the boundaries of our realms converge, and it is there that Lumina's family's magic holds sway. Their power is capable of nurturing even the most delicate of life."

Wilhelmina clapped her hands together, her smile broadening. "That is a wonderful idea! From there, we shall meet Seraphina. She will show us the way to the Whispering Woods and the Guardian."

She gestured toward Selenus. "Your brother is right. Seraphina's sanctuary is both a haven and a convergence of Solarae's strength and the magic of renewal. The Love Blossom could thrive there."

Phaethon's eyes drifted to a point beyond the palace spires. "Forging unity is difficult, regardless of your claims. Even now, divisions linger."

“Divisions can be mended,” Wilhelmina countered. “But only if we choose to do so. Your light and your brother’s shadow are complementary, not opposed. One cannot exist without the other.”

For a moment, silence stretched between them. The only sound was the rustle of the arid wind.

Phaethon sighed, his shoulders relaxing slightly. His golden eyes, though still wary, held a glimmer of something akin to understanding, or perhaps just a deeper weariness of conflict.

“Very well. At dawn, we will journey to Lumina’s family home and plant this blossom. But let me be clear. This is not an act of submission. It is a test.”

“A test of hope, then. For all of us. Now that you both are here, our chances of restoring balance are even greater with your complementary gifts.”

A trace of a smile formed on his lips as he bowed his head.

“I suggest you get some rest. The servants shall provide all you need. I bid you good night.” Without another word, he pivoted on his heel to the palace interior, his golden form fading into the shadows of the archway.

With a deep sigh, Wilhelmina exchanged a glance with Selenus and gestured for him to follow. They made their way toward the awaiting chambers, the wind’s murmurs accompanying their steps.

20. Seeds in The Desert

Wilhelmina sat before her dressing table, brushing her hair in measured strokes. She wore a gossamer nightgown—soft as the down of a dove—wrapping her in gentle comfort. Her distant, preoccupied expression stared back at her in the mirror. The flicker of the lantern beside her cast her reflection in muted tones.

From the nearby balcony, a melody drifted, delicate and poignant.

Aria's voice rose and carried with it a sweetness that wove its way through the air like a silken thread.

Wilhelmina paused, the brush stilling in her hand as the song's bittersweet strains called to her. Rising, she stepped outside onto the balcony, the cool stone beneath her bare feet a quiet anchor.

Longing infused every note as Aria's ballad unfolded. The lyrics spoke of Quill, her distant companion, and painted a portrait of devotion that was both intimate and universal.

Brave heart who writes truths yet untold,
Your pen etches futures in whispers bold.
May safety guard your every breath,
For love endures beyond all death.

The melody swelled, ascending to a crescendo. As the final refrain faded, its echoes remained like a prayer offered to the vast night sky.

Wilhelmina sighed. "That was beautiful."

Aria turned her head slowly toward where Wilhelmina's voice had come from. She called softly from the next rail. "Wilhelmina? Is that you?"

"Your music moves my heart! How you describe your love for Quill... It has awakened a feeling within me... like a yearning. Not for a grand, sweeping romance, but for true companionship."

Aria nodded. "You're thinking of him. Despite what you first thought, Selenus has surprised you... and all of us. He's been there through each trial and peril."

"Yes." The words Wilhelmina spoke aloud were almost tentative, as though she sought to give voice to a truth that had been forming. "Something has settled. I believe him now—not the image he presented, but the man revealed beneath it."

A smile played on her lips. "It's the little things... His fumbling with the runes in Miragwyn..." A laugh escaped from her throat. "I found his exasperation more endearing than frustrating. It made him unexpectedly human."

Aria's features softened. "It sounds like you're seeing him for who he really is."

Wilhelmina's smile faded as she gazed out at the night. "Phaethon spoke of his isolation. I'm not unfamiliar with that kind of solitude. It has also shaped my understanding of duty and sacrifice. I have long believed that true connection is a luxury reserved for others—those unencumbered by the burdens of leadership."

"You still doubt it could ever be something you could experience. My love for Quill... Know that it is more than an illusion or a fleeting hope amidst the shadows of our quest. I will not succumb to the fear that such a thing is fragile, doomed to fade beneath the weight of our greater responsibilities. I simply won't."

Wilhelmina turned, her eyes glistening. "Your song... It reminds me of what we fight for."

"And you remind us why we keep fighting." Aria's tone was imbued with a gentle conviction. "We wouldn't have come this far without you. You see the path, even when the rest of us falter."

Wilhelmina inclined her head; a small but genuine smile crossed her lips. "And I'd lack the courage to walk it if you weren't by my side."

"We are in this together," Aria said before retreating to her chamber, the soft click of her door marking the end of their exchange.

Wilhelmina lifted her face toward the heavens. The night stretched, its vast quietude at once daunting and reassuring. She closed her eyelids, inhaling deeply as if the cool desert air might bring clarity to her tangled thoughts.

The sound of footsteps drew her attention, and she turned to see Selenus emerging onto his adjacent balcony.

"Wilhelmina... are you well?" The moonlight gentled his features, lending him an intensity that spanned the space between them.

She hesitated, her fingers tightening on the terrace railing. "I'm... uncertain. This quest, this mission—it feels as though it demands all of me, and I wonder if I will be enough."

She lifted her head to look at him. "I'm surprised at myself to even speak this way."

His countenance softened. "Your strength has guided us, even when doubt threatened to overtake us."

She blinked. "Did you hear Aria's song?"

"Yes... It spoke of hope and that something better awaits us."

Wilhelmina's breath caught as the moonlight reflected in his eyes, illuminating a depth that left her momentarily unmoored.

"This journey has bound the group in ways I never expected. Tomorrow, we take a step toward a future we've dared to imagine. The Love Blossom will be the beginning—for Solarae, and for the wounds we carry."

"No matter the challenges, we shall face them." Selenus extended his hand, his gesture one of solidarity and quiet encouragement.

Their eyes met, the unspoken emotions between them a palpable presence.

Slowly, he leaned closer, his movements tentative but certain. She found herself drawn to him, her heart quickening as the distance between them dissolved. But just as their lips nearly met, a sudden sound—a bird's cry from the desert—shattered the moment.

The orb in Selenus's pocket pulsed like a golden glow spilling into the night. His attention lifted to the sky, and there, the star he had once sought gleamed.

They both drew away, their breaths unsteady.

Wilhelmina laughed, the tension easing. "Good night, Selenus."

He released her hand slowly, the lingering touch a silent promise.

"Sleep well, Wilhelmina."

As she entered her chamber, she paused, glancing back toward him. He remained at the railing, his focus turned to the horizon, as though searching for something beyond the stars. Against the vast expanse of the night, his silhouette appeared changed—no longer cloaked entirely in the shadow that had long defined him.

A delicate glow emanated from his form, pressing against the darkness that sought to envelop him. It was no grand illumination, but the first flicker of a new emotion, fragile but persistent.

Wilhelmina's hand rested on the edge of her balcony entrance. She sighed deeply and turned away, her steps carrying her back into the solitude of her room. The door closed behind her, leaving the courtyard to its quiet. Yet the image of Selenus, standing against the night with shadow and light in subtle tension, resonated in the air, an impression as lingering as the song that had so recently filled the evening.

❧

At first light, the companions gathered to break their fast in the dining hall, where the hum of conversation blended with the rustle of fine linens and the clink of goblets against porcelain. It was a tableau of civility amidst the desert's harshness.

Phaethon presided over the grand table. His laughter mingled with his guests, though his smile faltered, fleeting like the light of dawn. His eyes wandered to the Love Blossom, shining fiercely at the table's center.

A goblet of golden nectar rested in his hand, its liquid catching the first rays of the sun. He breathed deeply and let out a long sigh. He raised the cup with calculated warmth, though a crease in his brow betrayed a mind less certain than his next words.

"To Solarae's dawn and the promise of rebirth. May the Love Blossom's roots bring life to these sands and healing to all who dwell within them."

The group raised their goblets in unison and drank, but Lumina's gaze sought Phaethon. A warmth that suggested more than mere admiration illuminated her expression. Whether he shared this sentiment, however, was uncertain. For all his brilliance, he seemed wholly preoccupied by shadows that neither daylight nor affection could dispel.

Wilhelmina watched her friend's light take on a heightened radiance. Yet Lumina clasped her hands tightly against her breast as if to guard her heart.

She then shifted her attention to Selenus, whose usual stoicism softened into a smile. Even Phaethon's solemn gaze remained on his brother for several heartbeats, though he said nothing.

She cleared her throat and turned toward Phaethon. "To see Solarae cradle this bloom will restore our faith in a future forged from the embers of the past. Your support, Your Highness, strengthens our will."

Phaethon's eyes met hers briefly before a servant, cradling a sword forged from sunlight and its polished sheath, approached. He turned and rose to accept it. With practiced ease, he secured the sheath around his waist and retrieved the sword, lifting it high. The sleek blade radiated fiery brilliance as if infused with the essence of dawn.

"Then let us sow this emblem of hope. May its roots defy even Solarae's harshest trials."

His focus remained fixed on the Love Blossom, as though he were willing its success. With a deliberate motion, he sheathed the sword.

"Come. Let us depart for Seraphina and Lumineon's sanctuary."

The companions rose and made their way to the courtyard where the firesteeds awaited, their blazing forms reflecting the morning light. As they departed the hall, the dawn illuminated their faces, each expression—resolve, hope, uncertainty—etched in its glow.

From daybreak to midday, the firesteeds carried the companions from Solarae's searing sands to an oasis where life defied the desert's cruelty. At the heart of this verdant haven stood the sprites' home, a welcome respite nestled within the valley's embrace. The modest yet enchanting abode seemed a natural extension of the landscape. Blooming flowers and fresh earth perfumed the air surrounding it, while golden light filtered through the canopy of ancient trees nearby.

As they dismounted, they were greeted by Lumineon and Seraphina. Their smiles held both warmth and gravity.

Lumineon's long silver hair shone in the filtered sunlight, cascading over the shoulders of his flowing robes, which were adorned with subtle cosmic patterns. His thin, wiry frame conveyed quiet resilience, and his pointed chin and sharp features gave him an air of ethereal regality, as if carved from ancient stellar essence. His piercing aquamarine eyes gleamed with an almost diamond-like quality.

Beside him, Seraphina's presence was no less striking. Silver strands, threaded with twinkling stars, framed her luminous face, and her gown flowed around her like a living entity, shifting like air or waves on the sea. Her amethyst eyes were radiant and multi-faceted, revealing a world of dreams and possibility in their depths. Her features seemed sculpted by astral forces, and she carried an air of both timeless serenity and quiet power.

“Welcome,” Seraphina said, her tone warm. “This sanctuary has awaited your arrival, and now you are here.” She drew Wilhelmina and Aria into a joyful embrace.

Lumineon extended his hand to Phaethon and Selenus, his grip firm. “The land speaks of your journey. It has witnessed your trials and whispers of the challenges yet to come. But please come inside. You’ll want to shed the dust of the desert before we share a meal.”

The group followed, but their steps slowed as they took in the cozy home. Delicate fabrics, carved wood, and sentimental keepsakes filled the space with a magic that spoke of love and history.

❧

After they’d washed away the desert grit and rested in the shade, Seraphina guided them to an outdoor seating area where low tables held a simple but abundant feast. The atmosphere here was refreshingly different. While more spartan than the palace, the spread was cozy and inviting, showcasing the land’s bounty in dishes made with love.

As they settled, she paused beside a vine-clad wall. Her attention fell on a withered tendril with brown leaves.

“Oh! You poor little one,” she cooed to the lifeless plant. “The desert still reaches for us, even here.”

She brushed her fingers along its brittle stem. In an instant, the vine stirred to life, and tender green tendrils spread across the stone in a cascade of life.

Wilhelmina’s lips parted. “It’s extraordinary... Your touch has awakened life from stone!”

Seraphina then stepped back to admire the cheerful verdure growing before her. “Even in desolation, life persists in Solarae.”

Nearby, Lumina chuckled, “Good thing you caught it in time, Mother.” She stepped closer, though hesitant, as she examined the new vines still growing on the stone. “Your touch restores life so effortlessly. I wonder if... there’s more we could do to prevent the desert’s reach.”

Seraphina responded, her serene smile unwavering. “The land teaches us patience, Lumina. Not all change comes through force. Sometimes, it requires gentle harmony.”

Lumina’s lips pressed into a line, but she nodded. “Of course. You’re right.” She glanced down, her chartreuse eyes revealing a hint of frustration.

"This land is as much a teacher as it is a home. This reminds us that growth, even from the tiniest beginnings, requires careful nurturing," Seraphina explained. "It's always revealing its truths to those willing to listen." She then gestured toward the table. "Come, everyone. Please find a seat, and let us share in the land's bounty."

Wilhelmina looked to Lumina. "Your family's guardianship of Solarae is remarkable—a true legacy of hope."

Lumina nodded, her lips curving into a wistful smile as she glanced at Phaethon's quiet strength. For a brief moment, their eyes met, and his expression grew peaceful, though he said nothing.

As the companions settled around the low tables laden with a simple yet abundant feast—a spread of fruits, herbs, and bread—the warm glow of lanterns cast gentle shadows across their faces. The scent of fresh herbs mingled with the evening air.

Seraphina, seated at one end of the long table, unfolded her linen napkin and spread it across her lap. "Tonight, we weave together our past, present, and future. These bonds will strengthen the path ahead."

Lumina, seated at the center of the table, turned her attention to her mother and then to the guests. "Beneath the stars' watch, let us seek the harmony we've yet to find."

Her father walked to the other end of the table and sat down. "Let us remember that unity is our greatest strength. It has carried us through the trials of the past and will fortify us against the darkness that threatens our future."

As people passed around serving bowls of food, Seraphina turned to Wilhelmina, seated at her right, and touched her arm. "There's a question in your heart." Seraphina leaned forward, lowering her voice.

Wilhelmina hesitated, her hands trembling slightly as she met Seraphina's piercing gaze. "How do you balance it? It feels... impossible, but you make it look so easy."

Seraphina's brows drew together in confusion. "Balance what exactly, child?"

Wilhelmina cleared her throat, matching Seraphina's posture. "Love... with duty."

Seraphina's expression deepened into one of quiet understanding. "Duty gives love direction." She lifted a hand, cupping her palm. "And love gives duty courage." She cupped the other hand. "Together, they weave a tapestry that endures." She joined her palms together, pausing before holding Wilhelmina's uncertain look. "Do you see now?"

Wilhelmina's lips parted. "What if the moment comes when I have to choose, and I get it wrong?" She looked down at her lap. "What if we must sacrifice one for the other?"

Seraphina put a hand on her shoulder. "Then you weigh the moment and trust your heart to choose the greater good. It will not always be easy, but it will always be true." Her gaze drifted across the table. "You lead many, Wilhelmina, but your strength does not lie in solitude. The friendships you nurture will guide you when the path seems unclear."

"Yet you've merged love and duty so seamlessly." Wilhelmina's lips trembled. "How?"

Seraphina glanced at Selenus, then back to Wilhelmina. "Long ago, when I first beheld Lumineon, love struck me like a thunderbolt. I thought I had to choose between honoring my father's wishes and following my heart. But I learned that love is not a distraction—it is integral to our duties. In the end, love strengthened and helped me lead with compassion."

Wilhelmina stole a glance at Selenus, whose gaze beheld her, unreadable yet steady.

"The journey wasn't simple," Seraphina continued. "There were sacrifices and moments of doubt. Yet love became my beacon, guiding me through every storm."

Wilhelmina swallowed slowly, her hands stilling in her lap. "The ancient texts, the ones Gwydion taught me, forewarned that the wedding fairy cannot allow such an occurrence to happen, or the magic will dissipate."

Seraphina tilted her head and scowled. "He told you this?"

"Gwydion has been good to me," Wilhelmina said, her tone sharper. "After the Enchantress and Lambda—my mother and father—had to abandon me, he... took their place and nurtured me. He taught me everything I know."

Seraphina's eyes narrowed. "That may be, and I respect your loyalty, but the owl's assumption is false. The texts speak of love as a danger to your magic, but they warn against love untethered—reckless, selfish love. True love, rooted in duty and sacrifice, is the greatest force of all. It does not weaken your magic, Wilhelmina. It strengthens it."

Wilhelmina nodded, her expression thoughtful. "Yes... But Gwydion told me love would weaken me—that I must guard my heart to wield my power. What if he's right?"

Seraphina cut her off gently, her hand resting on Wilhelmina's trembling fingers. "Gwydion may have acted out of love, but fear often disguises itself as protection. If you look closely, you may find that his warnings reflect his own insecurities, not yours."

She paused, exhaling. "You are not meant to inherit his fears, Wilhelmina—you are meant to transcend them. And perhaps the texts were not as absolute as you were told. It may be that Gwydion believed you needed this warning to remain focused."

Wilhelmina shook her head slowly. "All this time, I thought my magic was bound by rules I couldn't break... but maybe there is another way..." Her words trailed.

"Our ancestors shaped these rules for their time. Their wisdom is a foundation, not a prison. The world has changed, and so must we," Seraphina said as she sat back, folding her hands in her lap.

"In truth, our magic is similar. Mine binds and grows living things; yours does the same for those who wish to bind their love in matrimony and grow a family." Seraphina pointed towards Wilhelmina's heart. "Your magic is not bound by its limits, but by the belief you have in yourself."

Wilhelmina nodded slowly. "To wield such energy as ours is both a gift and a burden."

"Indeed, each decision we make ripples through eternity and shapes every realm." Seraphina's hand rested on Wilhelmina's cheek, her touch anchoring the young fairy in a truth that transcended words. "You already carry the strength you seek, child. Let love guide you—it will never lead you astray."

Wilhelmina sat motionless, her expression shifting as though years of teachings loosened their grip. The moments when warnings loomed like shadows—steering her away from the light of connection—seemed etched upon her face. Yet now, under Seraphina's even regard, those shadows faltered, their power diminished.

"Thank you for sharing your story with me. I have much to think about."

Her shoulders eased, visibly easing her posture. Across the table, Selenus's gentle smile caught her gaze, and for the first time, she did not look away.

❧

The murmurs of conversation between bites of food and sips of drink continued. Wilhelmina set down her fork and exhaled. She looked down the length of the table at Lumineon, who sat at the end of the table. "Your home is truly a haven, and we are grateful for your hospitality."

Seraphina patted Wilhelmina's hand, tutting. "It is our pleasure. But tell us more about what brought you to us."

Wilhelmina squeezed her hands together. "The Enchantress entrusted us with the Love Blossom, and we seek to plant it here in Solarae in a place where it can thrive."

Phaethon nodded. "Selenus believed your sanctuary would offer the best chance for its success."

A knowing gleam shone from Seraphina's face. "It will flourish here, protected from harm. These are consecrated grounds, and ancient forces will rise when the balance is disturbed."

Wilhelmina's expression grew serious. "It is a beginning." She glanced at Selenus and met his eyes. "The shadow Selenus brought to Aetherwyn has catalyzed an imbalance between the realms, sickening the lands and people."

Seraphina shook her head. "But the blossom's planting alone will not be enough to heal the rift between realms."

"Indeed, it will not, unfortunately." Wilhelmina furrowed her brow. "We need to do more. To restore the balance, we must replenish the reserves of the Omega Energy."

Seraphina nodded slowly and took a deep breath. The candlelight reflected in her eyes. "Ah, yes. I understand. You need to reach my father."

Wilhelmina leaned forward, nodding vigorously. "Yes, exactly. Without him, we cannot save Crispin, heal the realms, or free the Enchantress... my mother." Her chin sank as her voice faltered.

"Our friend Crispin looked into a mirror meant for Wilhelmina and is now spellbound," Aria offered. "Flora chose to stay with him, and she still cares for him under the protection of the Enchantress. She told us that the Elixir of Lost Dreams alone can save him."

"And that the Guardian holds the key to mending the Dreamscape," Wilhelmina added. "Without his help, we cannot create more of it."

Seraphina's lips pressed into a thin line as she listened. "The Elixir is vital, both for your friend and for the restoration of harmony itself."

A somber silence settled over the group.

Selenus's deep voice interjected. "Forces seeking to deter us have shadowed our path. We encountered resistance at every step."

Seraphina's eyes gleamed as she folded her hands tightly in her lap. "It is an honor to witness your courage in pursuing this path. It is a righteous one, but it involves significant risks." She glanced at Selenus. "Your return, despite the dangers, speaks volumes."

Lumina, seated beside her mother, leaned forward. "Our powers may have limits, Selenus, but together, we're stronger than any one of us alone. The simple fact that you made it this far attests to that. The trials you've faced must have been terrible, but you worked together to overcome them."

Seraphina turned to her daughter. A flicker of light crossed her features. "Well said, Lumina."

Selenus nodded. "Agreed. It took all of us, leaning on one another, to arrive at your door intact. But there is still much ahead before we can claim success."

"Indeed." Seraphina paused. "In three days, the major cosmic convergence will occur. It is a rare event that will thin the barriers between realms. We had planned to leave tomorrow for my father's retreat and help him prepare for the harvesting of the Omega Event," she said. "It is well that you came when you did."

A ripple of unease passed through the companions. Wilhelmina glanced at Selenus. "Then we have less time than we thought."

"Time is running ahead of us." Lumineon's tone grew serious. "This could either aid your mission or amplify the dangers you face."

A profound stillness followed before Phaethon broke it. "I would rather you did not risk going. Instead, I will join this quest in your place and do all I can to thwart the darkness's threats against the harvest."

Gasps arose, but he raised a hand, silencing them. "As a prince, it's my duty. As one who believes in protecting our dreams, it's my calling. And perhaps, as a brother, it's my path to redemption. Therefore, Seraphina, Lumineon, I ask you to oversee Solarae in my absence. Let me take your place in the harvest."

Surprised murmurs swept through the group. Lumina's eyes widened. But then she raised her eyebrows, and a slight smile played at the corners of her mouth as she tilted her head, her focus fixed on Phaethon.

Seraphina's brows knit together. "Are you certain?"

He nodded firmly. "Solarae will be safe in your care."

"Very well." Seraphina exchanged a thoughtful glance with Lumineon. "We will guard Solarae and strengthen its defenses."

“You honor us, Phaethon.” Lumineon nodded. “We shall ensure Solarae’s endurance.”

“The challenges you face are grave, and we shall direct you,” Seraphina added. “But if the darkness threatens the haven or you fail to reach my father in time, he will invoke the Final Veil—a protection spell sealing the refuge for a century. The preservation of magic depends on the Omega Energy, and it must be harvested before he is forced to speak the last words of the spell.”

Lumina rose from her chair, standing tall. “I will accompany them.”

Seraphina’s brow creased. “Lumina!” she exclaimed, her voice sharp with alarm. “The journey is perilous.”

Lumina shook her head, her expression resolute. “I understand, but I cannot remain here while our world’s future hangs in the balance. I believe my abilities can aid our mission, perhaps in ways tradition has yet to explore.”

Lumineon raised a brow. “You speak of new methods?”

Lumina met his eyes. “Yes, Father. Combining what I’ve learned here might be the key to transforming not just the desert, but the way we fight against the darkness. Solarae’s balance taught me patience—but perhaps it’s time to act.”

Seraphina exchanged a glance with Lumineon before nodding. “Very well.” She gave Lumina a pointed look. “You’ve always sought harmony in innovation, but your path will not be easy. Our connection with this realm is as ancient as the stars, and our ancestors united here long ago to restore harmony when negativity and pessimism—the underlying energies of darkness—threatened. My daughter, if you go, I ask that you carry those lessons and the legacy of our ancestors forward.”

Lumina’s eyes glowed, mirroring the golden hues of the valley. “I’ve learned from this land—the moon’s guidance and the constellations’ melodies taught me to revive life in barren places, where all seemed lost. I’ll carry that knowledge with me, Mother.”

Seraphina stared at the horizon, where the sky hinted at twilight. “The Great Alignment is both an opportunity and a risk. If the darkness gains influence during this time, it could seep into all realms.”

Lumineon, eyes focused on the guests, added, “This event is a nexus of power. If you fail to act in time, the barriers between realms will weaken.”

“Then we must act swiftly,” Phaethon said. “We’ll plant the Love Blossom to bolster Solarae’s defenses and then depart for the Whispering Woods.”

Selenus stepped forward. "Every moment counts. Our actions now will shape the future for many."

Seraphina scanned the group. "The bonds you've forged will guide you. Trust in them, for they are your greatest resource and the magic to see you through the challenges."

To emphasize her point, Lumineon knelt and touched the sand beside the table. A single bloom erupted from the barren ground, its petals vivid against the desolation. "And sometimes, discovering our resilience involves embracing the vulnerabilities we fear. As the desert blooms after rare rains, so too must you find courage in adversity."

Lumina watched the new bloom, and her fingers twitched as if tempted to touch it herself. She took a measured breath and stepped back.

"The land speaks of change," Seraphina said, her focus on the earth beneath them. "The stars converge, and with them, the balance tilts. Our window to act narrows."

Phaethon's voice cut through the tension. "Then we complete the planting and prepare for what lies ahead. The future of the realms demands nothing less."

When the meal ended, conversation thinned into a reverent hush, as though the sanctuary itself had begun to listen.

Twilight now painted the valley in hues of gold and purple. As lanterns dimmed and the valley cooled, Seraphina rose—quietly—and the others followed. Gentle tremors rippled through the earth, and the stars above flickered like distant warnings.

She led the group to the sacred clearing, carrying a basket filled to the brim with gardening tools. The air here was different—heavier, as though imbued with ancient power.

"Long ago, this land was blessed with Solarae's first light," she said, her eyes distant. "But even in the most sacred places, shadows wait."

Lumineon took Seraphina's basket from her and set it at the side of a patch of open, loamy soil for the planting. "These grounds are consecrated by the light of Solarae's first dawn," he explained. "Here, the magic runs pure, a gift from our ancestors."

Lumina had drifted toward a flowering bush and knelt beside it. She brushed her fingertips against its petals with reverence.

Phaethon approached her, his usually confident demeanor tempered with curiosity.

"You seem to thrive here," he observed.

"This is where I learned to bring life to barren places… and where I found my inner fortitude."

Phaethon's expression softened. "It's rare to meet someone who finds power in creation rather than conquest."

She looked up at him, her face alight. "And it's even rarer to meet someone who can see the value in that."

For a brief moment, the burden of his title seemed to fall away, and a smile tugged at his mouth. "Perhaps there's something I can learn from you."

Lumina looked away before the moment could linger. She rose and walked toward the group where the planting would take place. Phaethon followed her, watching her back in silence.

Wilhelmina knelt beside Selenus with the Love Blossom cradled in her hands.

From Selenus's pocket, the orb thrummed like a distant heartbeat. Its radiance seemed to harmonize with the blossom's light, perhaps hinting at an ancient bond.

"Let's see what wonders this little plant's presence will bring." Phaethon's gaze softened when his fingers brushed Lumina's as she passed him the trowel.

Wilhelmina watched their silent interaction as Phaethon shaped the earth with care.

There appeared to be an unspoken tension between them—one rooted not in rivalry but in the stark contrast of their natures. And yet, in that fleeting glance, there was a fragile understanding, a shared yearning for something neither had yet named.

"In this place, the desert's barrenness meets the promise of renewal." Lumina took the cutting from Wilhelmina's hands and, with a flourish of her wrist, the seedlights from the blooms rose into the air and landed in Wilhelmina's palm. "Together, we bring hope to where it is most needed."

Aria's clear voice became a song of blessing for the new growth.

While in this hallowed, quiet place,
Where desert sands and gardens grace,
We plant a seed beneath the sun,

A journey ended, yet begun.

With tender care, the earth we part,
A blossom blooms, a beating heart.
A song of unity we bring.
To life's vast tapestry, we cling.

Wilhelmina cradled the seeds in her hands, and when she pressed them into the soil, a resonant hum from them spread outward, harmonizing with Aria's melody.

From the barren ground, new life ascends.
In harmony, our spirits blend.
Through whispers of the wind's soft call,
Joined we rise. Joined we fall.

Selenus firmed the earth above the seeds. A rhythmic energy then pulsed from the soil between them, responding to the magic. From the ground, a soft light emerged, weaving through the cracks like threads of gold.

The companions exchanged uneasy glances as the light's intensity grew.

"Do you feel that?" Lumina's voice grew quiet as her stare fixed on the glowing earth.

Seraphina's voice cut through the stillness. "The roots of the Love Blossom take hold—but they've stirred forces far older and deeper than the land's magic."

Beneath the endless, starry dome,
We find a place to call our home.
A single bloom, in silence, stands,
Uniting all with gentle hands.

As Aria's song ended, the ground beneath their feet shuddered, and a discordant melody echoed from the horizon.

The new planting and the soil around it pulsed like an erratic heartbeat. A low hum emanating from its roots reverberated through the clearing, a warning cry.

As if in response to the Love Blossom's call, a chilling breeze carried with it a murmuring of sighs that grew louder with each passing moment. Tremors rose from the land, emitting a resonance that both repelled and drew energy closer. The energy, however, carried a dual nature—a force of revitalization and disruption.

Selenus stiffened. "Something stirs."

The sands glistened, and shadows coalesced at the edges of the clearing, becoming spectral forms that shifted in a menacing display.

Lumineon grew still, his expression hardening.

"The guardians have awakened."

The companions instinctively drew closer together, their breaths frosting in the sudden cold. They watched as the guardians loomed larger, armed with ghostly weapons glinting with an otherworldly light.

Seraphina's expression hardened. "These are the guardians of Solarae—protectors of the realm's deepest secrets. The blossom's integration into the sacred sands must have triggered them. Stay alert, for they will test you."

The companions' brows raised in alarm, their faces brightened by the planting's eerie glow. The light flared brilliantly one last time before the clearing descended into chaos.

The spectral guardians launched a full-scale assault, their wisp-like arms reaching with unnerving precision. Each ghostly limb seemed to penetrate the companions' very beings, clawing at their hearts with a terrible, pulling force. Screams erupted as they clutched their chests against the unbearable pain.

Wilhelmina's knees buckled, her resistance fading.

Selenus collapsed beside her, his heartlight wrenched from his chest—a radiant orb glowing like the pale moon—clutched in the smoky fingers of a larger guardian. The spectral figure tightened its grip, and Selenus's breath escaped in a strangled gasp.

"Selenus!"

The scream tore from Wilhelmina as she seized his arm, desperate to pull him back, but the force holding him was unyielding.

Nearby, Aria flailed, her voice reduced to a gurgled sound as another spectral form coiled its wispy fingers around her throat, choking her.

Only Lumineon, Seraphina, and Lumina remained untouched. The protective magic coursing through them seemed to repel the guardian's onslaught. But the sight of their companions writhing under the spectral attack galvanized them into action. They surged toward the breach, their movements synchronized, as though guided by an unspoken plan.

Lumina stepped forward, positioning herself between her parents. Her body emanated a brilliant, transcendent glow, powered by Solarae's stars. Together, the three sprites raised their voices in a harmonic chant, their words reverberating with ancient power—a lost language from a time long forgotten.

Under the light of Solarae's enduring stars
And the depths of the timeless sands,
We call forth the shield of daybreak
To banish the darkness at hand.

As guardians of the dawn and dusk, united,
We weave this spell,
Let this barrier of light encircle our home,
Where peace shall dwell.

The words they spoke flowed like a river of light, casting a brilliant dome around their dwelling. The trio's outstretched hands pulsed with pure energy, weaving the barrier's brilliance into an unbroken shield.

By the boundless light that courses through our veins,
May this sanctuary of strength and hope remain,
In unity, our powers merge, a fortress of light we claim,
Against the dark, we stand as one, our legacy to proclaim.

As the incantation soared to its crescendo, Lumina became the spell's focal point. Her radiance enveloped the clearing, pushing the shadows back into the void from which they came. The guardians' wispy, forceful chokehold around Aria's neck and arms, pulling at Wilhelmina and Selenus's hearts, recoiled. Their spectral forms dissolved into wisps before vanishing. But their whispers remained, echoing ominously.

Wilhelmina, Selenus, and Aria exhaled in relief, huddling together in the clearing's newfound calm. Their eyes glistened as they checked each other—still whole, still breathing.

The new Love Blossom planting shimmered steadily again, but its light now seemed to contain an almost imperceptible shadow, signaling the precariousness of the returned order.

Lumineon broke the silence, his brows drawing together. "This disturbance was merely a prelude." Though his voice was even, he appeared visibly shaken. "We've made things more dangerous by awakening the protector spirits."

Lumina straightened, standing taller. "Father, this shows that our defenses must evolve. It is time for innovation."

Seraphina interjected gently. "Daughter, harmony has always been our goal, not dominance."

Lumineon added, "That's right. Our resilience lies in harmony, which gives us the strength to adapt and overcome the darkness."

Determination edged Lumina's words. "I'm not speaking of dominance, Mother, Father. The guardians attacked us because they couldn't discern our intentions. Their inability to distinguish friend from foe created a new crack for the darkness to exploit."

Lumineon nodded, gripping his chin. "You're right. Solarae and the Whispering Woods must become more than just strongholds—they must embody adaptability. Light and shadow must support one another, not battle endlessly."

Lumina straightened, shoulders squared, her words flowing with quiet certainty. "If we heal the rifts and weave bridges between us, the guardians, and other realms, we can create defenses rooted in understanding rather than walls of division."

"A noble vision, my child." Seraphina held Lumina's face. "But the path forward will demand more than just resolve—it will require trust and unity. These are the ingredients required to create the bridges you speak of." Her expression turned grave. "As you already know, time is of the essence. My father is probably already preparing to invoke the Final Veil."

Wilhelmina's brow furrowed. "The spell you mentioned earlier—one that will seal the Whispering Woods for a century?"

Seraphina nodded. "Yes. It will shield the Sanctuary from all threats but also block any aid from entering."

Selenus exchanged a glance with Phaethon, whose countenance imbued tension.

"Such a measure may preserve the Sanctuary, but at great cost. It would suspend time and freedoms alike," Selenus said, his voice low.

"Exactly," Seraphina replied. "It is the last resort against the darkness."

She reached into her robe and withdrew a glowing object—a crystal vial swirling with the fire of starlight.

Aria's breath caught as the vial's illumination filled her face, and Selenus's stern demeanor softened as he witnessed the eddying nebula within.

"What is that?" Wilhelmina whispered, leaning closer.

"This is the Essence of the First Dawn." Seraphina held the small bottle aloft. "A droplet of creation's original light, preserved for when its power is most needed. It will guide you through the veils between worlds and protect you from the siphoning shadows."

Wilhelmina's hands tightened into fists at her side, her lips slightly parted as she watched the vial's luminescence flicker.

"This magic is as ancient as the Guardian himself. It carries the whispers of the first dreams—the sparks that ignited imagination across the realms." Seraphina paused, her words settling. "You must carry it with care."

Wonder flickered across Wilhelmina's features.

Seraphina handed the vial to Lumina. "You carry the hope of our mission—the potential for creation and change. Guard this well."

"The planting showed me how fragile rebirth can be," Lumina said as she accepted the vial. "Carrying this... It's more than a duty. It's a chance to weave together what has been broken. For the desert, for Solarae, for us all. I will not fail you, Mother."

Seraphina's lips curved in an encouraging smile. "I believe in you, my child."

Lumina curled her fingers protectively around the vial. She cast a fleeting glance at Phaethon, who stepped closer. He stood taller, gripping the hilt of his sword, sheathed at his side. "Let us be swift." His golden eyes met hers. "We embark united—for dreams, for balance, and for the future."

21. The Starbound Path

Seraphina led the companions to the sanctuary's heart—a circular chamber suspended in time, a nexus between what was and what could be. The walls shone with countless constellations and planetary figurations, drifting in a celestial expanse. She stopped before a smooth surface of stone and, raising her hands, traced the shapes of runes in the air. They sparkled, illuminating the companions' stunned expressions.

An indistinct outline of an arch flickered into existence. Streams of iridescent energy lined the archway, humming as if awakening. Their brows lifted when, from beyond the archway, a surreal, ethereal panorama swirled into view.

"This gateway leads to the Whispering Woods." Seraphina's voice resonated with an almost musical cadence. "There, the lines between dreams and reality blur. Possibilities take form, and your choices will echo across the realms."

She turned and touched the Sphere of Golden Thread resting in Wilhelmina's hands. "This is no ordinary relic. The Sphere is both compass and conductor—a sacred tool for weaving light when the forest dims. Let it guide you when your own sight fails."

The companions' lips parted, unease flickering in their expressions as they exchanged glances.

"The woods are not just a place," Lumina said. Her eyes reflected the shifting light coming from the gateway's opening. "They are a tapestry woven from the dreams and intentions of all who walk through them. Each step shapes the strands of reality."

"Indeed. Your journey will take you through the Forest of Echoes, a passage my family has traveled for centuries to reach the Whispering Woods. Here, the light of potential flickers as it leads you to my father's sanctuary."

Seraphina surveyed the companions, giving them each a pointed look. "The route will test you, however, as it tests all who enter. First, you will see the great forked path of the Whispering Woods."

Her features eased as her gaze came to rest on Lumina. "You know this realm better than anyone here. I know you have always wanted to take the easier, brighter trail, and we have always refused your wish to go that way. The easy course is not always the best one, but it is your choice to make. I hope you will make the best one... as long as it comes from your heart."

"Thank you for trusting me to guide them." Lumina squeezed Seraphina's hand. "I won't let you down." She straightened, and the faintest trace of doubt melted from her face.

Wilhelmina pressed her lips together, her focus locked on the shimmering arch. "You speak as though the forest is alive. How does it test us?"

"This is no ordinary forest," Seraphina replied. "It breathes with your intentions, shaping itself to mirror your fears and hopes. But know this—hesitation or discord will unweave its balance, inviting darkness to take hold."

A palpable unease settled over the group, manifesting in ways as varied as their natures. Wilhelmina bit her lip while Aria folded her arms tightly, her jaw set. Selenus allowed his hand to graze the Sword's pommel. His broad shoulders squared, used to bearing the gravitas of leadership. Phaethon's expression appeared as though he was about to approach a storm head-on. Lumina alone appeared unshaken.

"You must walk the path as one." Lumineon's deep voice resonated in the chamber. "The forest will try to fragment you, to divide your wills. But unity will anchor you, and your choices, made together, will light the way."

"And if we falter?" Aria's question hung heavily in the chamber.

"Then the forest falters with you," Seraphina said solemnly. "And the darkness gains a foothold."

Selenus adjusted the Sword at his side, his lips curling into a wry smile. "We've faced shadows before."

Lumina brushed fingers against the vial at her waist. "We will meet whatever awaits us together."

Seraphina embraced each of them in turn, lingering briefly on her daughter. "Go forth with courage, and remember, every step is a choice, and every choice shapes the outcome."

❧

The sanctuary's warmth fell away as they stepped through the gateway into the Whispering Woods. A tingling sensation crept over their skin. The space they found themselves in had a strange air that hummed with possibility.

A path wound in front of them through a living grove made solely of ethereal energy. Here, tall trees with branches trailing luminescent, vibrating strands emitted gentle harmonies that wove through the air. Dappled with the light of scattered stars, the ground beneath their feet served as a map to guide their way.

Aria turned in a slow circle, her fingers brushing the air as though she could catch shimmering notes chiming in the luminous expanse.

"It's... like stepping into a melody," she breathed. "Everywhere I look, I feel a rhythm, a song waiting to be played."

Wilhelmina's voice lowered to a hush. "While it's quite beautiful, it feels fragile, as though one wrong step could break the harmony."

"That's because it can." Lumina grazed her hands against a tree cloaked in glowing moss.

"These strands of light—these vibrations—are the dreams that shape existence. Though they are malleable and respond to intention."

Phaethon's jaw set. "What happens if we make the wrong choice?"

"The forest will show you." Lumina's tone was even but edged with caution.

The footpath seemed to ripple beneath them as they ventured deeper. The trees leaned toward them. Their glimmering strands cast shifting patterns on their faces, as if the forest itself were watching their every step.

Breaking the silence, Selenus said, "Wilhelmina, does this not remind you of the first time we stood under the Celestial Arbor?"

Her lips curved. "It does. But the Arbor felt... eternal. These woods feel alive yet mortal... and like they are waiting for us to act."

Aria paused, her gaze focused on a grove of glistening tendrils reaching skyward. "These vibrations are out of sync." She pressed her hands to her ears as a discordant hum rose from the ground.

"It's the forest's way of testing us. It reflects the imbalance within us." Lumina's expression remained calm, yet her hands were clenched at her sides. "If we hesitate or falter, the instability grows."

"Then we need to keep our wits about us." Selenus's jaw tightened. "Every choice must be deliberate."

Lumina nodded. "Even hesitation is a choice, and the woods react to it."

The grove's luminous beauty gave way to darker hues as shadows crept among the branches. The dim light made it harder to see as they navigated the shifting path.

"The forest sang in harmony when I last walked here. But this is new," Lumina murmured. "Now it struggles, and its echoes misalign and cling to the past. The darkness is feeding on that stagnation."

She stopped abruptly, and the companions followed suit behind her.

The road now diverged into two distinct trails, both rippling with a peculiar, sentient energy.

One trail, resplendent with blossoming flowers and vines, climbed skyward in a riot of color.

The other, cloaked in muted sepia tones, exuded a subdued glow. Its ancient roots pulsed like the embers of a dying fire and a wisdom long held.

"Two paths and only one choice," Wilhelmina said at length.

"And if we choose wrong?" Phaethon asked, glancing at Selenus. "Do we risk everything?"

Lumina crouched down by the shaded track, her fingers brushing its roots.

"These aren't mere paths," she murmured. "They're reflections of intent—manifestations of what we hold most dear."

She rose and faced them, her expression tense. "The shaded path speaks to tradition and resilience, finding strength in what has endured."

Her steps carried her unconsciously toward the bright route, her feet aligning with its pull.

"The bright path," she declared, gesturing toward the blossoms, "represents boldness—embracing the unknown, the willingness to create anew."

"My family has always chosen the traditional path, refusing to let me explore the brighter one." She stopped, faltering mid-step, caught between longing and restraint. "The land responds to our intentions." She shook her head, pacing back and forth before the fork in the road.

A quiet deliberation settled over the group, their faces lit by the dual glow of the paths. Their silence stretched until Phaethon broke it.

"The shaded path is reliable and enduring. Our ancestors laid these roots with purpose." He folded his arms across his chest. "Forsaking them now would insult their wisdom and possibly create a grave risk."

"And yet," Lumina countered, her tone restrained but impassioned as she turned to him. "Clinging too tightly to the past risks stagnation."

She planted her hands on her hips, her expression taut. "The bright path is alive with potential—unpredictable, yes, but isn't that the essence of growth?"

Selenus leaned on his Sword, his expression thoughtful. A smile played at the corner of his mouth. "You both have a point," he said, scratching his chin. "Tradition offers safety, while innovation offers hope. But can we afford to sacrifice either?"

Fidgeting with her sleeve's hem, Aria stood slightly apart. "What if the bright path is too bold? We've only just found harmony as a group. What if boldness disrupts more than it creates?"

Wilhelmina stepped into the circle, sweeping her gaze over her companions. "This choice isn't just about us. It's about what we're trying to achieve. The realms are fractured, caught between old wounds and the need for renewal. Whatever path we take must honor both where we've come from and where we hope to go."

Aria drew nearer to clasp Lumina's hand. "As your mother said, the easy trail isn't always the right one, but as long as you choose with your heart, it is the best one for you."

Lumina's focus lingered on the bright path and grinned broadly. "It's time for a change."

She took a step and then another. The path brightened, as if her determination illuminated it.

The others exchanged hesitant glances before following her, some with resignation, while others did so with reluctance. As their steps fell in sync, vivid blossoms, their petals trembling like a sigh of relief, unfurled along their path.

But a shadow darted between the trees, its presence unshaken by their decision.

❧

The forest breathed. Branches of light swayed, and whispers wove through the air like fragments of a forgotten melody.

"The Whispering Woods hold more than echoes," Lumina said, leading the way with deliberate yet hesitant movements. "They unveil dreams, hopes, fears, truths we might not wish to face. But it's through clarity that we find unity."

"Dreams?" Wilhelmina glanced upward at crystalline trunks. "Can we trust what we see?"

"The price would most likely be too steep," Selenus replied.

The whispers grew louder, their tones shifting from gentle hums to sharp, discordant notes. A glowing fog suddenly coalesced, rippling through the woods. It wrapped around them, cold and heavy, severing their connection with the outside world.

Aria stilled, straining to listen. "Do you hear that?" Her expression grew tense. "It's like a song I've forgotten, but somehow still know."

With a sudden surge of fog, the companions found themselves abruptly separated before anyone could react.

❧

Lumina stood alone, the fog swirling like a restless tide. The whispers sharpened, focusing on her. Words now emerged from the cacophony: "Innovation. Tradition. Break. Build. Change."

The air shimmered before her, forming an image of her grandfather standing tall, his stern gaze fixed on her as he wove intricate patterns of light. Lumina realized she was no longer on the path, but trapped in a tangle of thorny, ancient roots.

She watched as the image of herself as a child appeared. Her younger self eagerly imitated her grandfather's movements, but she faltered, her patterns imperfect. His expression darkened, and his words, harsh and unyielding, echoed.

"You must preserve the roots of the legacy, not reshape the branch."

The scene shifted, showing an older version of herself, standing alone amidst a copse of decaying light. The strands of energy, once thriving, lay brittle and fragmented at her feet.

The ancient roots now tightened around her ankles, threatening to trip her.

A surge of defiance rose within her. "No," she said aloud, her voice firm. "The past guides us, but it cannot bind us. Growth demands change."

As she spoke, the tangled roots snapped, receding into the earth. The image faded, and the fog thinned. Even the whispers softened to an almost approving murmur.

She exhaled, and the path cleared ahead as she placed one foot in front of another.

Wilhelmina found herself on a tight, crumbling path that split into two steep slopes. The fog had thinned, but the air had become heavy, and the silence was absolute.

A figure cloaked in rigid silver armor stood on the slope to her left. His voice was a harsh echo. "The Sphere is your burden. Leadership requires sacrifice. You must forsake the bonds that distract you."

To her right stood a figure whose clothes shimmered with soft gold light. Her voice was warm, but her gaze was relentless. "The Sphere is your heart. To lead others, you must first trust the depths of your own tenderness."

Confusion swirled, but her hand instinctively went to her chest, where the memory of Selenus's quiet strength and unwavering belief in her burned like a brand.

She straightened, planting her feet on the unstable path. "I am not divided," she declared, her voice ringing clear. "My heart is not a weakness to be purged, but the beacon that illuminates the path of my duty."

The figures on the slopes dissolved into wisps of fog. The crumbling path beneath her feet solidified, and a single, steady light—the constant, pure glow of her own resolve—guided her way forward.

The fog around Selenus thickened, diminishing the world into a suffocating, ink-black void. The whispers here didn't chant; they snarled in a singular voice—his own, laced with a bitterness he had long tried to bury.

"You think light absolves you?" the voice hissed. "The darkness within is the only truth you possess."

A towering monolith of obsidian rose from the ground, its surface rippling like black water to form a mirror. As Selenus stepped forward, his reflection stared back—not as he was, but as a monstrous wraith clad in armor made of smoke and jagged glass. Its eyes burned with a cold, predatory malice.

As he watched, the ground beneath his boots decayed, the starlight path turning to ash wherever his shadow touched. The wraith in the mirror raised a spectral blade, mimicking his movements with a mocking sneer.

"That is the ghost I have outrun," Selenus said, his voice a low, dangerous rumble. He didn't just clench his fists; he reached out and pressed his palm flat against the cold surface of the obsidian.

"I am not the damage I have caused. I am the protection I provide."

Under his touch, a vein of pure gold light erupted from his palm, spider-webbing across the dark stone. With a sound like a great bell tolling, the monolith shattered into a thousand harmless shards of light. The decay at his feet vanished, replaced by a path that glowed with a steadier, more resilient luster.

Aria stood at the center of a literal whirlwind of sound. The fog here didn't just swirl; it vibrated, the chaotic echoes assaulting her ears like a shattered instrument.

Images flickered in the mist, but they arrived as staccato, jarring notes: a lonely child sitting in silence; a creature with wings too heavy for flight; a girl standing on the dark fringe of a campfire's glow, watching others laugh. Each memory was a string snapping within her chest, the old ache of isolation threatening to pull her under.

The wind shrieked, a discordant gale that tried to drown out her breath.

"You are a solo note," the wind seemed to howl. "Forgotten as soon as you are played."

Aria trembled, her hands flying to her ears. But as she closed her eyes, she searched beneath the noise. She looked for the rhythm she had sensed back at the gateway.

Slowly, she hummed—not a new song, but the steady, low tone she heard whenever she walked beside Wilhelmina, or the sharp, bright cadence of Lumina's laughter. One by one, she layered the "sounds" of her friends into her own breath.

"I am not a solo note," she whispered, her voice cutting through the gale. She looked up, her eyes bright with tears. "I am a movement in a symphony. My song is only beginning, and it is written in the hearts of those I love."

The discordant wind then didn't just fade; it resolved into a perfect, resonant chord. And now, the fog didn't just lift; it harmonized with the light, turning a soft, warm amber.

Aria stepped forward, her gait light and rhythmic, as if she were walking to a beat only she could hear.

Phaethon stood in the heart of a blinding golden gale. It wasn't just a storm; it was the sky itself tearing apart over the foundations of a magnificent, shimmering kingdom. Below him, his people cried out as the marble structures of their home crumbled into dust.

He saw himself at the center of the ruins, crowned and desperate. He was throwing every ounce of his power against the wind, his muscles straining until they burned, but the storm merely laughed. With every blast, more of his city dissolved into the overwhelming force.

A voice boomed from the thunder—his own, distorted by a frantic need for control.

"I must be the shield! If I falter, everything dies!"

He braced his shoulders against a falling archway, the weight of the stone crushing him into the dirt. His breath came in ragged gasps.

He was the king of nothing but falling ash.

Just as his knees buckled, a hand appeared in the gold-dust haze—not to take the crown, but to help hold the stone. It was Lumina's hand, followed by the steady grip of Selenus, then Wilhelmina's and Aria's. The weight didn't vanish, but it suddenly became bearable.

"I am a pillar," Phaethon whispered, his eyes narrowing as he looked at the hands joined with his. "But I am not the only one. To lead is not to be the sole foundation, but to be part of the structure."

As he accepted their strength, the storm's fury didn't just stop—it became the very energy used to rebuild. The archway he held didn't fall; it locked into place, stronger than before. The blinding gale dissipated into a clear, steady warmth.

Phaethon now stood tall, exhaling a breath he felt he'd been holding for a lifetime. He adjusted his stance, no longer bracing for a hit, but ready to walk alongside his peers.

The individual visions dissolved like salt in a rising tide. One by one, the companions stepped out of the thinning fog. No one spoke at first; the air was thick with the weight of the truths they had just faced.

Lumina was the first to emerge, her stride certain as she reached the center of the clearing. She looked back to see Wilhelmina standing tall, the Sphere in her hands pulsing with a heartbeat of pure gold. Selenus joined them, his hand no longer white-knuckled on his sword but resting there with calm readiness. Aria followed, her eyes bright and her head tilted as if she were finally hearing the forest's true song.

Finally, Phaethon stepped into the light. He didn't lead with his chin as he usually did; he looked at his friends with a quiet, profound humility.

No words were needed. The discord that had hummed through the woods earlier had vanished, replaced by a deep, resonant harmony that seemed to vibrate from the very earth beneath their feet.

Lumina met each of their eyes, acknowledging the shadows still lingering in their expressions before voicing the truth they all felt. "This path showed me the decay of staying bound to the past." Her voice sounded older, more thoughtful. "It showed me that the roots can become a cage if we don't let the branches grow."

She pressed a hand to her chest and straightened her posture. "I choose to move forward. To create something new."

"We stand beside you," Phaethon said. It wasn't a boast this time, but a promise.

The others nodded in silent, ironclad agreement. As their resolve locked into place, the trees' whispers shifted, no longer discordant but a gentle, guiding hum that led them toward a grove bathed in a deep, cerulean light.

"The way is open," Lumina murmured, showing the trail. Now, the bright path they had chosen shimmered, beckoning with intensity. The blossoms along the edge turned toward them, their petals luminous.

But at the very edge of that beautiful blue glow, the shadow they had glimpsed before stretched long and thin across the path, waiting.

❧

The canopy overhead filtered the luminescence into ebbing pools of color, shifting like tide-pools under a moon. At the heart of the grove stood an ancient tree, its bark veined with glowing strands that pulsed with a slow, heavy heartbeat. Nestled within its boughs was a single, immense crystalline orb, flickering with the ghosts of a thousand possible lives.

The companions approached, drawn forward by the orb's resonant hum. It trembled as though aware of their presence. Then, with a sudden burst of light, it fractured with the sound of breaking glass—not a crash, but a chime. Dozens of now smaller orbs—dream seeds—drifted toward them, deliberate and purposeful.

One settled before Wilhelmina. As her fingers grazed the surface, she saw herself speaking before gathered realms. But then, the image of her as a compassionate leader wavered. Smoke-like whispers curled around the vision, and for a moment, she saw the faces of those she loved turned away in doubt.

"They are not just dreams," she whispered, the cold reality of consequence sinking into her bones. "They are the weight of every 'yes' and every 'no'."

Lumina's seed spun with frantic energy, its patterns a kaleidoscope of ancient sigils merging into new, shimmering designs. For a moment, she saw a world where her innovations brought light—but she also saw the fragility of that beauty, a glass structure that could shatter without the strength of the old ways to hold it.

Aria's orb emitted a soft, pulsing glow that vibrated against her palms. In its depths, a symphony played—a song that bound the realms together—but the notes were hollow, lacking the depth that only a shared journey could provide. She realized the melody wasn't hers to sing alone.

Selenus didn't speak. He watched his indigo orb swirl with silver, showing him a throne of shadows and a crown of absolute power. It was a tempting, solitary peace. He reached into his pocket, his fingers brushing the cold, dimming orb that held his father's waning life. The contrast was a physical ache—the dark power in the seed versus the selfless sacrifice in his pocket.

"The forest knows my fears," he said, his jaw tight. "But it does not know my will."

Phaethon focused his gaze on a golden kingdom that flourished even as a storm gathered on its horizon. He didn't describe it; he simply looked at the others.

"The question," he said, his voice grave, "is not which dream we nurture. It's which one we are brave enough to release."

A heavy silence fell. They stood like statues, each holding a fragment of fate. They realized that even the right choice exacted a toll—that to choose one future was to murder a dozen others.

One by one, they made their peace.

Selenus was the first to act. With a steady hand, he released the indigo seed of power. It didn't shatter; it simply dimmed, sinking into the ancient roots to become nourishment for the earth instead of a burden for his soul.

Phaethon followed, releasing his orb with a reverent bow. Aria pressed hers to her heart, her breath hitching as the melody merged with her own pulse. Finally, Wilhelmina drew her orb close, embracing the vision of leadership—shadows and all.

As the last choice was made, life surged through the ancient tree. The heartbeat quickened. The chosen seeds rose, merging into a single radiant sphere that hovered like a new sun before sinking deep into the ground.

❧

A chill settled over the companions as they pressed onward. The air didn't just cool; it soured. The forest's once-harmonious whispers twisted into a jagged, discordant snarl, and the luminescence dimmed to a sickly, flickering gray. Shadows didn't just fall—they writhed across the ground like oil on water, inching closer with every step.

Lumina halted abruptly, her hand raised. "Something's wrong," she murmured, her voice sharp.

The path before them splintered into a wall of gnarled ebony roots and vines that hissed like serpents.

"The forest isn't testing us anymore," Lumina said, her hand raised to halt Selenus as he reached for his sword. "It's reacting to the shadow at our backs. It's feeding on our lingering hesitation."

A low growl echoed from the distance, vibrating through the ground.

"Then we give it no more food," Wilhelmina declared, stepping forward. The Sphere of Golden Thread in her hands thrummed, sensing her resolve.

The vines then surged toward them, weaving into a dense, writhing barrier. The ground trembled, and the dissonant hum swelled into an almost taunting crescendo.

Selenus drew his Sword, the blade flashing in the dim light. "We can cut through," he said, his jaw clenching. "If we're quick enough—"

"Wait." Lumina stopped his action, placing her hand on his sword arm. "These vines aren't just physical. Look at how they're moving—they're connected to the forest's energy. If we attack them recklessly, we could make things worse."

Aria crouched, her fingers brushing the rough, vibrating tendrils of the barrier. "There's a rhythm here," she whispered. "It's a scream of fear. If we cut it, the entire forest will feel the wound. We have to... we have to sing it back to sleep."

Phaethon frowned, scanning the encroaching vines. "What happens if we're wrong? What if waiting just gives the forest more time to trap us?"

Wilhelmina turned to face the group, her expression firm. "This is a test of our unity," she said. "How we face this—together—will determine the outcome."

Selenus's grip on his Sword tightened. "And if calming it doesn't work?"

"Then we'll face the consequences," Lumina said simply. "Rushing in without understanding the forest could cost us more than time."

The barrier loomed closer, and the vines hissed, their movements growing frenzied.

"We need to decide," Wilhelmina said, her voice cutting through the hiss. "Cutting through is destruction. Retreating is defeat. We choose harmony." She turned to Aria. "Find the melody."

Aria straightened, her fingers tracing the chaotic rhythm beneath the bark. "I'll need all of you. It's responding to us, but we need harmony to fully unravel it."

Selenus and Phaethon moved to the flanks, weapons ready—not to strike, but to shield the others as the vines lashed out like whips. Wilhelmina held the Sphere aloft, its pulse quickening.

"I'll weave the connection," Wilhelmina declared. The Sphere's light erupted into golden rays that intertwined with the ebony vines.

"Aria. Now!"

Aria drew a grounding breath and let out a single, pure note. It was a thread of sound that sliced through the discord. Lumina's hands moved in a blur, her fingers catching the golden rays from Wilhelmina's Sphere and weaving them into the air, creating a shimmering lattice that mirrored Aria's song.

As they worked, the vines writhed violently, their edges gleaming with a lethal, crystalline sharpness. But as the melody swelled—a symphony of Aria's sound, Lumina's structure, and Wilhelmina's light—the menace bled out of the wood.

The obsidian blackness of the vines faded back to a healthy, deep green. With a final, long tremor, the barrier didn't just break; it unraveled, the vines retreating into the earth like a bated breath finally released.

"We did it," Aria whispered, her voice tired but clear.

Wilhelmina smiled, lowering the Sphere, and exhaled slowly.

Lumina watched the retreating vines. "The forest reflects us. Our unity shapes its harmony."

The forest whispers returned to a gentle hum—a reminder that harmony was their greatest strength, but also their most fragile defense.

Selenus clapped Phaethon on the shoulder, a silent acknowledgement of the balance they had found between force and patience.

But as they stepped past the former barrier, the light of the Sphere caught a flicker at the edge of the grove. The shadow was still there—silent, watching, and undeterred by their victory.

Curving into darkness, the path prompted wary glances between companions; the forest's lesson tempered their victory—that harmony, once achieved, needs guarding, and unity, even within, can be tested.

22. A Split in the Labyrinth

The moment the light vanished, Wilhelmina's world didn't just go dark; it collapsed. Sound, sight, and the presence of her companions were swallowed by an absolute, hungry void. She was left with nothing but the frantic whisper of her own breath and the icy, phantom touch of walls that seemed closer than they should be.

"Selenus? Lumina?" Her voice sounded small, a fragile thing in the vast silence. "Aria? Phaethon? Where are you?"

No echo returned her cry. The silence was a physical weight, pressing against her eardrums until the rhythm of her own heart sounded like a funeral drum. A cold, metallic scent–like old blood and wet stone—clung to her lungs. She reached forward, her fingers trembling, seeking purchase in a world that had become a grave.

"What is happening?" Even her words sounded crackly in her ear. "Is this real or a cruel dream?"

A breeze curled around her, caressing her skin like icy fingers, sending a shiver racing down her spine. Somewhere in the distance, a sigh—an exhalation too low to be real—brushed past her ear.

Startled, she lost her footing and slipped on a slick, uneven floor. She went down hard, the splash of a shallow puddle soaking through her skirts and biting into her skin with a bitter, unnatural cold.

Water trickled down her fingers, and then—a sharp movement. Something small and quick scurried over her hand. A wave of revulsion washed over her. She recoiled with a cry, shaking her fingers violently.

On hands and knees, she crawled through the muck until her palms scraped against damp, jagged stone. As she hauled herself up, she gasped as her temple struck a protrusion. A sharp, dull throb radiated through her skull. Her hand darted to her hairline, finding a sticky warmth that turned her stomach. The blood was the only real thing in a landscape of shadows.

She pressed on, time beginning to stretch and warp. Minutes bled into what seemed like hours as she trailed the uneven stone. Every turn led to another identical corridor. The labyrinth wasn't just a place; it was a loop of her own rising despair.

A whisper of air, cold and deliberate, brushed her arm. Then came the sound—not a cry, but a soft, rhythmic *thud-step, thud-step* from the darkness behind her.

"Who's there?" She spun around, her voice cracking.

The footsteps stopped. The silence that followed was worse; it seemed expectant. Then, a low whooshing sound filled the air, and a hand—strong, slender, and impossibly cold—latched onto her arm.

Wilhelmina lunged back, her tendons straining against the unyielding grip. A dim, sickly light filtered through the murk, not from a torch, but seemingly from the figure itself. Her head jerked upward, a soundless gurgle escaping her throat.

The figure stood with rigid, terrifying grace. The silhouette was a mirror of her own—from the slope of the shoulders to the tattered hem of the dress. As the light grew, it revealed the truth with a cruel, clinical clarity.

Wilhelmina was staring into her own face—but the eyes were hollow, reflecting a version of herself that had already given up. This wasn't a dream. This was a split in the world.

❧

Wilhelmina's breath remained frozen in her throat. The face before her was a cruel distortion–her own features, but filled with a predatory malice that turned her blood to ash. It wasn't just a nightmare; it was her own identity stolen and corrupted beyond recognition.

"No!" The word tore from her throat, raw and desperate. She lunged, gripping the being's ceremonial gown—the very one she wore for weddings in Aetherwyn—in a bid for release.

The light flickered out. In the sudden pitch, something dragged her with brutal force. Pain surged through her shoulders as the being's grip tightened. The sound of tearing fabric rent the air.

Her feet barely kept pace as she was shoved through narrow, weeping corridors until they burst into a vaulted chamber. The air here was heavy and clung to her skin, thick and fetid. It reeked of acrid decay and stagnant water.

Wilhelmina crumpled against a slick wall, her palms scraping against the craggy stone. Shadows pooled in the corners like living ink, pressing against a weak, sourceless light. She scrambled backward, clutching her arms to her chest as the being loomed over her.

"Who are you?" she demanded, her voice a ragged ghost of itself. "H-how a-are you m-me?" she stammered.

The doppelgänger stood silent, but then a guttural growl escaped from its throat as it stepped into the center of the room. An otherworldly glow bloomed around them.

It smoothed the tattered silk of its gown with a deliberate, mocking grace. Its eyes—Wilhelmina's eyes—glittered like shards of broken glass, studying her with a cruel curiosity. It took a deliberate step forward, its smile widening as if savoring her fear.

"How indeed?" it sneered, the voice a perfect, chilling replica of her own.

The doppelgänger crouched slightly, its muscles coiling as if ready to pounce. Wilhelmina's pulse thundered in her ears, but she forced herself to meet its gaze, unwilling to cower.

The being shoved Wilhelmina into a wall, the impact knocking the breath from her lungs and sending her sprawling to the ground. For a moment, she stayed on her knees, gasping. A spark of defiance ignited within her, fragile but bright.

"No. Not like this." Drawing a shuddering breath, she pushed herself to her feet.

It circled her with the precision of a wolf. With a flick of its wrist, it summoned shadowy tendrils that snaked across the floor. As Wilhelmina scrambled back, the creature raised a hand. A bolt of dark, crackling energy hissed toward her.

Instinctively, Wilhelmina threw up her arms. To her shock, a barrier of pale golden light flared between them. The dark bolt glanced off, illuminating the room in a serrated flash.

She rose and staggered back a step. "W-Was that me?"

"You're weak." The doppelgänger hissed, unfazed. "You think you're a leader? They don't follow you out of loyalty—they pity you. The orphan fairy. The mistake left in an egg in the mud."

The words cut deeper than any physical blow. Wilhelmina's knees buckled. "That's not true," she murmured, shaking her head, but her voice wavered.

"And Selenus?" The creature laughed, a sound like grinding stones. *"You think he loves you? Oh, poor, naïve, foolish girl."* Another cackle of laughter

gurgled from its throat. *"He only pities a broken thing, Wilhelmina. Who could truly love someone so common? So uncertain?"*

The armor she had built around her heart cracked. Each word was a shard of glass slicing through her resolve. A strangled sob escaped her lips as she fell to her knees. Then, the shadows in the corners shifted and grew. They didn't just move; they molded themselves into familiar shapes. Wilhelmina's head snapped up, and relief flooded her face.

"Selenus? Lumina?" she gasped. "Aria?" Her eyes held a flicker of hope.

But as they stepped into the light, the hope died. Aria's face was twisted into a sneer; Lumina's eyes were cold and vacant. Selenus stood with his arms crossed, his expression one of pure, mocking disdain. Their tittering grew, echoing off the chamber walls, joined by Selenus's deep chortling. Their words lashed out like whips, leaving invisible wounds that bled raw.

"Leader? You're a lost child playing at being a queen," Aria's voice echoed, dripping with venom.

"Every step you take pulls us closer to the grave," Lumina jeered.

Selenus stepped forward, his lips curling into his usual cold smirk as he loomed over her. "*We follow because we must, little bird. Not because we trust you.*"

Wilhelmina doubled over, clutching her head as the weight of their disgust crushed the air from her lungs. Their laughter—a dissonant cacophony—rose into a cruel symphony of her worst fears. Tears stung her eyes as the doppelgänger joined the chorus, adding to the terrifying harmony.

❧

The darkness was absolute—not just an absence of light, but a hungry void that echoed the hollow spaces in her heart. Wilhelmina collapsed, her knees striking the cold, wet stone with a jarring thud. She pressed her trembling hands to the ground, tears blurring her vision as the mocking words—*orphan, mistake, unloved*—clung to her like a suffocating fog.

She forced herself to breathe. *Inhale. Exhale.* The sound of her breath was a whisper, but it was there—a reminder of life still within her. Slowly, the panic ebbed, replaced by a fragile stillness. Her breath slowed.

And then she heard it—a single note, faint and pure, like a thread of sound piercing the abyss. It rang in her ears as though it had always been there, waiting for her to notice. But it wasn't a sound from the labyrinth. It was a sound from *within*.

The note rippled through the air, invisible waves brushing her skin like the softest breeze. It thrummed in the earth beneath her, reverberating outward as though the labyrinth itself were alive with its resonance.

Her chest tightened as an unexpected wave of warmth swelled within her, chasing away the chill that had gripped her bones. The sound grew louder with each breath, not harsh but insistent, wrapping around her like a ghostly embrace.

The suffocating grip of the darkness loosened as the note's warmth seeped into her marrow like a sun-soaked morning. It was a balm that coaxed her trembling soul back to life and awakened parts of herself she hadn't known were sleeping.

Tears spilled, unbidden, down her cheeks. Her pulse slowed, her heartbeat syncing with the note's rhythm. She placed a hand on her breastbone, as though trying to contain the flood of emotions bursting forth—a bittersweet ache, tender and euphoric.

"I-I've heard this s-sound before." Her voice shook, but the note continued to ascend into full resonance, like the timbre of a memory calling her home. It carried her thoughts to places she had long forgotten.

A smile trembled on her lips as the note swept through her mind, soft as a whispered promise, painting vivid images with every beat. She saw herself kneeling beside a young fairy, her hands cupped gently around a trembling butterfly. The child's tears gave way to laughter as the butterfly took flight, its iridescent wings catching the light.

The note played deeper now, each wave bringing another memory—a cascade of laughter, wonder, and small moments of kindness.

"I gave," she whispered, her voice gaining a melodic strength, "and they gave back."

Other memories surfaced, each one carried on the note. The golden threads she wove, not for herself but for others. Laughter with Selenus under the moonblossom trees in Aetherwyn, their shared wonder at the stars above. Aria's hand clasping hers during moments of doubt, Phaethon's reassuring nod when the weight of leadership threatened to overwhelm her. And the way Lumina's voice always seemed to lift the surrounding air, even in the darkest times.

Her memories were the threads that wove her life together, the unspoken truths that even her shadow self could not take away. The words she spoke aloud, so simple, resonated like a second note, harmonizing with the first. The being stiffened, its cruel features softening as if caught in the melody of truth.

The note now pulsed in rhythm with her heart—a reminder of her place in the symphony of life. It wasn't just a sound but a part of her—everything she had cherished, everything she had ever been.

She filled her lungs and spoke into the void. "I am not broken." Fragile at first, the words gained strength. "I am *love*... I am *joy*. I am *hope*."

Uncertain, the void trembled and flickered. While the darkness remained, she was no longer drowning in it. Wilhelmina met her doppelgänger's stare head-on.

"It would be easier to let the labyrinth decide for us... to hand over our will and escape the burden of choice. But no. The labyrinth wasn't created to define us—it was created to remind us we alone must decide."

The creature still wore her face, still held that cruel sneer, but it was smaller now—less like a monster and more like a frightened child. It bent its head toward its shoulder, as if hesitating. But it took a step closer.

Wilhelmina stared at it without flinching. "You are a part of me." Her voice resonated in harmony with that internal note, and she reached out her hand. "But you are not all of me. I see you. You are loved... I understand. I *forgive* you."

The moment their hands met, a rush of energy surged through her. She gasped as the sensation spread—not just over her skin. The porous membrane of her being—once riddled with fractures and gaps—sealed itself. She sensed every cell, every tiny receptor that governed the flow of her life-force, align with the rhythm of her heartbeat.

The light within her expanded, pressing outward, filling every crevice until her form was whole, unbroken, and impenetrable. The once-discordant energies within her—the fear and the hope—danced together in fluid, perfect motion.

The shadow, stripped of its malice, dissolved into her light like ink fading into clear water. Yet it didn't vanish entirely; instead, it became a soft hum within her—a reminder of her own depths. No longer a source of fear, it transformed into a reservoir of strength.

The note reached a crescendo, a symphony singing from every particle of her body. A blinding light burst forth—not from the Sphere, but from *her*.

A luminous warmth spread outward from her heart, radiating through her limbs, her mind, her soul. The merging wasn't a collision or resolution; it was a communion and rebirth. Darkness and light were no longer opposing forces. They were the weave of her existence, bound in profound harmony.

"We are one," she whispered, her voice a declaration that shook the void. "And together, I am whole."

The light dimmed, leaving her crouched on the chilled surface. The labyrinth's whispers faded into a respectful silence. She blinked, and the world flickered between the dark corridors and the familiar forest path. The phantom of the nightmare dissolved, leaving her standing in the soft glow of the woods, her spirit finally, inviolably complete.

❧

"Wilhelmina!" Selenus's voice jolted her back to the physical world. She looked up to see her companions encircling her, their faces etched with sharp worry.

"You've been crouched there for ages," Lumina said, her brows furrowing. "We thought the forest had claimed you."

Wilhelmina rose, her legs trembling, half-numb with pain. Yet, the labyrinth's last echoes hummed in her marrow—a resonant farewell that lingered as Wilhelmina steadied herself.

The labyrinth had been a creation of her own making, though the pulse beneath her feet signaled that its power was not entirely gone. An eerie calm still lingered in the air.

Even so, a laugh bubbled from her lips—soft at first, then growing into a jubilant melody. She spun, her arms outstretched, shaking off the remnants of the labyrinth's grip.

"You didn't lose me." Her lips curved, her tears spilling. "I found myself."

The companions exchanged glances, their brows knitting.

Wilhelmina burst into infectious laughter. "I am not just the light you see or the shadow I fear. I am both, and that is what makes me whole."

Her expression softened as she looked toward Selenus. "Selenus, I understand you better now. You were just experiencing the split, just as I have... And you are whole, as am I. As we all are."

Selenus exhaled, his lips curving. "Hearing you say that... that feels so good. And coming from you, it can't get any better." He grasped her and lifted her, spinning her around.

Their laughter burst forth, and as it faded and Selenus set Wilhelmina back on the ground, Lumina approached her. "I don't know what just happened, but you're different—stronger somehow."

"And you all didn't experience it?" Wilhelmina asked. Lumina shook her head. "Then… the labyrinth must have had a purpose for me. But I don't know what that is."

Selenus looked at Wilhelmina with tenderness. "Whatever it is, Lumina's right. You're even more beautiful."

Wilhelmina returned his gaze, but from the corner of her eye, a strange light flickered. An outline of the labyrinth's passages appeared, thrumming like a fading heartbeat, before vanishing entirely.

"Wilhelmina… seriously… what really happened to you?" Phaethon asked, his voice cautious.

She touched her chest, feeling the lingering hum of the symphony within her. "I think… the labyrinth wasn't a place. It was me. A part of me I needed to understand… and to forgive."

Before they could celebrate, the air soured. A powerful gust of wind screamed through the canopy, snuffing their fire and scattering their gear. The phantom outlines Wilhelmina had seen didn't fade; they darkened, turning into inky black threads that stitched themselves into the physical trees.

"It's back!" Wilhelmina choked. "But how is that possible?"

An ashen residue suffocated the luminous trees. Their radiant branches sagged, their glow dimmed to a dull flicker. A grimy, gray film cloaked the once-crystalline bark, as if remnants of a long-dead forest fire had settled upon every surface. Leaves, once alive with iridescent hues, now curled inward like desiccated husks.

The air grew heavier and laden with the scent of burned wood and decay, searing their nostrils, clinging to their throats. Beneath their feet, the ground was cold, barren, and unyielding.

A hollow, dissonant sound replaced the sonorous melodies that had danced through the forest, now mourning its collapse.

Aria jerked her head toward the sound. "What is happening?"

"The labyrinth has entered our reality. I think the darkness must have discovered it when you went through the inner dimension, Wilhelmina," Lumina said. "It's using its power to bring it to life in this one."

Though Selenus and Phaethon rapidly drew their swords, the living monster continued to enlarge, emitting low growls. Tendrils of blackness coiled around them, blowing the swords out of their grasp.

Wilhelmina spun her head. "Swords won't work." She searched each face; the encroaching darkness shadowed each one. "The labyrinth isn't just testing me now. It's feeding on our fear."

Aria pressed a hand to her throat, coughing as the acrid air clawed at her lungs. "What do we do?"

Lumina's usual glow dimmed, her light flickering like a candle struggling against the wind.

"We don't fight it," Wilhelmina said. "We outshine it. Think of something that makes you laugh or fills you with wonder."

"I don't know..." Aria said, hesitating. "But I guess we could try."

"I remember my childhood, climbing a tree so high that I thought I could touch the stars in the farthest perimeters of the universe," Phaethon said, chuckling. "A mischievous squirrel once stole my crown during a game, and I had to bribe it back with nuts."

"I love that," Lumina said, smiling. "I remember when one of my new spells... something I had been inventing for a long while... finally worked!" She clapped her hands, her glow flaring brighter. "It went beyond magic."

Selenus chuckled, then doubled over with laughter. "I remember Wilhelmina's first attempts at enchanting, how she once accidentally made a bird sing backwards for an entire afternoon!"

Wilhelmina covered her face with her hands, attempting to smother a laugh. "I remember that... how embarrassing!"

Laughter rippled through them, light at first, then growing stronger. Contagious. Infectious.

As their joy peaked, the darkness recoiled. The inky threads shrank until they dissolved, unable to maintain their structure against the resonance of their unity.

The forest exhaled, and the ashen residue vanished, leaving the stars visible once more.

"Laughter, love, and curiosity," Wilhelmina breathed. "They're the threads that bind us."

Lumina walked toward Wilhelmina and rested a hand on her shoulder. "And you have shown us how to weave them."

Wilhelmina took Lumina's hands in hers. "We found it together—" Her words trailed off as, high above, a sudden motion streaked across the sky. It was a meteor, its colors shifting from serene blue to fiery crimson. The starry canopy warped and pulled, forming a celestial pattern that chilled the air. A spellbinding glow bathed the still forest.

"The Omega Constellation," Wilhelmina whispered.

Lumina nodded. "The Zenith soon approaches." Her voice blended with the forest sighs. "And it means that our time is dwindling."

Wilhelmina nodded, her hand over her heart where the symphony still played. "Then we keep moving. And we leave no soul behind."

23. Division in the Forest of Light

Deep within the Whispering Woods, the companions found themselves ensnared in an eerie stillness. Twisting vines and the glow of bioluminescent moss obscured the path ahead. Their shifting patterns created unsettling illusions.

The air hung heavy and damp, thick with a metallic tang that caught in their throats. Every rustle of leaves seemed deliberate.

Wilhelmina shivered, rubbing her arms. "It feels like the forest is watching us."

Lumina's wings twitched, catching the dim, sickly light of the moss. "It's just a forest, Wilhelmina. You're imagining things." But her gaze darted nervously to the shadows as she spoke.

The ground beneath them hummed with a low, uneasy tremor. Suddenly, a luminous white vine—one of the predatory light-snakes—slithered down a trunk and coiled around Wilhelmina's arm. She cried out, shaking her limb with all her strength, but the entity squeezed harder.

Thwack! Selenus's blade severed the vine in one clean motion. The entity recoiled, hissing as it vanished back into the bark.

"Disgusting," Wilhelmina whispered, her heart hammering against her ribs.

"Those are light-snakes," Lumina snapped, her voice tight with a stress she was trying to hide. "Have a care where you step!"

Wilhelmina pressed her lips together, her fingernails digging into her palms.

The tension between them was a spark in a dry forest. When Selenus pulled out the map, the spark caught fire.

"We should rest while I get my bearings," Selenus suggested, his voice forced and calm. "Seraphina's map shows—"

"No!" Wilhelmina barked, surprising even herself with her sharpness. "We've wasted enough time. I'm going to find water."

"I'll come with you," Selenus offered, stepping toward her.

"I don't need your help," she cut him off, her pride flaring. "I can handle it myself."

But the forest was already reacting to her anger. The ground beneath her boots turned to a treacherous mush, sucking her down. As the princes rushed to pull her free, the argument didn't end—it only shifted targets.

Wilhelmina brushed the mud from her boots, the cold dampness seeping through the leather. "Let's mark the spot so no one else steps there."

They worked together to roll heavy, lichen-covered stones over the treacherous patch of earth. The physical labor was a brief distraction from the growing tension, but the silence between them was brittle.

Phaethon gestured toward Wilhelmina, his eyes meeting Selenus's with a measured, princely weight. "Let her lead, but we'll stay close. It keeps us together without stepping on anyone's toes."

"A compromise, then," Selenus agreed, though his jaw remained tight.

Wilhelmina exhaled a long, shaky breath. "Fine."

They pressed on, but the forest seemed to feed on their forced politeness. Before long, frustration mounted again. A chilling breeze encircled them as their voices rose.

"We've been going in circles," Aria said, rubbing her arms, a restless attempt to chase off the weakness she remembered all too well during her time in the desert. The forest gloom triggered those memories. "And we still don't have water."

Selenus's grip tightened on the map until the parchment crinkled. "There's a stream marked here." He tapped a line on the map's contours with forceful precision. "Old travelers' tales promised safer passage along waterways. If we follow the current, we'll save time and effort."

Phaethon leaned over Selenus's shoulder, his brow knitting as he studied the map. "And if the stream leads us into a trap? The terrain is too confined near the banks. This clearer path over here is safer," he argued, pointing to a location where the trees thinned. "Open space will give us more visibility and fewer surprises."

Selenus let out a sharp, mocking chortle. "Visibility? That's what you call stumbling around aimlessly in the open? The stream is marked for a reason." His tone grew sharper. "We should trust the signs and our instincts."

Phaethon crossed his arms, his posture rigid. "Your instincts? They've led us into enough trouble already!"

Selenus's expression turned hostile. The air hummed with agitated energy. "And your caution is slowing us! Time won't wait for your second-guessing." He took a step forward, his face inches from Phaethon's, the map forgotten in his hand.

Phaethon's shoulders tensed, his voice rising to a serrated edge. "And your recklessness will be our undoing!" He ripped the map from Selenus's hand. The parchment shrieked as it crumpled in his grip. "Maybe if you listened for once, we'd actually get somewhere without risking our lives!"

The ground beneath them didn't just tremble; it groaned, a low-frequency growl that resonated through the soles of their boots.

"Stop it!" Wilhelmina's voice was urgent, her head spinning between the two brothers. "The forest is reacting to us!"

But the princes were locked in their own orbits. Selenus stepped closer, his eyes flashing with a dangerous, rhythmic pulse. "You think leadership is about standing still? You have to act, Phaethon!"

"And you need to think!" Phaethon jabbed a finger at Selenus's chest, punctuating his words with the force of a blow. "This isn't just about your ego!"

A loud crack split the air. The ground rippled violently. Wilhelmina, Aria, and Lumina grasped each other's arms as the stable world turned into a shifting sea of mud. Shadowy tendrils crept from the fissures like ink in water.

Selenus suddenly doubled over, clutching his chest as if his lungs were burning. When he looked up, his eyes were bloodshot with strain. "I'm trying to lead us to safety," he gasped, his voice struggling against the whipping branches that now flailed around them like a wooded duel.

Nearby, oblivious to the brothers, another friction was sparking. Aria reached down and picked up a colorful feather, its iridescent barbs glowing against the gloom. "Strange to see something of such spirited colors in this land of white light," she mused, her voice wistful. "It's a reminder that beauty still exists, even here."

Lumina set her hands on her hips, her light flickering with irritation. "We need more than beauty, Aria. We need a tactical advantage." She gestured toward the dense thicket. "Thick boughs will give us shelter. This moonlight... it feels like a trap."

"A trap? Or a reprieve?" Aria's shoulders stiffened. "Do you really think we'll find peace by hiding in the dark? This clearing feels like a balm."

"A balm won't protect us from what's watching!" Lumina's wings shifted restlessly, casting jagged shadows. "The forest is uneasy because *we* are uneasy."

"Then maybe we should find hope instead of fear!" Aria clenched her fists. "What's the point of surviving if we lose sight of what we're fighting for?"

The earth finally surrendered. A giant crack zigzagged through the clearing, physically separating their footing. Above, the star flickered erratically, casting fractured crimson light that made the scene look like a broken mosaic.

Lumina marched up to Aria, standing nose to nose. "And what good is a reminder if it threatens us? Use your head!"

"Why are we even here?" Aria shouted back, her frustration boiling over.

Lumina whipped her head toward Wilhelmina, her voice sharp as a blade. "Ask her! She's the one leading us into this nightmare!"

In that instant, the ground underfoot turned to a hungry, viscous slush. Aria and Lumina cried out as the earth swallowed them to their waists. Wilhelmina spun around, watching in horror as the shouting princes were also claimed—the earth drinking them down like a straw.

"This forest feeds on our doubt," Wilhelmina whispered, her mind racing. "Like what happened in Miragwyn, it reflects what festers inside us."

She looked up, her eyes widening as she noticed the vines dangling overhead. They weren't just moving; they were hunting.

Wilhelmina spun around to see her companions batting at shadowy tendrils that whipped from the muck like black lashes. Curdling screams and panicked shouts filled the clearing.

"I've got to try!" she cried.

She ran toward them, but the crack in the ground had widened into a gaping maw. Without thinking, she leapt across the chasm. She landed hard on the far side, her boots skidding on the slick moss. She teetered over the edge for a heart-stopping second before flinging her weight forward, barely catching her balance.

Nearby, she spotted a cluster of thick vines. She grabbed at several, but two hissed and bared light-filled fangs; she recoiled, letting them go, and seized the inert ones. She stretched and pulled with every ounce of her strength, throwing the lengths toward her friends.

"We're too heavy! It won't hold!" Selenus shouted, his voice strained as the mud claimed his chest.

The bioluminescent moss dimmed erratically and in cadence with their desperate grunts. As the seconds ticked by, their bodies inched further down into the unforgiving earth.

Wilhelmina's gaze swept the clearing until it snagged on a circle of stones nestled among the roots of ancient trees. She dropped to her knees, tracing the etched patterns with trembling fingers.

"These stones... they amplify harmony and balance," she whispered. "Like my marriage spells." She closed her eyes, channeling the resonance of light and shadow through the stones, just as she had for the couples in Aetherwyn.

By the light and shadow's weave,
Grant us freedom, let us leave.
Bind this chaos, still its might.
Guide us back to balance, bright.

As the incantation left her lips, the stones vibrated. It was a familiar resonance—the eternal dance of opposites seeking equilibrium. This was her calling—to bind what threatened to break apart.

Overhead, the Omega Constellation flickered, its crimson glow pulsing in rhythm with her spell. For a fleeting moment, it steadied, its hue momentarily softening to a pale gold.

The vines she held didn't just tighten; they fused with the stones, glowing as they anchored themselves into the deep earth. With a collective heave, the earth seemed to exhale, and the companions were pulled from the muck.

"It's working!" Aria cried.

Mud-streaked and gasping, Lumina, Phaethon, and Selenus staggered onto solid ground. But the forest wasn't finished.

Aria's shrill scream pierced the air.

The others turned—she was still waist-deep, thrashing against a swarm of light-snakes that writhed around her arms and throat. Their glowing white forms dimmed with every coil, as if they were literally drinking her life-force.

"Aria, hold on!" Wilhelmina shouted. "Selenus! Lumina! Phaethon! Help me!"

They were doubled over, trying to catch their breath, but Phaethon and Lumina lunged back over the crack. A massive tendril lashed out, knocking them away.

Selenus's grip slackened on the Sword of Truth's hilt, and his expression clouded as if he were caught in a sudden, internal fog.

"Selenus!" Wilhelmina's voice cracked like a whip. "We need you!"

Selenus shook himself out of the stupor and drew his blade. In a blur of motion, he joined Lumina and Phaethon.

"Focus on the tendrils!" he barked, his eyes scanning the chaos. "Cut them cleanly, but don't let them touch you!" He slashed at the light-snake choking Aria.

The entity screamed—a hollow, dissonant sound—as Selenus severed its head.

Aria gasped, her face flushing as the air finally returned to her lungs.

During the melee, Wilhelmina returned to the stone circle, her fingers tracing the glowing geometry once more. She whispered a second incantation, which sent ripples of light through the ground.

Sacred stones, your power I call,
Bind the darkness, stand as a wall.
Light and shadow intertwine.
Seal this breach, and hold the line.

"The stones can hold them," she muttered, her sweat dripping onto the ancient rock.

"But not for long!" Lumina stepped forward. Her hands glowed with a beam of concentrated inner light. "We'll hold the tendrils! Pull her out—now!"

Selenus and Phaethon gripped Aria's arms, while Lumina's light clashed against the dark tendrils, burning them away. But the shadowy forces fought back with renewed vigor.

Wilhelmina staggered back, her breath stuttering as she watched the chasm continue to expand. Its dark interior hummed with a hungry energy. "Hurry!" she cried. "If it gets any wider, we'll be trapped on the wrong side!"

"Aria, grab my arm!" Phaethon grunted, digging his heels into the earth.

Selenus gripped Aria's other arm, bracing against the force.

With a final, desperate tug that made their tendons snap with tension, they hauled Aria free of the chasm's lip.

Aria collapsed into their arms, gasping as the last of the light-snakes dissolved into the dark. Dirt and tears streaked her cheeks as she looked up at her rescuers. "Th-thank you… that was awful!"

Wilhelmina rose, her legs shaky and her face pale. "The circle's energy is fading. The forest will not forgive us so easily." She watched as the retreating shadows slithered back into the widening crack like oil retreating into a drain. Her gaze shifted to the vein of shadow running through the crack.

Selenus followed her line of sight. "Why does it feel like the fissure was just an invitation for something worse?"

He didn't see the ring of black smoke until it was coiling at his feet. It was nearly weightless, an imperceptible anomaly in the dim light. He swiped at it with his blade, but the vapor evaded the steel, slithering toward his ankle. As it brushed his skin, a sharp jolt shot up his leg—cold and searing all at once.

A gasp escaped him, and his body reeled.

"You will never escape this," a dark whisper curled around his mind. *"The shadow is who you are."*

Lumina's head swiveled sharply toward the sound. "What was that?"

Selenus stumbled, his head reeling. "Nothing," he snapped, though his hand lingered on his ankle where the cold remained, throbbing like a brand.

Above them, the Omega star pulsed a deep, violent crimson. Seeing the worry on his brother's face, Selenus walked toward him. "We could have died," he admitted, his voice low.

Phaethon didn't answer with words; he pulled Selenus into a fierce, grounding embrace. Nearby, Lumina held Aria's hands. "I almost lost you," she murmured.

To break the heavy silence, Selenus managed a weak chuckle as he looked at their muddied robes. "We need to find that stream—and wash off this mess."

Wilhelmina smiled, though her eyes remained serious. "Do you think we can learn to compromise now?"

Her eyes darted between the two brothers.

Phaethon faced Aria and Lumina. "What do you think?"

"Both your instincts are good. But in this case, Selenus's idea makes more sense," Aria said.

Phaethon bowed his head. "Very well. A good leader knows when to listen to common sense." He clapped Selenus's back. "Your instincts were right, brother. The stream is the best choice."

He turned to Aria and Lumina. "I overheard your ideas, and you're both right as well. Let's find a place on the map where there are boughs bordering a clearing. We'll set up camp there."

After a moment of shared realization, the group finally listened to each other. They found a spot on the map where the stream met a clearing wide enough to see threats coming, yet sheltered by thick boughs—a perfect synthesis of everyone's ideas.

Their renewed laughter mingled with the whispers of the luminous forest. As they set forth, Wilhelmina glanced back. A dark red glow was emanating from the crack in the earth, a perfect, mocking mirror to the star above.

❧

Later, encamped under the shadow of the mountains, the companions watched the flames of their campfire. The Guardian's Sanctuary was a jagged silhouette on the horizon.

"You did what was needed in the moment." Lumina glanced at Wilhelmina. "But how did you know what to do with the stones?"

"Gwydion taught me about the sacred geometry of stone circles," Wilhelmina explained, poking the fire until sparks danced like tiny stars. "They harness the natural ley lines of the earth to stabilize balance. It's what I used for marriages... to unite what was at risk of fracturing."

She looked at the brothers. "Something to remember if we ever find ourselves at odds again."

Selenus nodded, the firelight softening his features. "Phaethon, I know I can be difficult. My fears have always clouded my judgment. I'll endeavor to listen."

"And I will respect your instincts," Phaethon replied, his hand steady on his brother's shoulder. "But to be fair, it must be annoying to have an older brother under pressure to always be right."

Selenus grinned. "Your power comes from the courage and wisdom you already possess. I've always admired that."

"From now on, we share the burden of leadership." Phaethon extended his hand, and Selenus grasped it warmly.

The peace was short-lived. Lumina pulled her focus toward the sky, where the meteor heralding the Omega Event was positioned, no longer a siren blue but an urgent crimson. At a near distance away, Wilhelmina's stellar imprint mirrored the chaos spreading across the cosmos.

"The meteor's colors are changing. It was calmer earlier, but now it's growing angrier. I've never witnessed such hostility from the forest. It's reacting to its changes."

"Aaahhh!" Selenus suddenly arched, clutching at his chest. His face went ash-white as a sharp pain coursed through him with every pulse of the star.

"Selenus!" Wilhelmina dropped to her knees beside him.

"It feels like something is tearing me apart from the inside," he wheezed, shielding his face as if from an invisible blow. A flash of anguish crossed his face. "Every pulse... It's as if... it... echoes... in my soul."

Lumina's expression turned grim. "This is new." She turned to Phaethon, her brows knitting tightly. "It is possible that the chaos of the Omega Event is awakening the Curse of the Shadow's Heir."

Phaethon rubbed his face, his voice heavy with a long-held fear. "I thought we could avoid it... but you're right. The star must be forcing it to the surface."

Wilhelmina looked up at the menacing red light mocking them from the heavens. "We must get to the Sanctuary," she commanded. "Let's break camp. We move now, before the shadow takes him completely."

The meteor throbbed again, a deep bass note that made the very air quiver with pressure.

24. Curse of the Shadow's Heir

Dawn's weak glimmer failed to pierce the heavy canopy as the companions resumed their march. Though unity had returned, an unsettling tension coiled beneath their steps, mirrored by the forest itself. Beneath Selenus's calm exterior, a darker flicker pulsed—a shadow hidden from most, but not from Wilhelmina. To her, it looked like he was being pulled toward an invisible brink. The rift in the earth had been sealed, yet a deeper one festered within the roots of the woods.

Oppressive darkness pressed in. A chilling wind carried haunting murmurs, and the bioluminescent flora flickered intermittently, casting eerie, lace-like patterns across the shifting forest floor.

Wilhelmina and Phaethon moved as one, their hands gripping Selenus's arms to keep him upright.

His condition worsened with every step. Jabbing pains wracked his body, leaving him staggering and clutching at his chest. The forest watched him; the glowing moss dimmed in time with his labored gasps, and the murmurs of the trees sharpened into mournful sighs that echoed his suffering.

"Leave me here!" Selenus suddenly cried out, his voice raw, piercing the forest's fragile calm. "I cannot come back from the shadow I conjured. There is no penance for me!"

"What's happening to him?" Phaethon's voice broke as he struggled to hold his brother's weight.

"I don't know," Lumina said, her focus narrowing on spectral wisps that swirled around Selenus like smoke. "But the shadows are hunting him."

Aria nodded, her face pale. "It's like the curse is growing stronger the nearer we get to the Sanctuary. It's not just an ailment—it's a tether, pulling him away from the light."

"Selenus, please, just hold on," Wilhelmina pleaded, her voice trembling. "This is the darkness trying to thwart us. We have to stay focused."

But her words barely reached him. His legs buckled, and he collapsed onto the luminescent moss, convulsing as gasps tore through his chest.

"Go without me..." he rasped, the sound broken and small. "You must reach... the Guardian."

Wilhelmina crouched beside Selenus, her hands shaking as she watched him writhe. She looked up at the churning heavens, her voice cutting through the discordant whistle of the wind. "Even if the Omega Event has started, Selenus, your life takes precedence over this quest."

"I can't... bear... to fail you all," he gasped, his fists clenching until his knuckles were white. "Promise me... see this through. Everyone is depending on us."

Above them, the sky deepened to a bruised purple as the star's crimson pulse quickened.

"Not without you." Phaethon knelt beside his brother, ignoring his protests. With a grunt of pure determination, he hoisted Selenus over his shoulders. "Let's go!"

The group broke into a desperate run, the path twisting and narrowing before them like a closing throat.

❧

The woods seemed alive, their shadows stretching like clawed hands to grasp at the companions as they pushed forward in a race against time. Finally, the trees thinned. The faint glimmer of the Guardian's domain appeared ahead like a beacon, but its light shimmered erratically—a frantic echo of the Omega star's angry pulse.

"There might be spells or charms hidden here we haven't thought of yet."

Lumina's brow furrowed, her light flickering with caution. "We can't risk using dark magic without fully understanding its consequences, Phaethon. If we miscalculate, it could accelerate the curse."

Aria folded her arms, her gaze moving from the mountains back to Selenus. "There may be other answers besides a magical cure," she reminded them softly. "Remember what we've overcome with just our hands and our heads. Magic isn't the only way home."

Despite their debate, exhaustion claimed them. As the group collapsed into a restless sleep, the fire crackled, casting jagged light against the encroaching mist. Wilhelmina stayed awake, her heart quickening.

Through the fog, a voice—obscure and ethereal—echoed in her mind: "*Beware the tangled roots in the darkness and a betrayal misunderstood.*"

"What was that?" Wilhelmina whispered, but the others lay still, their breathing rhythmic. Only Selenus was awake. He sat apart from the circle, a slouched figure staring at a distant, invisible point.

She approached him softly. "Selenus, talk to me."

"It's not just a curse, Wilhelmina," he said, his voice hollow, as if coming from the bottom of a well. "It's a reflection. The shadow I conjured... my stupid fears."

Wilhelmina reached for his hand, her grip firm and warm. "Your past doesn't define you." She nudged his chin upward, forcing him to meet her eyes. "You've been a light to us. Especially for me." She brushed a damp lock from his brow, smiling through threatening tears.

Selenus held her stare, but his voice grew heavier. "Long ago, my father received a prophecy... a dire warning of a great imbalance threatening Aetherwyn. He believed it would arise from our lineage."

Selenus sighed, his shoulders sagging. "Hidden texts in the palace archives spoke of a scion—someone doomed to lead the realm toward destruction by succumbing to darker impulses.... Jealousy, envy, fear... The Curse of the Shadow's Heir."

Phaethon's eyes fluttered open. He rose without a sound and stepped into the firelight. "I always feared I was the heir," Phaethon admitted softly. "I envied you and sought power, thinking it would make me worthy. But my pride made me someone I didn't recognize."

"No, Phaethon!" Selenus's voice broke. His tears brimmed unchecked. "It was I. The night the Enchantress untethered me... I told her you despised her. I wanted her to favor me alone. I hoarded her attention like a thief."

A heavy silence stretched between them, fragile as a silken thread.

Phaethon's voice was a mere whisper. "I didn't know. I wish you had told me... I would have helped you carry it."

"I was ashamed," Selenus sobbed. "I thought handling it alone was the best way. I thought I could bear it. But now I see how wrong I was. Hurting you was never my intention."

Phaethon knelt, placing a firm hand on his brother's shoulder before pulling him into a fierce embrace. "We've both made mistakes. But we're still here."

Selenus pulled back, his hand drifting to his robe. "I think this is the root. And then... I stole her wand."

"You *stole* it? I thought she gave it to you!"

"I wanted a piece of her," Selenus admitted, his hand shaking as he dragged the artifact from his robe.

"When the Enchantress forged it, she meant to bestow it upon someone worthy," Phaethon said, breaking the uneasy silence. "She searched for it after it went missing, but she must have had some idea you took it." His eyes softened. "The irony is that I believe that was her intention—to let you have the wand all along."

Wilhelmina's mouth opened slightly, then closed as if she were searching for words. Instead, she inhaled deeply, steadying her voice. "May I see it?"

Selenus's hand drifted unconsciously toward his robe pocket, as though something inside pulsed with weight. "It's... here," he admitted, tone almost apologetic. He patted his chest. "I believed I might need it for the journey... had hoped to give it back to Demiurge... but that wasn't possible."

As the wand emerged, it pulsed with a parasitic malevolence. A jolt of dark energy lashed out, making Selenus gasp. He forced the wood into Wilhelmina's palm. It was unnervingly cold. Wisps of black smoke seeped from the tip like necrotic, tangled roots pulled from poisoned soil.

"This wand... has been poisoned by shadow, and it's been feeding on you," Wilhelmina whispered, tracing the gnarled, blackened fibers embedded in its surface. "It's alive. Forged for balance, but twisted by a betrayal misunderstood. I am sure it is the source of the curse."

She looked at the roots. "These are from the Celestial Arbor. Snarled by misuse."

"The prophecy became a self-fulfilling one," Selenus realized, running his hands through his hair. "The warning planted the seeds, and I let them take root."

"Then we uproot them," Phaethon said firmly.

Lumina and Aria, now fully awake, stepped forward. Lumina's gaze darted to the incandescent trees. "We're surrounded by light, but this will take more power. Both Phaethon and I can help. Wilhelmina, rebalance it. Use our light to harness the opposite of that shadow."

A chilling breeze hissed through the camp, extinguishing the fire. A low, mocking snigger rose from the very dirt.

"The darkness is here," Wilhelmina said, her face taut. "Hands together. Now!"

Phaethon and Lumina seized Selenus's hands, placing the wand between them. Wilhelmina whispered an incantation, drawing the silver radiance of the trees and merging it with Phaethon's outer glow and Lumina's inner brilliance. This power shot into the thick shadow intertwined with Selenus.

The wand resisted, vibrating with a violent, coarse energy, but the light pressed in.

Suddenly, the black roots whitened. The smoke transmuted into radiant, silken strands. A soft pink glow—the true, heartbeat-throb of the Celestial Arbor—pulsed through the wood.

"This is love," Aria whispered, blinking back tears.

Selenus inhaled deeply, his chest finally moving at a normal, rhythmic pace. "I feel... lighter," he breathed.

Wilhelmina stared at the wand. Its transformation was incomplete but unmistakable. The roots glowed pale and pure; the smoke was gone. But its core hummed with power, even now. "The wand is quiet now, but its power has not diminished. We must guard it carefully."

The wand lay in Wilhelmina's hand, no longer colored or heavy, but a glowing ember of peace. Above them, the angry crimson of the star faded to a steady, watchful white, bathing the weary companions in a warm, protective light as they finally settled into a dreamless rest.

25. A River in Reverie

An expansive sky, dotted with the light of several moons, domed the open valley. Below, a flowing river meandered across the landscape like ribbons of blue and silver. While it appeared serene, the stream was a sentinel, blocking the path to the Guardian's Sanctuary. Beyond it, a forest of intense, vibrating hues stood in stark contrast to the monochromatic white woods the companions had only recently escaped.

The red sun climbed higher, signaling the dawn. They had left the oppressive woodland hours earlier, guided by the looming presence of the Omega star. There, the shadows that had threatened them finally failed.

Selenus, still weakened and pale, managed to keep pace only with Phaethon's support. Though the wand was healed, the brothers avoided eye contact; its revelation had sparked a new tension between them that even the morning light could not dissolve.

The alizarin sunlight bathed the tops of their heads and shoulders as they stopped to take in the river's expanse. Wilhelmina paused at the water's edge, staring into the depths as they shifted like liquid glass. A strange, heavy stillness emanated from the current—a silence that seemed more an observation than peace.

"This water is like a mirror, but it's more than that," Wilhelmina whispered, a chill tracing her skin. "It seems to something deeper than our images... as if it knows us."

Lumina and Aria drew close beside her. "It's the River of Reverie," Lumina said, her voice tinged with the gravity of memory. "I've crossed it many a time, and you're right. The river is sentient, Wilhelmina; it carries the collective dreams of the realm toward the Sanctuary."

Aria leaned over the bank, her wide eyes reflecting the river's iridescent brilliance. To her, the water held no malice. "It's magnificent," she breathed.

"We have to cross if we want to reach your grandfather," Wilhelmina said, her nod firm despite the uncertainty in her chest. "But how?"

"There." Selenus, his voice hoarse from the lingering shadow, pointed toward the distance. An elegant bridge spanned the current, its arc forged of luminous solid light. "We can cut across from there."

The companions hurried toward the structure. Its surface gleamed with a slick, glass-like polish beneath their boots—a beautiful but treacherous path. Halfway across, the fragility of their state took its toll. Phaethon shifted his weight to better support Selenus, but the sudden movement unbalanced him. His foot slipped on the frictionless light, and Selenus's weakened grip failed to catch him.

Phaethon's body lurched. In a heartbeat, gravity claimed him, pulling him into the river's icy embrace. The splash broke sharply against the still air, shattering the river's mesmerizing hum like a stone through glass.

"Phaethon!" Selenus's cry was raw as he reached out helplessly toward the churning wake.

Lumina dove without a second's hesitation, her sprite-glow slicing into the water like a falling star. But the river's current surged, an unyielding grip of frost that dragged her down as quickly as it had taken Phaethon.

Underwater, a nightmare turned into reality. Phaethon's limbs flailed as dark forces—sentient and hungry—dragged him into the depths. The cold was a physical assault, like thousands of needles piercing his skin, and the fire in his lungs grew as he fought the instinct to inhale the freezing brine. His struggles only sapped his strength, and terror twisted his features as the river moved to consume him whole.

Lumina's radiance flickered in the dark pressure like a fragile, dying beacon. She kicked with desperate force, propelling herself through the heavy currents until she finally reached him, her frozen hands grasping his arm.

But the river resisted. Its tendrils of glistening water coiled tighter around their ankles, a liquid noose that held firm. High above on the bridge of light, the others watched in a paralysis of horror as seconds swiftly bled into minutes.

Aria remained on her knees, her knuckles white against the bridge's edge, while Selenus stood frozen, his body trembling as much from the curse's lingering shadow as from fear. "They've been under too long," he choked out, clenching his fists. "The river isn't natural. It's fighting them."

Underwater, shadows danced in maniacal patterns, casting eerie, shifting shapes that mocked the survivors above. Suddenly, a faint glow pierced the murk.

"Look! Lumina's still there!" Aria pointed, her breath hitching. "She's holding his hand!"

But the river was drawn to Lumina's celestial sprite-nature. It churned with renewed spite, seeking to extinguish her inner flame.

A low, rhythmic hum vibrated in the depths, a sound like a thousand voices whispering in the fathoms below.

"Do you hear that?" Aria's voice trembled. "The water—it's competing with Lumina's light!"

The riverbed shuddered, sending a tremor up into the light-bridge. Wilhelmina and Selenus threw their arms wide for balance, but Aria used the sway to propel herself upward.

She rose and kicked off her shoes, her face hardening with a resolve they had never seen. "They're not coming up... I have to save them."

"No! Aria, you don't know how to swim!" Wilhelmina's hands reached out to snag her, but the girl was too quick.

Aria pivoted, her expression severe, her eyes reflecting the silver moons above. "Look after Selenus," she commanded, her voice strangely calm. "Quill would have done the same for me." Without waiting for a response, she jumped. Her small form vanished underwater with a sharp, final splash.

Minutes stretched into an unbearable silence. Selenus and Wilhelmina stood as statues, staring at the rippling wake.

"We have to do something!" Wilhelmina's body shook with the force of her panic. "But what can I—"

"Go, Wilhelmina," Selenus urged, placing a hand upon the bridge to steady himself. "I'll be fine. Go!"

Wilhelmina dove. As she opened her eyes in the viscous, biting water, the scene was a nightmare in motion. Aria, pale and wide-eyed, was pointing frantically toward the others. Phaethon and Lumina's bodies twisted against the river's relentless grip as strands of light—coiled like serpents—anchored their ankles to the silt.

In her satchel, the Sphere of Golden Thread pulsed with an immediate, hot intensity. As she pulled it free, its brilliance spilled into the murky depths, causing the river to recoil as if burned. With desperate movements, Wilhelmina unraveled a length of the thread, fashioning a lasso even as the suffocating pressure of the water crushed her chest.

To her left, Phaethon's eyes were rolling back, his bubbles thinning to a final, silver stream. To her right, Aria's small hands clawed at the empty current, her frenzied movements already slowing into the lethargy of the deep.

An impossible decision: *who to save?*

The river mocked Wilhelmina's hesitation. Its tendrils tugged like the hands of fate, indifferent to mortal love or the agony of choice.

She surged toward Phaethon and Lumina, her golden lasso trailing behind her like a streak of captured sun. As she looped the thread over their twisting forms, its light flared with a violet brilliance. The vines writhed, hissing into the silt as if scalded. Freed from the river's spite, the two companions kicked toward the surface, leaving Wilhelmina to turn her desperate focus to the melody-siren who could not swim.

She propelled herself toward Aria. The Sphere pulsed in her hand as she lashed a second lasso over her friend, the thread burning through the clinging tendrils. Nearly all were loosened from the river's grip.

Save for one.

Wilhelmina's lungs screamed for air, and her vision blurred into a kaleidoscope of dark blues and grays, but she refused to let go of Aria's hand. She kicked, her muscles burning with a lactic fire, hauling them both toward the shimmering ceiling of the surface.

Yet the final tendril—a vine woven from the cosmos's unwept sorrow—refused to yield. It didn't just hold; it snapped tight around Aria's ankle with a sickening tug. Wilhelmina lunged, her fingers brushing Aria's sleeve.

The melody-siren's hand, slick with river water, slipped from Wilhelmina's grasp.

Their eyes met for one fleeting, eternal moment.

Aria's gaze was not of terror, but of serenity—a silent goodbye before the vine dragged her into a swirling funnel of blackness at the river's floor.

Wilhelmina froze, the image branding itself onto her soul. Her lungs could bear no more; the black void nipped at her skirts, threatening to claim a second prize, and she was forced to surge upward. The river released her with a lingering reluctance, and she broke the surface with a gasp that tore at her throat.

She drank in air in ragged, sobbing gulps, but her reprieve was a hollow thing. An anguished scream rose unbidden—raw, primal, and wrenching. It echoed across the valley, scattering birds from their perches. Other animals fled into the shadows, stunned by the sheer magnitude of her grief.

On the opposite shore, Phaethon and Lumina collapsed into each other, trembling and pale, coughing the river's ice from their lungs.

Relief washed over Selenus as he staggered to them. "Oh, thank the Eternal Ones—you're alive!" He spun his head toward the water, searching for Wilhelmina and Aria. All he saw was Wilhelmina's form bobbing in the current, resembling a frozen iceberg buoyed in glacial waters.

She did not move. Her skirts clung to her as she stared into the churning spot where Aria had vanished as if she were silently begging the river to return what it had stolen.

Finally, she turned to face the bank. Her strokes were slow, mechanical. The river had sapped not just her strength, but her will.

After what seemed an eternity, Wilhelmina hauled onto the damp ground. Tears blurred her vision as she crawled forward a few paces before collapsing onto her hands and knees. Raw and unrelenting, her sobs broke through the fragile silence.

"It should have been me," Wilhelmina choked out, the words thick with river-silt. "I've failed her... I've failed them all." Her shoulders shook, and the sound of her sobs mingled with the eternal, indifferent whispers of the river.

The forest canopy shuddered as the companions huddled on the riverbank, their breaths shallow, uneven, and heavy with the scent of silt. The import of their loss pressed down on the atmosphere as a smothering fog would, dampening the trees' flourishing colors. Wilhelmina sat hunched by the water, peering at a single, unmoving point on the ground, her eyes glassy and distant. Beside her, Selenus crouched in the dirt, his arm moving in a mechanical, rhythmic motion as he rubbed her back, trying to provide a warmth he didn't truly feel himself.

A familiar voice rang out from the distance, strained and frantic, yet carrying an unmistakable note of hope.

"Aria? Wilhelmina? Selenus?"

The companions turned toward the sound, their movements sluggish and hesitant, as if moving through deep water.

It was Quill.

He emerged through the kaleidoscopic trees, stumbling over roots with quick, unsteady steps. He wore a cloak adorned with mirrored fractals that caught the alizarin light, splintering into a thousand tiny rainbows.

In his hands, he clutched a small, weathered journal. "There you are! I can't believe I've found you!" His radiant smile burst through the gloom, his chest heaving with exertion. "You will never guess how I managed... Never mind. I'll tell you... It was the Book of Truth! Goodness, it has more magic than anything I've yet to see."

His head spun, and he turned in a circle, searching the riverbank for his North Star. "I've got to tell Aria—"

He stopped. His gaze bounced from Selenus's dripping tunic to the way Lumina wouldn't look up from the mud. The color drained from his lips, making them appear bruised and waxy white.

"Aria?" he whispered, the name small and hollow. "Where is she? Where's Aria?"

No one answered. The silence was absolute.

Selenus looked down at his boots, unable to meet the elf's gaze. Lumina tightened her grip on her own arms, her light dim and flickering. Phaethon turned his head away, staring at a distant, empty point across the churning river.

Wilhelmina rose unsteadily to her feet, her shoulders slumped under an invisible mantle of lead. Her tears flowed anew, hot and salty-bitter. "Quill, I—" Her voice cracked, the words splintering before they could form.

"Why are you all wet?" Quill's tone sharpened, a defensive edge born of sudden, keen intuition. His face paled to a chalky shade of white as his stare locked onto Wilhelmina's tear-streaked features. He saw her breath hitching, her lips blue from the cold. "What happened?"

She opened her mouth, but the air in her lungs seemed to turn to stone. No sound emerged.

"Aria...?" Quill's voice grew thin and uncontrolled. He stumbled forward, the mirrored fractals on his cloak clashing as he gripped Wilhelmina's shoulders. "Tell me. Where is she?"

Wilhelmina's lips trembled. Finally, in a hoarse whisper that barely carried over the river's hum, she choked out the truth. "She... she's gone. The river... took her."

Quill staggered back as if she had struck him. His arms dropped to his sides, and the journal slipped from his numb fingers, landing soundlessly on the damp earth.

"No." His chest heaved, and he took another step back, bobbing his head in agitated denial. "That's not true. She can't be gone. She can't—she wouldn't!"

Wilhelmina reached out, her hands shaking, but he spun away from her touch.

"You let her go—" Quill's voice broke, accusation hanging overhead like a poisoned mist.

"I tried," Wilhelmina sobbed, her words splintered. "I tried to save her, but I—"

"She fought with everything she had," Selenus interrupted, his voice firm as he stepped forward to place a steadying hand on Quill's shoulder. "But the river's magic was stronger than any of us. Aria... sacrificed herself."

Quill's gaze snapped back to Wilhelmina, his eyes rimmed with a sudden wild grief. "How could you—how could any of you let this happen?"

"Stop!" Selenus moved between them, shielding Wilhelmina from her friend's misplaced rage. "This isn't helping."

The fight left Quill at once. He sank to his knees in the mud. "Nor can she now... She always said her song carried the essence of those she loved." Streams of tears spilled unchecked down his cheeks. "Not anymore..."

Wilhelmina stumbled backward, her head shaking. Every word from Quill was a dagger to her chest, twisting in the wound of her own guilt. "I can't... do this."

Before anyone could stop her, she turned and fled, her boots thudding against the moss as she escaped into the forest's deepening shadows. The companions watched her go, her sobs fading into the distance until only the river remained.

For a fleeting moment, a gentle breeze brushed past those remaining on the bank. It carried a strange, impossible warmth and a flicker of soft light that lingered near the water's brink. It resembled a bird's wing grazing the air, a final, ethereal caress. Then the warmth vanished, leaving only the cold silence of the woods.

Selenus stared into the darkness where Wilhelmina had disappeared. He hesitated between going to the broken elf on the ground and the broken fairy in the trees. Finally, his feet moved.

Quill remained kneeling, his head buried in his hands, while quiet, hollow sobs racked his body. Lumina and Phaethon stepped closer, hovering like ghosts, but no words came to their lips. There was no language left in any realm that could fix this.

The forest stilled. The colorful leaves ceased their shivering, and for a long, heavy moment, the world stopped its natural rhythms in honor of the light that had gone out.

❧

Selenus found her slumped against a tree with bark the color of turquoise and yellow, her sobs muffled by the damp cerulean moss. He approached cautiously, his own heart heavy as lead, his voice low and trembling. "Wilhelmina."

"Go away," she rasped, her face hidden. "You were right. I'm not strong enough. I never was."

He knelt beside her, meeting her gaze, and placed his large hand over her delicate one. "I didn't mean—"

"Don't," she snapped, her eyes blazing through a veil of tears. "Do not try to fix this. I failed her. I failed everyone."

"You didn't fail," he breathed, though his own guilt seemed like a collar around his neck. "The river's magic—"

"No." She cut him off, her voice rising in a jagged spike of despair. "It is over. I'm not the leader you all think I am." Her body shivered, and she dug her fingers into the earth. "I have ceased to care. It is not worth the pain."

"Please... do not give up," Selenus murmured, leaning closer. His hand brushed her shoulder. It acted as a spark to a fuse.

She lifted her head sharply, her gaze locking onto his lips. A breath passed between them, heavy and charged with the static of a thousand unsaid words. Without warning, she simply lunged, her mouth crashing against his with a desperate, bruising force that tasted of salt and the freezing river.

For a moment, Selenus froze. Their first kiss—the mirrored illusion in Miragwyn—was a distant, fragile dream compared to this wildfire. Devouring and uncontrollable.

But something else stirred. The residual curse of the wand, dormant but potent, slithered up like a shadow. It touched his lips and coiled around the love they shared, sensing the darkness in Wilhelmina's heart. It poisoned the connection, turning the fire between them into a bitter taste of ash.

Selenus broke away abruptly, gasping as if he had been submerged again. He took her by the shoulders, holding her at arm's length. "No! Wilhelmina, we can't. Not like this."

Her expression crumpled, and she pressed her quivering fingers to her lips. Her gaze searched his face. "Why not? Aria and Quill had love—and now it's gone. Why keep pretending there's time? Why should I keep denying what I want?"

Her next words tumbled out like a flood through a broken dam. "I want you, Selenus. I want a future and a life where we aren't running from shadows. And I know you want me too. I feel it in every look, every touch."

Selenus's grip loosened. He rubbed his face with unsteady hands, the furrows on his brow deepening. "The realms need us," he whispered, his voice cracking. "You were the one who told me that once."

Her shoulders stiffened, and her once-vivid gaze hardened to steel. "The realms take everything from us! They demand our lives, our souls, and leave us with nothing. I won't let them take this, too."

"Wilhelmina," he pleaded. "Aria was brave... just as you were. You tried—"

"I let the river take her!" Her fingers bunched the fabric of his tunic. "If you'd been there, you would've saved her. You wouldn't have failed her the way I did."

Selenus reached out, raising her chin so she had no choice but to see the truth in his eyes. "You told me once that I wasn't alone... that my past doesn't define me. Why can't you believe that for yourself?"

She looked down, her voice a hollow echo. "It's different with me."

Selenus caught her wrists. Redness rimmed his eyes, the corners crinkling as he fought back his own flood of emotion. "I'm not a savior, Wilhelmina. Neither are you. We're just...trying to hold on."

She froze, her chest rising in an uneven, shallow breath. Slowly, her grip loosened. She released him as if he were made of the same ice that had filled the river.

"Fine," she whispered. "You don't want me. I'll go. Do what you will."

"You're wrong!" He grasped her shoulders again, desperate to make her understand. "My love for you has always been there. Even when I was too blind to see it. If you just have faith—"

"It changes nothing." She closed her eyes, and a lone tear escaped. "It's too late, Selenus. The darkness has already won."

He extended his hand to touch her cheek, but she stepped back into the shadows.

"You're better off without me," she said, her voice thin, like a dying ember of a fire.

Before he could respond, she swiveled and ran further into the forest, her figure swallowed by the strange, colorful trees. The leaves quivered in her wake, their rustle fading with every step.

Selenus remained rooted in place, his outstretched hand trembling before falling limply to his side. His shoulders slumped, and his breath faltered. He stared at the empty space she had left behind until the crunch of approaching footsteps broke his daze.

Phaethon pressed his lips together, his brow furrowing as he looked at his brother. "What happened? Why is she leaving?"

"She did nothing but save us!" Lumina cried, running up beside Phaethon, her light flickering erratically. "I am the one at fault. I should have known the river would fight me."

Phaethon laid a quieting grip on the sprite's shoulder. "Lumina, this wasn't your fault. There was something darker at work. I've never seen anything like it—an evil that clings to everything here."

"This is true," Lumina whispered. "The darkness has nearly saturated the Whispering Woods. But Aria... I couldn't save her. And now, Wilhelmina... I have to go after her."

"No." Selenus cut her off. He leaned heavily against the turquoise bark, his head tilting forward as if it were too heavy to lift. But then, a resounding will pulled him upright. He drew in a deep, ragged breath, the dark circles rimming his eyes clearing. "I will find her."

Without looking back, Selenus broke into a run, the crunch of leaves beneath his boots marking his path as he vanished into the forest after her.

26. The Observatory

A faint, diaphanous light shone above Wilhelmina as she ran, its glow cutting through the Forest of Colors' high-spirited, shifting hues. The radiance intensified, coalescing into a translucent, gleaming form of Gwydion.

She froze, her breath hitching as she looked up. Perched on a high branch of a tree with bark dappled like a painter's palette, the ageless owl peered down at her with eyes that held the depth of ancient nebulae.

"Gwydion! H-How...?"

"My body is fast asleep in Aetherwyn," the owl's voice resonated in her mind, a low vibration of wisdom. "Within my dreams, our bond allows me to see you in your greatest time of need."

"It's too late." Wilhelmina pressed her palms to her face, the silt of the river still dry and chalky against her skin. "Aria is lost to us..."

Gwydion bowed his head low toward his talons. In a silent ripple of magic, the forest's flamboyant colors dimmed in solemn accord, the turquoise and yellows fading into bruised violets. Then, he rose, expanding his wings until they seemed to span the very sky.

A trill of birdsong responded from the deep woods—a sharp, clear requiem that echoed through the canopy. Once the exchange of nature's music faded, Gwydion ruffled his feathers and met Wilhelmina's eyes with a piercing, unblinking gaze.

"Grief grips you, as it did when the Enchantress left you as a tiny chrysalis. Then, as now, do not despair or let the darkness take root in the soil of your heart."

Wilhelmina sank to her knees, the damp moss soaking into her skirts. "I've lost everything and everyone... I'm so ashamed."

"The river has claimed much, but love is not lost—it is remade," Gwydion said, his voice dropping to a soothing hum. "It transforms, just as you must. You stand at the edge of creation itself, Wilhelmina. Let its infinite patterns remind you that what is broken can be woven anew. Let your heart be the loom. Your path continues—into the next measure of what you are meant to compose."

Wilhelmina reached toward the spectral owl, her lips parting to speak, but the ground beneath her feet thrummed with a sudden, rhythmic tremor.

"Wilhelmina!" Selenus's voice rang out, raw and desperate, from the shadows behind her.

In the blink of an eye, before she could cry out, a radiant light erupted around her. The world blurred, dissolving into a kaleidoscope of brilliance—and she was gone, the light swallowing her whole.

Selenus didn't hesitate. Seeing the golden flare begin to collapse, he surged forward with a final, long-bursting effort, diving into the heart of the brilliance just before it vanished from the forest earth.

❧

The lush forest dissolved into a radiant corridor of light—a prismatic continuum where time stretched and folded like heated glass. Wilhelmina, and now Selenus—hastening to narrow the distance between them—had stepped into a realm suspended between dimensions, where the boundaries of the known world blurred into a luminous infinity.

Selenus stared at the back of Wilhelmina's head, his hand white-knuckled on the hilt of his sword. He angled his posture forward, his boots striking the floor with a rhythmic echo that sounded like a heartbeat in a vacuum. Each step was laced with an unnamed but undeniable urgency.

"Wilhelmina! Wait!"

She stood at the edge of a great threshold and spun at the sound. Her eyes were red-rimmed and narrow. "What are you doing here? Why did you follow me?" Her voice wavered, thin as a reed. "You shouldn't have come, Selenus."

She wrapped her arms tighter around herself, a physical barricade against the crack that ran through her very soul. As she did, the corridor walls rippled with faint, unsettling whispers—echoes of grief or perhaps the future—and the light momentarily flickered.

"I told you before." Selenus halted, standing as an immovable pillar before her. "I will always stand beside you, no matter what you choose."

A jagged laugh escaped her. "You may regret that."

She took a sharp, bracing breath and stepped forward. The path beneath her feet solidified into ancient, thrumming stone the moment her weight touched it. Selenus followed at a distance, silent and watchful.

"I won't," he murmured. The words left him like a vow—meant for her, and perhaps for himself as well. He gestured toward the shifting brilliance. "Now that we're here... what is this place?"

"I have no idea—Oh!" Wilhelmina gasped, her head tilting back as she looked upward.

In a reflex of pure instinct, she reached back and clasped Selenus's hand. He looked down at their joined grip—silt-stained fingers against his calloused palm—and pulled her beside him.

Beneath a kaleidoscope canopy, a symphony of color and motion unfolded. Unbridled energy wove through the air in viscous ribbons, making the space come alive with the electricity of unspoken possibilities. Their lips parted in unison. Wonder bloomed across their faces, momentarily eclipsing the sorrow of the riverbank.

The forest had been replaced by an arcane Observatory, its weathered stones thrumming with a latent, tectonic power. The ceiling had vanished, and in its place was a living tapestry of stars, planets, and nebulae. Each celestial body was tethered to the room by invisible strands of magic, like pearls on a string of golden thread.

Wilhelmina's breath caught as they entered the heart of the chamber. On the floor lay a glowing circle—a mosaic that appeared unbroken yet fundamentally incomplete.

Voices rose from the shadows, not as sounds, but as vibrations in their bones.

"Welcome, Wilhelmina. We have been waiting. It is time for you and the one who safeguards your heart to awaken."

Two intensely shining points of light in the heavenly ceiling grew brighter, detaching themselves and descending in a graceful, sweeping arc like falling stars. When the light hit the stone surface, the orbs materialized into two beings.

Stellara materialized first, the familiar twinkle in her eye and that lopsided, irreverent smile as sharp as ever. Beside her stood a man who carried the quiet gravity of a master mason. He looked like someone who had shaped stars with his bare hands and still had silver stardust under his fingernails.

"I've been meaning to introduce you," Stellara said, nudging the stranger with her elbow. "This is Zografos. He's meticulous, maddeningly methodical—and my mate."

Zografos now bowed his head, a heavy chisel resting loosely in one hand. "Master artist of creation, they say. I just work with raw potential and broken things."

He studied Wilhelmina—not with judgment, but with the clinical, attentive gaze of a restorer. He noted the invisible fractures of grief already shifting beneath her skin.

Wilhelmina and Selenus bowed their heads in greeting.

"I am happy indeed to see you both," Stellara said, her eyes meeting Wilhelmina's. She grinned with a mischievous glint in her eye. "You have come far, but the path narrows. The choices before you carry implications not just for your journey, but for the mechanics of every realm."

Wilhelmina faltered, her knees threatening to give way. "What... choices?"

"The Moon Prince's love for you," Stellara's features gentled, "and his desire to atone, drew him from his post. In his absence, the Moon remains untethered. The balance his father upholds is fraying under the strain."

"The tides of Lunarae have begun to stutter. Night arrives too early in some realms and never quite settles in others," Zografos added.

Selenus's expression tightened, his hand reflexively curling around the orb he carried. He withdrew it slowly, its glow dimming to a dull ember.

"I have carried this as a reminder of the weight I left behind," Selenus said, his voice dropping into a low register of regret. "I thought I could mend it by finding Wilhelmina and the Enchantress. How is my father?"

"Varytita grows weaker," Stellara replied, her tone grave but compassionate. "The strain threatens to collapse the gravitational bonds between the realms. Yet this imbalance is not his solely to bear. It falls to all of us to restore what has been unraveled."

Wilhelmina's knees buckled, and she reached out, her fingers brushing the cool, weathered stones for support. "Why would he take such a risk?"

"Love often leads us to choices that seem illogical." Stellara stepped closer. Her gaze held understanding, as though she spoke from a place of personal knowing. "But the threads of love, duty, and creation are never separate. They are woven together, where each choice pulls on the whole. It is not his alone to mend."

Behind her, Selenus released her hand and stepped back, his presence steady yet unintrusive. His shadow stretched across the chamber as if to shield her from the weight of her own history.

Wilhelmina's words spilled out in a raw confession. "I don't have anything left to give, Stellara. Aria... I've lost too much. I don't even want to care."

"Your grief is valid, Wilhelmina, but Selenus's orb has shown him the toll this imbalance has taken." Stellara gestured toward the dull glow in Selenus's hand. "Gravity diminishes, and the celestial forces weaken. If left unaddressed, King Varytita will collapse entirely."

Wilhelmina's head snapped up, her eyes blazing with a sudden, sharp fire. "How can I possibly fix this? How much more can the world demand of me? Why must I carry a burden I never asked for?"

"You are not alone in carrying these burdens, though the weight feels singular now," Stellara said, extending a radiant hand. "Creation is both a burden and a gift. It asks not for perfection, but for *possibility*. Your grief, your doubts—these are merely threads in the tapestry you are meant to weave."

Wilhelmina shook her head, her voice strained. "I don't want to weave anything. I've already lost too much. If this is destiny, then I reject it. I won't be a puppet to the universe's whims."

"Then don't be," Zografos said, his voice steady as a heartbeat. A wry smile curved his lips.

Startled, Wilhelmina pivoted from Stellara to him. For the first time, she met the Master Artist's eyes head-on. Her voice rose, fueled by a defiant strength. "I am tired of carrying burdens that aren't mine. If this is to be my destiny, then let it be one I choose. Let it be mine."

"Destiny is a suggestion, not a command," Zografos said, his steely gaze locking onto hers. "You are not here to fulfill a prophecy; you are here to *create*. To forge your own balance—not one dictated by stars or scrolls—but one born of your own will."

Zografos's voice softened, though its intensity remained, vibrating through the ancient stones. "Creation is transformation, Wilhelmina. It is not about fixing what is broken, but reshaping it into something new. You've already created simply by standing here and choosing to continue."

Wilhelmina's breath caught in a ragged hitch. "I-I don't believe that anymore."

She turned away, her fingers curling into her palms until her nails bit into her skin. The weight of the river was still in her lungs. "What if I choose wrong again? What if I break what little still holds?"

Selenus stepped beside her. He didn't reach out, nor did he offer platitudes. He simply stood there, steady and present, his silence louder and more grounding than any comfort could be.

For a long, suspended moment, Wilhelmina stared at the fractured pattern beneath her feet. The mosaic's shifting light reflected her own internal turmoil—a jumble of cragged edges where nothing held and nothing was certain.

"You have been told that your star is the key to balance, but the shape that balance takes is not dictated by destiny," Stellara said, her voice blooming with a sudden, radiant warmth. "It is yours to design."

She extended a glowing hand toward the center of the observatory, where the air shimmered with unformed potential. "Creation is born from intention. If this is your wish, you have the power to shape your future, and in this observatory, you may freely craft it."

"What do you mean?" Wilhelmina whispered.

"The observatory reveals not a fixed destiny, but the patterns within yourself." Stellara gestured to the floor.

The glowing circle shifted, the stones sliding over one another like liquid glass until their edges formed the outline of a heart. "What you see here—this mosaic—is your essence made visible. It changes with your thoughts, your intentions. What will you choose to weave into it?"

Wilhelmina folded her arms tightly across her chest, her gaze hardening with a flickering spark of resistance. "And if I don't want this? If I choose to let it all fall apart?"

Stellara nodded, her expression solemn and unwavering. "That, too, is your choice. But I ask you this: What will you leave behind if you surrender now?"

The question pierced through Wilhelmina, slicing through her doubt and despair like a surgeon's blade. She stared at Stellara, but no words came. Her attention dropped to the mosaic, where the patterns beneath her feet swirled and moved in a dizzying dance.

The silence grew heavy, thick with the scent of ozone and ancient dust. Finally, Wilhelmina took a deep, shuddering breath, her shoulders rising as if bracing herself for the impact of a great battle.

"Maybe belief isn't the start," she whispered, her voice gaining a sudden, strange clarity. "Maybe it's the result."

She knelt. Her hands moved of their own accord, reaching for the broken fragments. As she touched the first stone, a memory returned—not of the river's cold, but of the warmth of Aria's laugh, the import of the decisions they had made despite the dark.

A sudden burst of light spiraled outward from her core like a tidal wave. It spun toward the Observatory's center and exploded into a thousand shards of crystallized stone, scattering across the floor. The ground trembled as the circular pattern's edges transformed into the shape of a Heart Circle, glowing with the soft, silver radiance of the moon. Two empty crossed lines appeared at its center, delineating its four distinct chambers.

Wilhelmina raised her hands to her cheeks, her eyes wide. "What is this? Why is this design appearing?"

"It is a reflection of you," Stellara said gently. "The heart represents your longing for connection. The cross, your ability to bridge and balance. And the empty center? That is the space for your choice."

Wilhelmina froze, her attention locking on the glowing mosaic. "A choice?"

"Only you must decide how to fill it." Stellara pointed toward Wilhelmina's heart. "You're not fated to this; it's a choice you alone can make."

"Look closely," Zografos added, stepping forward. "Creation is not about control but collaboration. Your star, if you choose, can become the cross within the circle. Together with the Moon, you can forge a balance that does not bind but shares. This is creation—not obligation, but freedom."

Wilhelmina's gaze drifted to the Sword of Truth's Eye, its hilt shaped like a radiant star. Slowly, she retrieved the Sphere of Golden Thread from her satchel. It pulsed with a hot, rhythmic intensity.

"The Star and the Moon... Not opposites, but complements." As the words left her lips, the very stones of the Observatory seemed to hum in agreement, as if a long-silent chord had finally been struck in the music of the spheres.

Selenus stepped closer, his voice low yet resolute. "Wilhelmina, you've carried the Sphere of Golden Thread, and I've borne the Sword of Truth's Eye. All this time, we've held pieces of each other's light."

Wilhelmina's voice broke, a last vestige of her shame surfacing. "B-But I don't deserve you. Not after all that has happened."

Selenus shook his head firmly. "You've guided me when I faltered. Let me stand beside you now." He took a step back, his posture steady but open.

"I don't think I can," she whispered.

"You can. Not because you are perfect, but because you are willing," he replied. "Creation begins with a choice. It doesn't demand certainty—only courage."

"The power is yours, Wilhelmina. Not to fulfill some imposed destiny, but to shape a new one," Zografos said, holding out his chisel and hammer like sacred relics. "The universe waits not for fate but for vision."

Wilhelmina approached the mosaic's center. She hesitated for one heartbeat, her breath shallow, then inhaled deeply and placed the Sphere atop the glowing heart.

The mosaic pulsed. Threads of light spiraled outward in radiant arcs. Selenus, his movement deliberate and reverent, approached and laid the star-shaped Sword beside the Sphere. Their light intertwined, violet and gold weaving together as if searching for the other across the void.

Wilhelmina knelt again, her hands shaking as she gathered the remaining scattered stones. Each fractured piece hummed beneath her touch. As she arranged them, a warmth spread from her palms, filling the air with the scent of earth after rain. The circle grew whole, its glow pulsing in rhythm with her heartbeat.

"This force that you wield is your birthright," Stellara's voice echoed. "Embrace this gift, Wilhelmina, for in your hands lies the skills to shape destinies, to bridge worlds, and to manifest your dreams into reality."

When the final stone clicked into place, a brilliant light erupted from the heart's center, surging upward through the open dome. The celestial expanse responded. Beside the Moon, a radiant star appeared—Wilhelmina's cosmic imprint. Its light wove into the Moon's glow, finally tethering the untethered.

Wilhelmina turned to Selenus. She looked exhausted, but for the first time, her eyes were clear. "Now we get to choose and create a new balance—one that reflects who we are and is not dictated by others. Although... I still don't know what that is."

Selenus reached out and took her hand, his gaze unwavering. "I will always be there for you as the answers come, however long it takes."

Wilhelmina managed a small, genuine smile. "Then let's start with this: we'll face the unknown together."

She squeezed his hand, and for a moment, the light of the mosaic shone between them, a silent promise of the work yet to be done.

❧

The Observatory's brilliant light dimmed, leaving only the steady, rhythmic gleam of the completed heart-mosaic. A quiet stillness settled over the chamber, broken by the low, tectonic hum of magic reverberating through the stones.

Stellara's radiant expression had shifted—serene but edged with gravity. "Wilhelmina, Selenus, the balance you've forged here is a beginning. But the path forward grows darker."

Selenus's hand moved instinctively, his fingers brushing the hilt of the Sword. "What do you mean?"

Stellara extended a hand, and the air between them shivered like a disturbed reflection. A vivid, haunting image formed—a crimson constellation glowing ominously in the night sky. The Omega constellation pulsed with feverish energy, its light seeping into the void like veins carrying poisoned blood. Around it, the heavenly tapestry flickered and frayed.

"The zenith of the Omega Event approaches," Stellara said. "The Omega is not merely a celestial anomaly. It is a force born from the same primal energies that threaten the realms—the manifestation of chaos. If harnessed for the good of all, it is benign. But as the ancient darkness grows stronger, it seeks to consume the Omega, and, with it, creation itself."

Wilhelmina inclined her head, her gaze fixed on the bleeding red stars. "If this darkness is so powerful, how can we possibly stop it?"

"Creation is the only answer," Stellara replied. "Darkness thrives on stagnation, on fear, and on the absence of vision. Your creativity—your ability to imagine and manifest—is its only true adversary."

The chamber trembled, a low vibration that rattled Wilhelmina's teeth. Her eyes flicked to the glowing heart beneath her feet. "But this balance we have created... isn't it enough?"

"It is the foundation," Stellara said. "But the darkness has reached beyond Aetherwyn. The Omega constellation marks its epicenter; its approach disrupts gravity and frays the bonds between worlds. It destabilizes the very forces you have just begun to restore."

Zografos shifted beside her, his presence a gentle yet grounded counterbalance to Stellara's celestial intensity. "The Omega Event is both creation and destruction, depending on the perspective of the one who harvests it, Wilhelmina. It is an opportunity—a canvas on which you must paint the vision of what could be." He gestured toward the glowing mosaic. "You've seen how creation bridges worlds, binds opposites, and forges new paths. Now, you must extend this understanding outward, beyond yourself, to the realms."

Wilhelmina stilled, disbelief flooding her. "How? How do I stop it—when it spans the cosmos?"

Stellara stepped forward, raising her hand to hover just inches above Wilhelmina's heart. "You have already begun. Creation begins within, and it is amplified through connection. The light you share with Selenus is a seed. Together, you must carry it forward, weaving it into the very fabric of the stars."

"The Omega constellation is not fixed," Zografos added. "It pulses with potential energy—a void waiting to be filled. If you can reach its core and project your star's essence into it, you will not destroy the chaos. You will transform it."

"But the Omega Event is approaching faster than we can travel," Selenus interjected, his brow furrowed.

Stellara's expression became unreadable. "The path will be treacherous. The darkness will resist. It will twist your fears and your doubts against you. But your bond—the covalent tether you have forged—gives you a strength the darkness cannot understand. You can create something the darkness cannot destroy."

Wilhelmina straightened her shoulders. "Then we have no choice. We have to try."

Zografos smiled; the mosaic's light was mirrored in his features. "You do not merely try, Wilhelmina. You create. And in creation, you reclaim what the darkness seeks to erase."

The chamber shuddered one last time as the crimson constellation flared—a warning and a summons. Stellara and Zografos began to dissolve into the surrounding radiance. "Go forth with courage," Stellara's voice echoed. "The Omega is not an ending, but a start—the beginning of a new harmony, one you alone can create."

Zografos's final words echoed in the chamber. "You are the weaver of your destiny."

"If the Omega isn't an end..." Wilhelmina whispered to the fading light. "Then maybe it's a beginning no one has dared to imagine."

She turned to Selenus. He met her gaze, and as they linked hands, a blinding light surged around them. When it faded, the vivacious, whispering grove in the Forest of Colors encircled them once more.

❧

By the time they emerged from the trees, the sun had dipped low, casting long, amber shadows across the clearing. The air seemed changed—more expectant, yet tinged with grief.

Wilhelmina paused at the edge of the open field. She spotted Quill seated at the base of a great tree, his back hunched and his head bowed. His journal lay unopened in the dirt beside him, its pages untouched for the first time since their journey started.

Lumina stood nearby, her light dim but steady, watching him with a mournful hope.

Wilhelmina met her gaze and offered a gentle nod before turning her attention to Quill. She took a steadying breath, her steps faltering as she drew closer.

Quill's hands rested limply on his knees, and the lines of grief etched into his face deepened as she approached.

"Quill," she said softly, her voice quivering.

He looked up slowly, his eyes dull. "What do you want, Wilhelmina?" His tone was flat, the music gone from it.

"Quill." She knelt before him, her tears spilling down her cheeks. "I'm sorry. For everything I couldn't do. For what we've lost."

Quill shook his head, his jaw tightening. "Sorry doesn't bring her back," he spat, his fingers curling into fists. "She was the best of us, and now she's gone."

Wilhelmina reached for his hand but stopped. "Her light hasn't gone out, Quill. I choose to believe...she's still with us. Maybe not as she was... but she's here."

Quill's eyes snapped to hers. "How can you say that when it's your fault she's gone?"

Wilhelmina flinched, but she didn't look away. "Because I saw her bravery. She didn't hesitate, Quill. She jumped into that river because she believed in us, in this mission, in what we're trying to save. That kind of courage—it doesn't just disappear."

"You don't know that." The fight had drained from Quill's voice. "You can't know that." His chest heaved as he struggled against the tide of his emotions. "But I should've been there. I should've found you sooner."

A melodic trill suddenly echoed through the clearing.

They both froze. From the shadows of the canopy, a small, radiant bird emerged. Its feathers shimmered with iridescent hues—blue, silver, and a faint, celestial gold. It glided down with impossible grace, its wings dabbing a soft rhythm before landing gently on Quill's shoulder.

Quill went rigid, his breath hitching. The bird tilted its head, its eyes bright and knowing. It let out another trill—a melody so achingly familiar that Quill's tears now broke and fell freely.

He raised a trembling hand. The bird pressed its head against his fingers. "Aria?" His voice broke. "Is it... you? You are beautiful, just as you always were."

The bird's song swelled, weaving a tune of hope and renewal that filled the clearing with light.

Lumina gasped, her hands clasped to her chest as the bird took flight, circling once before landing lightly on Wilhelmina's outstretched hand. Its song quieted, but its warmth remained.

Quill wiped his eyes, his breath coming slow and deep. "I don't know how to go on without her," he admitted softly. "She was my guiding light."

"Then let her light guide us now," Wilhelmina said, her voice steady. "Let her bravery remind us why we fight. We can't let this darkness win, Quill. Not after this."

The bird soared upward, disappearing into the top branches, though its song lingered like an echo. Quill stood, squaring his shoulders. "Let's honor her," he said. "And finish this."

Wilhelmina rose to join him, Lumina and Selenus stepping in beside them. As they turned toward the darkening path, a faint golden glimmer rippled through the moss at their feet—a subtle, unmistakable thread weaving toward the horizon.

27. Sanctuary of Lost Dreams

The radiant bird flitted through the skies, returning with soft trills none could decipher. It brought a smile to Quill's lips—a glimmer of hope breaking through his somber demeanor. His pace was heavy but determined. Selenus and Wilhelmina kept their gazes fixed on the ground. Behind them, Lumina and Phaethon moved with stoic grace. Occasionally, they would steal glances and link hands when no one was looking.

Bioluminescent plants lined the path, their neon glows illuminating the companions' features with an eerie, shifting radiance. As they neared the Sanctuary of Lost Dreams, the atmosphere curdled. The hum of dark energies grew from a murmur to a thrumming vibration, resonating through the ground like a distant, ominous heartbeat.

Lumina halted, inclining her head to hear the buzzing noises in the air. "The darkness has already converged on my grandfather's home... his power is weakening."

"How can you be certain?" Phaethon asked, his hand tightening on his weapon.

"The very geometry of the woods is changing," Lumina replied, gesturing to the trails that coiled and warped like melting wax. "The paths, I knew as a child, are being corrupted."

"The Omega Event nears its zenith," Wilhelmina added, her voice carrying the weight of the Observatory's revelations. "It offers immense energy—a cosmic gift that renews and transforms. But the darkness is eager to twist that light into something hollow."

She looked toward the horizon and gasped. "There! The flickering light—that must be the Sanctuary!"

Lumina followed her gaze, a faint, hopeful curve touching her lips. "Indeed. Grandfather is waiting."

Conscious of time's rapid erosion, they ran. The landscape grew increasingly hostile; the sky darkened into a deep violet, and the air crackled with the static of a world being pulled apart.

As Selenus quickened his steps, a coil of dark smoke hissed up from the earth beneath his boot.

"We must reach the gates before the paths seal!" he urged

Without warning, the earth groaned. A jagged chasm split the path, a yawning abyss of nothingness that threatened to swallow them whole. Lumina stumbled at the crumbling edge, her body wobbling over the void.

"Lumina!" Wilhelmina lunged, her fingers catching the sprite's arm and hauling her back just as the ledge gave way. Rocks and debris vanished into the darkness, the sound of their fall never reaching the bottom.

"Another way—quick!" Phaethon shouted.

The landscape transformed before their eyes. Familiar trails were choked with thorns that grew with unnatural speed, their barbs dripping with shadow. Every step became a struggle against a physical, resisting force.

Quill paused, pressing his palm against the bark of a shuddering tree. The bird circled above, its wings frantic. "The forest is ill," Quill murmured, his eyes wide. "It's sick with incoherence. It knows we are its last hope, yet it is losing the strength to hold the way open."

Suddenly, the shadows curdled. A swarm of ghostly creatures drifted from the timber, their pupils glaring with ancient malevolence. They hissed, lunging with claws made of smoke. Selenus dropped into a defensive stance, the Sword of Truth's Eye humming in his grip.

"The Final Veil has begun!" Lumina cried over the din of the creatures' shrieks. "My grandfather has invoked the defense. These were once guardians, now warped by the strain!"

"We cannot stop!" Wilhelmina shouted, dodging a spectral lunge. "We must push through!"

The luminous bird sang a desperate, warbling melody, its feathers flapping in defiance of the approaching gloom. An oily, smoke-like tendril lashed out, striking the small form with battering force. The creature gave a sharp cry, its wings fluttering unevenly as it was forced to retreat into the safety of the deeper forest.

Heartened by the bird's bravery but terrified by its injury, the companions pressed on. The path beneath them pulsed with a rhythmic light, simultaneously guiding them and threatening to pull them into the soil—a viscous, living barrier that demanded every ounce of their will.

❧

As the companions passed through the gates, they stepped into a reality that had begun to buckle. The air was no longer a gas but a weight, thick and distorted, pressing against their chests until every breath felt like a labor of will. Even the light seemed exhausted, struggling to pierce a gloom that felt less like shadow and more like the absence of hope.

The environment wavered, a heat-driven mirage that refused to hold its shape. Every tree they passed was a contortion of wood and agony, their branches warped toward the sky as if desperate to escape the very soil that anchored them.

"It's starting," Phaethon murmured, his knuckles white against his sword's hilt. "The Final Veil is no longer just a shield; it is overwriting the dreamscape."

They breached the Sanctuary's outer threshold—a monumental archway of white crystals that hummed with a crystalline frequency. As they crossed, a cascade of brilliance shattered the gloom, and the bird soared back into view. Its feathers were ruffled, yet its flight was steady.

Tears carved tracks on Quill's face as he watched it; the bird's melody had shifted, growing rhythmic and purposeful, acting as a needle trying to stitch the unraveling reality back together.

To their left, a grove of bone-white trees pulsated with a slow, rhythmic thrum. They breathed in unison, exhaling a silver mist woven from the raw fabric of dreams and the ragged edges of nightmares.

Selenus glanced back at the path they had traveled, which now resembled a smear of oil on water. "The land is testing us," he said, his voice grim. "It is testing our ability to perceive what is real."

"We're too late," Wilhelmina cried, her voice cracking as she felt the surge of a Great Closing. "The Guardian has quarantined the Whispering Woods. The seal is setting."

"No one will be able to get back in," Selenus agreed, his expression hardening like stone. "And nothing will get out."

The stones beneath their boots began to liquefy, the path smearing into the surreal colors of a dream. They hurried forward, driven by Lumina's mounting dread. "My poor grandfather," she whispered. "The pressure he must be enduring to hold this together... I pray we reach him before the tremors break him."

The earth beneath them shuddered in response.

"The old trees... they are whispering in tongues I haven't heard since the cradle," Phaethon noted, scanning the shifting horizon.

"They speak of the first dreams," Lumina replied, her voice tinged with awe and terror. "The ones that existed before there were minds to dream them."

Reality folded in on itself, and infinite dimensions layered one atop the other in a chaotic, multidimensional dance. The veils between worlds thinned to transparency, offering flickering, kaleidoscopic glimpses of other lives and other deaths that vanished as quickly as they appeared.

"Look!" Wilhelmina pointed to a grove where the bark had turned to polished silver.

The path below them hardened into a flawless mirror, reflecting their frantic movements against the backdrop of a sky that was now a whirlpool of stars. The temperature plummeted with a sudden, violent snap. Their breath didn't just mist; it crystallized into tiny ice particles that tinkled like glass against the ground.

Quill rubbed his arms, his teeth chattering in a frantic rhythm. "It's growing... so cold," he managed to gasp.

At last, they burst through the last layer of the dream-fog and into a clearing that defied description—a surreal tapestry of chaos and breathtaking beauty. A sea of bright red poppies flooded the landscape, reaching across a horizon that didn't end but curved upward. Bioluminescent vines wove through the flowers like veins of neon light, and the air was saturated with a thick, heady mist—the scent of blooming life clashing with the metallic tang of arcane power.

❧

At the heart of the clearing stood Somnius, the Guardian of Lost Dreams. He was a commanding presence, draped in robes woven from the very stuff of the deepest layers of sleep—shifting textures of moonlight, shadow, and blurred memory. His lips moved in a frantic rhythm, spilling a torrent of silver whispers into the air.

This was no mere prayer; it was an arcane incantation. Swirling dream fragments and the dark, static murmurs of collective thought coiled around his aura like a defensive storm. He stood with one hand thrust skyward, clutching a staff of ancient, polished driftwood that vibrated with a life of its own. His form shimmered and blurred, appearing less like a man and more like a silhouette buffeted by an invisible, psychic tempest.

As he worked, the atmosphere around them became translucent. The poppy fields faded, revealing a spectral glimpse of the Void—the great cosmic tapestry pulsating with the raw light of unformed stars. Threads of brilliance wove through the encroaching shadows, forming a delicate, universal web that shuddered from the pressure of an immense external force.

"It is he," Wilhelmina whispered, her voice barely audible over the drone of the spell. "Somnius."

The Guardian sensed their presence and broke the incantation. Then he turned as the swirling fragments settled like falling snow. The sharp, etched lines of exhaustion on his face softened into relief as his gaze fell upon the companions. He moved toward them with a terrifying grace, his feet gliding inches above the poppy blossoms.

As if governed by a shared instinct, the companions bowed.

"Brave souls," Somnius said. His voice did not come from his throat, but resonated from the very depths of the earth and the height of the stars. "You have arrived at the precipice of the end. The breach before us, born of ancient grievances and nourished by dark energies, threatens to unravel the very threads that bind existence."

"The Final Veil..." Wilhelmina's voice rose, tight with dread. "Are we too late? Have you already sealed us in?"

"I had no choice," Somnius replied, his shoulders sagging under the weight of his office. "The darkness did not merely knock; it consumed. This Veil is a desperate measure—a temporary cage to contain the chaos."

Phaethon's brow furrowed, his eyes searching the Guardian's face. "Are you saying our journey was for nothing? That we are to be preserved in a tomb of light for a hundred years?"

Somnius shook his head, a spark of ancient fire returning to his eyes. "No. A sliver of time remains. The closure of the world hangs by mere threads, but those threads have not yet snapped. We can still avert a dire fate, but the window is narrowing."

As he spoke, the world around them wavered like a reflection in a disturbed pond. The Sanctuary's borders rippled, the white crystals flickering in and out of phase with reality. Somnius scanned the horizon, his expression turning sharp. "We must hurry. The unfolding has begun."

"What exactly is this 'unfolding'?" Selenus asked, stepping forward to steady Wilhelmina.

"The Final Veil was intended to mirror reality, holding it in a moment of suspended grace," Somnius explained, his brows knitting in a grim line. "But if the dissonance saturates the spell, the reflection will become the reality. It will become irreversible. The physical world will be transformed into a frozen, hollow echo—a suspended ghost of what it once was—until the magic finally recedes a century from now."

❧

Wilhelmina watched as Lumina stepped forward, her small frame silhouetted against the towering presence of her grandfather.

"We are here, Grandfather." Lumina's voice was a steady chime in the heavy air. She held aloft the vial of Essence, its contents swirling with a light that seemed older than the sun. "Mother gave me this. Can it save us?"

Somnius turned, the weary lines of his face softening into a look of profound recognition. "The Essence," he breathed, taking the vial with a hand that trembled slightly. "Born from the first sparks of creation, it is the only balm for a world being torn by dissonance. It can reinforce the Dreamscape, buying us the precious time needed for repairs."

He held the vial toward the wounded sky. The light within erupted, turning the dim clearing into a cathedral of brilliance. With a sharp, commanding gesture, Somnius released the magic. The droplets did not fall; they ascended, hovering in the air like a constellation of fragile, golden beacons against the encroaching murk.

"The Essence will bind with the unformed dreams within these borders," Somnius intoned, his voice swelling with power. "But light requires a shape. It requires your intention."

High above, the glowing bird—Aria's spirit made manifest—let out a piercing, melodic trill. In response, tiny squiggles of iridescent color danced to the rhythm of her song. The companions closed their eyes, focusing their wills into the melody. The sound vibrations began to physically manifest, weaving together into a shimmering, translucent blanket of light that grew with every note.

"The land is answering," Somnius cried. "Let the harmony guide the barrier!"

As the melody reached a crescendo, the dream-blanket soared outward, hitting the edges of the Sanctuary. Somnius struck the ground with his staff, and the fragments burst into a wall of pure, blinding radiance. The surrounding darkness recoiled, an audible scream of frustration echoing through the trees as the shadows found themselves unable to penetrate the newborn barrier.

Wilhelmina turned to Lumina. "It's working."

"The light... it feels as though it has merged with us," Lumina said, her eyes reflecting the golden pulse of the shield.

"The bitterness is gone," Selenus added, watching the slithering shadows retreat into the deep woods. "I can breathe again."

Somnius returned the vial to Lumina's palm. "There are several droplets remaining. Use them wisely, for they are the last of their kind." He then turned toward a path flanked by the earliest oaks—trees so ancient their gnarled branches seemed to hold up the sky itself. "Come. The barrier is but a reprieve. Now, we must reset the cosmic metronome."

❧

They emerged from the eternal forest into a mystical henge of towering monoliths. These were not mere stones; they were the guardians of prehistory, aligned with the shifting pulse of the stars. Energy crackled between the pillars, casting long, geometric shadows across the moss.

"This is the nexus," Somnius explained, pointing toward the firmament where the constellations danced in violent anticipation. "Every thousand years, the Omega Event pours the raw energy of life into our universe. This Sanctuary is the conduit. To protect it, I invoked the Final Veil—a seal intended to last a century."

His gaze sharpened, settling on Wilhelmina. "As I told you, the Final Veil is a cage—but it is also a forge. In the remaining buffer of time, the spell is still fluid. We must use this energy to defeat the dissonance now, or the seal will lock, and the world will stay silent for a century."

He gestured into the air, and the breeze rippled with spectral visions—stars dimming, worlds fraying like old cloth. "The universe is a web, and the dark energies have already begun to snap the strands. You must reweave the tapestry using the very dreams you carry. Your choices and your bonds are the threads."

The stones vibrated with a low, tectonic hum.

"In the Dreamscape, reality is a song," Somnius continued. "We will use the alignment's energy to restore the harmony."

"And to sustain the pulse of all life," Quill added, his voice ringing with a new, quiet authority.

Somnius turned to the elf, a flash of recognition blazing in his ancient features. "Yes. Exactly."

The Guardian led them to a glowing archway formed between the two largest monoliths. The hum rose to a roar, vibrating in their very bones.

"Beyond this portal lies the Archive—the library of all that was, all that is, and all that still dreams of being. Within its halls, creation holds the memory of wholeness. There, you will find the tools to repair the fabric of the cosmos."

As they stepped toward the portal, the distance between worlds vanished. The breach was before them, but for the first time, the path was illuminated by a light that could not be extinguished.

28. The Price of Dreams

The portal vanished behind them, sealing the companions in the surreal expanse of the Archive. Towering shelves, laden with glowing scrolls pulsing like caged stars, stretched into the silver haze of this timeless realm.

The air carried the scent of ancient parchment, tinged with the sweetness of honey and the dampness of rain. Beneath their boots, the ground was a dark, glass-like expanse. It did not reflect their weary faces, but rather flickering fragments of dreams they had long forgotten or had yet to imagine.

Wilhelmina trembled, her skin buzzing as she adjusted to the Archive's high-frequency vibration.

"Somnius," she called, her voice echoing through the endless stacks.

From the shifting shadows, the Guardian emerged. His form was no longer a solid silhouette but shimmered like light refracted through a prism. His eyes, infinite and piercing, locked onto Wilhelmina. "I have waited," he intoned, "to ensure your spirits were tuned to the vibrations of the unfulfilled dreams and the forgotten tales. Only those in harmony with loss may walk these halls."

Wilhelmina walked forward, lifting her chin. "Our friend Crispin is fading. If he does not receive a cure soon, the darkness will claim him." Her voice faltered for a heartbeat, then steeled. "Somnius, we seek the Tears of Lost Dreams. They are the only hope he has left."

Somnius looked at her, then swept his gaze over the others. "Alas," he sighed, "the Elixir of Tears is depleted. Its vessel is dry."

As hope drained from Wilhelmina's face, he raised a finger. "But its essence can be restored—if you are willing to pay the price of its distillation."

"What price?" Quill asked, his brow furrowing as the radiant bird shifted on his shoulder.

Somnius gestured toward the center of the Archive, where a massive, glowing loom hung suspended in mid-air. Threads of light—the literal fabric of the Dreamscape—spun around it, though their radiance was choked by craggy, shadowy fissures. The loom didn't just move; it sang a haunting, low-register melody.

"This is the Dreamscape, the weave of all sentient realms," Somnius explained, his eyes clouding with an old sorrow. "It holds the magic required to manifest the Elixir. But the weave has frayed. It has been torn not by age, but by the fear and doubt currently poisoning the world. To mend it, you must offer threads of your own creation."

"What kind of threads?" Wilhelmina asked, her shoulders sagging but her focus remaining sharp.

Somnius raised his hand. In a flash of silver light, a spindle whorl appeared before each companion—disk-like stones etched with intricate, pulsing runes.

"These whorls will allow you to spin filaments from your own dreams, your secret fears, and your deepest desires," he said. "But creating a thread is more than a labor of thought. It is a labor of loss. You must decide what you are prepared to sacrifice."

Selenus caught his whorl, the stone humming against his palm. "Sacrifice? What does that mean for us—in truth?"

"It means relinquishing the chance to realize certain futures," Somnius replied. "The threads you spin must be born of truth, not ambition. To mend the Dreamscape and restore the Elixir, you must surrender a piece of what you hoped to become."

Wilhelmina took a deep breath, her fingers closing around the hovering stone. "For Crispin," she whispered.

"For Crispin," the companions echoed, their voices bonding into a single, resonant vow.

As Wilhelmina held the whorl, it warmed, the runes glowing in response to her pulse. Somnius's voice became a tectonic rumble. "To spin a thread is to confront your truest self. You must grasp the dreams you cherish most deeply and decide which ones to release. To weave the world together, you must first let a part of yourself fall away."

Wilhelmina closed her eyes, and a deluge of imagery surged to the surface of her mind. She saw the lively, swaying meadows of Aetherwyn, heard the chaotic laughter of Lumina and Crispin, and felt the steady, sunlit presence of Phaethon.

Then, the focus shifted. She saw Selenus. His shadowed gaze had always haunted her thoughts, and the memory of his touch sent a fresh shiver through her. These were the yearnings she had buried beneath the armor of duty—the life she wanted versus the life she was told to lead.

The spindle whorl glowed with a fierce heat as these images swirled. Her fingers trembled. To release even one of these dreams felt like tearing a stitch from her own psyche.

"What holds you back, Wilhelmina?"

Somnius was suddenly there, his presence as pervasive as the air. He didn't just hear her; he seemed to inhabit the silence between her thoughts.

She breathed in. "I dream of the destiny I calculated in the Observatory... a life where I marry the one I love, where we raise children in a home filled with peace. I dream of a world where leadership doesn't demand the death of the heart. But... I don't know if those paths can ever converge."

"The thread you spin will reflect your truth," Somnius said. "It need not be perfect; it only needs to be honest."

She nodded and set the whorl spinning. Filaments of light unraveled from her fingertips, shimmering in hues of gold and violet. The golden strands radiated the cold, bright energy of resilience and hope; the violet ones were softer, carrying her unspoken desire to be free from the wearying role of the Wedding Fairy.

As the colors intertwined, a sharp snap echoed through the hall. A violet strand disintegrated into a wisp of smoke.

"No!" Wilhelmina's breath turned shallow.

Somnius placed a steadying hand on her shoulder. "A broken thread is not a failure, little weaver. It is a sign that your intentions are conflicting. You are trying to bind two futures that the current weave cannot support."

He looked around the room. The other companions were struggling as well, their own threads flickering and snapping like dying sparks. The confusion on their faces was palpable.

"Your threads are breaking because the decisions you have made require more careful weighing." He paused, and blank expressions appeared on the companions' faces around the room. "I have an idea." From a leather-bound satchel, he withdrew sheets of parchment and quills tipped with starlight-infused ink. He gestured for them to gather around a stone table etched with the maps of the constellations.

"Choices are threads in life's tapestry, each branching into new paths." Somnius's voice resonated like a soft melody through the cavernous hall. "Alas, the outcomes are seldom clear. I will teach you the art of the Vision Tree, a tool to map your choices and foresee their consequences."

"Let us begin." He unrolled a piece of parchment and dipped his quill into the ink. "The first step is to draw a question at the root of your tree—one that embodies your choice. Write this question at the top of your parchment."

Somnius watched them write, then continued. "From there, draw branches, or vision nodes, representing each choice you could make. Let them split and grow outward, reaching for the unknown."

With a flick of his wrist, he drew a branching diagram on his parchment. "For every branch, consider outcomes, or leaf nodes—the final fruits of your choices, rich with potential and risk alike."

As he drew, the companions' eyes widened, but they soon nodded in understanding. "Trace them carefully, for the paths you choose will shape your destiny and the fates of countless others."

He set his quill down momentarily, letting the companions catch up. "If you wish to delve deeper, you may assign probabilities to these outcomes and calculate their worth."

He paused, his expression softening. The companions, noticing the shift in his demeanor, glanced up.

"Perhaps," Somnius said, his voice dropping to a gravelly whisper, "it would serve you better if I shared a decision of my own—a choice that once tormented me and almost cost me everything I hold dear."

The companions breathed deeply and sat back, the vast Archive seeming to shrink around them as they leaned into the unfolding story.

"My daughter, Seraphina, came to me many moons ago with a request that shattered my understanding of our traditions. She wished to marry not for duty, but for love—with Lumineon, a stargazer of humble origins who held no claim to our celestial line."

He ran a hand over the parchment, smoothing it as though soothing an old physical wound.

"At the time, her choice seemed reckless. Our family had always been the keepers of the ancient ways. How could I allow her to sever herself from that lineage?" He drew a deep breath and dipped his quill into the shimmering ink. "At the root of my Vision Tree, I wrote the question: *Should I accept Seraphina's choice, or refuse her to preserve the legacy?* Two branches emerged. One led to acceptance, where I would bless a union that might let our traditions fade into obscurity."

"The other," he continued, his quill scratching a sharp, jagged line, "led to rejection. I would disown her, erase her from my life, and uphold the legacy at the cost of my daughter's happiness."

A murmur of disbelief passed through the companions. Their sharp expressions softened, and a hand reached out to squeeze Somnius's arm, a silent gesture of compassion for the impossible weight he had once carried.

Somnius's hand trembled slightly as he mapped the outcomes. "From the branch of rejection, the leaf nodes grew dark: *Legacy intact, but daughter lost.* Another grew darker still: *I destroy her spirit, and with it, my own heart.* It was a path born of rigidity, one I am ashamed to have even considered."

He looked up, his eyes heavy with the shadow of that past regret. "But on the branch of acceptance, a different outcome appeared, like a beam of light piercing a storm. If Seraphina flourished, her happiness might bring a new, unforeseen strength to our line."

A soft smile touched his lips as he turned to his granddaughter. "I did not yet know then that her joy would lead to you, Lumina. You, who now stand at a crossroads much like hers, wishing to weave something new into our family's fabric. You remind me of her courage, and I would not trade that decision for anything in the heavens."

Somnius gestured to the group. "The Vision Tree forced me to confront my fears. It showed me that even the darkest branches can lead to the brightest leaves. Draw your trees with care, but do not fear the choice. For even the most painful branches give rise to unexpected beauty."

He stood back, his story lingering in the air like the fading resonance of a song. He pointed to his parchment, which now displayed a fully branched tree of light. "This is but one example. Now, it is time to create your own."

He leaned forward, his eyes searching each of theirs. "Do not rush. Ponder each branch. A hasty decision can fell the mightiest tree, but a carefully chosen path may lead to unimagined glory."

As the companions bent over their parchment, the only sound in the Archive was the soft, rhythmic scratching of quills.

Somnius stood back, a silent guardian over their work. "Write, my friends. Draw your trees and let the paths reveal themselves."

29. Threads of Becoming

With their vision trees carefully mapped, each companion returned to their spindle whorls to spin the essence of their choices into being.

Wilhelmina closed her eyes and exhaled, her gaze flickering to the gold and violet branches she had drawn. "My fear and doubt have no place in this weave," she murmured, releasing the fragment of herself that clung to old hesitation. With renewed focus, she set the whorl in motion. The thread grew luminous, no longer brittle, but flexible and strong.

When she finished, the strand rested in her palms, vital and alive. She held it up to the light of the Archive. "It is not the path I once imagined," she acknowledged, "but it is the one I have chosen."

Somnius's voice resonated from the shadows. "And it will mend more than you know."

Quill approached his spindle, his movements heavy. "I mapped the nodes... but my dreams feel like ash. When Aria died, the music died with her." He glanced at Wilhelmina's glowing thread.

Somnius appeared near the elf's shoulder, his presence like a soft cooling breeze. "Loss is a mirage, Quill. Nothing created is ever truly destroyed; it only changes its resonance. Spin from the love you still hold, and the thread will find its purpose."

Quill took a deep breath. Filaments of silver and deep blue emerged from his fingertips, vibrating with the echoes of Aria's melodies. Each strand carried her longing for a symphony of joy and unity, interwoven with his quiet poetry about truth in all things. But as the strands formed, they faltered, turning to gray mist.

Quill's hands shook. "I cannot hold them! They are breaking apart!"

"You seek a flawless song," Somnius countered gently. "But the Dreamscape is not built on perfection. It is built on truth. Embrace the fraying edges—the imperfections. They are what make your message real."

Quill hesitated, then slowly loosened his desperate grip. He stopped fighting the friction. The fraying strands did not dissolve; instead, they merged into an intricate, stunning pattern. When the work was complete, the thread glowed with a harmony that resonated through the Archive.

Quill smiled, a short, sharp cough hiding the burgeoning tears as he looked at the snaggy harmony in his hands. "Perfectly imperfect," he whispered. "Like me."

Somnius moved through the Archive's shifting light to stand beside Selenus. The warrior held his spindle whorl with white-knuckled intensity, his jaw set in a hard line.

"What if my dreams are unworthy?" Selenus asked, his voice low and raspy. "What if they only bring more despair to the weave?"

Somnius met that dark gaze with a look of profound patience. "Dreams are neither worthy nor unworthy, Selenus. They are simply the raw energy of the soul. What matters is the geometry you give them."

Selenus hesitated, then set the stone spinning. Filaments of deep silver and shadowy black emerged, their interplay reflecting the war within him. The silver strands shone with a quiet, desperate yearning for connection—for a place in the light. The black threads carried the cold bite of his jealousy, the old fear of being forever overshadowed by Phaethon's brilliance.

The threads did not weave; they clashed like iron, threatening to snap. Selenus's hands faltered. "I cannot control them," he hissed, his face contorted in pain. "The dark is too heavy."

"You do not need to master them," Somnius said, stepping into the heat of the warrior's struggle. "Let them guide you. Balance is not found in victory, but in acceptance. Let the shadow breathe alongside the light."

Selenus closed his eyes and loosened his grip, relinquishing the need to dominate the thread. The tension eased. The silver and black stopped fighting and spiraled in a graceful, obsidian-mist pattern.

The thread in his hands glowed with a tempered, steady light. "It is not the pure light I wanted," he murmured. "But it is the truth of who I am. And that is enough."

Somnius smiled. "It always is."

Across the hall, Phaethon stood beside Lumina, the spindle whorl cradled in his hand. His eyes reflected the soft glow of the Archive as he watched the light of her green and silver thread reflect in his golden whorl. He then glanced at her, his usual mask of leadership slightly askew.

"I have always viewed my dream as a straight line," Phaethon confessed. "To uphold the legacy. To be the guide. But looking at my vision tree... I wonder if I have left any room for a life of my own."

Lumina tilted her head. "You carry the sky on your shoulders, Phaethon. I have watched your light reach everyone else, but I realized it rarely touches you. Duty should be a shield, not a shroud."

"And yet, I see the same tension in you," Phaethon said, his voice dropping to a gentle register. "Innovation and tradition—aren't they the twin tethers pulling at you, Lumina?"

Lumina nodded, squeezing the spindle whorl in her delicate hands. "It's true. I've always felt caught between honoring the past and shaping the future. Perhaps they can coexist, like the sun and moon."

"Perhaps," Phaethon agreed. "Let's see what the threads reveal."

Side by side, they spun their threads. Phaethon's threads emerged in radiant gold and deep amber hues. The golden strands expressed his unwavering sense of duty, the light he carried for others. The amber, darker and more subdued, reflected his longing for freedom—a life beyond expectations.

Lumina's threads gleamed with silver and budding green. The silver carried the wisdom and reverence for her heritage, while the green pulsed with the vitality of her creative spirit, her desire to build something new.

Their threads wove together in the air, luminous and dynamic. But as they worked, tension rippled between the strands. The gold threatened to overpower the amber, and the silver and green clashed in a battle for dominance.

"I'm having trouble finding the balance," Phaethon confessed, his jaw tightening. "One consumes the other."

Lumina's brow furrowed as her threads twisted unevenly. "Mine are fighting, too."

Somnius stepped closer. "Balance does not mean eliminating tension. It means embracing it. Let your threads dance together, not compete."

Phaethon exhaled deeply, loosening his grip on the spindle. The amber threads grew stronger, weaving with the gold to create a spirited harmony. "Even the sun sets," he murmured, the tension easing from his shoulders. "Balance is not a weakness—it is a necessity."

Lumina adjusted her touch, her silver and green threads intertwining in a fluid, dynamic motion. "Tradition and innovation aren't enemies. They're partners, each strengthening the other."

When they finished, their threads glowed—Phaethon's like the warmth of dawn, Lumina's with the glimmer of starlight over a meadow. Their eyes widened simultaneously as they admired the result of their efforts.

"You see?" Somnius said, approval woven into his tone. "This balance you've found within yourselves will strengthen the Dreamscape and the realms beyond."

"Perhaps we are not so different," Phaethon mused, leaning toward Lumina, his lips curving. "Our paths may diverge, but our dreams share the same roots."

Lumina's face lit with a smile. "And together, we can weave something stronger than either of us could alone."

Somnius touched the side of his nose, a twinkle of light appearing in his eyes. "Choice still requires refinement even after the vision tree is drawn. But eventually, you will find satisfaction, and your heart becomes less heavy."

He gestured towards the great Loom, where its threads glistened around fissures. "And now... your task is to restore faith in dreaming, to mend what has been broken, and to restore what has been lost."

"This is the Dreamscape—a living tapestry—connecting all realms. It is woven from the threads of countless dreams—realized by some, eternally sought by others."

He walked the length of the Loom, grazing its surface. "It hums with the energies of creation. Sound, music, and the vibrations of life."

Wilhelmina's lips parted as she watched the interplay of light and shadow in the tapestry. "This is a living reflection of what we hold within ourselves—our vulnerability to fear and the strength it takes to dream beyond it."

Somnius paused, studying the fissures. "Yet its vitality is fleeting, weakened not by time but by the shadow of doubt. Without renewal—without belief—threads fray, and the tapestry unravels. Death becomes inevitable, but... the threads you hold may yet mend what is broken."

Selenus leaned forward. "Tell us what to do. Every moment is precious."

"Each strand you integrate, each knot you tie, must reflect your purest intentions."

"If our intentions are pure," Quill's voice was small, "will our lost pieces return?"

"Yes," Somnius confirmed. "The tapestry reflects reality, and it reshapes it."

Wilhelmina held her golden thread high. "Let's begin. For the realms, for each other, and for all we've fought for."

"Hope is the seed from which all dreams grow," Somnius said, watching them approach the Loom. "Believe in the cycle, for in every ending, there is a beginning." His lips curved as he watched the companions embark on giving new life to the ancient tapestry.

30. A Melody's Encore

As twilight's embrace deepened, the meteor dominated the sky, its hues shifting with frantic urgency from tranquil blue to fiery crimson. Above, the Omega constellation locked into its final formation, signaling its galactic return. It was a cosmic metronome counting down the seconds to the zenith.

The surrounding environment subtly changed. The Archive buckled under the celestial pressure. A reflective sheen crept over the high shelves, turning thousands of tomes into silvered mirrors.

"The Archive is changing," Wilhelmina warned, her voice tight.

Quill reached for a scroll, but the paper turned to glass in his hands, the primeval ink reflecting the meteor's bloom. "Knowledge itself is being sealed behind a barrier," he said, his fingers sliding over the slick surface.

At the loom, Selenus and Phaethon watched as the frescoes of old legends on the ceiling lost color and bled into a monochromatic silver. "Everything is retreating into the void," Selenus growled. "Faster!"

The clatter of the loom rose to a deafening rhythm. Wilhelmina's thread glowed with the light of a dawning sun as she fed it into the weave. Its fibers branched out like the roots of a mighty oak, spreading its internal force across the Dreamscape.

"I offer my dream of a peaceful realm," she declared. "But dreams require more than hope; they demand action and, sometimes, the greatest sacrifices."

With every pass of her shuttle, blooms of light sprouted where dark fissures had marred the fabric. "There, I've created a home, a haven for the family I will build with my beloved—cherishing him, our children, and offering service to the realm."

Each companion added their threads, reinforcing the fabric and infusing it with their experiences and aspirations. Colors intensified, and images came alive. Each stitch was a plea, and each thread a promise, weaving a powerful spell of protection and restoration.

The Dreamscape pulsed with renewed energy, its surface alive with the hum of power and reflecting the past, present, and possibilities.

"You have done well," Somnius's voice resonated, his aura flaring. "The Dreamscape is whole again. Your sacrifices ensure that these dreams will influence realities seen and unseen. Your actions will carry your legacy far beyond your lifetimes, shaping the world yet to come."

Wilhelmina turned to him, pressing her palm to her hammering heart. "The Elixir of Tears. Can we restore it now?"

Somnius pointed to a solitary shelf on which an empty vial lay. "The original supply is gone; your woven dreams may bear fruit." The empty vial began filling with a gleaming liquid drawn from the Dreamscape itself. "Your collaboration has created a new source."

The air glowed at the room's edge, and a blinding white light enveloped the room. From that brilliance, silhouettes began to take shape.

Wilhelmina squinted; her breath caught at the sight emerging before her. Slowly, two familiar forms materialized, and tears welled in her eyes. "Crispin? Flora?" Her voice trembled as the cherished names poured out.

Summoned by the magic of the weave, Crispin and Flora stood before them, their forms hearty and whole. Crispin blinked, his impulsive energy replaced by a quiet wonder.

"The pain... It's gone," he whispered, looking at his hands. "Am I alive?"

"Very much so, old boy," Selenus said, his own voice thick with relief.

Crispin bowed his head low, turning to Wilhelmina. "I'm so sorry that I put you through so much anguish because of my impulsiveness."

"All that matters is that you and Flora have returned to us safely," Wilhelmina whispered, her voice thick with emotion.

"We were never apart." Crispin turned to Wilhelmina and swept his gaze over the group. "What you've woven here is magic—proof of the love we share for one another."

Flora walked over to the loom, touching the Dreamscape's new surface. "These patterns... are extraordinary. I can see how they mirror our journeys. Opposing forces of destiny and will, and the complexities of choice."

Wilhelmina chuckled, the sound a sharp, joyful contrast to the humming tension of the Loom. "Indeed, that is exactly right!"

Flora's eyes widened as she took in the silvered walls of the Archive. "I almost cannot believe the change. Miragwyn's energy buckled the moment you finished the weave... Demiurge warned me that the world would shift once the threads were tied."

Wilhelmina's smile faded. Her gaze moved to the newly filled vial of Elixir. "Flora, how is my mother?" Her voice dropped, turning somber. "I had hoped the Elixir's restoration would reach her, too."

"Not yet," Flora said, her expression softening. "She remains trapped behind the glass, though she is well for now. But we must be swift—we have to harness the Omega energy before the mirrors dissolve."

A soft cry escaped Wilhelmina's throat. Flora stepped forward, raising Wilhelmina's chin with the tips of her fingers, forcing her to look into eyes that had seen the depths of the Dreamscape. "Don't let the doubt take root now," Flora whispered. "We will free her. The threads are strong enough."

Wilhelmina nodded, her eyes glistening with a mixture of exhaustion and renewed steel.

❧

The ground trembled. The Dreamscape's restored brilliance, clashing with the encroaching void, caused the Sanctuary to shudder. From the corners, shadows stretched unnaturally long, their smoky forms twisting, though drawn by the light.

"With each flame we ignite, the darkness grows more desperate," Somnius warned, his voice cutting through the hum of the Loom as he raised a glowing staff.

Quill hesitated, staring at the glimmering silver and deep blue strands in his hand. Their light was dim compared to the brilliance of the others' threads. He swallowed hard, his knuckles white as he gripped them.

"I... I need to try something," he whispered.

"What is it, Quill?" Wilhelmina asked, pivoting toward him.

"Aria. Her music—it's part of me. If the Dreamscape reflects our truths, then her song isn't gone. It's just... waiting."

Somnius stepped forward, his expression unreadable. "The Dreamscape responds to intention, Quill. If you weave her essence with an open heart, it may serve as a tether."

Quill approached the Loom, his hands trembling. "She was more than a friend, more than a companion... she was our hope. I won't let the darkness take that from us."

He wove, not with the precision of a scholar, but with the raw ache of a poet. He summoned every memory: her laughter in the forest, her voice lifting them in the dark, the way her eyes never wavered in the face of danger. "Aria," Quill's voice trembled. "You believed in us when we didn't believe in ourselves. Come back to us. Please."

As his thread entered the fabric, the silver and blue strands flared. The air around the loom exhaled a long-held breath, and a melody rose—a familiar tune that carried the salt of the sea and the sweetness of the woods.

"It's her," Wilhelmina gasped, her hand flying to her mouth.

The melody swelled. Light from the tapestry surged toward the vibrant bird on Quill's shoulder. The creature let out a trill that harmonized with the Archive itself, pushing back the shadows. The sound wove through the air, filling the Sanctuary.

Then, the bird's form blurred. Her iridescent feathers, as if born from the stars, carried her aloft. And in this strange magic, she dissolved into a radiant mist that coalesced into a human silhouette, emerging from the brilliance. The light faded, leaving Aria standing before them.

"She's back," Lumina whispered. "And stronger than ever."

Quill stepped back, his breath hitching. "Aria?"

Aria rushed toward Quill, her head resting against his cheek. "I missed you," he whispered through his tears.

"Our love is stronger than any law of magic," Aria replied, her voice still holding the warm, melodic cadence of the birdsong that had carried her.

Wilhelmina lingered at the edge of the light, her hands pressed against her chest as if to hold her heart in place. The sight of the two lovers struck her like an unresolved chord finally finding its key—a vibration that hummed through her own bones. She took a tentative step forward. "Aria."

Aria turned, her form still shimmering with the residue of the starlight that had birthed her. "Wilhelmina. You carried me with you, even in the silence. It was your strength that kept the path open."

"I thought I had failed you." Wilhelmina's voice was a mere whisper, breaking under the weight of months of secret guilt. "I carried your loss like a physical wound."

Aria reached out, her hands warm and solid as she caught Wilhelmina's trembling fingers. "You didn't fail. What you wove into that loom—what you all sacrificed—is what pulled me through the veil. The darkness had no anchor because of you."

Wilhelmina closed her eyes, a single, hot tear tracing a path through the dust on her cheek. "I thought the ache would never heal."

"Then let it change," Aria said, her voice firm with the wisdom of the transition she had just survived. "We are here now, and we are more than we were. Let that wound become a scar, Wilhelmina. Scars don't speak of the blow that fell; they speak of the strength it took to endure and close the gap."

Quill stepped beside them, his arm a steady weight around Aria's shoulder, bridging the group together. "She's right. We all carried pieces of one another through the dark. That is why the weave held."

In the background, the Tapestry responded to the unity. It didn't just glow; it exhaled. The threads of light exploded with color, racing through the darkened fissures like wildfire through dry grass. The Dreamscape finally breathed anew, a rhythmic pulse of vitality that shook the stone floor beneath their feet.

"This is the geometry of connection," Somnius said, his gaze sweeping over the gathered companions. He stood as the silent architect, watching his students surpass the lesson. "Through unity and the willingness to lose a piece of yourselves, you have reborn the light. Even in the deepest void, truth creates its own dawn."

31. Darkness Attacks

"The darkness grows bolder. It bends the brilliance against us." Somnius's voice cut through the rising chaos, steady despite the tremors. "This is the eye of the storm."

"Stay vigilant!" Wilhelmina shouted. "Aria, send out your melody—build us a barrier!"

The shadows surged like a black tide, tendrils clawing at the light. Selenus and Phaethon moved in a blur of steel, flanking the group as Wilhelmina took the center. She lifted the Sphere, her incantation pulling Aria's silver notes into a physical web of protection. Every note carved a sanctuary out of the gloom, but the darkness retaliated. It spat back discordant echoes, twisting Aria's song into grating, metallic tones that set their teeth on edge.

"Keep close!" Wilhelmina's voice rose above the din. "We mustn't let them break our formation!"

The mirrored walls turned the Archive into a kaleidoscope of chaos. Reflections of the companions clashed with reality; every swing of a sword was echoed back a dozen times until allies and enemies blurred into a silver-and-gray haze.

"Hold the line!" Selenus's Sword flashed, cleaving through a writhing form that dissolved into smoke.

Lumina raised her arms, throwing an inner dawn across the stone. The radiance acted like a lightning flash, freezing the shadows in place and revealing their oily, shifting forms.

"Sing with me!" Aria's voice soared, her melody transforming the clamor into a thread of unalloyed silver. The shadows recoiled, their edges flickering as if burned by the purity of sound.

"Now!" Wilhelmina held the Sphere high.

She gritted her teeth as she whispered spells, drawing out what light remained. It finally cascaded outward, amplifying Aria's song into a triumphant crescendo. Selenus and Phaethon struck in unison—twin suns of steel—while Lumina's beam pierced the heart of the swarm. The combined force shot forward, overwhelming the darkness in a blinding wave of white.

The Sanctuary fell still. The echoes of the fight lingered like fading stars, but the silence was wrong. Wilhelmina surveyed the walls; the cracks in the stone looked like fresh, uneven scars.

Somnius lowered his staff, his face etched with gravity. "This was but a prelude. The darkness retreats, but it does not surrender. The Final Veil nears its threshold, and the enemy will come again—stronger."

A sudden distortion twisted the room. The dynamic colors of their victory curdled into sinister, oily hues. The ground shuddered, not with a crash, but with a deep, sickening groan.

"What's happening?" Flora whispered, her voice trembling as the air became static with dread.

New shadows, unfamiliar and heavier than before, began seeping through the cracks. They weren't just attacking; they were being *drawn* to the newly mended Dreamscape like magnets.

Aria clutched her chest. "I have no idea, but it's not good."

"I would agree," Crispin gulped, his eyes widening with alarm as the ground shuddered beneath their feet.

"Together!" Somnius commanded, his staff swelling with brilliance. "Guard one another—the light will hold if we do not break!"

Phaethon stepped in front of Lumina, his grip tightening on his hilt. "Stay behind me."

Somnius pivoted, his eyes blazing with a celestial resolve that shook the chamber. "I must get the Dreamscape to safety!"

He struck the stone floor with the butt of his staff. A resonant, low-frequency hum surged through the room, charging the air until it tasted of copper. The Dreamscape shimmered violently—its threads didn't just break; they unraveled into a thousand firefly sparks that swirled into a vortex before vanishing into the void.

A screeching, metallic hiss—*CChhhshsssssss!*—erupted from the walls as the shadows lunged for a prize that was no longer there.

"What happened?" Crispin cried, his voice trembling. "Is it gone?" His shocked expression echoed the disbelief on everyone's faces.

"Where did the Dreamscape go? Don't we need it to defend it?" Flora's attire of leaves and flowers dulled, losing its intensity as she glanced around, fists clenched.

"It is hidden," Somnius declared, his voice echoing against the quaking stone. "The Dreamscape rests in a secret realm, beyond the reach of claws—safe, but only for a time."

He swept his staff in a wide arc, casting a golden dome of light over the companions. The warmth pressed into their bones, a sharp contrast to the writhing, shrieking shadows that scorched themselves against the barrier's edge.

Phaethon's eyes narrowed, and his grip tightened on his sword, the blade gleaming in the shrouded glow.

Selenus exchanged a glance with Wilhelmina, his jaw clenched and his posture tensed, ready for any impending threat. She touched his arm, her grip steady. Her other hand strayed toward the Sphere in her satchel, her breath shallow.

The darkness shifted tactics. The temperature plummeted to a bone-chilling degree, and the acrid stench of burnt ozone mingled with the musty rot of old parchment.

The hair on their skin lifted.

Spectral darts, smoky and crackling with malevolent energy, shot from the corners of the ceiling. Each dart moved with eerie precision, trailing black vapor as it targeted the companions.

The atmosphere grew heavy and oppressive, making breathing difficult. Each blow triggered a surge of strength-draining, icy dread that wove a tapestry of despair. A high-pitched keening wail accompanied the volley.

"What is that?" Crispin croaked, reeling back. A look of pure terror crossed his face as the dark projectiles closed in.

Wilhelmina winced as a dart grazed her arm; instantly, a mist of frost rose from the skin, turning her veins to blue ice. The metallic odor of her sweat filled the air. "Stay strong...," she commanded, though her voice shook. "Don't let them break us!"

The darts multiplied, their screeching sounds piercing their ears. Aria's melody faltered under the sonic assault, but she forced out a series of pure, defiant notes to counter the growing lethargy.

Phaethon stepped forward, his sword carving arcs of light that sizzled upon impacting the spectral vapor. "We've faced worse!" he roared, his blade singing with a resonant hum as it scattered sparks of white fire.

Lumina gripped her vial, looking at her grandfather. "What else can we do?"

"We can't let fear win." Quill's words echoed against the stone walls.

"Look inward!" Somnius's voice rolled through the chamber like thunder. "The light within you is not fragile—it is your shield. Let your hearts burn against the shadow, and it will break before you!"

Selenus stood as a sentinel beside Wilhelmina, his movements swift and surgical. His blade cut through the air, a sharp, clear ring against the din of the keening darts.

As the Final Veil thinned, the sanctuary morphed, distorting the very landscape. The trees of the Archive twisted into gnarled claws, and a thick, silver mist shrouded the grass.

"This is the moment!" Wilhelmina shouted against the gloom. Her rallying cry briefly stilled it. "Our courage is the light that darkness cannot extinguish!"

❧

The shadows quivered and surged again, their forms bleeding into a disquieting, absolute blackness. They shifted their focus, narrowing like a predator's gaze onto Wilhelmina. Their intent was clear: to sever the bond of light she embodied and shatter the unity that held the group together.

An unsettling hush fell over the room—not a true silence, but a heavy, pressurized atmosphere thick with a thousand murmuring voices. The scent of musty earth and rotting leaves grew cloying, closing in on them.

The companions drew inward. Crispin's head jerked about, checking for signs of movement. Aria's song wove a protective barrier, and its melody was a soothing counterpoint to the rising tension.

"Hold fast!" Somnius commanded. His staff flickered, casting long, dancing shadows across the chamber.

Selenus stood at Wilhelmina's shoulder, his knuckles white against the hilt of his Sword. "We will not falter," he vowed, his voice a low rumble that vibrated through the floor. "Not now, not ever."

In a coordinated strike, a barrage of spectral darts zeroed in on Wilhelmina.

They trailed plumes of icy vapor and emitted high-pitched, supernatural shrieks. *"You cannot escape your fate, little fairy! It is you who forged this path! Your choice—your denial of love—tore the first fissure,"* the venomous voice spat, seething with primeval malice. *"You cursed yourself, and now your price is due! Surrender to the darkness!"*

Selenus lunged, his breath fogging as he threw himself between Wilhelmina and the onslaught. The clang of his steel against the ghostly projectiles rang out with a piercing, metallic rhythm, each deflection sending a spray of white sparks into the gloom.

But one dart, swifter and darker than the rest, slipped through. It didn't pierce her like a needle; it dissolved into her chest like a drop of ink in water. "Oh!" A gasp escaped her lips as a mist of ice rose from the point of impact.

Wilhelmina exhaled a sharp, jagged breath. She winced, clutching her chest as the poison began its crawl, icing her veins and dimming her heartbeat. Her knees gave out.

Selenus caught her, lowering her gently behind a fractured stone pillar. "You're hit," he said, his face bleached white.

"I'm fine," she snapped, her tone curt even as her voice frayed.

Selenus pinched the bridge of his nose, a flash of raw, helpless terror crossing his features. "You're not fine."

"There isn't a choice," she whispered, her head lolling as dizziness threatened to pull her under. "I must keep going."

"She is weakening," the sinister voice cackled, the sound echoing from the very cracks in the floor. *"The light within her dims. Soon, she will be ours."*

To the others, Wilhelmina appeared to be holding onto her will by a thread. But inside, the world was slowing down. The numbness was creeping toward her center, blurring her vision until the Sanctuary faded.

She clutched at her chest, where the wound pulsed cold, but she kept her gaze focused ahead of her.

Yet, through the encroaching cold, a memory pierced through the dark.

The battle dissolved into a blurred periphery. The Sanctuary faded, replaced by the ghost of a morning in Aetherwyn—sharp, clear, and agonizing.

She saw Selenus again. He was taking her hand, pressing it to the steady beat of his heart. She heard his voice, soft but aching: *"Is this not the realm of love's magic? I have need of it... to quiet some turbulence."*

And she saw herself. Firm. Retreating. *"I can't let them down... I mustn't..."*

In the present, Wilhelmina's heart stuttered against the ice in her veins. "I… did this," she whispered.

The memory rushed back, bittersweet and terrible—his outstretched hand, her retreating steps, her denial. Her fear. Her choice.

In choosing duty, she had thought she was saving the realm, but her silence had carved the very first wound. The first break. The first curse. She hadn't meant to wound him, yet he had stayed. Every time.

"Feel it, little fairy," the darkness hissed, its voice curling around her like oily smoke. *"The curse you spawned now consumes you! Your denial sealed your fate, and there is no escape."*

Wilhelmina froze, tears welling in her eyes. Nearby, Selenus's silhouette hovered, his Sword flashing like a sliver of moonlight—a sentinel for a woman who had turned him away. She looked at him now, seeing not just the prince or the warrior, but the boy whose heart she had fractured.

"*I severed the bond that might have saved us,*" she whispered.

The silence turned toward a painful dying. She felt her essence rise from her body, drifting toward the void. But in the hollow depths of that quietude, *she remembered.*

A single note sounded within her. It rose now, slow and defiant, against the bitter chill. It was the note from the labyrinth—the pure tone of selfhood, rising from her core. The one Aria had always recognized. The one Selenus had held within his heart.

"I didn't understand," she breathed, her soul whooshing back into her body with the heat of a furnace. She pressed her palm to the frost on her chest. "But I do now."

"The curse lives in your veins!" the darkness shrieked.

"Then let the curse become the cure," Wilhelmina countered, her voice weak but regaining its steel. Her body was failing, but her soul surged. "Let my weakness be my strength."

She raised the Sphere with trembling hands. "I made the first fissure. I will make the first mend."

The darkness screamed, hurling a new tide of spectral darts toward her faltering light.

Selenus struck them down with surgical precision, his breath fogging in the air. Between strikes, he glanced back at her. "Wilhelmina… please. You must retreat."

"No!" she cried, though she stumbled, the Sphere nearly slipping from her numb fingers.

The shadows snapped like hungry beasts. Selenus exhaled sharply. His eyes locked with Phaethon's across the chaos. He motioned with a quick tilt of his head toward Wilhelmina, urgency blazing in his eyes.

A split-second of silent understanding passed between them—a warrior's pact. Phaethon gave a resolute nod and shifted his stance, stepping into the breach to shield their retreat.

Phaethon's blade caught the fractured light as he held the line, providing the seconds Selenus needed to pull Wilhelmina into a shadowed nook. The cacophony of the Archive—the metallic ring of steel and the thunder of spells—reverberated off the stone walls, feeling miles away.

"You're in no condition to fight," Selenus huffed, his voice thick with exertion as he lowered her. "Rest—just this once."

Wilhelmina's limbs felt like lead, heavy with the icy poison, but her spirit unfurled. Through the resonance of their bond, her thought reached him, clear and unburdened: *I see it now. I should have said yes.*

Selenus's breath caught. His hand reached toward her—his fingers trembling as they moved between the shadow pulsing in her veins and the light radiating from her heart. He dropped to his knees. "You're not too late," he whispered, his eyes searching hers. "You're still becoming."

Her cracked lips parted. The shadow swelled, threatening to pull her into the void, but instead of recoiling, Wilhelmina drew the darkness deep into her lungs. She didn't surrender; she transformed it. She shaped a note from the very core of her being—a sound that wove the curse with meaning.

"Let it become the bridge," she breathed. "Not the end."

In that instant, the dark energy flickered. A soft, golden resonance stirred—defiant and raw. The note was imperfect, but it was honest, and the Archive trembled in recognition. Magic, she realized, didn't require her to be perfect or whole; it required her to be true.

She squirmed in Selenus's arms, her wavering smile a spark in the dark. "And leave you to face this alone? That's not how we work."

He hesitated, his jaw clenching as he looked at the battlefield and then back to her. "The stars... they taught us balance," he reminded her softly. "Strength and vulnerability."

"And trust," she added, "You said you would trust me to lead—to trust us to guide each other."

"I haven't forgotten." The tension in his expression softened as his eyes met hers. "I can't lose you, Wilhelmina."

"You won't." She reached out, her hand brushing his arm. "We're still aligned, Selenus. Two lights in the same constellation."

The tension in his shoulders finally broke. He gave a sharp, appreciative nod. "Then we give it everything. But for now... rest."

He stood, his gaze lingering on her for a heartbeat longer than safety allowed before the cry of a companion snapped him back. He plunged into the chaos, his Sword a shard of moonlight.

Wilhelmina leaned against the cold stone, her breath shallow but her eyes burning with an internal fire. She wouldn't let the darkness claim her—not while her friends fought in the haze of burnt embers.

The respite was brief. A fresh tide of shadow rose, and the companions' strength waned to a dangerous low. Wilhelmina forced herself up, leaning heavily on Selenus as he returned to her side. One of his arms steadied her while the other carved a path through the dark.

With her hand white-knuckled around the Sphere, she summoned every ounce of magic left in her soul. Her defiance burned brighter than her failing body, a sun rising in a world of ice.

❧

Phaethon and Lumina held the left flank, their movements a synchronized dance of steel and starlight. Lumina clutched the chilled vial Seraphina had gifted her, its surface frosted and pulsing.

"The shadows are converging!" she cried as the air grew heavy with a predatory malice. "Oh! I understand now!"

"What is it?" Phaethon asked, his voice tight as he parried a spectral dart.

"The prophecy—the crossroads! The Essence is meant for this exact moment. Our light—the sun in your veins and the dawn in mine—must merge to wake it. We can call up the shield, but only Wilhelmina's touch can unlock the healing at its heart!" She held the vial up; the liquid inside flickered like a dying candle. "There are only a few drops left!"

"We'll make them count," Phaethon said, stepping into her space. "Tell me what to do."

"Take my hands."

They interlocked fingers, cradling the vial between their palms. As their magic touched, the Essence didn't just glow—it roared. A searing arc of brilliance burst outward, refracting against the Sanctuary's walls and carving dazzling, geometric patterns of light into the shadowed stone. The air hummed with a low-frequency power, and a rippling barrier unfurled like a living lung.

"It's working!" A radiant smile transformed Phaethon's face.

The light swelled into a protective bubble, casting long, defiant silhouettes against the Archive shelves. Spectral darts hissed through the air, but as they struck the barrier, they dissolved into harmless cascades of golden sparks.

Lumina looked down at their joined hands. A single, shimmering drop remained at the bottom of the glass.

"Why do I feel so weak?" Crispin staggered, his legs buckling as if the floor had turned to lead. "It's like... something is draining us."

Heavy lethargy settled over the group. The air became viscous, turning every movement into an agonizing struggle. The magic was keeping the shadows out, but it was feasting on their very spirits to stay alive.

Wilhelmina gritted her teeth, the blue frost of the poison still tracing patterns across her skin. She forced her lungs to expand, her voice a ghost of a whisper. "Focus, Wilhelmina. Be strong... for the Dreamscape. For everyone."

A spark of fierce resolve returned to her eyes. The companions closed ranks, their breaths clouding together in a single, defiant mist in the frosty air. They stood as a lone island of light, refusing to falter even as the shadows pressed against the glass, waiting for the final drop to fall.

32. The Maze

The companions huddled within the flickering barrier, their faces pale under the golden light. They watched the Sanctuary's dream-grounds blacken through a chamber window. The verdant greenery was gone, replaced by a sinister, reflective sheen.

"*The darkness is coming back!*" Flora whispered, her voice a thin thread.

With renewed ferocity, the darkness retaliated. Inky black tendrils spiraled around the barrier, hardening into towering walls that formed a vast, shifting maze. The boundaries vibrated with a low, malevolent hum. The air became a choking fusion of burnt ash and frost as the ground groaned under the strain of the dark magic.

"This is no ordinary barrier," Somnius warned. "It is the *labyrinthos maleficarum*—a punishment for those who challenge the cosmic balance. It preys on fear and doubt, feeding on the hope it seeks to extinguish."

Wilhelmina's grip on the Sphere tightened. "We won't let it," she breathed, though her voice shook. "But... will it never stop?"

The walls lurched inward, answering her. Frantic, the companions bolted through the narrowing corridors. The passages twisted unnaturally, blocking paths the moment they were chosen. Each turn was like a betrayal, and the companions' desperation mounted.

The pressure frayed their fragile unity. Their voices rose into a panicked clamor: "It's this way!" "That's a dead end! Turn back!" "Keep your right hand on the wall!" "It's hopeless! We're never getting out!"

"Stop!" Wilhelmina's command cut through the rising hysteria. She doubled over, her body straining as her breath came in ragged gasps.

She pressed her palms against the cool, sentient surface of the walls. "This maze isn't just stone and shadow. It's testing us—our unity, our ability to rise above the fear. Like the stone chamber in Miragwyn." She turned toward Aria, her eyes bright with sudden clarity.

"The harmony!" Selenus said, catching her meaning. He let out a weary, breathless chuckle. "I thought it odd at the time, but Aria's melody was the only thing that worked. *The mystic chord.*"

"Exactly," Wilhelmina nodded, her voice gaining strength. "It wasn't escape that freed us. It was our connection."

As she spoke the words, a translucent light glowed from the black walls. "Aria, can you create the first note?"

Aria's brows knitted together in concentration. "We may need a conduit to amplify our harmony."

Somnius wove his hands through the air, and a lyre materialized, its strings glinting with captured starlight. "This is deeper magic," he said, handing it to Aria. "We must find the chord that binds us."

Aria traced the graceful lines of the instrument in wonder. "The right chord... one that binds us, as it did in Miragwyn."

She plucked the strings. As if awakening something dormant, the vibrations seeped into their bones. The sound rose like a sunrise—tentative at first, then growing into a bright, assured glow that brushed against their skin like a warm breeze.

The maze shuddered. The oppressive weight of the ceiling lifted ever so slightly. Then, Aria's fingers shifted, adding a deliberate dissonance—a wavering D# that hung in the air like an unspoken fear. The companions tensed as the sound reverberated off the stones.

Quill stepped forward, his voice blending with the vibration of Aria's strings. The dissonance didn't feel like a threat; it felt like a shared heartbeat, a bittersweet ache that acknowledged their struggle before lifting them beyond it.

From the darkness, we find light.
In our unity, strength takes flight.
We stand as one, we sing as one, our voices one,
As the walls take wing.

"Sing, everyone," Wilhelmina urged, her voice a steady anchor despite her weakening frame. "Turn the doubts into a clear, fresh harmony."

As they modulated their tones, adapting and harmonizing, the dissonance, in slow waves, transformed into a greater, more beautiful whole. When Aria resolved the wavering D# chord into a pure, shimmering E major, the shift was tectonic—a total transformation of the atmosphere. Runes flared to life, glowing upon their faces in ancient scripts of water, fire, and moons.

The maze walls didn't just fall; they quivered and shuddered, their solid forms dissolving into pulses of daybreak.

Somnius raised his staff, his eyes reflecting the transformation. "You have rewritten the stars. This melody transcends time and binds all creation with hope."

The resonance of the E major chord lingered, vibrating through the stone until the very air breathed with it.

Flora exhaled, her shoulders losing their tension for the first time since the Archive fell. "It's like the air is alive with our spirit." Beside her, Crispin nodded vigorously, a grin spreading across his face.

Quill stood close to Aria, the quiet radiance in his eyes reflecting the silver glow of her lyre. "With every end comes a new beginning," he said softly, his gaze locked with hers. "And this is ours."

"This... this is what freedom feels like," Aria murmured. The spectral light of the runes danced in her wide eyes, no longer reflecting a maze, but a possibility.

As Wilhelmina leaned into the solid warmth of Selenus, he opened his arms to steady her. The glowing runes surrounding them pulsed in time with their shared heartbeat. Selenus looked past her to Phaethon; the two brothers, smiles curving their lips, exchanged a look of raw, unshielded affection—a silent bridge built over years of distance.

Phaethon's grip on his sword finally relaxed, the white-knuckle tension vanishing. "This music—its vulnerability—is stronger than any blade," he admitted, his voice a low rumble of awe.

Lumina stepped into his space, pressing her palms against his heart. As she did, their connection flared, a golden glow that harmonized with the silver light of the others.

The companions drew together into a circle, their hands reaching out instinctively until they formed an unbroken chain. As the light intensified, the spectral colors swirled, shedding the jagged shapes of the maze and settling into new, fluid patterns.

A breeze swept through the corridor, carrying a crystalline ringing like a thousand stirred chimes. The walls of the *labyrinthos maleficarum* quivered, then pulsed. With a final, resonant thrum, they imploded with a spectacular burst of brilliance that scoured the dark energy from the air.

The luminous cascade surged outward, enveloping the group in a blind wave of white before the world shifted, unraveling the stone and revealing the impossible realm beyond.

❧

The transition was instantaneous. One moment, they were anchored by stone; the next, they were suspended in the galactic ether. Here, physical existence thinned into translucence, and the heavy pull of the earth vanished. They had entered an interstellar limbo, a realm unbound by the mundane constraints of time or gravity.

Stars hung suspended like burning jewels, close enough to touch, casting long, prismatic beams of light through the group. Around them, planetary nebulae swirled in silent, violent plumes of violet and gold, while distant galaxies spun in intricate, clockwork patterns. The sheer brilliance of it painted the void with an uncanny, terrifying beauty.

The air hummed, vibrating with the harmonic frequencies of the spheres. It didn't just carry sound; it carried a scent—a sharp, clean mingling of ozone and ancient starlight, as if the cosmos had just exhaled a long-held breath.

The companions stood frozen, their forms slightly shimmering in the starlight. They were awestruck, silenced by a splendor so overwhelming it made their previous fears seem like shadows in a candle's flame.

"Look at that." Lumina pointed toward a cluster of stars that pulsed with a rhythmic, golden heartbeat, perfectly in sync with the energy of the group. "It's... beautiful."

Selenus's eyes were silvered by the reflection of the expanse. "It is like the night skies of my childhood," he murmured, his voice carrying a wistful, grounding note. "But now, I see it with wisdom gained. The stars aren't just distant lights anymore; they're the map of where we've been."

Wilhelmina reached for his hand, her fingers interlacing with his. She cradled his palm as though anchoring her very soul to him amidst the infinite wonder. "I almost didn't believe we would ever come to this point," she whispered, her eyes glistening with the light of a thousand suns. "But we did. And we will keep going, Selenus. To the very edge of it all."

Phaethon nodded, his gaze unwavering as he traced the slow, majestic spin of a nearby galaxy. The warrior's tension had finally left his frame. "I finally understand it now," he said, his voice resonant in the thin air. "This is what we're protecting—not just a kingdom or a throne, but a future of hope and light."

As the companions stabilized in the shimmer, Somnius and the other Eternal Ones descended from the higher reaches of the glow. They did not walk; they drifted like slow-moving constellations, their forms translucent and pulsing in rhythm with the galaxies behind them. They stood as silent observers, their faces masks of celestial neutrality.

Around them, the star-space pulsed in response to their unity. It was a harmony forged from the grit of their sacrifices and the shared magic of their bonds. In this ether, their connection resonated with the very essence of existence—an unbreakable, luminous chain that defied the encroaching dark.

But even in this unbound realm, the darkness was a predator that refused to be left behind.

A new, sinister force zeroed in on Selenus. With a sudden, vicious surge, shadowy tendrils struck him with the lightning swiftness of a serpent. He didn't just fall; he collapsed inward as the shadows enveloped him like a suffocating shroud, dragging him down into the endless void.

"Selenus!" Wilhelmina's cry was raw, tearing through the harmonic hum of the ether.

Though she was still wingless, she didn't hesitate. She dove into the abyss, every muscle screaming in a jagged protest against the poison and exhaustion. Her vision blurred into a smear of starlight, but she refused to stop. Her fingers brushed the rough edge of his robe, slipping once, twice, before she finally caught hold. Sweat glistened on her brow, her gasps sharp and uneven as she clung to his dead weight.

The dark matter around them pulsed, regaining tension, and their bodies floated back toward the circle of companions, cradled by cosmic forces Wilhelmina scarcely understood.

She lowered him onto a bed of swirling stardust that felt like spun silk beneath her knees. She knelt over him, her hands still glowing with the fading embers of the maze's magic. "Selenus... p-please stay with me..." Her voice broke, a hot tear trailing through the frost on her cheek.

"The prince is prickly, but I've grown fond of him," Crispin said. His voice was forced and light, but his fists were clenched white at his sides. He knelt beside her, whispering into the silence, "We're not losing him now. We'll bring him back."

Lumina hovered over them, her eyes flickering toward the silent Eternal Ones. "The bond you share is stronger than this darkness," she whispered. "Trust it, Wilhelmina."

Phaethon stood apart, his back turned as he stared into the swirling void. His jaw was set so tight it looked like stone, unable to look at his brother lying so still.

"It is the curse's final bind," Flora murmured, her face bathed in the subtle shimmer of a distant nebula.

Lumina's voice tightened with a sudden, sharp realization. "The wand... the darkness must have reactivated the old magic through the void." She grasped Wilhelmina's shoulders, her touch grounding. "Your love is woven into this moment. Do not let doubt unravel what you've built together."

Wilhelmina bowed her head, her shoulders trembling as she rested it against Lumina's. Then her gaze fell to Lumina's lap, where the outline of the vial glinted beneath her cloak. She straightened, new energy lighting her tear-streaked face.

"Lumina, the Essence of the First Dawn... please, let there be some left—it might save him."

"There's only one drop left." Lumina placed the vial in Wilhelmina's open palms.

She uncorked it, her hands shaking as she held it over Selenus. She let the final, golden drop fall onto his lips. "Please, please, please..." Her voice was a low chant, a prayer to a universe she was only beginning to understand.

But nothing happened. The rise and fall of Selenus's chest had stilled. His face remained ashen, a cold marble statue in a field of stars.

The silence thickened. Wilhelmina hunched forward. Through a choked sob, she whispered the words she had once been too afraid to say in Aetherwyn: "I love you, Selenus. We will find each other again."

As she leaned down to kiss him, brushing her lips with his, a single tear—heavy with the honesty of her regret and the heat of her hope—fell from her cheek. It merged with the golden drop of Essence still resting on his lips.

At the point of contact, where her tear and the golden Essence met on his lips, a flare of light erupted. It wasn't the cold, distant silver of the stars, but a warm, living amber that rippled outward, bridging the gap between her heart and his.

A sudden, violent gasp tore through the silence of the ether. Selenus's chest heaved, his lungs pulling in the stardust-laden air with the desperation of a drowning man reaching the surface.

"Selenus?" Wilhelmina's breath caught, her heart hammering against her ribs.

His eyes fluttered open—no longer ashen, but dark and silvered with returning life. His hand reached weakly, his fingers searching for hers. "...Wilhelmina..."

Relief spilled from her in a tangled mess of tears and laughter as she gripped his hand, pulling him back from the edge of the void.

"W-what happened?" he whispered, his voice raspy and thin.

"I don't exactly know..." Wilhelmina breathed, still trembling.

Lumina touched Wilhelmina's shoulder, her voice a hushed, celestial melody. "The Essence can shield, yes, but its deepest magic has always been bound to your touch, Wilhelmina. Your tears held the dreams you feared losing. When joined with the Essence and your love's kiss, they created a magic beyond compare—a magic only you could unlock."

Phaethon, who had stood like a statue of grief behind them, now rushed forward. The warrior's mask had cracked, revealing a raw, brotherly relief. He offered Wilhelmina a subtle nod and a smile that carried a new level of respect. "You've shown us love's true power," he said softly.

Somnius swept his gaze over the exhausted companions, his staff pulsing with a slow, steady rhythm. "It is through your light, born of unity and love, that the cosmos shall find harmony again. But do not be lulled by this victory. Be steadfast, for the journey is not over. The shadows linger, and the window to reverse the Final Veil narrows. Your courage is vital."

Wilhelmina clasped Selenus's hand, her fingers locking with his. "Together," she said, looking at him with a clarity she hadn't possessed in Aetherwyn before their quest began. "We've transmuted light into our greatest ally."

She turned to her companions and the Eternal Ones, her presence a quiet flame binding them together into a single, defiant unit. "Love and unity brought us here, and they'll guide us forward—to whatever lies ahead."

She lifted her chin, her eyes burning with resolve even as the poisonous fire of the dart still flickered in her veins, a reminder that time was still running out.

33. The Omega Event

Beneath the swirling cosmos, a resonant vibration filled the void as the stars above aligned. But a sudden beam of radiating sheen enveloped Wilhelmina and Selenus, lifting them from their companions and pulling them upward into the heavens.

They drifted through a vast, star-strewn expanse where galaxies spun like distant, phosphorescent wheels. Then, the landscape blurred, snapping into focus as they entered a dimension where the celestial bodies blazed with a fierce, blinding urgency. Here, the very fabric of reality rippled, taut and vibrating with the pressure of a final, cosmic moment.

Ahead, a colossal tear yawned in the cosmos—a jagged wound carved into the dark skin of existence itself. Its dim, wavering effulgence bled into the void, casting long, hollow shadows across Wilhelmina and Selenus's weary faces.

Wilhelmina's gaze fixed on the rift. She forced herself to stand tall, though the poison in her veins pulsated with an insistent, molten burn. In her hands, the Sphere of Golden Thread became strangely alive, thrumming in harmony with the Sword of Truth's Eye at Selenus's side. The artifacts grew heavier by the second, as if they were impatient to be released.

Two silhouettes materialized within the swirling ether. Celestia and Varytita emerged, their forms beaming with the radiant energy of the cosmic balance they upheld. Celestia raised her hands, commanding the threads of reality to respond. She wove a shimmering veil of light around Wilhelmina and Selenus—an impenetrable, radiant protection against the chaos of the rift.

"It is time," she said, her voice a calm yet undeniable force. "Your journey shall bend the arc of destiny."

Varytita floated closer, his presence a bridge between divine wisdom and mortal resolve. "The trials you have endured were but preparations for the task before you."

Selenus reached into his pocket and removed the orb, which now cast a pure, honeyed glow. He exhaled, the sharp, defensive lines of his face softening into the expression of a prodigal son returning home after a lifetime in the cold.

"Father, is your burden lifted?" he asked, his voice hesitant and thick with years of unspoken weight. "Have I finally eased the grief I caused you?"

Varytita's eyes gleamed, his celestial form pulsing with a brighter, warmer light. "Indeed, my son. The grief is gone. I am proud of you for overcoming your jealousy and for rediscovering the love between you and your brother."

"Thank you," Selenus said, his voice breaking under the weight of his relief. "I'm sorry for the pain I caused. I sought your approval, failing to realize I'd never lost it."

With a fierceness that belied his ethereal form, Varytita wrapped his arms around his son. It was a grounding embrace, one that knit together the broken pieces of Selenus's past. "You have done well, Selenus. The cosmic journey is but a school of lessons. You have learned. You have loved. That is all that matters."

Wilhelmina watched them, her breath catching in her throat. Despite the poison singing through her veins and draining her strength, a small, genuine smile softened her face.

"Father," Selenus said, finally turning his gaze toward the vast, weeping tear in the sky. "We're ready."

Varytita gestured skyward, where the Omega constellation loomed, its stars shifting into their final alignment. "The celestial clock ticks toward the final hour," he warned, his voice echoing like distant thunder. "The Final Veil's activation is imminent. If left unchecked, it will solidify its hold on existence. Time to act is slipping away."

"What must we do?" Wilhelmina asked, her features shadowed by a fresh wave of pain.

"The harvesting of Omega Energy and the repairing of the cosmic tear will decide the fate of all dimensions," Varytita said somberly. He pointed toward the rift, where the edges writhed and flared like frayed silk.

"And how can we mend it?" Selenus asked, his hand tightening on his sword.

"The artifacts you bear are no mere tools." Varytita's gaze shifted between the Sword and the Sphere. "They are the Needle and Thread of Destiny—ancient instruments of celestial repair, imbued with the unity you share and the love that sustains you."

At his words, the surrounding space shimmered with a sudden, violent brilliance. Both gasped as the relics vibrated, the unexpected shift leaving their hands trembling. The Sword of Truth's Eye in Selenus's hand elongated, its heavy blade narrowing and sharpening into a fine, flaming point—a Needle of celestial perfection. Simultaneously, the Sphere of Golden Thread in Wilhelmina's grasp unraveled, its concentrated light spinning out into a spool of a silken strand that shimmered with an inner, embedded radiance.

Selenus tightened his grip on the Needle, as though reassuring himself it was real. Wilhelmina's lips parted in awe. "So, existence really is like a fabric... its threads made of vibrations."

Varytita inclined his head. "Precisely. Your journey has mirrored the cosmos itself—fragmented and healed through love and trust. Just as you've mended your own spirits, so too must you mend the universe's fragile weave."

"How did this tear come to be?" Selenus asked, staring at the jagged abyss.

"It is a manifestation of fragmented dreams and unresolved conflicts that have plagued our realms," Varytita explained. "Your quest has been about healing these root causes. Now, you must complete the work before the cosmos unravels entirely."

Celestia floated down, standing beside Varytita. Her voice resonated with a divine authority tempered by an almost imperceptible warmth. "Do not be afraid, children," she said, her gaze steady, as if she were reading the very lines of time. "Your love is a power the darkness cannot rival. It shall rewrite even the stars."

She reached out to embrace Wilhelmina, a touch that felt like a cool breeze on a fevered brow. "Before you begin, I wish to thank you, Wilhelmina, for saving my son."

She glanced at Selenus, her expression brimming with a mother's pride. "He has always loved you, and that love—combined with the magic within you—is invincible." She stepped back, bowing her head low before the two demi-mortals who held the fate of the stars in their hands.

"Ascend," Varytita commanded. "Weave the Thread of Destiny through the eye of the Needle—stitch closed the wound that bleeds chaos."

"Have faith in each other, and let your spirits guide you," Celestia added. As their luminous forms dissolved into stardust, a final cascade of light trailed behind them like a blessing.

Selenus turned to Wilhelmina. He gripped the Needle, its edge glinting with a cold, astral silver, while she slowly unraveled the Thread. They rose into the expanse with synchronized motions, their ascent resembling a slow, gravity-defying dance.

The tear loomed—a swirling vortex of jagged darkness and fractured light. The seething abyss radiated a storm of dissonance so loud it was nearly a physical blow, threatening to pull them into its maw. Their hair and garments snapped and whipped in the stellar gales, yet they pressed on without wavering, bracing their bodies against the resistance of the void.

With precision born of absolute trust, they began. Wilhelmina threaded the flaming Needle, guiding the silken strand with trembling fingers. Selenus then pierced the Needle through the first frayed edge, beginning the first stitch.

With each pass they made, the tattered borders of the cosmos drew closer together, creating a luminous, silver-gold seam. But the cost was becoming clear. Wilhelmina's fingers shook as she pulled the Thread through the jagged edges of the rift. The poison coursing through her burned like liquid fire, making her vision swim in a haze of gray and gold.

At one point, the Thread slipped. It drifted, lost to the ethereal currents of the void, but Wilhelmina lunged, her hand snatching it back just before it vanished into the abyss. Her breath came in shallow, labored gasps as her fingers tightened around the glowing strand.

As the new seam lengthened, the surrounding chaotic energy abated, the tempestuous winds softening into a shimmering haze. The void danced with hues of gold and silver, like a cosmic Borealis reflected in a dark mirror. Still, there were many stitches to go.

Selenus paused, glancing at Wilhelmina. His brow furrowed as he saw her deathly pallor—the strain written in every line of her face.

"What's happening to you?" His voice cracked, the Needle in his hand trembling for the first time.

She lifted her head, her lips curving into a weak, heartbreaking smile. "The dark energy from the maze... it wounded me more than I admitted." Her breath hitched. "I thought victory would heal us both, but... I'm fading, Selenus. My essence dims."

Selenus's hold on the Needle tightened until his knuckles turned bone-white. "Why didn't you tell me?" he asked, anguish bleeding through his words. "We could have found another way. We could have—"

"There was no time," she interrupted, her voice a thin thread of sound. Her fingers clung to the Thread as if it were the only thing keeping her soul from drifting away. "And there's no choice now but to finish this. For the universe... for our friends... and for every moment we've dreamed of sharing."

Her eyes, though shadowed with exhaustion, locked onto his with a fierce, final resolve. "Please... we have to finish this."

Selenus swallowed the lump in his throat, his eyes shimmering with unshed tears. He nodded, a silent vow passing between them. "All right. Then we will—together."

He drew her close with one arm, anchoring her trembling frame against his own as he resumed the delicate, agonizing work with the Needle. Their movements synchronized once more, a desperate ballet performed on the edge of the abyss. Though her weight pressed heavily against him, Selenus did not falter; he became her strength as she became his guide. Each stitch was a shared vow, an act of defiance against the encroaching darkness and a testament to the future they refused to surrender.

Wilhelmina's world narrowed until there was nothing but the radiant Thread. She poured the last reserves of her spirit into it, weaving her very essence into the cosmic fabric. Every pass through the tear felt like a final gift—a piece of herself left behind to hold the worlds together, and a legacy for the man who held her up.

"Please," she whispered, her voice carrying like a prayer reaching beyond the dimensions of time and space. "Give us the strength to finish this."

As the last stitch pierced the darkness and sealed the cosmic tear, a resounding thrum reverberated through existence. It was like the final, triumphant heartbeat of a long and weary struggle.

The Eternal Ones, who had watched with bated breath, let out a collective ripple of relief. Their shimmering light pulsed with unspoken pride. Tears of starlight glistened on Celestia's cheeks.

"They have fulfilled their destiny," she murmured. "The universe shines brighter because of them."

"Unity and love have triumphed." Varytita nodded solemnly. "Their connection has healed both the cosmos and their inner wounds."

Suddenly, the void exploded with radiant, multi-hued radiance. The chaotic energies that had once threatened to unravel existence vanished, replaced by a symphony of renewal. The glow painted the expanse in colors never before seen—a dawn of creation and hope.

☙

But as the light of the new dawn flared, Wilhelmina's knees buckled. Her body folded like a marionette with its strings cut, her breath seizing in one last, trembling gasp. The strength she had held onto by sheer force of will ebbed away, pulled from her by the immense toll of the mending. Her life force flickered, dimming like the last embers of a dying star against the infinite dark.

Selenus, still absorbed in the finality of the repair, remained momentarily unaware of the peril. His hands stayed steady as he ignored the ache in his bones and the crushing weight of his own exhaustion. With a decisive motion, he tied the final knot, securing the cosmic weave, and cut the glowing Thread.

Suspended in the stellar expanse with the Needle still clutched in his hand, beads of sweat traced paths down his forehead. His tousled, damp hair framed a face lit with pure, unadulterated triumph. He exhaled deeply, his radiant smile reflecting the universe—a universe that was now humming with a newfound, perfect harmony.

"We've done it," he whispered, his voice heavy with overwhelming relief.

But when his gaze shifted to find her, the triumph turned to a sickening horror. Wilhelmina's crumpled form lay lifeless beside him; her light waned to a faint, gray ember. A visceral cry tore from his throat, raw and frantic, echoing into the vacuum.

"Wilhelmina!"

He gathered her up, his hands trembling so violently he could barely hold her. "No, no, no," he muttered, his voice a frantic, broken rhythm.

Below, Celestia's face contorted as the cry reached her. Her gaze locked onto Varytita's, her eyes pleading. "My love, please... guide him. He must harness the Omega to save her."

Varytita appeared instantly at his son's side, an anchor in the prince's storm of panic. He rested a steady, glowing hand on Selenus's shoulder, forcing him to focus.

"Listen to me," Varytita said, his voice firm. "You've mended the great tapestry, but the work is not yet finished. To save her, you must acquire the Omega Essence."

Selenus looked up, his eyes bloodshot and burning with a terrifying resolve. "I won't let her go."

"Then act swiftly," Varytita urged. "We will watch over her until you return."

Varytita gestured to the shimmering void, where an Omega vessel materialized from the ether. Its exterior resembled polished stone, gleaming with captured constellations and swirling patterns forged from the remnants of ancient nebulae. Yet, as Selenus reached for it, the vessel quivered with a rhythmic, pulsing heat—a heartbeat of unbridled power.

"Take this vessel," Varytita instructed. "It is crafted from the cores of fallen stars, capable of containing the vast energies you will collect."

Selenus took the vessel in trembling hands. Its surface was cool, yet it strummed with a latent, hungry power. Casting one last, aching glance at Wilhelmina's pale, still face, he surged into the expanse. The interstellar weave of the cosmos rippled in his wake, the universal tapestry responding to his urgency as he raced toward the heart of the near-waning Omega Event.

At last, he reached the source. Here, energy gushed like a wild, untamed river of white and violet fire. Without a moment's hesitation, Selenus plunged the vessel into the pulsating heart of the torrent.

Luminescence flared in a dazzling, blinding burst. The reflections danced across his sweat-streaked face as streams of raw creation and renewal poured into the vessel. It vibrated violently in his grip.

"This is for Wilhelmina!" he cried, his voice a defiant roar against the vacuum. "Her light has guided us all—it cannot end here!"

His desperate plea reverberated through the expanse, entangling with the golden currents of the Omega as if his sheer will could force all creation to listen. From the void, his father's voice drifted to him: "*Guide the energy, Selenus. Let your will shape it. Bind it with your love and your resolve.*"

The celestial clock, which had been ticking toward the Final Veil, stilled at last. With the vessel brimming and glowing with a fierce, iridescent fire, Selenus turned. His silhouette stood framed against the radiant core of the universe. As he surged back to the others, the hum of the cosmos fell into a respectful silence.

Each beat of his heart echoed the fading flickers of Wilhelmina's spirit. He could feel her essence holding tenuously to the precipice of existence, a thin thread ready to snap. With the swiftness of a falling star, he descended, reaching for her crumpled form.

Her chest barely moved now; each breath was a wheezing, agonizing strain against the silence. The cosmic winds whispered around them, a ghostly chorus urging her to hold on for just one more second. Varytita knelt beside her, his glowing hands steady as he propped her up with fatherly care. He turned a solemn, expectant gaze to his son.

"You possess the strength and the love needed to bring her back," Varytita said. "Trust in yourself, as we trust in you."

Celestia's luminous gaze met Selenus's, her eyes shining with an ancient hope. "You can save her, Selenus. Bring her back to us."

Selenus knelt before Wilhelmina, the Omega vessel pulsing in his hands like a trapped sun. Each iridescent bead of its contents shimmered with the power to rewrite destiny itself. He looked at her—the woman who had mended the world—and prepared to mend her heart.

"Let love bind," he breathed, his voice steadying, "what darkness tried to sever."

Celestia's voice rose, a balm to the tense atmosphere of the moment. "Let the light inside you reignite what the cosmos yearns to preserve."

With hands that no longer shook, Selenus tilted the vessel. He watched, breathless, as the luminous essence flowed, falling drop by drop onto Wilhelmina's lips. Each droplet sparkled like a microscopic fragment of a collapsing star, carrying within it the boundless, raw potential to breathe life back into the fading spark of her soul.

The Omega energy seeped into her, an intelligent glow searching through the darkness of her veins for the one tiny ember of life that had refused to extinguish.

Time stretched unbearably, the entire universe holding its breath as the moment balanced on the razor's edge of eternity. Then, the light found its mark. The gold-violet essence entwined with her spirit, weaving through the cold void between life and oblivion. It was the final act of mending—rekindling the fire that had nearly been lost to the dark.

A soft, rhythmic pulse glowed beneath her skin.

And then, from the profound stillness of the stars, a voice rose once more—quiet, spectral, and inexorable. It echoed not from the mouths of the Eternal Ones, but from the very foundations of the ether:

"The heir of shadow and light has stitched the wound shut with her own hands, and the age of renewal begins."

34. Renewal and Reunion

The awakening warmth surged through Wilhelmina's chest—not the searing poison of the maze, but the steady, gentle pulse of the Omega. As she drew a ragged breath, the deathly gray in her cheeks dissolved, replaced by a bloom of living color. Her eyes snapped open, pulling life back from the threshold of the abyss. She looked around, piecing together fragments of a fractured dream—then landed on Selenus's tear-streaked face.

"Selenus...?" Her fingers twitched, catching his sleeve to anchor her spirit to the physical world.

"I thought I lost you." His voice broke as he tightened his grasp. He touched his forehead to hers, his labored breath mingling with her own. "You're safe now. We... we held the line."

Tears misted Wilhelmina's vision, and a sob of joy tore from her throat. She rose and embraced him as her strength had returned in a sudden, golden surge. Around them, the cosmos—once a battlefield of starlight and shadow—now lay serene, the previous discord replaced by a low, harmonic hum of rebirth.

Varytita gazed upward. The Omega's nebulous glow coalesced into a canopy of weaving strands that cascaded downward like solar rain.

"The Omega Energy is more than a force—it is the breath of creation itself," Celestia said with reverence. "It falters where shadows encroach and flows where harmony reigns."

Where its beams touched, the Dreamscape unfolded, vast as a scroll in the hands of the cosmos. Just then, a filament of brilliance shot from Wilhelmina's fingertip, tracing a path across the heavens to her cosmic imprint. From there, another descended, striking the grand tapestry, illuminating its intricate, woven fabric.

"What is happening?" Selenus asked, his hand instinctively going to the Sword's hilt, even as he pulled Wilhelmina closer.

Celestia's smile was one of ancient pride. "A sacred triangle. Wilhelmina, her cosmic imprint, and the Dreamscape are finally one. The circuit of her destiny is closed."

"Our friends..." Wilhelmina's voice was small, her gaze searching the swirling ether. "What has happened to them?"

"Where are Phaethon and Somnius?" Selenus asked, furrowing his brow. "Are they safe?"

Celestia gestured toward the Dreamscape. As if answering her call, the tapestry rippled, revealing small windows of silver light. In one, the Sanctuary appeared fully restored, its grounds vivified and whole; the Final Veil's effects had vanished. In another, Somnius stood inside the Archive among his family—Seraphina, Lumineon, and Lumina. Phaethon stood beside Lumina, interlocking his fingers with hers. Next to them, Quill and Aria embraced, while Crispin and Flora turned their faces toward the brightening sky. Their laughter emerged from each window like a trill of birds in the protective glow of a new dawn.

"They are all safe, children," Celestia replied. "They have returned to the Whispering Woods where Somnius and his kin will harvest the remaining Omega and ensure that its magic flows to all realms."

Varytita nodded. "They will invoke a new Veil—not to hide this power, but to protect it from the shadows that seek to unravel all we've rebuilt. But for you, the work remains. You must return to Miragwyn."

"The Arbor requires the heir of shadow and light," Celestia added.

Wilhelmina blew out a long exhale. "I can finally free my mother... and father."

"The Dreamscape will carry you." As Celestia spoke, the tapestry surged. From its silken folds, a luminous orb materialized—a window through space. Within it, the Celestial Arbor towered, its branches casting long shadows over the Enchanted Mirror where Demiurge remained entombed.

Varytita watched the image, his voice resonating with a king's authority. "The Dreamscape is more than a memory; it is a bridge. Demiurge's confinement was a bastion, a shield interlaced with the weave of dreams. She wove her spirit into its very grain to safeguard herself from the dark, waiting for the day it would guide you home, Wilhelmina."

He held out an empty flask that glinted like frozen starlight. "Zografos crafted this vessel from comet cores," he explained. "It will temper the Omega's raw power, ensuring it will flow gently into the Arbor's roots."

As he decanted the liquid Omega into the vessel, the radiance cast long, dancing shadows across their faces. He corked it with a decisive snap and pressed it into Wilhelmina's hands.

"The Omega Energy you now carry is a promise," Celestia said, her gaze lingering on the pair. "Let it now flow through the Arbor, and it will breathe life where despair has lingered. But heed the warning: the Arbor's roots bind as much as they nurture. Approach with care."

Wilhelmina held her grip tighter, her eyes flashing with a fierce, new clarity. "I understand. The love that mended the rift will mend the tree."

Selenus anchored Wilhelmina against him, his strength supporting her fragile frame as they stepped onto the weave. The Dreamscape thrummed beneath them, a living current of light sensing their purpose. As it surged forward, cutting a white-hot path through the expanse, Wilhelmina and Selenus stood as one, their eyes fixed on the horizon where the ancient boughs of the Arbor waited in Miragwyn.

❧

The solid earth of Miragwyn was a mercy beneath their feet. Before them, the Celestial Arbor loomed as a silent titan, its silver-veined leaves rustling with a sudden, anticipatory shiver. The air was thick, charged with the scent of ozone and crushed violets—the perfume of ancient magic.

Wilhelmina uncorked the flask, its light dancing in her eyes as she looked at Selenus. "It's time."

"I am with you," he said, his hand resting on the hilt of his Sword, not in a threat, but as a silent anchor.

Together, they approached the gnarled base of the tree, circling it. Wilhelmina tilted the vessel over, and the liquid Omega spilled forth in a shimmering ribbon. As it touched the roots, the ground didn't just drink—it pulsed. A low, rhythmic drone reverberated through the earth, the heartbeat of a world waking from a long, cold sleep.

Glowing tendrils of energy spiraled upward like climbing vines, igniting the silver bark with a soft, internal fire. In the center of this new brilliance, the Enchanted Mirror appeared, its dark, obsidian surface finally cracking to reveal the silhouette within.

The ground groaned as the ancient roots heaved. The old spell—the bastion Demiurge had woven to protect herself—did not recognize the end of the war. It fought the light, its thorns scraping against the air.

Selenus moved instinctively, his blade a flash of steel between Wilhelmina and the shifting timber. "It's resisting!"

"It isn't resisting," Wilhelmina corrected, her voice steady even as the earth quaked. She stepped past him, her hand outstretched. "It's waking up."

She pressed her palm against the trunk. Under her touch, the frantic thrashing of the boughs slowed to a rhythmic sway, and the aggressive roots wove themselves into a gentle, ascending path toward the Mirror.

Nearby, the Dreamscape hovered, its silken fabric rippling in a sympathetic rhythm with the Arbor's pulse.

Wilhelmina's breath caught as the flask and the tapestry's vibrations harmonized. "The roots, the Dreamscape... they're all connected," she whispered. "Just like the realms."

A soft chime—like a finger circling a crystal rim—echoed through the woodland. The Omega energy surged. Inside the Enchanted Mirror, the threads binding Demiurge unraveled like burnt silk. Raw golden power rippled across the glass, shattering the enchantment's hold.

Wilhelmina stood paralyzed for a heartbeat, clutching Selenus's arm as the last of the dark energy dissipated into nothingness. Then, a brilliant flash heralded the return.

Demiurge emerged—not as a ghost, but as a living sun, radiant and whole. She set foot onto the solid earth and took a deep, triumphant breath, her lungs finally tasting the air of Miragwyn.

"Freedom," she shouted, her voice a melody of joy that resonated with the trees themselves. She moved with the grace of a dream made flesh, her gown a tapestry of moving constellations, her eyes finally finding the daughter who had traveled through shadow to find her.

"My beautiful child," Demiurge whispered. "Your bravery has achieved what I could only imagine in the dark. I see you, and you are magnificent."

Wilhelmina choked back a sob and threw herself forward, burying her face against her mother's silken robes. The scent of starlight and home enveloped her as her tears soaked into the fabric.

"Mother," she choked out. "I never stopped looking. I never stopped hoping."

Demiurge stood back slightly, her hands framing Wilhelmina's face. "Every challenge you faced led to this moment. Your courage and the bonds you forged unraveled the spell that bound me. You have done more than free a mother; you have restored hope to the cosmos."

Selenus stepped forward, his hand finally leaving the Sword's pommel. "What were you protecting so fiercely that it required such a sacrifice?"

Demiurge's gaze drifted to the towering Arbor. "The Celestial Arbor is not only Miragwyn's heart—it is the loom from which the Dreamscape was spun. To guard its truths, I wove layers of dreams around it when I entered the Enchanted Mirror. My prison became its shield, concealing the heart of creation from the darkness—what it most desired."

Selenus nodded, the weight of the lore finally settling into place. "It's one intricate web. Your sacrifice preserved the threads."

Wilhelmina glanced at the glowing roots beneath her feet, a sense of awe settling over her. "All our struggles, the trials, the choices... they weren't just for us. They were for this—restoring what you protected."

"And now," Demiurge whispered, brushing a stray hair from Wilhelmina's forehead, "the darkness is pushed back. But vigilance must be our constant companion, for the shadows never truly vanish; they only wait."

Before the gravity of her words could sink in, the Arbor's branches rustled, sounding like ancient, wooden laughter. A beam of pure Omega light shot from the roots, streaking across the horizon, resembling a fallen star returning to the sky.

Wilhelmina shielded her eyes, squinting at the distant point where the beam struck. A familiar figure emerged. At first, he was a mere shadow against the gold, but with every step, the silhouette sharpened.

"It's him," Wilhelmina breathed. "It's Lambda."

The air left Demiurge's lungs in a ragged gasp—a sound that carried the weight of a thousand lonely years. For a heartbeat, she stood frozen, as if she couldn't believe the earth was solid enough to hold them both. Then, the light seemed to propel her. She broke into a run, her constellation-streaked robes billowing like a nebula behind her.

Lambda quickened his pace, his own cloak catching the solar fire of the Arbor. They were two celestial bodies, finally pulled back into each other's orbit.

Wilhelmina watched them, feeling the interlocked strength of Selenus's fingers in her own. "*Love is never lost*," she whispered.

"No," Selenus agreed, his voice thick with a rare, quiet warmth. "It seems we fought for more than just balance. We fought for this."

Wilhelmina nodded, her eyes glistening as she watched her parents collide in a distance blurred by light. "They deserve this moment. The universe is finally whole."

When Demiurge and Lambda met, their embrace was a convergence of long-separated souls. As they embraced, a ripple of pure white light expanded from them, smoothing the grass of Miragwyn and causing the Arbor to hum in a deep, melodic bass.

"You returned to me," Demiurge whispered, her voice trembling as she clung to him.

Lambda's tears spilled, his voice thick. "I never left, my love. Not truly. You were always the North Star in my heart."

Demiurge pulled back, her hands searching his face as if to memorize every line. "But how? I thought the void had taken you."

Lambda cupped her face with a hand that still bore the faint, silvery scars of his confinement. "When I realized I could not stop the darkness from reaching you, I chose to remain as close as the shadows allowed. The ruins where I was bound became my sanctuary—a place where I could sense your presence through the stone, even if I could not reach your hand."

"All those centuries," Demiurge breathed, and her tears fell freely now. "Alone yet near."

"I would have waited an eternity more to keep hope alive," Lambda said, his gaze shifting to Wilhelmina standing a few feet away. "But now, the waiting is over."

As they walked hand-in-hand toward Wilhelmina, their laughter rang through the air—a sound so bright it seemed to chase the remaining shadows from the grove. When Lambda reached her, he didn't say a word at first; he simply pulled his daughter into an embrace that felt like the closing of a cosmic circle.

"My brave girl," he choked out, his tears wetting her hair. "Your courage has made this dream a reality."

Wilhelmina leaned into the strength of his arms, her own tears flowing freely. "Father... I nearly lost my way, but I learned I was never truly a prisoner. I was always free."

Demiurge circled her arms around them both, resting her head on Wilhelmina's shoulder. "Our family is whole," she promised. "The thread will not break again."

Selenus stood nearby, the prince's usual stoicism replaced by a look of profound awe. "Indeed, it will not," he murmured to himself. "Never again. This I vow."

Wilhelmina turned to him, her face glowing. "And it's the light that will guide us home." Then, looking back at her father, she whispered, "The ruins... The crystalline palace... That was your doing, wasn't it?"

Lambda nodded, a flicker of pride igniting in his eyes. "I poured my fading strength into transforming that desolation into a place worthy of your journey. But it was only when you and your companions unlocked the Mirror of Truths that my magic could finally wake. Our magic catalyzed yours, Wilhelmina. We transformed ruins into a palace, together."

Wilhelmina's hand flew to her mouth, stifling a soft cry as the last piece of the puzzle clicked into place. They had never been alone. Every step of the journey had been a collaboration between the past and the future.

Lambda's voice carried the resonance of a foundation set at last. "Your courage and unity were the key. I could only lay the stones and wait for the cosmos to draw the family home."

"This is not an end," Demiurge added. She pivoted toward the Celestial Arbor, her gaze moving skyward where the pearly leaves bathed in the light of Miragwyn's two suns. The tree shimmered, casting a double shadow across the moss. "The light you've kindled must continue to shine. But first, the roots must be known."

She stepped to the trunk and pressed her palm flat against the bark. A glow moved through the wood, visible through the translucent silver. "The Arbor has stood as a guardian through the eons. Like you, Wilhelmina, it began as a mere seed and has become an embodiment of strength and resilience, sheltering the dreams of the cosmos. But she is more than a witness. She has kept a secret, shared only with her lineage."

Demiurge's voice deepened, carrying the gravity of the ancient. "The Celestial Arbor is life itself. She is the Great Mother—the Original Creator. And she is my mother."

The air in the grove grew still. A heavy thrum vibrated through the soil, matching the sudden, hard beat of Wilhelmina's heart.

"Your grandmother," Demiurge finished. "We are the fruit of her boughs. Her essence is the pulse in the wrist and the spark in the mind; it is the life in every leaf that thrives across the realms."

As if in confirmation, the roots beneath their feet flared with a low, golden hum. A current of energy passed from the soil into Wilhelmina's skin, setting her nerves alight.

"As a child, I wandered here," Demiurge mused, her eyes reflecting the silver of the boughs. "The stars whispered through the bark. She showed me the infinite tapestry—the warp of fate and the weft of choice."

Wilhelmina clenched her grip on Selenus's hand. "The cosmos has nurtured us through her, through you, and through every trial."

Demiurge nodded, a smile gracing her features as the Arbor's branches swayed without a breeze. "Your courage has reaffirmed her faith in the caretakers of the light. She reveals her truth because you have earned it."

"You carried the legacy, Wilhelmina," Selenus said. "But you went beyond it. You chose connection over duty."

"Indeed," Lambda added. "A choice for oneself creates threads stronger than fate."

Wilhelmina looked toward the horizon, the perspective of her role shifting. The wedding fairy of Aetherwyn was a shadow of the past. "My duty did not end at the borders of the upper realm," she said, her voice clear. "I used to think my purpose was to protect one world... but now I am a steward of a legacy, bridging the upper and lower realms."

"You are so much more, Wilhelmina." Selenus's smile radiated with an unshakeable pride. "You are a guardian, a bridge between worlds, and a keeper of harmony."

Nearby, Demiurge and Lambda exchanged a glance of silent understanding.

"Remember," Lambda intoned. "The path of light is never-ending. Each step taken must nurture the harmony fought for with such courage."

Wilhelmina and Selenus nodded with reverence. Demiurge reached up to a lush branch of the Great Mother, her hands selecting a shoot that emitted a subtle, rhythmic glow. With a firm twist, she broke the limb free and held it out to her daughter.

"This bough carries life, dreams, and the hopes that survived the eons," she said. "Like the Arbor itself, it bears a legacy of endurance. As I once gave you a planting to sow in Solarae, I give you this for Aetherwyn. Let it bloom as a living testament to the unity restored between the heavenly and terrestrial realms."

Wilhelmina accepted the branch. The wood was warm, vibrating against her palms. "It will stand for everything we have fought for. Every blossom will serve as a reminder of the connections nurtured and the future safeguarded."

"And when those blossoms open," Demiurge added, her eyes catching the light of the two suns, "they will echo the resilience you have shown. Generations to come will be inspired to continue the balance established here today."

In response, the Arbor's leaves shimmered with a metallic clatter, and a beam of light cascaded across the landscape, striking the crystalline palace in the far distance.

Demiurge followed the path of the light, her gaze finally settling on Lambda. A twinkle of joy replaced the ancient sorrow in her gaze. "I think," she said softly, "it is time for us to go home."

❧

The Dreamscape carried them, traveling the long stretch from the Celestial Arbor's grounds to the palace of crystals, its gleaming walls shining like the facets of a star.

"This palace has become a sanctuary," Demiurge stated as the tapestry lowered them to the shimmering terrace. "A home to nurture the bonds sustained through centuries of separation."

Lambda stepped forward, his expression warm. "It is more than a home. It is a symbol of the resilience that defines this family."

Wilhelmina smiled toward the gleaming spires. "It is perfect. We shall return soon to visit, but the planting must be sown in Aetherwyn before the current of the Omega fades."

Lambda turned to Selenus and extended a hand. Their grip was firm, and as their palms met, a faint glow emanated from the contact. With a silent nod, Lambda pressed a small, cool object into the prince's hand.

Within Selenus's palm rested an intricately crafted box of starlight-silver. Inside, a pendant lay against dark velvet—a crescent moon cradling a bright star within its curve. The metal gave off a low, rhythmic thrum, a heartbeat sealed in starlight.

"Zografos and Stellara crafted this long ago," Lambda said. "A symbol of love that transcends time. It has waited through the centuries for the right receiver. It belongs to you."

Selenus swallowed hard, his gaze fixed on the ancient craftsmanship. He gave a sharp, grateful nod. "Thank you."

"Take it," Lambda said, with a knowing smile curving his lips. "Let it serve as the reminder that love, once found, endures every trial."

He clasped Selenus's shoulder before stepping back beside Demiurge. "The Dreamscape shall bring you to your next destination."

"They have discovered their balance," Demiurge murmured, her voice soft with pride as the luminous weave lifted the pair away.

"And their love will guide them through whatever lies before them," Lambda replied.

Wilhelmina waved farewell to her parents and the towering silhouette of her grandmother in the distance. She looked onward, expecting the Dreamscape to bank toward the portal of Aetherwyn. Instead, the tapestry hovered, then descended into the Garden of Love Blossoms.

"Oh!" Wilhelmina's eyes widened. "This is where I found you."

"Indeed," Selenus said, his tone dropping an octave. "For which I am forever grateful. Imagine if you had passed by."

Wilhelmina tried to suppress a smile, but a laugh broke free—a bright, clear sound that rang

through the grove.

"We couldn't have that," she managed.

Selenus led her to the center of the garden, their steps slow and deliberate. Blossoms that had once been muted now vibrated with iridescent hues, their petals acting as tiny mirrors for the starlight. Vines of golden light wove through the branches, casting intricate, shifting patterns across the ground like a living lace.

Where a once-barren patch had stood, life at present surged in a riot of color. Multi-hued flowers erupted under the light filtering through budding, luminescent leaves. As Wilhelmina ran her fingers over a petal, the blossom opened wider, its glow intensifying as it released a heavy, sweet fragrance into the air.

"It has changed," Wilhelmina said, her voice a gentle echo in the grove. "It is no longer merely beautiful; it is awake."

The garden breathed with them. The petals displayed a dynamic spectrum: deep reds for passion, soft pinks for care, and golden blooms for enduring loyalty. Rare white blossoms stood like striking sentinels of purity. Together, the hues wove a visual narrative of the trials endured and the bonds forged.

Nearby, a small brook ran clear, the water splashing the boulders with a sound like wind blowing through crystal chimes. Wilhelmina bowed down by the bank, letting the cool current flow through her fingers.

"Everything here is alive with magic," she noted, looking up at the starlight spilling through the canopy. Silver stones, smooth and iridescent, lined the path through the garden, each one reflecting the celestial glow from above.

At the garden's center, there was a new fountain. The water within sparkled like liquid gold, capturing the effervescent colors of the surrounding blooms. Selenus crouched beside the basin, the golden reflection dancing across his features.

"The garden has been waiting," he said.

A gentle breeze stirred, carrying a chorus of fragrances that hummed with the history of their journey. Wilhelmina stood, her gaze sweeping over the transformation. "This place is more than a garden now. It is a memory made flesh."

Selenus slowed his pace as they arrived at a clearing where the Love Blossoms framed the clear sky. He faced her with a quiet, focused intensity. "Wilhelmina... do you remember what you said when you first found me here?"

Wilhelmina's fingers brushed the velvet surface of a nearby bloom. "I said you were a pebble in my shoe."

Selenus chuckled, a low, warm sound. He reached into his cloak. "And you turned that pebble into a purpose. You turned it into love."

He produced a small, ornately crafted box and clicked it open. Within, a ring captured the radiance of the entire cosmos. The band, forged from the silver of a fallen star, was interwoven with the preserved fibers of the very first Love Blossom they had saved—a union of the heavens and the earth.

"Wilhelmina, you have shown me that strength lies in vulnerability and that love is the greatest force we possess," he said, his voice steady despite the emotion behind it. "Here, where our journey began, the next chapter of our story begins."

He knelt on one knee. "I love you, Wilhelmina. Will you share all tomorrows with me and continue weaving light into the cosmos, together?"

Tears welled as she kneeled to meet him, her hands clasping his. "Yes, Selenus. In all ways, through any challenges, my heart has chosen you. You are my destiny, my light, and my love."

Selenus pulled her into an embrace, their foreheads touching in the quiet of the grove. "Each star and every blossom pales beside the radiance you bring."

"I choose... us," she whispered.

They shared a kiss that sealed the promise beneath the flowering canopy. The garden responded, exhaling a swirling dance of petals that caught the wind in a celebratory spiral. As he slipped the ring onto her finger, the celestial brilliance above intensified, illuminating the silver and flora of the band against her skin.

Walking hand-in-hand back toward the Dreamscape, Wilhelmina looked over her shoulder one last time. The flora swayed in the cosmic glow, its flowers watching their departure. The path they had walked remained marked by the glistening stones, a permanent record of their footprints.

"Do you think the branch might bloom as beautifully in Aetherwyn?" she asked.

"It shall surpass even this," Selenus replied, his eyes reflecting a vision of the future. "A new tree will represent all we have overcome. I can see it now—the branches heavy with blossoms, carrying the hopes of both realms."

Wilhelmina nodded as she cradled the sacred bough in her arms. "And when it blooms, we'll stand beneath it and say our vows. Under the stars, just as we promised."

He squeezed her hand, his smile beaming with unwavering devotion. "We will. The constellations above and the flora below shall bear witness to our story as it unfolds. All in good time... Come. We have a wedding to plan."

The Dreamscape, its silken surface resplendent with celestial hues, lifted them into the darkening sky. The stellar gems rippled in response, their light weaving a silver pathway toward the skyline.

Below, the Garden of Love Blossoms offered a final, glowing blessing. Ahead, the crystalline palace glistened, its facets catching the first rays of Miragwyn's twin suns. On the horizon, the dwelling built for their family rose larger, a sanctuary for the future. For this moment, Wilhelmina and Selenus shared the silence, their hearts alight with the love and hope that had carried them this far—and would guide them home.

35. Dawn of Harmony

As the group stepped through the final shimmering veil back into Aetherwyn, a sudden, crystalline chiming filled the air. One by one, the four Aetherwynian companions gasped as the weightlessness returned. The dragonfly wings of Crispin unfurled with a sharp, mechanical snap; Flora's leaf-veined sails bloomed into vibrant green; and the feathered pinions of Quill and Aria shimmered back into existence, shedding sparks of prismatic light. They hadn't lost their gifts in Miragwyn as a sacrifice; they had simply been waiting for the air of home to breathe them back into being.

But while the others stretched their newfound limbs with joyous shouts, Wilhelmina's wings behaved differently. They manifested at will—silver-spun glass that appeared with a thought and faded as naturally as a sigh. The shift in her magic flowed with unerring clarity; each time they appeared, they left a trail of luminescent frost in the air. She was no longer just a resident of the light; she was its master.

Selenus stood beside her, his gaze sweeping across the rejuvenated horizon. "We have left fragments of ourselves in the realms we traversed," he mused, "and gained the universe in exchange."

Later that day, they walked hand in hand to meet the magical folk who had safeguarded Aetherwyn in their absence. The once muted fields now gleamed with cobalt-veined moss and petals that hummed when brushed. Wilhelmina filled her lungs with the new air that bore the fresh scent of blooming moonblossoms.

"To come back here, where everything began," she announced, her voice echoing over the revitalized meadows, "and find nothing as it was."

A fairy child approached, her crown of daisies sliding over one ear. Tugging at Wilhelmina's skirts, the girl looked up with wide, trusting eyes. "Did you bring back the light, Wilhelmina?"

Wilhelmina knelt, meeting the child at eye level. She cupped her hand, and a soft, rhythmic glow—pulsing like a second heartbeat—emanated from her palm, casting a warm light on the child's face.

"We returned with more than light," Wilhelmina said. "We brought back a promise—that as long as unity stands, Aetherwyn will thrive."

The child's expression lit with delight, and she skipped back toward the village.

As Wilhelmina and Selenus, known only as the enigmatic Moon Prince to the villagers, continued toward the village center, their presence drew a crowd. While their love story had traveled ahead of them, whispers regarding Selenus's origins still lingered, creating a low, persistent murmur—like the buzzing of hornets in a dry field.

Selenus tightened his grip on Wilhelmina's hand, his expression resolute. He stepped forward to address the crowd, and his voice, deep and resonant, cut through the murmurs like a cloche bell ringing.

"People of Aetherwyn, I am no longer a prince from a realm of shadows, but a man transformed by light, love, and the weight of loss. I regret the fear my presence once caused, and I stand before you to seek the understanding and forgiveness I have had to find within myself."

Wilhelmina stood tall next to him, her posture mirroring the strength of the bough she carried. "Selenus battled the darkness within his own spirit," she declared, her gaze sweeping over the throng. "Beside me, he strove to restore the balance we now breathe. He has earned my trust... and my heart."

As her words settled, a surge of golden light heralded a new arrival. Demiurge materialized near Celestia, her form shimmering with a gentle, starlit radiance. A collective gasp rose from the gathering, followed by the awed name: "The Enchantress!"

The crowd bowed as one.

Demiurge spoke with the gravity of ages. "It takes bravery to battle perils from without, but greater courage to face the shadows within. Selenus has done both. Let him be judged not by the darkness he left behind, but by the path he walks today."

At her words, the rigid shoulders of the townsfolk relaxed. An elder elf at the front nodded slowly, his hands coming together in a quiet, rhythmic clap that was soon joined by the rest of the throng. Selenus turned his gaze to a group of young lads at the periphery.

"Let my journey be your lesson," he called out. "Shadows hold power only when fear sustains them. Stand in the light, and you stand with strength."

From the heart of the throng, a fairy grandmother stepped forward. Her movements were slow, her back bent by time, but her smile was as bright as the morning. She approached Demiurge with trembling hands.

"Enchantress," the elder breathed in a quivering voice. "Your magic was the shield of Aetherwyn. To see you returned... it is the honor of my lifetime."

A tidal wave of gratitude swept through the gathered folk in an enthusiastic shout. Demiurge bowed her head, her words laced with a fragile tremor. "I have sought to serve and to protect... but to be accepted is more than I ever dreamed."

Wilhelmina moved to clasp hands with Demiurge. "When I first read of you, you were the Forgotten Enchantress. Yet here you stand, forever vital to this realm. Thank you, Mother. I am proud to be your daughter."

Demiurge's eyes glistened as she cupped Wilhelmina's face, her touch warm and solid. "My heart is full. I have no regrets about the risks taken to protect you. Now, let us forgive the past. Let us plant the Love Blossom in Aetherwyn. It will serve as a living seal of all that has been restored."

❧

Beside the sparkling Serene Waters, the air grew thick and hummed with the resonance of gathered realms. Zografos and Stellara stood before the assembly, their presence radiating the stillness of ancient stars. Above them, the moonblossom tree's silver leaves rustled, moving in a rhythmic shiver that mirrored the excitement surrounding the gathering.

"This moonblossom tree, joined with the bough of Miragwyn, embodies rebirth and continuity," Zografos began; his deep voice resembled an echo from a mountain peak. "It is rooted in your courage and vision; a testament to all that has been overcome."

As Stellara stepped forward, her gown shone like moonlight on water. "Each bloom carries the enchantment of the stars that shaped your destinies. Let this act illuminate the horizon as a beacon of hope for all."

Wilhelmina and Selenus knelt at the base of the trunk. Their movements were deliberate as they molded the loamy soil around the Love Blossom. The crowd leaned in, the silence so absolute that only the lapping of the lake remained.

As the bough settled into the earth, a ripple of energy coursed through the ground, vibrating through the soles of every onlooker. Its pale petals ignited, transforming from moonlight-white into bursts of iridescent rainbow light. A unified gasp swelled from the grove.

Wilhelmina rose, her voice clear and audible to the outer edges of the audience. "This branch marks the culmination of our quest. This Love Blossom, born from sacrifice, carries the force of creation itself."

"Across the epochs, the Celestial Arbor endured," Selenus added, his expression solemn as the light of the just-emerged blossoms caught in his eyes. "Guarded by Demiurge's sacrifice, it harbored this life through the darkness. Today, it wakes."

Wilhelmina extended her arms. "The joining of the Moonblossoms and Love Blossoms will spread vibrancy throughout Aetherwyn, creating a restorative Elixir of Love."

"The end of old battles," Selenus finished, "and the dawn of a hopeful era."

Stellara intertwined her fingers with Zografos and chanted in a forgotten tongue that pulled the magic from the very stones. As he joined her, the soil glowed a deep, pulsing gold.

As if waking from a long slumber, the tree's roots stirred beneath the moss. The crowd watched in wonder as its branches unfurled with a melodic creak, and its petals cast silvery beams of light that danced across the lake. A pixie child at the front reached out, her fingertips catching the warm breeze created by the enchantment. Beside her, an elder fairy's weathered face broke into a toothless smile, her eyes glistening with awe and hope.

Demiurge approached the planting, her presence commanding yet tender. She stretched out her hands toward the trunk to weave a final spell. "May this blossom represent our enduring pledge to live in harmony," she intoned, her voice resonating through the grove. "A living symbol of the peace we vow to maintain."

A wave of magical energy rippled outward. The dynamic colors of the Love Blossom seeped into the silver moonblossoms, multiplying and cascading until the entire woodland was a swirl of iridescent light. The first petal arced into the air, followed by a thousand more in a dancing spiral.

A great cheer erupted—a joyous blend of voices that wove into the music of the trees, signaling that Aetherwyn was finally whole.

❧

With the sun at its zenith, Wilhelmina and Selenus rejoined their companions. The Octet of Heroes—as they would be immortalized in the annals of the realms—began the procession toward the reconstructed Meridian Bridge.

The path was a riot of laughter and sprightly colors; the air physically tingled with a surplus of joy and magic. Crispin stumbled as a playful pixie darted between his legs, her mischievous giggle ringing like a cascade of silver bells.

"Well, that is one way to be welcomed home!" he exclaimed, catching his balance and grinning.

The pixie hovered, meeting his eyes and with her tiny hands on her hips. "We wanted to see if the glorious hero still had his footing!"

Crispin chuckled, ruffling the pixie's luminous hair. "Not quite, it seems."

Flora, walking a step behind, handed him a small, fragrant sprig of lavender. "Perhaps this will help keep you grounded," she teased. She looked toward the horizon, where the plant life pulsed with a new, animated rhythm. "Everything flourishes. The land itself celebrates."

Aria plucked a wildflower and hummed a tune that the breeze immediately carried and amplified. "The air is singing," she noted. "Aetherwyn has waited long for this day."

Lumina surveyed the revelry, her eyes gleaming. "The beauty and peace here reflect the harmony we fought to protect. Tradition and change are finally in bloom together."

Phaethon gave a solemn nod. "The land mirrors the light we restored. It is our duty now to uphold the balance."

Crispin's voice grew solemn, though his smile remained. "There were moments I doubted we would ever see Aetherwyn like this. Every challenge was worth it to reach this dawn."

A young elf scampered forward, holding a garland of vivacious flowers. He stopped before Crispin with wide, reverent eyes. "For you, Sir Crispin! You've earned it!"

Crispin took the garland and placed it atop his head with a mock-serious expression, striking an exaggerated warrior's pose. "Do I look like a proper hero now?"

Laughter flowed through the Octet and the gathering crowd. "You look perfect!" the child declared, clapping his hands.

As the merriment settled, Quill approached Wilhelmina. His steps were hesitant, but his smile was steady and warm. "Your bravery turned this from a dream into reality, our dear, determined protector. That is the meaning of your name—I found it in the ancient texts," he said, adding a wink.

Wilhelmina's eyes glistened, and a bright laugh escaped her. "Thank you, my friend. But it was not my bravery alone. It was all of us."

She held his gaze. "Especially you. Your choice to remain in the library, preserving stories and lessons—that, too, is courage."

Quill's cheeks flushed a deep crimson. "It was nothing," he mumbled, his eyes dropping to the pearlescent stones beneath his feet.

"Not nothing," Wilhelmina countered, her tone firm. "Historians etch truth into memory. You safeguard wisdom for generations. Like our swords and spells, your pen has waged a silent war against oblivion."

Quill straightened. His blush remained, but his eyes now shone with a clear, steady pride. "Thank you, Wilhelmina. It is heartening to believe our stories will be told through time, guiding those who come after us in ways we can but dream."

Wilhelmina gave a slow, thoughtful nod. "Without each tale shared and every truth recorded, future generations would lack the wisdom to choose the light over the shadow."

Amid the growing revelry, Somnius—accompanied by Seraphina and Lumineon walking arm-in-arm—approached. The Keeper of Lost Dreams carried a presence both calm and profound.

"Your journey, child of light and shadow, mirrors the dreams of countless realms," Somnius intoned. "You have proven that even the faintest spark reignites the cosmos."

Wilhelmina inclined her head. "And you reminded me to dream boldly. Seraphina, you showed me the courage to follow my heart. Lumineon, your guidance lit the way. Thank you."

The illuminating sprites—those who had shown the fortitude of family and the persistence of light—bowed deeply. Their forms shimmered, softening at the edges until they faded into the crowd like mist into a golden morning. As they vanished, the mirth and music swelled, a palpable wave of sound that wove the joy of the moment into a living tapestry of celebration.

❧

Dusk descended over Aetherwyn, casting long shadows that dissolved into a peaceful, violet twilight. At the Meridian Bridge, the crowd spanned the history of the realm, from the smallest shimmering sprites to the eldest elves. They waited in charged silence for the ceremony that would mark the end of the old world and the birth of the new.

The bridge stood as a marvel of inter-realm craft. Each stone bore a unique hue, its iridescent surface shifting beneath the radiance of moonflowers and sunburst lilies that entwined along the rails in a living mosaic. Above, lanterns housed bioluminescent creatures and sunlight-absorbing crystals, bathing the structure in a fluid, undulating radiance. The wind, tracing arcane meridians, carried a scent of rain and nectar, aligning the natural world with the magical.

Near the perimeter of the congregation, Gwydion the owl spread his wings wide, his venerable silhouette commanding an immediate hush.

"People of Aetherwyn," Gwydion began. "We stand upon the cusp of prophecy. Long ago, it was foretold that a bridge would one day connect light and darkness, uniting realms divided by fear. Today, that prophecy is no longer a whisper from history, but the stone beneath our feet."

Wilhelmina stepped beside him, her presence radiant yet anchored. "This bridge is evidence of the harmony we fought to achieve," she stated, words reaching the furthest reaches of the gathering. "It is a promise of a united future."

From the crowd, Demiurge and Celestia emerged, flanked by Varytita and Lambda. The assembly bowed in an instinctive, rolling wave of reverence.

"You have shown immense resilience," Demiurge intoned. "This ceremony marks the beginning of an era where light and shadow coexist."

"May this bridge stand as a lasting tribute to the beautiful intertwining of unity and diversity," Celestia added, her warmth suffusing the air like a hearth-fire. "Let the love that guided you here inspire every step you take across it, Wilhelmina."

Wilhelmina began her walk. Her gown was a living canvas—woven from dream-strands and infused with magic, the fabric danced with rainbow light. Intricate motifs of the Dreamscape's boundless wonders adorned the hem and sleeves, shifting with her movement.

From the opposite end, Selenus approached. His robes of deep midnight reflected his transformation; buttons crafted from smooth pebbles served as silent markers of his journey from the shadow he conjured to the light he now embodied. His stride was steady, his presence exuding a quiet, forged strength.

On the flanks, Phaethon and Lumina joined them. Phaethon's robes gleamed a lush green like leaves kissed by a new sun, while Lumina's gown captured the dappled interplay of light through the foliage.

At the bridge's middle, the four stood as one.

"My children of Aetherwyn," Demiurge said, her voice rich with emotion. "Today, we witness a union that transcends realms. Born from love and fortified by trial, you reflect the journey from adversity to triumph."

"In unity, we find strength. In love, we discover the source of our existence." Celestia raised her arms. "Let us carry forth the lessons learned. Embrace diversity, cherish bonds, and strive for understanding and compassion."

As the four heroes linked hands, the Dancing Lights of Jubilation exploded in the sky. Bursts of emerald, gold, and violet painted the heavens, the colors reflecting in the wide, awed eyes of the spectators below.

A short time later, amid the revelry, Wilhelmina caught sight of Selenus. The prince was laughing—a sound free of his old burdens—as the villagers' children taught him the steps of a traditional dance. He caught her gaze and beckoned her forward.

"Come, Wilhelmina!" he called out. "Dance with me!"

Wilhelmina's laugh was light as she joined the impromptu circle. Around them, the celebration thrived—an endless canvas of joy where the luminous aurora overhead gradually faded into the deep peace of a permanent night, charged with the hope of all that was to come.

❧

Excitement infused the morning air as Aetherwyn awaited the union of its Wedding Fairy and the Moon Prince. The preparations of the past days had woven a tapestry of magic and merriment, a physical herald of a new era.

The melody-sirens sang, their harmonies weaving a luminous spell over a new wedding song penned by Quill. Each note resonated like ripples on the sea, infusing the shores of the Serene Waters with an ethereal warmth.

Demiurge and Lambda, Phaethon and Lumina, and Quill and Aria stood at the forefront, their expressions radiant with joy. Among them, Grumblefoot's gruff exterior softened with a rare smile.

Under the starlit sky, Wilhelmina walked with deliberate grace, each step casting an iridescent glow that mesmerized the crowd. In her hands, she carried an exquisite bouquet, a vibrant bough from the Celestial Arbor radiating from its center.

At the water's edge, Selenus stood beneath a young Love Blossom tree. Its glowing branches extended toward him in a silent welcome. His gaze remained locked on Wilhelmina as she approached, his presence radiating a quiet, profound reverence. When she reached him, they joined hands—a silent affirmation before the first word was spoken.

For centuries, Wilhelmina had orchestrated the unions of others. Today, the realm returned the gift.

"Beloved Aetherwyn, we gather to honor this extraordinary union," Demiurge began, her voice carrying across the hushed assembly. "Today, you serve as officiants, blessing the one who has spent her life uniting you." She opened her arms toward the couple. "You may now speak your vows."

Selenus squeezed Wilhelmina's fingers, his voice steady. "Wilhelmina, you are my guiding star and my light of hope. Even when the shadows seemed insurmountable, you stood by me. United, we are whole. With every breath, I vow to honor and protect you, love and cherish you."

Wilhelmina had choreographed countless weddings, never daring to imagine that her own could take form, that one day she would stand here ready to pledge her love. Now, she embraced the truth of her value and the worthiness of the love she desired.

Her radiant smile widened as she looked upon the man who had once been her greatest challenge. "Selenus, I have seen your shadows and embraced them. You have brought light into my life, and today, I vow to cherish, to love, and to stand by you—in light and shadow, in joy and sorrow—for all the days of our lives."

Demiurge raised her hands to incant the wedding enchantment. As they exchanged rings, the magic of Aetherwyn's blessing took flight. It enveloped the Love Blossom trees and branched outward, a wave of light traveling to the farthest reaches of the universe. Their choices reached the interstellar fabric of the Dreamscape, merging with it for all eternity. When they sealed the vows with a kiss, the crowd erupted in a joyous roar.

Wilhelmina tilted her head skyward. The astral expanse twinkled with her cosmic imprint—a solitary star embraced by the crescent moon. Once distant, the celestial body now rested jubilantly in the moon's protective glow. A beam of light descended from the star to Wilhelmina like a luminous galactic bridge, while another streamed from the moon to Selenus. The two rays ricocheted outward, meeting in midair to coil into a heavenly sailor's knot, securing their eternally entwined fates within the stars themselves.

At that moment, Wilhelmina and Selenus understood that destiny had planned for their union—a union that could not have come to fruition without the challenges they had faced and only because they had chosen it.

As tradition dictated, Wilhelmina tossed her bouquet. Lumina and Aria caught it together, their giggles mingling with the wedding guests' cheers and applause. Behind Aria and Lumina, Quill and Phaethon shared a knowing smile, an unspoken toast to the paths yet to open.

All about them, the joy was palpable. The Love Blossoms' sweet scent mingled with the laughter and songs of a people reborn, while above, the Dancing Lights tinted the sky with iridescent hues, captivating both children and elders alike.

Wilhelmina turned to Selenus, interlacing her fingers with his as they watched the revelry unfold. "I was once the Wedding Fairy, weaving dreams for others."

"You were a dreamer who believed in the impossible," Selenus replied, his voice tender. "And your dreams have shaped your destiny and illuminated the cosmos. I am the luckiest of men to be your husband."

"And I... your wife." Wilhelmina wrapped her arms around Selenus. "And so, we bring in a new dawn of time under the Celestial Arbor's gaze."

Selenus leaned down, meeting her lips in a kiss that carried the light of a thousand stars.

What was once imagined had become reality—a design crafted with care by the Celestial Arbor. Across the realms, the blooms now swayed in the gentle night breeze, their sprightly petals releasing a faint, rhythmic glow that pulsed in time with the stars. It was no longer just flora; it was a revival of imagination, a living map of the victory they had won.

A calming aura enveloped Aetherwyn as the celebrations faded into the deep peace of night. Under the eternal watch of the Celestial Arbor, Wilhelmina and Selenus stood with their companions at the edge of the Serene Waters. They watched as a single luminous petal drifted from the tree, caught the wind, and began a long journey toward the horizon—a spark of silver and rainbow light against the dark. The tale of Wilhelmina did not truly end; like that drifting petal, it remained a guiding light, a story of enduring love and unity that would catch the wind and echo through the ages.

THE END

Acknowledgments

To my late mother—beautiful, eccentric, and an author herself—who brought me books when I was very young. She instilled in me a love for story and its ability to touch the human heart in magical ways.

To my family: thank you for your unwavering support, laughter, and belief in the world I was quietly building.

To my wonderful friends: thank you for believing in me, always bringing encouraging words, and offering a guiding light to illuminate the path.

To the creative power of discovered tools that acted as quiet co-editors and imaginative catalysts throughout this journey.

To my dedicated beta readers—your insights shaped this tale with care and clarity.

To my professional editor, George Jreije: thank you for your wisdom, precision, and encouragement.

And finally, to the mystical whisperers who have walked with me across the past twenty-five years—thank you. This book blossomed from the threads you helped me find.

About The Author

M. Turandot is a genre-blending author and narrative alchemist whose stories shimmer at the edge of fairytale, satire, and soul. Drawing on a background in computer science, theatre, and narrative design, she brings a refined instinct for structure, tone, and emotional resonance to every page. She holds a Bachelor of Science in Computer Science and a Master of Business Administration from the University of Michigan.

A former screenwriter and story editor, she has served as a judge for the Austin Film Festival for eight years. Her work has also been recognized by international screenplay competitions.

Wilhelmina is her debut novel. Her writing explores themes of memory, identity, and transformation across time and genre—ranging from luminous fables and mythic fantasy to sharp satire, urban mysticism, and metaphysical mystery. Across all forms, she invites readers into worlds where wit, wonder, and wisdom collide, and where the heart always finds its thread.

Through her Substack, *The Joy Weave*, M. Turandot shares reflections on storytelling as soulcraft, weaving radiant threads of creativity, curiosity, and coherence across time.

She believes the greatest magic is not what you inherit—but what you dare to become.

www.ingramcontent.com/pod-product-compliance
Lightning Source LLC
Chambersburg PA
CBHW020915310726
48980CB00011B/896/J

* 9 7 9 8 9 9 9 4 6 1 7 0 4 *